All the best

Joshibhawishach

Nosodes & Imponderables come alive!

By

Dr. Bhawisha and Dr. Shachindra Joshi

Based on Bhawisha and Shachindra Joshi's
Imponderables and Nosodes Lecture Series

With additional cases, insights and comparison with
similar remedy groups

Title: Nosodes and Imponderables come alive!
Cover Page: concept: Bhawisha Joshi
Illustrations and design: Haresh Mesta
Edited by: Bhawisha Joshi, Rima Desai

Printer:

Greeshma Arts
23, Milan Industrial Estate,
Abhyudaya Nagar,
Cotton Green, Mumbai-33.

Publisher:

Dr. Shachindra Joshi (HUF)
501, Pelican, 311 Sant Muktabai marg, Vile Parle (East), Mumbai 400057, India
Tel: +91-22-26149922

Email: info@drjoshisclinic.com / homoeopathypatterns@gmail.com
Website: www.drjoshisclinic.com

First edition: March 2011

ACKNOWLEDGMENTS

First of all, we wish to acknowledge Rima Desai for her extensive efforts and dedication in editing the raw content of our lectures to bring shape to this book.

Our patients have been our best teachers. We are ever grateful for the faith that they have put into us. It is through them that we have received so many opportunities to learn and grow.

It has been our privilege to have had the opportunity to work closely with Dr. Rajan Sankaran. Through his constant encouragement and faith in us, we have crossed several milestones in our career. Our theories are based on his work on the 10 miasms. Both, we and the field of homoeopathy will be ever grateful to him.

Special thanks to Bettina Szilagyi who helped us in the final stages of the book.

Our thanks to Dave Housman for being such a wonderful and insightful friend and an inspiration for this book.

Finally, our heartfelt gratitude to Jan Scholten for his encouragement and critical review about the contents of this book.

CONTENTS

Preface 1

Notes to the Reader 3

Chapter 1 – The Idea of Kingdoms 5

Chapter 2 – Understanding the Nosode Kingdom 9

Chapter 3 – The Basic Understanding of Miasms 15

Chapter 4 – Different Nosode Pictures according to the Joshis 27

Chapter 5 – Difference between Nosodes, Minerals & Animals 41

Chapter 6 – A Case of Ringworm 45

Chapter 7 – A Case of Carcinosinum 81

Chapter 8 – Second Case of Carcinosinum 111

Chapter 9 – A Case of Malaria Nosode 131

Chapter 10 – A Case of Medorrhinum 141

Chapter 11 – A Case of Tuberculinum 147

Chapter 12 – A Case of Bacillinum 177

Chapter 13 – Joshis' Take on Miasmatic Relationships 185

Chapter 14 – Comparative Analysis of Nosodes with Identical 197
              Remedy Groups

Chapter 15 – Common Words and Themes of Nosodes 217

A Poem   – Beyond The Horizon 223

Chapter 16 – The Polarity in Imponderables 225

Chapter 17 – Imponderable Case 1: Sol 229

Chapter 18 – Imponderable Case 2: Sol 253

Chapter 19 – Understanding the Nature of Imponderables.............. 259
        & their Themes

Chapter 20 – Specific characteristics of Different Imponderables 267

Chapter 21 – Imponderable Case 3: Laser Beam 273

Chapter 22 – Positronium 277

Chapter 23 – Imponderable Case 4: Vacuum 285

Chapter 24 - The Themes of Black Hole 301

Chapter 25 – Imponderables at the Micro & Macro Levels 311

Chapter 26 – The Difference of Imponderables from other Similar 315
        Looking Remedies

Chapter 27 – Miasms of Imponderables.............................. 319

A Concluding note by Bhawisha & Shachindra Joshi 323

PREFACE

Each one of us as a child discovers things and has our 'eureka moments'. Later in life as we begin to believe that we know everything we need to know we lose this curious little child within us. But every now and then we are confronted with situations where we discover some truth. These are our eureka moments when we feel we have been touched by some mystical power in the universe and have understood something cosmical.

To us discovery of the sensation of nosodes and imponderables has been such an exciting moment. Needless to say that our patients led us to them. Hence the process of case-taking in cases where we gave imponderables and nosodes was like going on a discovery trip and finding something new.

We are a couple practicing and teaching Homeopathy since 1997 in Mumbai. We have been trained in Classical Homeopathy. We strongly believe and practice the Sensation method of Dr. Rajan Sankaran, since 2001. We have been part of this method since its very roots and have contributed to it by our own experiences and teachings for the past decade. In this book you will see how we have found the sensation of the imponderable and nosode remedies and how to use them using the Sensation method.

Our first interaction with these remedies was way back in 2003 and since then we have developed a deep connection and understanding of these remedies through more and more cases over the past eight years. There has been an increasing demand on us to put into a book form all our ideas and experiences so that we can reach many more people than the ones who have been lucky to have attended the seminars on these topics.

Shachindra and I have always liked the idea of discussions and dialogue in our teachings which has been clearly reflected in our previous book. We always attempt to strike a friendly chord with our readers, students and patients. In keeping with our style, this book feels like an informal talk as versus a typically formal book. Also, there are times in the book where we have written 'we' and there are times when we have written 'I'. This is just going with the flow of the book at that point.

Since we have given all the details of imponderables and nosodes very systematically in this book, it becomes a 'must read book' for even those who have attended our seminars.

NOTES TO THE READER

This book includes case histories for in-depth understanding. Most cases and follow-ups have been edited for the ease of reading. However, some illustrative cases have been kept unedited. Also, some personal details of patients have been changed to maintain confidentiality of cases. For greater introspection, we have included our analysis and understanding of the cases in italics.

The following abbreviations have been used while describing the cases:
★ P = Patient
★ D = Doctor
★ M = Mother
★ AC = Air condition
★ MIL = Mother-in-law
★ HG = Hand gesture
★ BP = Blood pressure

The concepts in this book are completely new and based on our experiences with the imponderables and nosodes rather than specific references from Materia Medica. We have clinically confirmed these ideas over the past eight years before bringing this book forth. However some books and references that have helped us in our journey until now with these remedies have been listed below.

Reference books
• S.R. Phatak's materia medica
• Keynotes to the Materia Medica by H.C. Allen
• Materia Medica of the Nosodes and Provings of X-ray, by H.C. Allen
• Synoptic vol 1 & 2 , by Frans Vermeulen
• Julian's Nosodes, by O. A. Julian
• Dictionary of Practical Materia Medica , by J.H. Clarke
• Foubister's Carsinosin, Donald MacDonald Foubister
• KHA's Reference Works & Mac Repertory Homoeopathic software program

We hope this book turns out to be a valuable source of learning to you.

THE IDEA OF KINGDOMS

I.   Introduction

II. The Kingdoms

III. The duality or the basic polarity in Plants

IV. The duality or the basic polarity in Animals

V. The duality or the basic polarity in Minerals

I. Introduction

Homoeopathic remedies are reflections of natural substances and hence they are made from plant, mineral and animal sources. As homoeopathic practitioners we know that the essence of the substance lays the remedial foundation. In other words, the remedy picture reflects the characteristics of the source that it is obtained from.

It fascinates me to see that patients needing remedies from different kingdoms express their deeper issues in manner corresponding to the kingdom that their remedy belongs to. You would notice that patients needing plant remedies are keenly sensitive whereas patients needing animal remedies are very vibrant and vivid. Interestingly, patients requiring mineral remedies are focused and target-oriented.

Let me tell you that this is only a glance of the resemblance that humans have to the world around them. At the core, we all resonate with or feel a duality that corresponds to the kingdom to which our remedies belong to.

We have discussed in detail the three kingdoms and the basic polarity of the three major kingdoms in our previous book namely **'Homoeopathy and Patterns in the Periodic Table (Part 1)'.** Here we are giving you a short glimpse of the kingdoms.

II. The Kingdoms

Everything in the universe can be seen as one 'thing', which can be defined by everything that it is not. This 'thing', whether the human mind, or a material object can also be referred to as the 'I'. The 'I' exists only in relation to what is not 'I' - the 'U'. Together the 'I' and the 'U' form the whole. Vice versa when you split the whole into 'I' you automatically create the 'U'. This is the concept of Duality.

Given this premise, every substance known to man can be looked at from the perspective of the 'I' – being the substance itself, and the 'U' – everything that appears separate from the 'I'. Everything separate from the 'I' can be seen as defining its existence. So, the experience of light can be looked at as being defined by experience of darkness, the experience of beauty can be defined by the experience of ugliness, a physical shape can be seen as defined by the space outside of the shape, and a life form can be seen as existing in relation to the environment which allows it to survive.

6

Below is a brief outline of how the kingdoms can be characterised within the framework of this duality or 'I' and 'U'.

III. The duality or basic polarity in Plants

We know that the most important thing that keeps the plants alive is their independence and their sensitivity to the environment around because they have the element of chlorophyll in them. All plants have chlorophyll which synthesises the food for the plant. Because chlorophyll needs light, plants need to be extremely sensitive to picking up or to absorbing this light to make their own food. In other words, the mode of existence for all plants is a reaction to the environment. All plants survive by synthesising their food with the help of chlorophyll, energy from a reaction with something in the environment. Energy is derived through chlorophyll, which reacts to sunlight. The roots too are sensitive to the contents of the earth. They analyse the nutritional, water and ph balances in earth and react very specifically to draw their optimum amounts. Therefore, in plants the deepest polarity, the deepest non-human issue is that of sensitivity and the opposite of that is of course reactivity.

In this way we can see the duality or 'I' and 'U' in plants as sensitivity and reactivity to the 'U'.

'I' am sensitive to 'U' and 'I' react to 'U'

'Sensitivity vs. Reactivity'

IV. The duality or basic polarity in Animals

The basic rule of existence for all animals in their natural environments is that they cannot make their food. They depend on other organisms as their source of food and energy. The herbivore depends on plants and the carnivore depends on other animals. The carnivore depends on catching its prey to survive while the herbivore depends on escaping the aggressor in order to continue life.

That is exactly the reason why sponges which look just like plants are not plants but animals because they cannot make their own food. They depend on planktons as their source of food and nourishment. In the same way, carnivorous plants do not become animals but remain plants because they do not survive on the insect that they kill for their food. They use the insects only to receive nitrogen and phosphorous that is required by them. They still make their own food by using the chlorophyll that they have.

For the carnivore, life is a situation of me against you or you against me. Either 'I' survive or 'U'. Whether 'I' need to beat 'U' or 'I' need to not be beaten by 'U', the crux isthe same: My survival is at risk because of 'U'. Thus, either 'I' survive or 'U'. It is a victim-aggressor conflict.

So the deepest polarity in the animal kingdom is not of sensitivity-reactivity, but the deepest polarity here is of *'Me vs. You'.*

V. The duality or the basic polarity in Minerals

The main thing about minerals is that they are unstable. They are lacking in the number of electrons in their outer most orbits and are constantly trying to complete their configuration. In order to be stable, the minerals need a very specific arrangement of electrons within their atomic structure.

Noble gas atoms are already stable. The atoms of all other elements need to make bonds with other atoms so that they can give, take or share electrons and reach the required stable configuration. Hence minerals are based on the 'I' need 'U' theme.

They have a need to be 'completed' by something other. They make bonds with what is outside of them in order to exist. So their deepest issue is the issue of stability and instability; that of incompleteness and its opposite is completeness.

'I' am incomplete without 'U'. Therefore, here the polarity is –

'Incomplete vs. Complete'

This was a brief of the 3 main kingdoms. Remember that the dynamic between the 'I' and what it exists in relation to 'U', not only creates its existence but also its disease. It is the apparent separation that causes the 'dis-ease'. As the polarity or the sense of separateness gets more and more intense, the disease gets more and more pathological.

2

 UNDERSTANDING THE NOSODE KINGDOM

I. Introduction

II. Nosode's Origin

III. An Example

IV. Nosode Features – Feeling & Polarity

V. The Words of Polarity

VI. Caution

I. Introduction

Over the years, homoeopaths have commonly spoken about remedies from the animal, plant and mineral kingdoms. It is now time to look at some other remedies from some other kingdoms. Remedies which have been present in our materia medica from decades or even from centuries! These remedies have been prescribed in the past but are not prescribed so often now. Although these remedies are very old, we haven't been able to give enough justice to them with the way in which we look at our cases today like with the Sensation method. We have not explored these remedies. These are remedies from the kingdom of Nosodes and Imponderables.

About 6 or 8 years ago we were asking ourselves that why we do not prescribe the simple Medorrhinums and Carcinosinums and Psorinums as often now. Is it because we have stopped needing them in our practice? Just like other remedies have a core essence the nosodes must surely have some core issue within them too. So we asked ourselves, "Have we not been able to understand this issue? With the Sensation method that we practice, how would we be able to see these remedies and recognise them?"

These questions inspired Shachindra and me to begin working, reading and exploring the nosodes bit. This exploration got us to look at remedies differently. We studied these remedies as we study the other remedies i.e. right at their origin or source. We directed our efforts in understanding how these remedies behave at their source because that is how they are reflected in the humans who need them.

Today we look at the remedies in their natural habitat. We try to understand the mode of existence of these elements in nature and what is the mechanism of survival that they require to continue to exist in nature.

II. Nosode's Origin

To understand nosodes let us look at the source of these remedies. The source of these remedies is a diseased tissue or a diseased secretion which is with or without the organism that is causing the disease. So the source itself in nosodes is a victim i.e. either a diseased plant or an animal tissue. It is a victim in a completely diseased state.

The nosode has the element or the essence of an individual suffering from that particular disease and therefore it has the feeling of the individual due to that disease. It does not have the feeling of the individual itself but it carries the feeling of the diseased individual - the individual who has either contracted the disease, been affected by the disease or has been totally taken over by this disease. Just like a person having the taint of a lion on his vital force experiences every human situation as a victim-aggressor situation, an individual needing a nosode experiences every human situation as the disease or defect within him.

III. An Example

Consider the **case of Lac Leoninum**. *He goes to the market where he is trying to park his car. The parking lot is totally full, there is absolutely no place. But this guy, who has walked in with the taint of Lac Leoninum on his vital force, sees this situation as a situation of competition. He perceives this situation as - 'I have a right to keep my car here and must have a parking spot here. I must have a space in this parking lot but there is no space left here for me. I am supposed to get this space. I am mightier and far more powerful. How come there is no place for me? I am going to show them who I am! How can it happen that a person like me doesn't get a parking space in this parking lot?' With these thoughts he goes and crashes his car into the first little car he sees. He perceives this whole situation as a victim-aggressor one which involves competition. For him, it is a 'me' versus 'you' situation, with a fight to the finish, a fight for survival!*

Let us now consider a person having the taint of a nosode, a diseased tissue on his vital force, walking into this parking lot and seeing that it is all full. His feeling within is - 'Oh! I am the diseased one, the abnormal one. Everybody here is normal. They have reached on time and hence they have a space in the parking lot. They are all normal individuals who know how to get their ways. I am the affected one, the diseased one. I am the abnormal one who cannot even get a space in the parking lot, shame on me.' He compares himself with the others and finds himself morbidly incapable of anything. The fact that others can do it and he can't constantly eats him. The nosode comparison is different from the animal comparison in that a nosode compares his wrong or inherently morbid character with others around who according to him are normal while in an animal it is a competitive comparison between strong and weak.

IV. Nosode Features – Feeling and Polarity

The feeling of a nosode in every situation is that – 'I am diseased. I am abnormal.' The source of these remedies is a diseased tissue; hence he feels – 'I am wrong from within.' His thoughts go like this - Something is wrong about me, it's not about others but it's about me. I am weak and so it happened to me, something is incorrect. Something is diseased within me, which needs to be mended, repaired and corrected. I am at fault. The whole issue is about me and not being incomplete but being diseased, incorrect and at fault. I have made a mistake somewhere.

So if this is one side, what is the other side? We need to discover the polarity in nosodes as well because we see everything in terms of polarity or duality, in terms of **'I and U'**. The polarity in plants is sensitivity-reactivity. In animals it's me versus you, in minerals it's incomplete-complete, in imponderables its matter and energy. What's the polarity in the nosodes?

The polarity in the nosodes is **disease and health**. There is on one side, a completely diseased tissue, an abnormal feeling within and therefore the person is striving to go to the other side and that is the healthy normal side. So his words are going to be 'I must change the situation myself or I am not able to change the situation myself. I must make amendments in my own system. There is a problem within me and it needs correction.'

The person may either feel he can change the situation or he cannot. In order to ascertain the nosode kingdom, it does not matter whether he can or cannot bring changes. The very fact that in his mind he wants to make amendments to health makes it the other polarity. The desire to change to health, points to the kingdom. The ability or inability to do so, points to the intensity with which he experiences the issue or points to the specific miasm within the nosode kingdom.

The distinct feature that differentiates nosodes from the animal kingdom is the feeling that: 'I' am abnormal and weak within to let 'U' overpower me. 'I' have something wrong within me and I need to be normal like 'U'.

In fact, the basic response of any diseased tissue is to fight the disease. Whether it can or cannot fight and win against the organism is a different issue but the need to correct and counteract against the disease is always present so that health can be regained.

'Disease vs. Health'

In other words whatever the nosode, the sensation within remains the same. He could be Anthracinum, Diptherinum, Pertussinum, Tuberculinum, Psorinum, Medorrhinum, Carcinosinum or any one of them or maybe more but the feeling, polarity and the sensation within will be that 'I am diseased. My own tissue is diseased from within'.

To conclude, the feeling of a nosode is:

1. **I am weak and abnormal**
2. **I am attacked**
3. **The fault lies within my own system to be attacked like this - now how can I correct it?**

V. The Words of Polarity
  * **Mistake on one side and rectification on the other**
  * **Fault on one side - correction on the other**
  * **Incorrect - correct**
  * **Problem - repair**
  * **Error - modification**

VI. Caution:

These words like a fault or an abnormality or a mistake or 'something is wrong within me' sound human. They could come up in any and every case as the patient is describing his disease or complaint. While any patient describes his complaint he is bound to say that the symptoms he experiences are not normal. He is bound to say that he is suffering from a disease, that something is wrong within the system. How do we know that these apparently commonly used words are not mere superficial human words, but belong to the core sensation of the case? One of the most important things is that these words in a nosode case constitute a pattern, a pattern that is universal or global to the case and repeats itself from the chief complaint to various human situations that the person describes in the case. It also percolates at the level of delusion while the patient is trying to explain his feelings behind every situation or emotion he experiences. When the homeopath probes deeper into the feelings or delusions he is confronted with the same pattern again which is - 'What is it that is wrong, faulty, abnormal or diseased in me. What is it in me that makes me different, weaker and abnormal as compared to other individuals who are not suffering and are normal.' Hence the pattern or the polarity of normal and abnormal runs through and through and emerges as the core polarity of the case. This differentiates a nosode case from a case of any other kingdom.

3

 THE BASIC
UNDERSTANDING OF MIASMS

I.   Hahnemann's Discovery

II. Understanding the Concept of Miasms

III. A Quick Example

IV. The Ten Degrees of Sensations

V. Nosodes in the past and their similarity and
difference to the way Joshis use nosodes

I. Hahnemann's Discovery

It was the great master, Hahnemann, who brought into awareness the 3 stages of chronic diseases and based on these states of disease, he introduced 3 chronic miasms namely - Psora, Sycosis and Syphilis. He also introduced another miasm - Acute miasm. As the name suggests, the acute miasm is an acute disease from which one can come out of completely. According to Hahnemann, miasms are obnoxious agents that influence the vital force of a living organism, thus causing a variety of diseases and disorders in an organism. He postulated that they can also be genetically transferred.

II. Understanding the concept of miasms according to Dr. Sankaran's approach

Shachindra and I follow the miasm approach based on the concepts of Dr. Rajan Sankaran since it is the Sensation method that we follow, practice and preach ever since its inception a decade ago. After years of having worked exclusively with this approach we have come to imbibe it and even modify it to develop our own flair and style yet sticking closely to the rules and parameters of the approach. In one line miasm can be described as thus.

Miasm is an ATTITUDE of the individual

Miasms are an inherent part of the deep state of the individual. They reveal the intensity with which the sensation is felt and also reveal what the patient is doing for that intensity of sensation or how the patient copes with the sensation. It is that predominant characteristic of a person which determines his overall outlook towards life, his reaction across various life situations and the diseases or the intensity of illnesses that a person suffers or goes through. The deeper the intensity with which the state is felt, the more intense and desperate is the coping mechanism. From Psora to Syphilis the state gets more and more intense and the efforts get more and more desperate too. Consequently, the miasms help us decide which remedy to give the patient out of the many remedies that are present in each family and kingdom.

If we were to define miasms in a single sentence, we would say that "A miasm is the behaviour that a patient takes to handle the situation." Hence we can say that the miasm is divided into two parts: the intensity and the coping i.e. the attitude. The sensation and miasm together make the cross point of exactly which remedy to give. It is needless to say that remedies also have intensities or miasms!

III. A Quick Example

The Ranunculaceae family (Staphysagria, Aconite, Pulsatilla) has a lot to do with humiliation and insult. Hence all the remedies of the Ranunculaceae family will have insult. How would we differentiate between all their insults?

 * *If the insult is felt as an acute shock and the person couldn't do anything, it is an acute way of reacting to that insult. The miasm is Acute as in Aconite*
 * *If the insult involves controlling with closed fist, the patient is controlling the intense humiliation and insult. – Here miasm is Cancer miasm as in Staphysagria*
 * *If he simply avoids the insult and is very sensitive by nature, he is hiding that insult. He is covering it up. Here the person is in the Sycotic miasm as in Pulsatilla*

In this way we have differentiated the insult being felt by all these three miasms. Hence, for each of these miasms the remedy will differ.

IV. The Ten Degrees of Sensation

Now we go to the ten degrees of sensation or diseases and the ten different ways of coping with the sensation. This will help us understand the ten different miasms. The first miasm is called by the name of Acute miasm. The name Acute would suggest that it is not chronic but when we look at miasms as being at the emotional or the mental level in their origin Acute miasm also becomes a way of looking at things chronically. Hahnemann said that the acute miasm has a base of chronic miasm in it .We believe that the acute miasm is also a chronic miasm where a person reacts acutely and intensely to every stimulus and then is back to normal as the situation passes.

Joshis take on miasms

Though Hahnemann believed that the influence of diseases in the past or in the previous generations caused miasms which remain permanently in an individual, we beg to differ. We believe that miasms or attitudes caused diseases. Tubercular miasm precedes tuberculosis; Typhoid miasm precedes typhoid and so on and so forth. Hence a person has a Tubercular kind of behaviour which makes him contract tuberculosis in the first place. He then passes it on to the next generation. Let us say that these attitudes were difficult to name in the past but the diseases they caused had a name. Hence the attitudes got the name of the diseases. Tubercular is an attitude which was always present in humanity before tuberculosis and caused other deadly

17

diseases then and causes many other deadly diseases even today. So, though the names of the miasms came from the diseases, these disease are typical of the attitudes and that the miasms in humans were much before the diseases. However due to these well-known diseases and due to the fact that we know the pathology of these diseases well, it is easy to stick to the names of the diseases for the miasms as well.

Therefore all of diseases present could be classified according to their behaviour and can be categorised into these ten different miasms.

E.g. Tuberculosis, diphtheria, pertussis can all belong to Tubercular miasm.
E.g. Typhoid, septic abscesses can both belong to Typhoid miasms.
E.g. Small pox, leprosy both can belong to Leprosy miasm.
E.g. Cancer, anthrax, autoimmune diseases can all be in the Cancer miasm.

Just as in plant cases Anacardium, Anhalonium, Ignatia, Ulmus, Agnus castus, Ornithogalum are all Cancer miasm remedies but have a different peculiar sensation depending on the family they belong to.

Similarly, Anthracinum and Carcinosinum belong to the Cancer miasm but will have a slightly different picture depending on the disease they belong to. We could say that there are certain nosodes made from the diseases representative of the miasms. Since every other disease also falls into the category one of the ten miasms, in each miasm, we can have many nosodes.

Let us look at the ten different miasms and their peculiar characteristics.

There are three main pillars of miasms – Psora, Sycosis and Syphilis. These three major miasms have peculiar differentiating characteristics and every consecutive pillar is more desperate than the previous one. Hence the desperation of Sycosis is more than that of Psora and that of Syphilis is greater than that of Sycosis. Any miasm can be intense but as you move away from Acute towards Syphilis the desperation and hopelessness increases.

1. The Acute miasm. Acute miasm simply means a situation that crops up acutely, instantly and suddenly and hence has the same kind of response. This situation also resolves itself completely and quickly. This miasm has words like acute, sudden, intense and great danger. Since the threat is too big and sudden, the response to this sudden intense threat is to escape. Either there is instinctive action or there is panic, shock and immobilisation. As such there is no coping, it is just panic. An individual in this miasm feels suddenly threatened or affected and does not act but only reacts to this immediate situation with panic and outburst and then the situation resolves as quickly as it cropped up. There is no chance and no need to cope here. Hence the person makes no effort to come out of the situation but nevertheless he comes out of it and almost without any permanent damage or marks. He only reacts overwhelmingly to it.

E.g. A person walking on the road gets hit by a foot ball coming from across a house on the road. A little boy kicked it too hard and it hit the man walking past his house. For a moment this man is shocked by this hit and he blinks his eye, he falls down and is in a state of shock but then he shakes his head, there is a small bump, he is back to his senses and he kicks the ball back so that the child gets it back. The child apologises and the man is hardly harmed or hurt and starts walking back again on the road to his destination.

2. **The Typhoid miasm.** The Acute miasm is characterised by shock and panic. In Typhoid, we see the panic and the suddenness but we also witness the hectic tremendous effort to do something for the situation and then be in comfort, complete rest and safety. So the picture here is not that of shock but that of 'a need to do'. The feeling in this miasm is that of losing one's comfort and hence they have to make intense but short effort. It is a situation of 'do or die' because it has the suddenness and panic of acute, but it also has the need to grab the situation and very quickly find a solution to avoid a collapse. A collapse would be felt as a completely given up struggle with a sinking feeling. It is a feeling of a man who is pushed into water and is drowning. He has to learn in those few minutes to come out of the water in order to save himself.

So the intensity with which Typhoid feels the situation is acute but the coping is not like Acute. The coping is not that of shock but the coping is effortful and hopeful to come to that point of safety where everything is calm and peaceful.

3. **The Psoric miasm.** This is the first chronic miasm according to Hahnemann or the first major pillar. The main theme here is that of a continuous struggle and trial with a lot of hope of reaching cure. The patient's response to stress is therefore that of continuous trials. Here the patient will try, try and try. He feels he must make effort to reach to a position of safety and health. So continuous and hopeful struggle is the key word for the Psoric miasm.

4. The Ringworm miasm. You know that there are three major miasms - Psora, Sycosis and Syphilis forming the three basic pillars or three basic miasms. In between these pillars we have several miasms. The Acute and Typhoid miasms precede Psora. Typhoid shows the suddenness of Acute but the struggle of Psora. Then Psora shows only struggle. Next, we have the Ringworm which lies in between the two major pillars of Psora and Sycosis. So what does Ringworm have?

Ringworm has the struggle of Psora on the base of Sycosis. Therefore the feeling in Ringworm is - 'This is a difficult situation and it is beyond any easy struggle or reach. The feeling that the situation is difficult and must be accepted belongs to Sycosis and the efforts to keep doing and trying belongs to Psora. Hence the element of struggle in Ringworm comes from Psora and the element of acceptance and resignation comes from Sycosis. As expected, Ringworm pendulates constantly between Psora and Sycosis or alternates between trying and giving up. A very typical example of Ringworm is the person who is obese. He loves to eat food and still wants to lose weight. Whenever he reads a magazine, listens to a health talk, visits somebody, goes to a party and sees everyone else fit and fine, he comes back home with the determination that 'I have to lose weight!' from the next day on he will go on a diet of fruit and salad. That is exactly what the Ringworm starts to think and do but the next morning when he is tempted by a delicious food plate in front of him; all the plans to lose weight are forgotten. The issue of the Ringworm here is that 'It's not so easy to start a diet and give up on good food'. And so the Ringworm pathology is very difficult to treat. It can go on and off constantly. Unlike the Acute and Typhoid miasms, the intensity is moderate. It is not acute or sudden and frightening and hence there is no need for an acute struggle. Like in the above example, it is ok if the weight is not lost in one minute. It's not a situation of drowning. Hence the coping or the pace of the effort is steady and continuous.

5. The Malaria miasm. This is a combination of Acute over Sycosis. The base is that of the Sycotic miasm whereas the panic and the feelings of being stuck and attacked come intermittently. The pathology in malaria is that of acute spikes of fever with chills intermittently. Between the spikes in pain and periodically the pain and fever worsen. Just like the malarial spikes, the Malarial miasm individual is periodically mournful and brooding. He feels that nothing is good and everything is miserable. It is just like the mosquito which is around you and nagging you, troubling you and you just want to get rid of it. The coping is that of brooding, complaining or of doing nothing about it. Here again, the situation is not fatal and hence the coping is moderate. There is an intense fear in this miasm which comes acutely and then settles, only to come back over and over again.

Let us take the example of being obese like we mentioned with Ringworm. In Malaria, the obese patient will tell the doctor that he is already over weight and now it's not at all possible to lose so much weight. After two days the patient will call the doctor to say that, "I just read in the newspaper that the people who are fat get diabetes, I am scared!" So we can observe a desperate anxiety here. Then after two more days he will call the doctor again with another anxiety like that of hypertension and then again two more days later at same time he will call up and tell the doctor that he is scared that he will get a heart attack, have high cholesterol and die. So although the patient will acutely call up the doctor with panic, he will do nothing about it, which is different from Ringworm where he will try to lose weight and give up after the first few attempts.

6. **The Sycosis miasm.** This is the second pillar. It is the other major pillar after Psora. Sycosis represents pure acceptance and nothing else. There is neither an acute attack, nor constant trial for improvement. The successful Sycosis simply accepts and avoids the situation. He covers it up. It is as if, 'As long as nobody sees it, it's fine.' Hence there is a constant avoidance of the sensation, the weak spot with the feeling that, 'Anyway I don't have the capacity to deal with it.' For example, you have a Sycotic who starts having urticaria by having rice then he will do nothing about the urticaria, what he will simply do is that he will wear a coat so that the world doesn't see it or he will constantly look for those rice items which cause urticaria and he will go hypochondriac over it. It's like - even if there is wheat he will keep checking if there is a rice item in it. So he will be hypersensitive and hypochondriac yet he will actually do nothing to help his urticaria.

On one side, the person shows such great avoidance of the sensations or sensitive spots that he is often labelled as being a hypochondriac or a hypersensitive individual. He lives a very restricted life. We could call this a 'failed Sycotic' reaction. The failed Sycosis will constantly complain of the weak spot, of the sensation with the feeling of guilt that he could do nothing about it and at the same time he will do nothing about it. There is guilt, remorse and self-reproach while also nothing to alter or better the situation. Notice that the pace or the coping of all miasms from Psora to

Sycosis is always moderate. Neither is it acute as in Acute or Typhoid miasms nor is it hopeless & nearing death as you see beyond Sycosis. With the same example of obesity, there could be a different reaction of the same Sycotic miasm which will say that, "I don't think I need to lose weight, there are people much fatter to me, and if I wear a dress in such a way, or if I wear a big coat then none of the extra weight is seen. So it's absolutely fine!" This can be called a 'successful Sycotic' reaction.

7. **The Cancer miasm.** The key words of Cancer miasm are - 'In control, never satisfied, pushing oneself to the limit with a constant feeling that the task is beyond one's limit'.

Since the Cancer feels that things are going out of control, there is a constant effort to keep things in control. This is the successful side. Here we have those people who work with a lot of precision in situations where others would lose control. On the contrary, the failed side feels immense chaos. It feels that everything is going to go out of control and feels that it is not possible to bring back that control. The intensity is very severe.

It is just like the athlete who is going to make that hundred-metre sprint in a very short time like that of just five seconds. He is making tremendous efforts to give his best performance. Here the patient over stretches himself beyond his limits to bring back control over the chaos. It is just like the cancer cells which keep growing. They create chaos in the adjacent area and there is no control.

8. **The Tubercular miasm.** Now we have the Tubercular miasm that lies between Sycosis and is closer to Syphilis. The intensity now begins to get even severe. The situation is not so hopeful. The chances to escape death are lesser. The intensity in Cancer is severe because it is moving towards Syphilis but in Tubercular miasm the desperation is even more severe. Tubercular is also closer to the Leprous miasm which lies just after Tubercular and before Syphilis. Because Tubercular is so close to Syphilis and death, the feeling is of intense suffocation and activity (like the last ditch effort) that is done just before death. There is a sense of hopelessness, a feeling that 'I might not be able to do it'. Hence, just before giving up and accepting death, Tubercular has a feeling of being caught in hectic activity, being compressed and suffocated. The gap seems to be narrowing and time seems very short which brings the experience of being choked by the force or the intensity of situation and efforts.

Let us take an example of the athlete. In Cancer, this athlete is the first guy who has made it close to the finish line whereas others are still behind. He now has the last five seconds before he reaches the finish line and has to keep full control of the mechanisms of his body. The Tubercular is different. He is the last guy there. His feeling is that in this last five seconds, I have to make a hectic intense effort to reach the finish line and that too first. Hence the pressure is intense. He knows he cannot cross all others ahead of him and make it to the finish line first but he still wants to do the impossible. It is the feeling of the lava that is coming out of the volcano. Tubercular puts in intense efforts in a near death situation. Tubercular activity is different and much more intense than Typhoid activity. In Typhoid the person feels that if he comes out of it he has reached to the point of safety. Typhoid has to struggle out of the pond, but for Tubercular the situation is more difficult. He has to fight the ocean! On the failed side, the Tubercular is completely burnt out and exhausted with all this tremendous activity; he is going towards destruction. He knows that all the activity only caused suffocation and compression and it leads to nothing and that he is very close to the fatal point. On the successful side the hectic activity is seen more clearly and vividly.

9. **The Leprosy miasm.** The Leprosy miasm is the second last miasm just before Syphilis. Here the hope is very low. To understand this miasm let us look at the situation of a person affected with leprosy. The leper as the sensations of being isolated, poisoned, destroyed, disgusted, despised, ashamed, hunted down and being pushed into a corner. He feels contemptuous of himself. A leper puts these thoughts away, shuns them off. We know that in Leprosy, the body begins to disintegrate, the fingers and the body parts get disfigured and self amputate eventually. The successful leper avoids sights of people. He cuts them off and isolates himself before the world can isolate him. But on the failed side the Leprous miasm individual cannot do that. He becomes suicidal, homicidal and self - destructive. He starts biting, tearing and destroying himself. The intensity is very severe and it deteriorates further as it goes to the last miasm.

10. **The Syphilis miasm.** We now come to the last pillar, the last point, the final destination, the final miasm. In Leprosy we begin to see disintegration and destruction of the cell, the biting, the tearing, the cursing, it is almost close to death. In Syphilis, one is dead, there is no hope; it as if death is the only choice, it's the only way out. The feeling is that 'It is completely beyond my capacity.'

23

Hence a person having a Syphilitic miasm has a very desperate and hopeless attitude towards life. In every situation he faces in life he sees failure and despair. Sometimes a Syphilitic individual could go to the exact opposite side of causing destruction outside as a reflection of the turmoil going on within him. Compensated individuals of this miasm would say that they do not make a single mistake or else they are doomed and destined to fail miserably and then there will be nothing left for them but to commit suicide. Hence you see that whether they are successful or failed they perceive everything as a desperate and near-death situation.

V. Nosodes in the past and their similarity and difference to the way Joshis use nosodes

Nosodes are popularly used as intercurrents or block removers.
An intercurrent as the name suggests is used in between the 'current' or regular flow of treatment. If in the regular flow of treatment there is a block or an obstruction which does not allow the improvement or cure to go forward an intercurrent is used.

What is an obstruction or a block? A block or obstruction in the treatment is a point where the patient stops to respond favourably to a well-suited remedy. There could be a block at the very beginning of the treatment as well where the patient gives certain disease or common symptoms only. In the classical way when a well suited remedy does not act any more or when there are hardly any characteristic symptoms the homeopath ascertains the miasm of the individual and gives a nosode. The nosode being representative of the miasm either clears this block and makes the patient more receptive to a well suited remedy or in cases where there are only disease symptoms it clears the miasm block and stirs-up the system or the vital force so that characteristic symptoms will now emerge. This kind of use of the nosode helps in forwarding treatment and clearing blocks.

We do not see nosodes merely as block removers, but as having specific characteristic states and symptoms of their own as well. However nosodes being disease products are extremely close to the disease or to the miasm that they belong to. Today we look at every remedy and every individual as having a deep sensation which is the very essence of the remedy and a miasm which shows the intensity of that sensation. Hence a remedy has sensation and miasm. Therefore if we were to consider the picture of the nosodes as sensation plus miasm their miasm characteristics are more predominant, more clear and stand out more vividly as compared to the sensation characteristics. This is also true of cases needing nosode remedies and hence you see more miasm characteristics in nosode cases as compared to sensation characteristics.

Because these miasm characteristics are so predominant nosode remedies work as partial similimums when you give them to a case who doesn't need a nosode but needs the same miasm as the nosode and therefore helps to treat the case to a certain extent. Therefore, according to us, intercurrent way of prescribing a nosode helps in the same way as prescribing a partial similimum, whereby the sensation is not taken care of but the miasm is taken care of.

Let's take the example of Tuberculinum. Let's say the patient needs Iodum which is a Tubercular remedy belonging to the mineral kingdom. Giving Tuberculinum to this patient would help him to a certain extent because both Iodum and Tuberculinum have the same attitude, which is Tubercular, however Iodum has the sensation of failure of achievement as a performer and he is restless as there is no time left before final destruction. Tuberculinum has a sensation that something is very wrong within him and there is no time before the final destruction. This component of 'no time before destruction' and the immense restlessness that goes along with it is common to both remedies because it is the miasm component of both remedies. Therefore giving Tuberculinum to this Iodum patient helps in relieving the restlessness and the next time the patient comes he is calmer and he talks about his inner feeling of failure, his inner desires of extraordinary achievement and his incapacity to fulfil them. The homeopath can easily see the Iodum state now, which was always there, but was probably difficult to elicit due to the immense restlessness. Therefore one could think that the Tuberculinum worked as an intercurrent and helped in clearing the case so that Iodum could be seen more clearly. Tuberculinum worked as a partial similimum. For several reasons Iodum could not be elicited in the first place so it becomes a zigzag way of cure like would happen with many cases.

Whether they are used as an intercurrent or any other way if a nosode is not indicated in the case or in other words if the sensation of the nosode is not present in the case, but the miasm matches then the nosode just helps to relieve the miasm symptoms but does not solve the case completely. Hence it works like a similar remedy.

Let's take another example. A patient needs Mercury for his follicular tonsillitis which is a remedy of the Syphilitic miasm and we give him Lachesis which is also a remedy of the Syphilitic miasm, but the two belong to different kingdoms. Here again Lachesis will help the Mercurius case. It will help the night aggravation, it will help the pain while swallowing and the immense throat inflammation that the patient has because both of them have the same miasm. But it will not totally cure the case. It will not totally cure the severe follicular tonsillitis that the patient is suffering from, however because it has helped some symptoms the patient feels relieved and the next time the homeopath will be able to see Mercurius symptoms more clearly. You could call it as Syphilinum worked as an intercurrent or partial similimum. Sometimes it often happens that we use the nosode because we haven't understood the case and come to the exact similimum. The use of the nosode in such cases works as a partial similimum because the nosode shares the same miasm as the similimum the patient needs.

4

 DIFFERENT NOSODE PICTURES ACCORDING TO THE JOSHIS

I.   Typhoidinum

II.   Psorinum

III.   Malaria Nosode

IV.   Ringworm

V.   Medorrhinum

VI.   Carcinosinum

VII.   Anthracinum

VIII. Tuberculinum

IX.   Bacillinum

X.   Pertussinum

XI.   Diptherinum

XII.   Leprominum

XIII. Variolinum

XIV. Syphilinum

XV.   Pyrogen

XVI. Lyssinum

I. Typhoidinum

Typhoidinum belongs to the Typhoid miasm. The pathology of typhoid is quite like a crisis situation. You have very high fevers, the intestines can get affected and perforations can develop in extreme cases. At the same time it's a pathology which is self-limiting and you can recover completely in less than a month's time. So here the feeling is -**'Yes there is a problem but with some intense efforts I can try to solve it. I can make an impulsive effort with my full strength and vigour. I am quite hopeful that I shall get a solution to this problem. The problem looks very intense but I am sure with some help around and with some kind of a desire within me to work this out, I am going to reach to a point of safety very soon'.**

We would like to discuss a case of Typhoidinum. A young girl, 19 years old, came to us three years ago with complaints of severe dysmenorrhoea. She tends to have acute illnesses before every exam, every presentation at high school and before any event. She often trembles due to anticipation and faints during such times. With the pain of the dysmenorrhoea she feels faint or fears she will almost collapse. Often she has been escorted home by friends from school due to these problems. Her mother is quite worried about her fragile, frail and nervous nature.

When we asked the girl about her pain she answered that she anticipates that something is grossly wrong with her. During the dysmenorrhoea it feels like she is going through something no other girl might have ever gone through. She fears she has some weak and abnormal constitution while others around her are strong and just healthy normal individuals. She feels herself to be very different from the rest. She feels embarrassed and that others might be laughing at her weakness. When asked about the embarrassment she says it is a feeling of being different from the rest. The rest of the group is just normal and fine while something is weird about her that is different almost like a disease, like something which differentiates her from the rest. She was weeping as she spoke about this. The fear according to her is that she will faint in public and create a big scene and everyone will know that she has this weakness and this fragile body. But often she calls her friends over every time she is worried and tries to divert herself. She makes it a point to go to school and elsewhere with her close friends so that they will always be there to help her in case she faints or collapses from nervousness or pain. When accompanied by friends the fear disappears as she knows she is well taken care of. Also, these episodes happen only when she has a presentation or when she has her menses. Otherwise she is very bubbly, enthusiastic and full of energy. She does not give these fears a second thought when there is no situation to precipitate them.

The feeling in the patient that she is weak, abnormal and different from normal people is the polarity of the nosode kingdom. This sensation however is a momentary one and crops up acutely every time she is faced with a situation that challenges her. She does not dwell on it constantly and also comes out of this sensation once the situation has been dealt with. This indicates an acute and a very hopeful attitude to the sensation. She makes efforts of taking help from friends and deals with the situation. This acuteness with taking efforts and asking for help to overcome one's sensation is the behaviour of the Typhoid miasm. She did extremely well on Typhoidinum 1M.

II. Psorinum

Psorinum is the remedy which belongs to the Psoric miasm. This remedy is made from the seropurulent matter contained in the scabies vesicle. Here the feeling would be that **'The problem lies within me and I am constantly struggling to solve this problem. There must be a solution within me. I must try. I must make an effort and struggle to solve this problem.'** Psorinum patients are worried all the time about every little single ailment or abnormal symptom that they develop because these little things make them feel they are far away from being completely healthy. Complete health is their goal and they cannot bear the slightest ailment. Hence they come across as very hypochondriac, anxious and ever-complaining individuals. They keep coming to the doctor for every minor development in their physical complaints. The effort to be near normal makes them want to read all about different diseases, health issues. This is exactly what we saw in a case of Psorinum that we saw a few years ago. We are going to summarise the case with the most important details.

A Case of Psorinum in brief

She has spotting. She does not have PCOD or any specific problem as such. She just has spotting in between her periods and especially spotting when she has overexertion or when she has done any kind of exercises. Generally it stops after one day or two days but rarely it continues till the end of the next period. This is the reason why she consulted us. The whole case was about nothing else but - 'Why do I have this spotting which is abnormal? I need to try and solve this. I need to be as normal as possible. I need to have no abnormality within my body. Why do I have this problem with me? Now that I have come to the doctor, it's not a big problem. But I struggle to see that I reach my levels of normalcy. I struggle to see that I don't have this kind of spotting. I should be rid of every ailment. I eat healthy, organic foods. I exercise regularly. I have all the healthy habits. Why should I have spotting? How can I get rid of it? 'That was all she kept saying at just a regular monotonous pace.

Remedy and Case follow-up
We gave her Psorinum 200C, just about 2 doses. We saw her for a year until April 2007 after which she was fine and discontinued treatment. She also felt more normal and not so disturbed by the feeling of abnormality within. If you see the earlier materia medica pictures of Psorinum, they talk of somebody who has a constant anxiety of poverty and a despair of recovery. It's a very complaining picture. We can understand that completely when we see Psorinum our way - the Joshis' way. Psorinum feels that something is wrong with him and hence has a constant need to reach normalcy. He is going to be complaining and fearful even though he is rich. He is going to have an anxiety about poverty and he is going to always want to continuously struggle and reach to a certain level of safety and security because there is a constant itch and a constant need within to reach a level of safety and health. These are mere reflections and expressions of a deeper feeling of 'I am not normal and I don't have enough.' Earlier, our patient kept going from one doctor to another, just struggling to get this spotting solved. When she improved, she said, "The need to constantly be normal is much lesser and therefore even if I do get spotting it doesn't affect me so much." She said that it was almost like a compulsion in her to reach that normalcy. In a couple of months the spotting and anxiety both had reduced.

III. Malaria Nosode

This nosode belongs to the Malarial miasm. The remedy is prepared from the combination of the 4 malarial species of Plasmodia: Plasmodium falciparum, Plasmodium vivax, Plasmodium ovale, Plasmodium malariae. The feeling in this remedy would be - 'There is a disease within, the problem is within. **I know nothing is really going to help me to come out of this problem, so why even give it a try**. I am already suffering so much with this issue within me. **I know from within that there is no hope. I am very abnormal, I can't change it and it just worsens.** When I see other people living a normal life I wonder why God made me like this, what is wrong with me? I mean why should he make me suffer like this? What is the problem with me? You know every time I look at someone or something happens, this feeling of anger and resentment within me gets aggravated'.

The Malaria nosode feels - **very tortured, tormented, nagged by his complaint every now and then in intermittent bouts and he cannot do much about it at all.** He therefore accepts his weakness within and at times gets into an acute frenzy of complaining and nagging.

A very important point is that Malaria has a combination of Acute and Sycotic miasms. Hence **after the acute nagging tormenting episode passes away, the individual becomes Sycotic in his behaviour where he accepts and avoids his faults and stays in this position until the next tormenting attack again**. Hence he is never out of it completely, he is either avoiding his faults or when they become too much to handle and to difficult to hide, he breaks down and bursts into acute episodes and then as the acute episodes settle the problem continues to persist at a plateau level or a tolerable level where he can start to hide it again.

IV. Ringworm

Ringworm belongs to the Ringworm miasm. This remedy is made from scraping of the eruptions of tinea taken from an infected patient.

A nosode with the Ringworm miasm would say - 'Yes there is a problem and **I am trying my level best to come out of it but somehow you know I don't think it really works. I am trying but I simply tend to give up at some point and let it be. But then I feel, no, there is a problem within and I do want to come out of it.** If that person has come out of it, why am I so abnormal? No, let me not give up, let me give it a try again.'

So there is a **constant trying and giving up.**

V. Medorrhinum

Medorrhinum is a nosode belonging to the Sycotic miasm. This remedy is made from the gonorrhoeal discharge. Here the deepest feeling within is just like any other nosode –'My system is at fault. I have a problem and there is some sort of weakness within me.'

So what will he do to overcome his problem and go to the health side?

Because he belongs to the Sycotic miasm, **he will do nothing about it. He will only hide it or avoid it and believe that if it is hidden, it is okay and it doesn't need any correction. He will anticipate and think of ways to avoid it**. 'I don't think I can do much to correct it. But if only I can hide it and avoid

31

it, don't make a big show of it then I think I can deal with it all my life, it is good enough.' This is the whole feeling of the Medorrhinum nosode which is the nosode belonging to the Sycotic miasm - 'I have a problem within me however I cannot correct it but I can definitely seem to accept and avoid it because nothing much can be done in this situation.'

VI. Carcinosinum or Carcinosin

Carcinosinum is the remedy belonging to the Cancer miasm. This remedy is made from breast cancer discharge. The nosode sensation in this remedy is - 'I have a problem within me. My own system, my own self has gone haywire'. While in the earlier Sycotic miasm, the Medorrhinum patient said I can do nothing to correct it and so I avoid it, hide it and cover it up. Here in Cancer miasm, the patient will say - **'Yes the problem is within me but there are other people who work wonders. Though there is a problem, I should try my level best to control and overcome it. I must check and look at every loop hole and rectify it so that I can get back to normal. There ought to be a way out. There are people who do superhuman things with their bodies, minds and souls. Why am I like this? No, I won't give up. In fact, I must not only be normal, I must be supernormal'.** This will be the way in which he will want to get to the other side of disease - to the health side. He wants to be super healthy and not just healthy.

Similar to Carcinosinum we can find more nosodes belonging to Cancer miasm like Anthracinum which will be discussed later.

Please note that along with this main sensation that I am diseased and I am not healthy, the specific quality of that disease will denote which nosode to give. The way in which he explains this sensation, copes with it and the intensity with which he sees the feeling – 'I have a problem within' will decide which miasm this nosode belongs to and will tell us exactly which nosode should be given to the patient.

Just as in the plants, e.g. the sensation in Hammamelidae remains the same: heaviness and lightness but the miasms of the ten different Hammamelidae remedies differ from one to the other and therefore we give completely different remedies, similarly the deeper sensation of abnormality and health remains and how the patient copes with this basic issue decides the miasm of the nosode the patient needs.

For example:

- ✶ The miasm in Cannabis indica is a miasm of Sycosis and therefore it avoids and flees into the fantasy of lightness believing that the world is beautiful and very brightly coloured.
- ✶ In Cannabis sativa which is of the Malarial miasm, the feeling within of heaviness and lightness remains the same but the coping is different. Here he feels 'Oh! I am always heavy. Why am I always heavy? Everybody else feels light and free but I always have this heaviness and I can never come out it.' The complaining, vehemence and the tortured feeling, puts him in the Malarial miasm.

So the heaviness and lightness remain common to Hammamelidae yet the miasm of Cannabis indica and Cannabis sativa being different, you can differentiate which one your patient needs.

VII. Anthracinum

Anthracinum has been taken from the spleen of an infected mammal. I was looking through the whole of the remedy because it has been listed well in our materia medica. It has been clinically used often in the past.

I wanted to know if there is a hint of this feeling and the polarity of the nosodes somewhere in the past like something that I have found out through many of our cases. Is it mentioned in the provings or in the clinical pictures of commonly known nosodes?

When I read about Anthracinum, I found something very interesting which I want to share with you. Vithoulkas says that Anthracinum holds so much grief deep inside that it can be seen as a remedy with the most silent grief and with the most serious emotional injury which also remains deep inside. It is as if all emotional and mental traumas of Anthracinum have been encapsulated in a huge dark tumour. He further says that it differs from Natrum muriaticum in the sense that it does not seem to be conscious of the trauma. It is as if he accepts the trauma and thinks that it is inherent to his existence. He will never discuss it with anybody. He can be extremely hard on himself and have a need to be in control. So the feeling in Anthracinum is just like any other nosode - 'The problem is within me, it is inherent to my existence and to my system. I was born with this disease and cannot do much about it. In fact, I was born with this inability to deal with the situation. Thus, Anthracinum is self-reproaching. So the miasm looks very Cancerous. From what we know about anthrax, the symptoms are those of necrosis and decaying. So the picture is very much that of cancer. The feeling here is - **'My system is so deranged that it is beyond repair. It is getting necrotic, spoilt and decaying but I really need to control it.'**

Therefore you may want to categorise a patient with a feeling – 'I have a problem within, I am hiding it', as Medorrhinum whereas you might categorise another patient as Carcinosinum if he says - 'I have a problem within, the situation is nearly hopeless but I am making superhuman efforts to come out of it or keep myself normal and fit even in such adverse circumstances.'

Both **Anthracinum and Carcinosinum will have a feeling that there is a problem within which is hopeless and needs superhuman efforts since both belong to the Cancer miasm.**

The next question then is about the difference in the picture of Carcinosinum and Anthracinum. We need to know how to differentiate between the two.

Anthracinum would have in its picture a lot of necrosis and destruction and decay whereas Carcinosinum will emphasise on the sensation of chaos within. Something like - 'Cells have gone haywire, my own system has turned against me and is creating new alien bodies and tumours within me and I must keep control in this hopeless situation or use tremendous will power.'

Anthracinum will emphasise that its own system is hopeless, that any attack from the outside will derange it and that there is such chaos within that it will begin to break down, melt, decay and putrefy. It then feels a need to take control in this adverse circumstance. This difference between the two nosodes is attributed to the disease picture itself and therefore also to the part of the source and remedy picture.

VIII. Tuberculinum

Tuberculinum belongs to the Tubercular miasm. This remedy, Tuberculinum bovinum, is prepared from tubercular glands of cattle. The feeling would be that - 'I know there is a problem within me.' But Tuberculinum is just some steps before Syphilis. It has a feeling that - 'There could be some effort I can do, let me try my level best. **There is hardly any time left to save the destruction or we are nearing death and therefore let me make my**

34

utmost efforts in whatever little time I have. I am out of breath, I feel suffocated. Let me hurry and make all kinds of efforts. Let me be very intense and very rapid, very desperate in my attempts and maybe that way I can do something to correct this problem.'

IX. Bacillinum

Bacillinum has a picture similar to Tuberculinum. **Bacillinum experiences the problem within him to be grave and almost impossible to repair. He feels the scarcity of time, he feels very suffocated and breathless from the intensity of the situation. He knows he has to make hectic and hurried efforts and he is fighting against time and that death is too close just like Tuberculinum** in the Tubercular miasm. But the difference between the two nosodes is that **the efforts are more in Tuberculinum whereas the sinking and collapse is more in Bacillinum**. A Tuberculinum patient desperately wants to do something to come out of the desperate unhealthy situation while the **Bacillinum patient is exhausted after hectic efforts and is panting breathlessly from the frenzy that he has just gone through**.

X. Pertussinum

This is the nosode of the Tubercular miasm, taken from the glary stringy mucus which contains the virus of whooping cough. The materia medica describes in Pertussinum, a forceful, strangulating, choking and resistant cough. Hence all this led us to think that this is more of a Tubercular taint with the sensation - 'My system is at fault and I am desperately trying to improve but I feel blocked and obstructed from within to bring about that change.' This blocked feeling itself causes aggression, desperation, violence and a violent whooping cough. The feeling here is **very similar to the Tubercular miasm. It is a feeling of being blocked and obstructed in the tunnel and then there is aggression and a desire to come out. The hectic activity, feelings of desperation, of choking, of being close to death, of running out of time are common to Pertussinum and Tuberculinum but in Pertussinum there is a feeling of being blocked and having to exert great force to break and destroy this block so that you can move or go ahead or reach health**. The block however is an expression of the intensity and not the sensation. Let us explain this. A Pertussinum patient will have the same sensation of a nosode that something within him is very much wrong and there is very little time left to rectify this. He has immense restlessness like that of a Tuberculinum patient. The feeling of having very little time at hand and not being able to rectify things is the component of the miasm. But in Pertussinum this Tubercular component of lack of time and hence having hectic activity is felt as a block or a wall in front of you which you want to break or push through. The intensity of wanting to get out is felt as a great force that one needs to exert and hence the feeling that you are being resisted and blocked further. Therefore you would give Pertussinum to a patient who has the basic sensation of a fault within himself, of a problem within or abnormality within him and he has to put great amount of force as if pushing toward a wall in trying to come out or rectify the faults.

XI. Diptherinum

If you look at the clinical picture of Diptherinum in our materia medica, it's one of weakness and collapse. The patient is very much weak to even complain. The tonsils and the glands of the neck are red and swollen, there is fetid expectoration, membranes are seen on the tonsils, the pulse is rapid and there are cold extremities. We get to see a prostrated patient. The state may end in collapse.

Diptherinum's picture as a nosode is that of a **collapsed Tubercular miasm**. It is very similar to Bacillinum since in Diptherinum too, the efforts made by the person are very poor. It's a completely collapsed state. Diptherinum differs from Bacillinum in the way that **the patient talks about a barrier or a membrane that is blocking and choking him** (similar to Pertussinum). **But unlike Pertussinum he is exhausted and has no strength left to break this film, layer or membrane that will finally suffocate him to death**. When Diptherinum talks of suffocation of the Tubercular miasm he gives you a picture of a barrier or wall or membrane that he is unable to breakthrough due to his exhaustion and collapsed state. The difference between the feeling of the wall in Pertussinum is that since Pertussinum has a more aggressive state (belonging to the disease picture itself), the wall is felt as a strong barrier like an iron or brick wall and the Pertussinum individual himself exerts a tremendous force or wants to exert a tremendous force to break it. Here force and strength are important key words, just as the aggressive nature of the whooping caught itself. Diptherinum on the other hand has a **picture of collapse and weakness** at the source level. Here there is a membrane like sensation in the throat, which makes swallowing difficult. Thus Diptherinum's **sensation of the wall is** not that of a very thick strong barrier, but more **like a soft layer or curtain which he has no capacity to go through because he is completely tired exhausted and collapsed**. You could say that Bacillinum is like a collapsed Tuberculinum and Diptherinum is like a collapsed

Pertussinum.

XII. Leprominum

The nosode belongs to the Leprosy miasm. This remedy is prepared from a
leprous nodule.

The feeling in Leprominum would be – 'I know there is a problem within me
and that I am abnormal. I know nobody wants me here. I don't know why I
am born with this? I worked out every possible way; I have tried my level
best but I don't think there is any way out. I feel that it's getting to a point
where I am so disgusting to everybody around that **I am treated as an
outcast.** I myself feel like I am an outcast. **I am so different, down trodden
and completely low as compared to the others around me. I feel like
harming myself**. I don't think I deserve to be around with this problem. I can
understand why people are trying to shoo me away because it is really such a
demeaning and disgusting thing, this problem of mine!' The nosodes of this
miasm have **resigned to faith and to destiny. They feel as if there is no way
out.**

We had a case of Leprominum who is doing very well now. It's almost three
years that she is following up with us and has steadily improved very well.
She had given us the entire picture of the leprous disease. She said her entire
complaint was a respiratory and asthmatic problem. But she said, "Every time
I go out with my asthma I feel like every other person thinks that I am
contagious. They think I am so terrible that I am a monster. It is as if I am
going to eat everybody up. Do I look like a monster to you? Do I look like a
deformed monster who is going to just spread this contagious disease to every
person he sees? I am just an outcast. I am not in the society. Nobody belongs
to me and I don't belong to anybody. I have a disease within me which is so
very disgusting that everybody throws me out."

XIII. Variolinum

It is a nosode made from small pox. I would put it in the Leprosy miasm. Here
the feeling would be – 'I am faulty within. **My system is so deranged that I
am going to lose my vitality or even my vital parts. I will die or I will have
to live with the deformities in my system forever.** I am no good and I am
going to bear the brunt of my faulty system for a lifetime. **People will always
have one look at me and know that I am abnormal, deranged and**

disgusting. They will shun me because once I had something so horrible and contagious; they will pity me like a beggar because of my state. Everybody looks at me. **They either want to shun me or pity me.'**

To understand the difference between Leprominum and Variolinum let us look at the diseases themselves. Small pox is a disease that affects in childhood. It has more of a sudden onset, a fatal result and for those children who survive they live either with a lifelong deformity or at least pox marks. Hence here the pace is sudden which turns fatal soon and in case one survives there is a deformity which does not grow or evolve slowly with time. In leprosy the pace is insidious and gradual and if left untreated it slowly and gradually proceeds to death. Hence in **Variolinum there is a feeling of sudden shame, hopelessness, shunned feeling and disgust, while in Leprominum it is more gradual feeling but it will take one hopelessly towards death**.

XIV. Syphilinum

Syphilinum belongs to the Syphilitic miasm. This remedy is made from the matter exuding from a syphilitic chancre. The feeling here would be – 'I know **there is a problem which is so much beyond hope that there is absolutely no way out or no way to correct it**. I know that **I am going to die with this problem**. There is no end to this problem, **no solution and nothing on the earth is ever going to make any change at all**. Not only will this remain like this, but **it's going to worsen day by day and eat me up**. This is the end of the story.'

A Case of Syphilinum in brief

We remember a case from our very early years of practice, rather from our years of learning when we were both studying in the homoeopathic college. It was a case of a very little child that we saw in our patient department at the hospital one day. He had come into the clinic with his mother. He looked very unhealthy. He had psoriasis. But it was all over his face and every inch of his body. He looked very unhealthy and dry, like a shrivelled baby. When he entered into the chamber, we were all the students sitting there, we almost felt disgusted at the look of the child as if he was dying. His mother put him in her lap and then he just got down of the lap and then took the pen and threw it at the doctor. I remember how all of us were surprised, confused and we were wondering what was happening.

The mother said, "He is such an angry child. He wants to **throw and destroy and rip every part of his skin**. He is always bleeding and it's almost as if he is so angry that it's not going to help anymore. He wants to destroy all this eczema that's there on his body." The mother's history during pregnancy was also one of anger and destruction. She had a very abusive husband and she hated him. According to her the child was a result of repeated rape by her husband. All through her pregnancy she felt that she wanted to kill herself and the child. There was no other way for her. The homeopath said that this was completely Syphilitic destructive thought and the child who had received several remedies in the past had responded to nothing at all. He then suggested that he would actually give Syphilinum as a last resort.

The Remedy
He was given Syphilinum 200C. We were amazed to see the result in the child within a month. The child recovered very well on the remedy.

The Sensation or Feelings
What we understood by looking back at the case is that the feeling of the Syphilinum nosode is – **'I have a complaint within me which is beyond hope. I am so close to death and destruction that there is no way out. I am getting destructive thoughts and with these destructive thoughts I want to destroy others. I will give into perversions of all sorts - homicide, suicide, doing any kind of a thing. I am going to die but before I die, I am going to destroy others as well.'**

XV. Pyrogen

Pyrogen we know is used for septicemia or during the course of diphtheria or typhoid. It was described as a polyvalent nosode in the past. It affects the blood, causes degeneration such as is met with in septicemic states with resulting fever, rigors and also interstitial and intestinal haemorrhages. We also commonly know that Psorinum is complementary to Pyrogen. The symptoms recorded in Pyrogen proving are hyperpyrexia, oscillating temperatures, a double rise of temperature and a feeling of euphoria which is also seen despite the fever. It has symptoms of drugs like Arnica, Baptisia and Arsenic all rolled into one and is indicated in a wide variety of fevers. It's a homoeopathic antibiotic. It's a wide spectrum antibiotic especially for puerperal sepsis. It can be prescribed when there is a septic focus in the body. Hence we put **Pyrogen in the Typhoid miasm** because it can be used in cases where there is acuteness of an attack. It can be used during the course of diphtheria, typhoid or typhus. **The feeling in Pyrogen is that its system will go into total deterioration if anything little goes wrong and it can die and never come out of the crisis. It is too quick and overwhelming to do**

anything. It might just have to totally surrender. We can use Typhoidinum in successful cases, i.e. where the miasm or the efforts are successful. On the other hand, we can use Pyrogen for the unsuccessful or failed Typhoid miasm. A Pyrogen individual looks at every situation intensely, acutely and thinks he is going to be doomed and will not come out of it, unless he does something for it. His pains are severe, his fever is very high, his physical sensation are intense, but at the same time, **since he belongs to the Typhoid miasm he comes out of it as soon as the situation passes and he is back to normal again till the next situation comes which can bring the sense of doom again**.

XVI. Lyssinum

We think the miasm of Lyssinum is an Acute miasm. 'I am so completely overtaken and overwhelmed by the outside that my system is behaving insane.' In Lyssinum the feeling is – **'I am so overwhelmed by the outside that I can behave even to the point of insanity. I don't even understand what have I done so wrong to be so badly affected? It came in so suddenly, so acutely and wham I am almost driven to insanity! I am going crazy.** Can I ever get help? I am even behaving berserk, crazy and violent. I don't think I can get any help. O my god! And I can't even control what's happening to me'. This is exactly the fear of Lyssinum that something terrible can happen to them. 'My system can never cope with an attack from the outside.'

Summary

So here we have spoken about some of the nosodes. We can read through more symptoms of each different nosode and also try to read the pathology of each disease to know what could be the exact picture of a patient who has as a specific nosode as a taint on his vital force. If we get a hold of how he could describe the source, symptoms and if we can grade them into different miasms, we can know how best we can work with them.

5

DIFFERENCE BETWEEN
NOSODES, MINERALS & ANIMALS

I.   The Themes Common to Nosodes

II. The Difference between Minerals & Nosodes

III. Differentiating Nosodes from Animal Remedies

I. The Themes Common to Nosodes

By now we know that **'abnormal'** and **'diseased'** are the most common feeling to the diseased tissue or to the nosode but the other important thing is a **'victim feeling'** because as you see in some of these nosodes, it's an infection from the outside. So the issue there is very animal like. The feeling is - Why me? Why was I attacked? Why am I born with this? Or sometimes they use the word 'attack'. Or in the case of nosodes of the autoimmune disorders, like we all know for cancer and also in SLE, or other diseases, the feeling is – 'I am born with these extra hypersensitive cells which react in a different way'. Of course cancer can be very clearly differentiated from the other auto-immune disorders because cancer has proliferation, metastasis and tumour formation which are not seen in other auto-immune disorders.

Constant comparison is another theme of the nosodes because they feel abnormal within. They are comparing themselves with the normal outside them but along with this they also have insight of a weak inner susceptibility. Somewhere the diseased tissue knows that 'I was weak within in the first place to attract these bacteria or to contract this kind of a disease.' The other interesting thing is the coping or the attitude of the nosode. In some of the cases you will not see the sensation of 'I am incorrect' but you will always see 'How can I correct it and in what ways can I correct it? How can I control or how can I overwork to correct this thing?' So the coping or the attitude or the miasm might be much more frequently seen than the incorrect sensation. Or the incorrect sensation might be seen subtly through the coping mechanism as you will read in a case later. She kept on saying - 'How can I correct myself ? I must make every effort to correct it.' Her desperation for correcting it is the coping. Implicit is the feeling that I am incorrect within, which is why she needs to correct it.

So the coping or the attitude can be predominant in nosode cases because the nosodes bring with them the essence of that tissue which was affected and the effort that the tissue is making or has made in the past to overcome the disease.

II. The Difference between Minerals & Nosodes

Minerals come very close to nosodes because in the minerals the feeling is - 'I am incomplete, I am lacking' and in the nosode the feeling is - 'The problem is within.' The nosodes might very often also use this word - 'Is there a problem? Am I lacking somewhere?' Hence to differentiate these two kingdoms, you must not analyse just in terms of words but really understand what the issue is within.

The feeling in the nosode is that 'Yes, the issue lies within' which is very similar to the feeling in minerals. But in the minerals there is a specific incomplete issue within, that they talk about. Whatever the situation may be, they come down to a specific issue of a specific row. Take for example when the problem within is the issue of one's own independence - 'Can I stand on my own two feet? Can I make it on my own?' You can clearly notice that this is an issue of an incomplete feeling of a specific kind.

It is the issue within of being dependant or independent, of being able to stand separately on your own which would take you to row two. Or the patient would say that the issue is within. 'Whenever I don't get appreciated in a situation and others do, I feel what is it that I am doing wrong or how can I change it?' If you ask the patient to describe further at this point, he says, "I always wanted to be recognised, to be accepted and acknowledged because then that makes you feel that you are an entity. It makes you realise that you are something by yourself."

So here the feeling that there is an issue within has a specific quality and that is the quality of needing identity which is an issue of the third row. The incompleteness in minerals is about independence, security, existence, or about challenges or power.

But in the nosodes, there is no specific quality like that of dependence-independence, challenge-power, existence, separation and identity. There is only a feeling that 'There is a problem within. I am abnormal whereas others are normal'. The polarity is that there is a problem within from which you need to come out. There is disease on one side and health on the other side where one wants to reach.

III. Differentiating Nosodes from Animal Remedies

Nosode remedies very often look like animals in the first few parts of the case. And it's completely understood because their source mainly is the animal tissue. It's a diseased victim which has been affected by another thing - by a virus or by an organism like by bacteria or something and he is now in this diseased abnormal state. Sometimes there is also an element of comparison that 'They are normal, I am not. They are healthy, they can do it

43

but I am the abnormal one. I am weak, deranged and abnormal whereas they are stronger, healthier and normal. I am incorrect and they are correct.'

In this comparison comes an element of weakness and strength as well. But the issue here is not that I am weak and I need to get back and fight. It's not about 'me versus you'. The issue here is 'Oh! I had certain susceptibility within me to contract this disease. There is a diseased tissue within me now. What can I change within me to increase that level of strength and to be as normal as the others are?'

Recently we have actually understood some of these nosodes exactly at the source level. The patient gave us the whole picture of the disease. Not only did he give us the sensation that 'I am diseased within' but he also gave us the complete pathology and mechanism of the disease development.

Now that we have covered the ten different intensities, the ten different miasms, the major pillars of Psora, Syphilis, Sycosis and the ones in between, from Acute right up to Leprosy, we will go to the cases. We will see what the sensation is and learn how we come to it. Side by side we will explain how we understand the intensity of the sensation, the miasm or the coping to the sensation.

6

 # A CASE OF RINGWORM

I.   Case Introduction

II. The Case

III. Remedy and Case Follow-up

IV. Summary

I. Case Introduction

It's a case that we took long ago in November 2003. This was the time when Shachindra and I were working with nosode source information and trying to ascertain the exact polarity in nosodes. It's a case which was taken under adverse circumstances because suddenly in the middle of the case there was a power failure and there were no lights. We were struggling to first use a candle, then use the camera light itself which added to our struggle to find the core issue of the case. When we understood the case, it was such a wonder that the lights came back! As you read you will know how this case is different from the cases of the other kingdoms.

II. The Case

She is a girl about 25 years old and her chief complaint is frequent headaches and episodic migraines, especially strong. She is also suffering from minor thalassemia and therefore she has undergone splenectomy when she was just about 14 or 15 years old. We ask her to tell us about the migraines.

P: Actually recently it is a little better. Initially when it started off, it used to be really bad. Almost every second day I would have a headache and nausea. So I went to a neurologist and I have taken some medication for that. I was told that if you continue taking migraine medication once it's like a lifetime thing. You kind of get addicted to it, which I didn't want. So then I tapered it gradually and then I stopped taking it. I discontinued. Recently I had a back problem. I had a pain in my left arm and you know the neck portion. So the doctor said it could be sometimes because of migraine. It is like you know a secondary effect of migraine. So then I had to start on migraine medication again which I took for about a month. Now again I have almost discontinued them. So headache that way is quite alright now but it does come up on and off.

D: Tell about the headache a bit more in detail.

She talks about headache and the nausea that is accompanied with it. Then we asked her to tell us more about this migraine because she just went more into the medication part of it.

P: I think it gets more regulated when maybe I have not had a good sleep or if I am in the sun for too long.

I think she didn't mean regulated. She meant that it gets aggravated.

P: Sometimes I eat something and immediately it feels better. Sometimes I pop in a pain killer and I get relief but sometimes it just goes on and on or if I go to sleep it goes away. My headache is always like a trial and error thing. I try different things what could help it, but I don't think I have got an answer to it.

She was trying to tell us more about the things she does to improve or to reduce the pain. We asked her to tell me more about the pain.

P: It gets really bad but you know I can't figure out where exactly is this pain. Maybe it's in the entire head. You can't really make out but more so it's at the temples. When I press my temples or around the eyes, or sometimes even the cheek bones and the bones of the face it hurts. I have even got an X-ray done. I don't think its sinusitis. Basically that's what the headache is, but when it's bad, it's quite bad. I mean it is unbearable.

Then she started telling us more about the migraine.

P: Like I can't really pinpoint as to where exactly it is hurting. It is not like how they would normally say -'Migraine is only on one side.' It is not really like that. It is just all over the head. And it is also at the back of the head. When I try and rest my head at the wall, sometimes I get a little bit of relief because it presses against the wall and sometimes if I take… if I drink maybe a hot cup of coffee or something, it does help. Or maybe if I just eat something, maybe have a chocolate or something. But then again, I was told not to have chocolates because they aggravate migraines. I feel a little nauseous sometimes because of the headache being so bad. My eyes hurt sometimes when the headache is there. I think that's about it.

So there was not so much about the character. She only talked about how her headache increased or reduced. She was still more intent on telling me the kind of things that aggravated or reduced the pain. She was more into modalities. We further asked her to tell us the character of the pain and she starts with some kind of shooting and throbbing.

D: Tell us more about the character of the pain that you get.

P: It's you know, more like a throbbing pain. It is like a shooting pain. I feel like literally banging my head on the wall sometimes, because it hurts so badly and it starts with a dull ache you know. I can make out that it's going to get into a migraine now. So I kind of get the feel that you know it's going to start now. Sometimes when I take a painkiller immediately when it is about to start, it does help, but not always.

D: Tell us more about this throbbing pain.

P: You know it is like… it subsides for a second, and then suddenly it shoots up. That throbbing pain I cannot explain it to you, but it's really quite bad. You know when it's there, it's really unbearable and you just don't feel like doing anything. When I have this headache, I just feel like being left alone or just trying to go to sleep or something like that.

Now she tells us a little bit about not the character, as in the type of pain but she talks more about the way in which the pain comes and goes. She says it subsides for a second but then it can suddenly shoot up. Again she goes back to trying to sleep or do something that will relieve the pain. Next, we asked her tell to us more, more about the fact that it subsides and it suddenly shoots up. This is the kind of pain she said she has –

P: Subsides in the sense, just like for a second or five seconds. Sometimes it feels like, 'Oh fine! It's going down.' But then suddenly you get this throbbing pain shooting up again that way.

D: Describe that.

P: I am not getting you; in the sense?

D: Whatever. Try and describe this - suddenly shoots up this throbbing pain. When it suddenly shoots up – just describe it.

P: I don't know. In the sense, it's like maybe I get the feel that it's going to subside but not really. It's still there. You know how a throbbing pain would be? As if it is throbbing on one side of your head. It is just that. It's just that throbbing pain.

D. Elaborate more on this throbbing. Just the word throbbing.

P: I don't know how to explain that but… how do I put it? It's like I cannot explain it to you I mean.

D: Just elaborate on the word 'throbbing'.

P: You know how you would have a normal headache or you know a muscle ache or whatever. It is not just like that constantly there. Sometimes it is aggravated. Sometimes it is a little less. It varies; you know the level of it varies. I don't think I can describe more than that.

Now you see these were the very initial years in 2003 where we were stuck with trying to understand more about throbbing. In those times we always tried to stay with a word like a throbbing, banging, hammering, heavy or light.

Here we are really trying to understand throbbing whereas what you can see from her answers is that throbbing is not what she is sensitive to. Her issue is more the way in which it comes and goes if you understand. Like in the chief complaint you have the location, sensation and modality. You have the character and in the character it's not only the type of pain but it's also the way in which the pain comes and goes. Both of these form the character. So it's very important to see what about the chief complaint the patient is more sensitive to.

What we can see here is that she is not more sensitive to the throbbing. We have probed throbbing several times. But she keeps coming up time and again with - "I don't know why it increases and reduces. I don't know why it suddenly shoots up and goes down." So for her what is important is the way in which the pattern of the chief complaint is coming - where there is an increase or a reduction, either sudden or non-sudden. Also what is important for her in her chief complaint, are the things that she is doing for her chief complaint i.e. the modalities - what is reducing or what is increasing the pain. She thinks of how she can reduce the pain further.

This is a perfect example of understanding what the chief complaint is. So it does not necessarily mean that if the patient says 'pain', you hold on to that word and try to find some character to the pain. No. The chief complaint means finding out the most sensitive and troublesome issue for your patient, hold on to that and then move forward. Here the most sensitive issue for her is the way in which it comes and goes and the modalities or the kind of things she does for her pain.

The more we go with throbbing, the more we are probing in vain. We are not going to get anything from it. But when we come to these points which she is

D: Describe this whole phenomenon of pain.

P: I just don't know it.

D: Describe the character, the throbbing that you are saying. This whole phenomenon that you are saying, that it throbs and you feel it subsiding and then it is not subsiding.

P: Subsiding in the sense, it's not like really gone because it doesn't go away in a second. But at times you feel like it's at a level where it's bearable, but then suddenly, there is this pain on some part of my head, somewhere, which is quite painful. It's just little more painful at that particular second and then it's at that level where it's constant.

D: So how does it feel when it's subsiding, and then it just suddenly comes up?

P: I guess here it is not like... maybe 'subsiding' is not the right word. It is not like subsiding, but it's at that level you know where it constantly aches throughout. But sometimes it just shoots up a little bit and then it comes back to the level where it's the same throughout that way.

So the kind of pain is that it is always there but then there are times when it shoots up and it comes back to that constant level. Next we asked her to describe her expression of - 'the pain shoots up'.

D: Describe this – 'it shoots up'.

P: I don't know... I mean, how else to describe this?

D: Just describe what you mean by 'it shoots up'.

P: I guess that it's maybe a level up than the normal pain. It goes up by one level, and comes back to the lower level; that kind of a thing.

So there is an up and down in the pain.

50

D. Describe that.

P: Describe in the sense, how it go up and comes down?

D: Whatever.

P: I think I have described as much as I could. I can't describe any more than this.

D: Describe this shooting pain.

P: What is it exactly that you are looking for? I cannot think of anything else to put it into words.

D. Just elaborate over the word 'shooting' in any way.

P: In the sense how the pain comes up or how I feel when it is a shooting pain or what?

D: Both, whatever.

P: I don't know how the pain comes up suddenly, because I try not to... maybe you know… like I am working in a lab. I am doing microscopy most of the time. So I avoid doing that for a while and see if it subsides. Yeah, I mean I try and get off work, or get some sleep or rest or just sit down and not move around. I think if I move around with a jerky movement it irritates and troubles more. Like if I am climbing a staircase or something… like I said that shooting pain… maybe that is triggered off when I am doing any kind of movement in the body that is jerky.

She is somebody who is more into the modality of the chief complaint. The focus for her is - how can I change this complaint or what can I do to get better. So we asked her to finally describe the character of the pain that she is getting. The more we will ask the character, the more her focus will be on the modality thus reinforcing that she is not so bothered about the character but what she can or cannot do for the complaint.

D. But describe this - the character of the pain that you are getting.

P: It's like I can literally feel somewhere inside the head, there is something

51

happening as if it is like you know, I don't know what you would call it. But it is definitely something that I don't want to be there; something that I would want to get rid of as soon as possible. It hampers the mind - the way I think or what I think or whatever I do. That's what I said - if I could maybe get off work and just be by myself, and try and get rid of it.

So then she says that it's something that she really wants to get rid off. We asked her to describe that to us. As you know in the earlier days, this was a way to enter into the generals to know what about the complaint bothers the patient.

D: Describe this - you want to get rid of it.

P: Yeah. I mean get out of that headache.

And then she couldn't go much forward from getting rid of the headache. So we asked her to elaborate on the symptom that there is something that is happening inside. This is because just a few paragraphs earlier she had mentioned that, "There is something that is happening inside which I don't know and I want to get rid of the headache." So we picked that up and asked her to describe it.

D: Elaborate on this sentence that there is something happening inside.

P: In the sense, like I said it is not like a regular pain, not a normal headache. I know this is a different kind of headache, which could be because of something else. But when this particular headache comes… which I don't know… I am told that it could be migraine. I am just using that word because that's what I have been told by doctors. But when it is that particular kind of pain, it is not something which is very tolerable. It's different than the normal headache you know. In the sense, it's more painful obviously and I guess it's just because it's so painful, you feel like there is something going on. There is something happening.

D: Describe that 'something'.

P: I think it's more like as if somebody is hitting on your head or I don't know what. As if it's like… it is a lot of physical pain. It's quite unbearable.

So she says it's unbearable as if something is happening. Hence we asked her to describe this - something is happening. It is now that she changes track. Now she really wants to explain the character. She says it's as if somebody is hitting on her head. We were jubilant at this point since now we had got something very interesting - beyond the modalities. We were curious to know where it was going to lead us.

D: Describe this - somebody is hitting on your head.

P: I mean I don't literally mean … as if somebody is hitting on my head but it's as if you are really… it's quite bad. I mean when it's there, it's really bad.

D: As if you are?

P: I mean this is what I feel like as if there is something majorly wrong in my head or in my brain or something because I have got these skull and sinus X-rays and all those things done. I just get hyper. I don't know why it's there. Not knowing the cause gets you to thinking all the more as to why it is happening so often, in spite of having taken the migraine course for six months and things like that.

It is interesting to know about the X-rays that she has done and that she feels something is majorly wrong in her head which is very discomforting. It is a mental and physical discomfort. So we asked her about this discomfort that she feels inside.

P: I think it is the pain, which is not letting me do anything else besides just sitting down at one place, and trying to…

D. How does it feel that the pain is not letting you do anything?

P: It's not a very nice feeling, because you can't really do much. You just have to wait till it goes down, and then get back to your normal routine.

D: How does it feel?

P: I think it does hamper your lifestyle to a certain extent if it's like they are more often, every second day or every third day. You kind of need to… you know like if I have to go out in the morning somewhere when it's too hot, then I would maybe not want to do that because you know it might cause the pain. I would avoid doing such things.

53

D: How does it feel?

P: It does hamper your kind of routine a bit.

D: Describe hamper.

P: You kind of feel a little tied up because...

A very interesting thing happened at this point. Till now the case was going so slowly that we were not getting any great characteristics. It wasn't going anything further in our minds. It had gone further but there wasn't something interesting coming up; like we would have expected a fantastic chief complaint and some gestures. We would have expected throbbing, hitting, hammering taking us somewhere but it wasn't.

It was just more about things that she was doing to reduce the pain and then more about something that is wrong inside, looking like a very normal complaint.

And then when we probed further, she said – "It hampers my lifestyle and I cannot do my normal routine." Then suddenly she went to – "You feel tied". This was a very interesting point. We felt that maybe now we were getting some character and that she was going to come up with beautiful gestures or with something nice. Finally we were going to get something interesting in the case and you know what happened, the lights went off! It was just that point of time where she had reached the point of delusion in the case. She was going from the fact, from the chief complaint not much into emotions but directly into the point that – you feel tied up with your complaint. At that important juncture in the case when we knew we had finally got her to say something interesting and important for which we had to focus a lot, the lights went off. We finally, with great efforts had got somewhere but the power failure, we were brought back to the ground from where we would have to start off again. We searched for some candles and started off from that point where she felt tied up with the complaint.

D: You said, 'I feel tied up'.

P: Yeah. Like I said, guess that you need to pre-plan your schedule because of not wanting to get a headache when you are out because you can't really enjoy what you are out for.

D: Just describe 'tied'.

P: It's like you know you are bound because of… I think I should stop using these words.

She says tied and bound and she immediately realised what she was getting into. She became aware of the kind of questions we were asking.

P: I don't want to go into this anymore.

We encouraged her to go ahead by saying that she was doing really well. We tried to focus on her hands and see some of her arms moving to pick up some gestures. But there were absolutely no gestures with tied or bound, so we motivated her to go on.

P: You just get bogged down because of this; that you can't really do what you would want to do.

She was again trying to tell us that she felt bound and tied. For her it meant that you can't do what you want to do. But we stuck to the bound, yes more bound, that's what we want to know.

D: Bound.

P: Normally I am at work in the morning. So it is not like it happens too often, but whenever it does, I need to like you know prepare myself beforehand. Like if I have to keep a fast, I would pop in a Crocin (paracetamol) the previous night so that I don't get a headache next morning, although it's not there the previous night. Yeah if I fast, then I get a headache very easily. I also get acidity because of that.

So again it's more about the kind of things that come with feeling bound - 'I need to prepare myself by taking a Crocin, as if it has happened in the previous night.' We were at such an important point in the case - 'tied, bound, you feel tied by this complaint'. It looked like she didn't want to go along the path of tied and bound though she had mentioned it herself. We were trying to really take her down that path.

D: More about bound.

P: It's like, for example, I can't fast if I would want to because I would easily get a headache. I used to do that earlier - fast, but now I can't because of the headache. Couple of things like these.

D: More about 'bound.' Just elaborate on the word bound.

P: I think it's like… I don't know how it feels to just go out and do what you want, when you don't have to worry about things like these. So I can't really compare between the two, because I have always had to… Like I said, it has been there for quite some time now. I have always had to think about it before I would want to plan something out. I mean it is not like a major issue that I have to every time think about it, but once in a while if I have already had a minor attack, maybe a day before, then next day I would want to maybe not do the things that would try and bring it up again. So in certain ways it feels like you have to think about these things before doing something which any other normal person may not have to because you don't have that kind of problem. But I don't know how it really feels without it because since a long time I have had this. So it is like more or less since a life-time kind of a thing.

We only asked her to elaborate on the word 'bound' but what came out was nothing to do with bound or tied or any kind of a sensitivity. What came out was the fact that - 'I don't know. I cannot compare this bound with anything else because I haven't felt anything else. I don't know how it would have been like a normal person'. The bound brought us to something which felt like it was a superficial and an unimportant thing that she was talking about. Why was she coming back to these very vague remarks? But remember if this kind of a comparison goes on further, it does not mean that the case is going further down. You then try to take it as not just a superficial remark. It's a feeling within her that she is comparing herself to other normal people. 'They can do it but I can't do it.' Like she said – "I had this problem for such a long time. It's almost a life-time kind of a thing." So she would tell us more about it. We asked her go on.

P: You know in school also I had the headache, but that headache was just a very normal kind of headache. At that time I never realised or we never really showed it to somebody who would tell us that its migraine.

We needed to understand this whole pattern at this time of the case. We were wondering what was happening. Here is somebody who sounds very boring as if she doesn't want to go into any kind of a pain or delusion. All she talks about are the things that she does for her pain and that something might be wrong inside; that she cannot do her normal things and feels bound because a normal person could do many things and she could not. We didn't understand what this was.

So we asked her - How did it feel to have this fact of constantly knowing her programmes, fun or enjoyment? She said that it was hampering, that she had to pre-plan and always do these kinds of things right. We wanted to probe into her feelings and get them out.

D: A normal person would be without it but for you, how does it feel to constantly pre-plan and have this hampering?

P: Like I said, it is not like a major issue - the pre-planning. It just happens sometimes if I have had a headache just the day before. If I have to go somewhere then I would try and avoid doing it the next day and maybe postpone it for a day or two or something like that.

D: How does it feel that you have to pre-plan, or that it hampers, or that it always needs to be like that?

P: That's when I feel like I am tied up because of this, that I can't really… I am not as free as I would be to do certain things.

D: Describe 'tied up'.

So it's back to bound and tied up, to the feeling that – 'I can't do all these things that others can do. I am tied up.' So then we asked her to describe tied up which she has brought up for the second time. We expected her to come up with something nice this time

P: I think it's the same thing. Bound by it or tied up.

D: Just elaborate.

P: It's like if I have a headache and I have to go for a movie, I would rather not go because I am not going to enjoy it with the headache. So I think just these small things here and there, which I don't do because I have a headache.

Again it is what she doesn't do or does because of the headache. Yeah it's never the description of tied up but the description of what she can or cannot do for the complaint or along with the complaint. We wanted to focus more on 'tied' and give it a full push. We wanted to see if 'tied' was going to take us somewhere...

D: More about just 'tied'.

P: I can't really think of much.

D: Just elaborate on the word 'tied'. Whatever comes to you?

P: Sometimes it just doesn't make you feel like a normal person because you know it hampers your routine or whatever.

Ah! "Sometimes it just doesn't make you feel like a normal person." So the tied brings us back to – 'Oh! You are not a normal person.' But we wanted her to give us an image of the word! We were so desperate to get a beautiful delusion out of this 'tied'. We weren't happy. This looked very superficial. It kept on coming back to- You are not a normal person; you compare yourself with others.' We wanted something really interesting. So we were going to give one last chance to 'tied'. We even told her to give her image, her delusion. We were eager to know what she would come up with.

D: 'Tied'. Just the word 'tied'. Give an image.

P: Sorry?

D: Give an image?

P: I don't know. I can't really elaborate much on that.

D: You are doing really well. Just be with it. Just try to tell more about this word 'tied'.

P: It kind of makes you feel like you are taking medication every now and then which I don't really like doing. I try and avoid doing that as much as I can. Sometimes this also makes you feel like you know you are tied up because of this; and I have been taking medications since my splenectomy. That is like when I was about twelve-thirteen years old. So since then I have been taking that already and plus in addition to that, comes this. So it's just these things which I don't like to do.

So what does tied bring us to? 'You have kept on taking medications, you have to keep on taking medications and you want to avoid taking medications that's something which I don't want to do.' So we thought - What is in this girl that we have to understand ? What is this feeling that you have this problem and that you have to keep on taking medications? She must be sensitive to this somewhere deep inside her...

She started to do something with her hands (bringing them together). Then she said that she doesn't like to take those medications.

D: You just did something with your hand?

P: Sorry?

D: You just did something like this with your hand?

P: Yeah …it was just.

D: Just describe what this is.

P: I don't know...

D: You have had your splenectomy. Since then you have been having this medication?

P: I am kind of avoiding eating my medication. Just skip it sometimes, because you know I feel like I have had enough of it.

D: How does it feel?

P: It doesn't feel very nice.

D: How does it feel to have these medications again and again?

P: It doesn't feel nice at all.

D: How does it feel?

P: Because for any other complaints that I have, the first thing I told you was about my past history that I am a thalassemia minor and my splenectomy has been done. So it comes up every now and then and not just that… I mean I am not like I mind talking about it but it's just the medication part of it for so many years now… it's like I don't like taking it anymore. Become a little lax in taking it, because…

D: How does it feel that you have to take this medication all this while?

P: Like I didn't mind doing it all these years. I have been taking it. Even now, it's not that I have completely discontinued. I do take it regularly. Sometimes I skip in between.

D: Yeah. You take it regularly. You don't mind it, fine. How does it feel?

P: Being on medication?

D: That you have to take it regularly. It's not a nice thing?

P: No. It's not, because no normal person would pop in medication every morning.

D: What about it is not nice?

You see with the gesture, she didn't go further. So we asked her to describe the feeling behind it. She said – "No normal person would have popped in medication like the way I do". At this point we thought that this was just something superficial that she was talking about.

D: Okay, you say you don't feel like a normal person pops in medication. So how does it feel to keep popping up medication?

The answer she gave was interesting.

P: It makes me feel weak.

60

We thought, "Wow may be weak will take us to something very interesting!"

You know it kept happening in this case that we would get something and then we would almost not get anything. It's only by the end of the case we realised that we were also in the same state that the patient was in. So anyways we will come to that at the end of the case.

D: Describe weak.

P: It just makes me feel like… like I said, just a bit weaker than any normal person would be. I mean any normal person would not have to take medication every day or every morning. So when I have to do that, it feels like there is something wrong with me that kind of a thing.

D: How does it feel?

P: It doesn't feel very nice.

And now you see this phenomenon has repeated itself far too often for it to be mere superficial words. She has said it so many times! What has she said? She said I feel weaker, but not weak as in 'me versus you' but weaker as in weaker than any other normal person. 'No normal person would have taken medication every day. So it feels like something is wrong with me.'

D: You said that "something is wrong with me". How does it feel that something is wrong with you?

P: Initially it was alright because it was okay but now it has been so long. I thought I will be able to discontinue it at some point but…

D: How does it feel?

P: I feel like I would have been better off without it; if I had not had these problems and been without medication.

D: What do these problems make you feel?

P: I think overall they just make me feel a bit weaker generally. Not just

61

physically, but overall it makes you feel like you are weaker than a normal individual.

So you see here what she is trying to say is that the chief complaint is migraine. The fact is that she is having these kinds of throbbing pains which increase in intensity and go back to a certain constant level. The emotion with it is just that she is upset. The delusion is that she is tied up and bound with these kinds of complaints that she has. But the pattern that's coming up even deeper is that 'I am tied and bound because I am weaker than any other normal person and therefore I feel tied and bound by this complaint that I have. What is wrong with me?'

You can see that this pattern is gaining clarity now.

D: What about this weak?

P: Like I said, I do have fatigue sometimes because of work or because of the headache. Sometimes that just drains you out. So I guess generally overall it's just something that you don't want to have happened. I could have been without it. It's like it shouldn't have been there. It's like I would have been better off without it.

D: How does it feel to be weak?

P: I mean I don't like really feel weak at the end of the day or tired at the end of the day, but whenever I do, I think it's because of me being thalassemia minor or whatever... that haemoglobin is low.

D: How does it feel to be in that state?

P: You don't feel very good, because you would want to be energetic all the time and do things. Maybe sometimes when I come back home and if I have to go out again, I would not feel like because I just feel tired and lazy to go out. Then it just maybe makes your life a little bit slower than the rest of them.

D: How does it feel to be slower than the rest, to be weaker than the rest?

It's always the same pattern – 'I am slow, I am weaker than the rest of them'.

62

P: I guess its ok because it's been there since a long time now but like I said, it would have felt better if I was without it. I don't really know how it feels without it because it's there.

She says, "I don't want it to be there."

D: How it feels to be with it? How does it feel that it is there, what's your feeling that you have this kind of a problem?

P: I mean how I feel in comparison with a normal individual or just generally how it makes me feel by myself?

She is automatically comparing herself with a normal individual. But that's not what we have asked at all. This is what is going on in her mind - 'Am I normal compared to others?'

D: Describe how does M (patient's name) feel with all these complaints, with all of them?

P: She doesn't feel very nice about it.

D: How does she feel?

P: I think it's just something, which also your family tells you - that you are weak, you feel tired and you are overworked or things like that which you don't want to hear. I mean you want to be as healthy and as energetic as possible.

D: How does it feel to hear all that?

P: It doesn't feel nice. I mean maybe sometimes I overdo things in spite of me not being able to do it just so that you know they should not say that "You are weak" or "You don't have enough strength" and stuff like that.

D: How does it feel to be weak in comparison with others? How does it feel when you are compared with others?

She says she wants to be as healthy and energetic as the others. So we asked her how it feels to be always compared like this. How does it feel to be weak in comparison with others? And she says that she does not feel slower but she definitely does not feel healthy and energetic and so she avoids doing extra things that other normal individuals do. So we asked her how it would feel to do these extra things you know because by probing in just one way we were not getting anything else except that 'you are not normal and that you are weaker than the rest'. We thought that maybe from the other side we will get something important. Hence we went to the other side. We asked her how she would feel to be able to do the things that others do.

Now you see this is a case where we were also very new with the concept. It is way back in 2003 when we were also trying to understand what this pattern was. We didn't clearly know at that point, the sensation of the nosode. In fact, we understood it through this case. We had already begun our study on nosodes. We had concluded that the source of the nosode is a diseased tissue and hence the problem could be somewhere within.

We were struggling with these kinds of issues till we were actually faced with a case like this where she was throwing this 'weak, abnormal, I am lesser than the others' kind of a pattern. But it was taking considerable time for us to pick it up and also that we wanted to confirm that this is not a superficially said thing but that this is the repeated pattern or sensation coming up in the case. So we were also really palpating every bit of the case.

On one side of the polarity is that I am weak, I am abnormal and others are normal. So let's see that if she would be full and strong, if she would be on the other side of the polarity i.e. if she could do the things that she wanted to do, how would she feel then?

If on the other side of this she says that 'I am strong, I can achieve what I want to do and I have an identity of my own', then we have already come to a mineral. Or if she says that doing the things that I want to do is going to make me feel stronger, I am going to be faster than the others, it is a competitive world, blah blah blah... it would take us to an animal. Our eyes were open. We were still unsure. We were trying to palpate the whole pattern that was coming up.

Let us see the answer that came from the other side.

P: If I could do those things? Definitely a lot better than what I do now.

D: How would it make you feel?

P: It would make me feel more content and happier.

D: Hmm.

P: ...and make me feel more normal.

So how would she feel to be able to do all the things that others do? She wouldn't feel stronger, achieved, more challenged or anything like that. She would feel happy, content and normal. The other polarity of abnormal is that I need to be normal. The repeated pattern that came up in this case, taught us the sensation of the nosode. It's not that the sensation has come in the superficial parts of the case. It came but then it went into bound and tied, then into her general routine and her life style and from there it came back to the feeling that 'I am abnormal'. You are going to see many more cases with exactly this pattern.

We will go a little further. We said just give us more about this picture of how will you feel when you are able to do everything that you want to do.

D: Had you been able to do all that?

P: Like I said, I would have been more active. I would have been not as dull as I feel normally in the evenings once I am home. I would have some more activities to do besides just staying at home and not doing anything. I think maybe I could progress better by doing something than just staying back by myself.

D: How would it feel to be in that state where you will be able to do all these things by yourself?

P: I am sure I will feel nice.

D: How is that nice feeling?

P: I feel I can't really describe it, because I don't know how it would feel, because…

D: How would you imagine it would feel?

65

P: I mean it would be nice to feel normal and to be able to do what you want to do whenever you want to do and not having to think twice before you plan to do something.

D: So how does it feel in a situation like that – can't do whatever that you want to do?

How is this nice feeling? What is this nice feeling? We repeatedly asked her and it came back to – 'It would be nice to feel normal and to avoid certain things or not want to plan them.' So now from the normal side we are going to try and elicit the abnormal side again just to be sure that the pattern is repeating itself exactly in the same way and it's not something else.

P: I sometimes feel a little disturbed because I am unable to try and have a normal life.

D: Describe this. Just forget the instances and the examples. Just give us this feeling - the feeling of being not ….the feeling of being behind, being slow and unhealthy. Describe these feelings.

It is very interesting that she is trying to have a normal life but she cannot have it. So the feeling within is – 'I am abnormal and I am trying to be normal somehow'.

That's why we asked her to forget everything that she was trying, doing this or that. We wanted her to concentrate on just how it feels to be unhealthy, to have this change of routines, to be slower than others, to be left behind and the feeling of not being able to lead a normal life. We just put all those negative things together and we said let's see if all this still comes back to 'I am abnormal' or it takes us to a further direction. What we were trying to elicit in this case was something new and so we wanted to be doubly sure. We wanted to understand every aspect of this sensation. So we told her to just go on and tell us how these things feel.

D: How do all these things make you feel?

P: I have tried to describe it best with the words that I used. I don't know how to further describe those words. You just feel like a different individual. You just don't feel normal.

It's very interesting that in every way that you probe her, she comes back to the same pattern of feeling abnormal from within.

P: If you sit down and think about it like I am doing right now, I think it's definitely not something that I want to live with. I personally feel I would have been much better off without these physical health problems that I have.

And in this next paragraph she also gave us the intensity of the feeling so we knew that the sensation now was that 'I am abnormal, I am not normal'. And as were trying to understand her a little bit further, she said "it's not to the extent of being very serious. I know I can live with it but I can be better without it." So the intensity, the gravity with which she feels the abnormality within her is not a desperate fatal intensity. In this way, we were already getting the hints of her miasm that she was quiet Sycotic in her acceptance but there was also an element of - 'But you want to come out of it'. We needed to elicit this a little more clearly. She further said certain things like - "It doesn't really bother you to be abnormal. I mean I am not really bothered about it, but I am just trying to right now, make a comparison between whether it is there and how it is, and if it is not there then how it is." We went to our next question.

D: It doesn't bother you?

P: No, not to an extent where I can really be flustered.

D: Then what about the whole problem bothers you? What about being thalessemia minor or having this problem or headaches or migraine bothers you? Because you say that it really doesn't bother you.

P: No, that doesn't bother me at all because it's not something... I mean you know it's alright. I can deal with it but as I said, it's not bothering me to an extent where I really feel like this is the end of it all and stuff like that. I am talking about it because I am being asked to talk about it. I am just trying to open up but it's not so distressing that I can't take it in my life. I can try and deal with it.

So when we ask her to describe it, she says – "Not just intellectually, even physically I am trying to deal with it. But I still feel that I would have been much better without it." She said that as a person she wants to be physically fit and mentally fit. So again you see the intensity is not a

67

desperate one. She only wishes that she could avoid it or reduce the problem.

Now if you go back to her chief complaint and with respect to this whole understanding of the slow development and of the sensation, she kept on telling us the things that she does to relieve her complaint and despite trying all those things she was not always successful.

So her sensation is - 'Somewhere I am abnormal, somewhere I have a problem. I am not normal.'

Her coping is 'I can deal with it. I can live with it but I try to come out of it time and again.' This makes her a combination of Sycosis and the Psoric element. It brings the trying of Psora on the base of the acceptance of the problem which is Sycosis. The combination of Psora and Sycosis is the Ringworm miasm. That is exactly what we now see and understand in the chief complaint.

In the chief complaint she said that the throbbing was not bothering her. What was bothering her was the fact that she was trying to really get out of it. She was constantly trying to see in which way she could reduce her pain and in which way it got worse. She was constantly trying to make amendments.

This is the whole coping of the Ringworm miasm - you try to come out of your problem. You try to help yourself in the sensation but you cannot help yourself to a very large extent and you come back and accept it. After sometime you try again and then you accept it.

This was also what she was trying to say about the pain. She says there are times when it increases and there are times when it goes back. There is a kind of an alternation even in the pattern in which the pain is coming but actually these things that she talks about in the chief complaint, are nothing but the reflection of her whole pattern in her sensation. Are you getting this whole gamete, this perfect reflection of the sensation in her chief complaint?
At this point when we started to understand this pattern, it was extremely beautiful and enlightening for us. We were very excited. We wanted to understand this miasm, this Ringworm, this nosode, this sensation little bit more. So we asked her to describe this. Then she said that it makes her

feel a little bit low.

D: Makes you feel low? Describe little more about this low feeling.

P: It depresses you sometimes because I have been trying to get out of it, but it hasn't really happened. Sometimes you feel like you know why is it happening so on and off, in spite of trying to take care of it and taking medication or whatever.

We wanted to get the nosode more clearly and this is exactly where it is when she is saying that it depresses you but you are trying to get out of it. But then it depresses you again that in spite of trying so much you don't actually get out of it. Now you will see the beauty of it, the more we ask about the miasm the more the sensation of 'I am weak, I am abnormal' will come up. It's a beautiful interplay between the sensation and the miasm in the next few lines.

D: How does it feel that you try to take care, you try to get out of it, but still it's not happening?

P: It sometimes makes me feel helpless, because I can't really do much about it. I mean I have to visit doctors and take medication as per what they prescribe.

Now you know that helplessness is another thing that we have seen with nosode cases because you know they are either accepting it or they are trying to do something and come out of it.

In the Cancer miasm they are really trying to overcome it by every means possible. In the Tubercular miasm they are making hectic efforts to come out of it so they are doing all these kind of things. The miasm is also the coping and hence often in nosode cases you find on the other side - a kind of helplessness. Notice how she comes back to the sensation of the nosode which is – 'I am weak'.

P: It just makes you feel weaker.

D: Just describe this. How does it feel to be weak?

P: Weak in the sense, just physically weak that you have a problem every now and then which you would not want to have. I constantly try to alter my diet, feel fit and stay healthy. It makes me do things like think about my health all the time.

What a beautiful interplay between the sensation of the nosode and the miasm of the nosode – 'I feel weak, I feel weaker than the others that I have a problem every now and then but I constantly try to alter my diet, stay fit and healthy so that I can be normal. I am thinking about my health all the time. I am diseased, I am thinking about health.'

But what is the coping of this nosode? The coping is – 'I am trying my level best to come out of it and yet at times I give in. I feel helpless. Despite of all this, nothing much happens and I do nothing but accept it'. This is the Ringworm miasm and that's exactly the nosode that we gave her.

But before that there was still a little more that we had to understand because this was something we were new to. We asked her to tell us something about her dreams. I must say it was a very interesting journey!

P: Off late I have had this sleep problem. When I come back from work, I try to get a nap. I think I don't know, is it because I am so fast asleep that I want to get up consciously, but I am unable to wake myself up. I don't know if that's just a dream in my sleep or am I actually awake and thinking? I can't really figure out between the two. But I am trying to consciously open my eyes and get out of the bed but unable to do that. So when I am up with the first chance that I get to get out of bed it feels nice that I could do it, which I was probably trying since last few minutes to do and I couldn't do, so…

D: How is the feeling that you are trying?

Isn't it very interesting that in the dreams she comes to a point where she says I try to wake myself up but I am unable to? The Ringworm aspect can be seen here clearly again - 'I am trying to open my eyes, I am trying to get out of bed but I can't.'

D: Describe this - you are trying to get out of the sleep or that you are trying to get sleep and you are not able to.

P: It feels as if something is stopping you from getting out of your bed.

70

We thought this doesn't look like Ringworm. What is this - somebody stopping you?

D: Describe this somebody stopping you.

P: It happened again just about ten days ago. I was trying to sleep at night and for quite some time I could not sleep. Then I hardly went to sleep and then suddenly the same thing happened that I wanted to get up. Maybe I was dreaming about something. I don't know. I can't recollect what it was but something was not giving me... I don't know… the dream wasn't giving me a nice feeling. There was this scared feeling which I had within me and I just wanted to get up from my dream but I couldn't do that. I felt like somebody was holding me down and not letting me get up.

D: Describe that.

P: It was very scary.

D: Describe this someone or something was holding you down. How did it feel?

P: I don't know how long it lasted, but for whatever time it was, I felt as if I was in an enclosed space and I thought - O My goodness!

We thought that we had found the entire pattern but now she is coming to something completely different. We have to understand this enclosed space now.

P: I felt almost as if the bed was closing on me. It was a feeling that somebody is holding you from wanting to get up.

D: Describe that.

P: I wanted to know what's happening. It's like it is happening but I know it's not really happening. It's just in my subconscious mind and I can't go against it. It's just for that little while you know and then I woke up.

D: Yes, but just describe this whole thing. What was happening to you?

P: It was not like I was dreaming about something. Just all of a sudden I

71

think it happened. As if you are in a bad dream and you want to get out of it. You want to really try and wake yourself up and that's what you are trying to do. But you simply cannot do it. You are unable to get up. You tell yourself this is not happening to you. Maybe that is what was causing the fright that you are unable to actually make your eyes open. You are trying. I think being unable to do that thing for a little while got me frightened. Is it happening or is it in my imagination that this is happening? I guess I couldn't differentiate between the two. I couldn't tell myself that it's okay, it's not really happening. I was really frightened at that time.

So what we figured out from this whole dream was not the enclosed, the space and somebody sitting on her or holding her. What was affecting her in the whole dream was that you are unable to do what you are trying to do. Another aspect of the Ringworm miasm is - 'You are trying to do something but you simply cannot get it done'. We asked her that if now she was in a situation like this how would she feel.

D: How will you feel now if you are in an enclosed space or if the bed is coming on you and you cannot move?

P: I am sure it would make me feel very helpless not being able to do what I want to do because I am put in a place where I can't do anything.

D: How does it feel to…in this place you are not being able to do what you want to do? How does it make you feel? Just describe this.

P: It just makes you want to go all the more against it because you want to do what you want to do but you are unable to do it, because of whatever reasons. So it does make you want to go ahead and do it all the more.

D: Yes. Because, what does that situation make you feel?

P: I think it's just that. The fact that you can't do what you want to do at that moment.

D: How does it make you feel?

The whole feeling in the dream is that you can't do what you want to do. You want to do something you are trying to but you can't do it.

P: It's scary.

D: What about it is scary?

P: That you can't do what you want to do.

D: Can you make a picture of what you want to do? How does it feel?

P: I am thinking why something like this is happening? I am sure it's not something normal.

'You can't do what you want to do' is the miasm. 'I am sure this is not something that's normal', that's the sensation. It's interesting that the dreams she has are exactly the dreams of a Ringworm nosode - It's not normal to not be able to get up. The sensation, the experience of every situation, every dream in her life is this - not normal. 'I am not normal, something is abnormal'.

D: So what did that concern make you feel? That scary thought you talked about...

P: What is it that was making it happen? What was it that is causing it? That is the fear which I would want to find out as to why I am…

The whole concern is inwards - What is wrong, why am I in this situation? What is happening to cause it? It's not common, it's not normal to have this kind of a dream. Why am I having it? What's the underlying meaning?

D: What is the worst that can happen? This is all imaginary. We are not talking of reality. When you are unable to do what you want to do, what will you feel in that situation?

P: I think I would just be depressed not being able to do what I want to do.

Isn't it interesting that when we asked her what is the worst that can happen if you are unable to do what you want to do, she said – 'That itself is the worst!'

That itself is the worst fear of the Ringworm nosode that they cannot come

73

*out of the situation. It's not a life-threatening or a fatal situation. It's a
situation that you accept and can live with and yet you want to come out
of it. Time and again you are trying your level best to come out of it. This
is exactly what the disease of ringworm is - it's a fungal infection.
However much you want to get rid of it, it's the most difficult thing to get
rid of. It's always there. And no matter what you do, you are going to get
stuck with it once again.*

*Interestingly at that point, the lights came back again! It was right at the
time, at the juncture when we had cleared everything.*

*Earlier in the case we were trying to get somewhere but we felt that we
kept coming back to a common pattern. Then when we probed further, the
lights went off. Gradually we came to the dream, we almost got it but then
the dream put us back again. After more probing we were finally
confronted with this whole Ringworm understanding. We had solved the
case, come to the remedy and come to the understanding. We were
enlightened! We were really joyous that we have understood the sensation
of the nosode; that we could understand this pattern very clearly. Just at
the time that we got the confidence that Ringworm will help her to very
large extent, the lights came back. Isn't this a very thrilling phenomenon!*

III. Remedy and Case Follow - up

*We will go to the first follow-up before which we had only given her one
dose of Ringworm in 200C potency. The reason for selecting the 200 potency
was the fact that she was not in her delusion or into images as much; there
weren't many gestures in the case. There was only a repeated pattern which
was related more to her entire situation than the sensation. She was telling us
how she was trying to do several things to reduce and increase or get out of
her pain. So we thought a single dose of Ringworm with a potency of 200C
would be the best thing. This is the first follow-up after that. Until September
2006 we have repeated Ringworm 200C only twice.*

First follow-up: 31 December, 2003

P: Few episodes of headache once in a while, but they were ok. Not so bad. They were kind of there since the time I woke up in the morning. It was a heavy head, probably because of late night and things like that. Otherwise I am doing alright.

D: In what way are you alright? Tell me more about the headache.

P: It was absolutely fine for a while after the medication. I didn't have a headache. It's because of the periods (menses) that it started again a few days ago.

D: How would you elaborate over that – 'feeling ok?'

P: I am not saying there is a very drastic change from what it used to be and what it is now but overall I feel fresh mentally. I mean I think I am fresher at the end of the day than I would be otherwise. Also because there is neither much acidity nor headaches, I feel healthier like the rest and can do more during the day.

D: Describe mentally fresh.

P: Mentally fresh in the sense overall physically as well as mentally you feel much more fresh than what you would as a routine otherwise.

She is much better in this follow-up. She has a headache since the past 3 or 4 days but it's not a migraine headache. It's just related to her menstrual cycles.

We had another follow-up with her a couple of months later in March 2004.

Second follow up: 5 March, 2004

D: How are you?

P: I am okay.

P: Yes, the constant headache or migraine has not been there. I had it once or

75

twice before my menstrual cycle but only related to the period and not for too long. Those were probably for only half a day or something or probably when I woke up in the morning the headache was there. It's nothing major like it used to be otherwise. No. Not like that.

D: No major headache?

P: No.

D: I want to assess as to how much better you are since the time we have started the medications.

P: I am feeling a lot better with regards to the headache and otherwise also the tiredness has reduced.

D: In what way are you feeling better?

P: I rarely get the headaches and even then the intensity is not so much.

D: Okay.

P: And the acidity also has not been there for all these months since November, since the time I have started your medication. In these last couple of weeks I must have probably had it just for three-four days for sometime in the morning.

D: No episode of cough and cold?

P: No.

D: The only time you had it was in the month of November?

P: Yes, that is the first time I took the medication and once after that.

D: Any other complaints?

P: Besides that no.

D: How has your mood been overall for the past two months?

P: I have been okay. In general my anger and irritability has reduced. I am trying to stay a little bit calmer.

She then talked about some kind of a situation in her office where she had to deal with her juniors and scold them about something that they had not done well. She was quite frustrated with the kind of work they were doing.

P: In the earlier days I wouldn't have been able to openly confront them and tell them that where they were going wrong. But this time at the end of the situation, I really felt very confident that I could handle it. For once I am satisfied with the change that I am trying to make in my situation at the office. I think I am able to do it more successfully.

D: Tell me about this.

P: Yes, because I am satisfied with the change that I am trying to make. I think I am being able to do it more successfully.

D: Could it have been possible in the past, six months ago?

P: Actually I could not even give it a thought six months ago. I probably did so only now.

D: Your sleep would be disturbed?

P: No. I am not having a disturbed sleep.

D: You are having a very sound sleep?

P: Yeah.

D: Good. Absolutely sound sleep?

P: Yeah, absolutely sound sleep.

D: Since the time that you have started our medication, which was around the 13th of November until date, how would you grade the changes that have happened physically, generally and the pain in your headache?

P: Overall there is a lot of improvement. Personally I feel with regards to my headache and even my mental status or whatever, I am quite alright.

D: In what way can you describe the changes at your level of mind?

P: I mean I am not disturbed. In the sense, things are probably going smooth in life. So you are not disturbed you know that's because of the medication or it's just generally with regards to day to day life how it is. With regards to the headache it has helped a lot. I don't have that much frequency and intensity like earlier. I am also feeling quite healthy and alright physically as well as mentally.

And then we saw her in September 2004 which was the last bit that we saw of her. By this time her weight had increased by 3 kilos in total. This was significant gain since one of her complaints when she visited us was low weight and low energy due to the problem of thalassemia minor. Her Iron-serum levels and her total iron binding capacity (TIBC) were well within normal limits. Her moods were way better. The frequency of headaches as you all read, have gone down but what was very interesting was this feeling that 'I have been able to make a change, I am healthy.'

After that she disappeared till somewhere in 2005 when my assistant got in touch her and asked her as to how she was doing.

My assistant had to call her up a couple of times because she would never be easily reachable on the phone. I remember when she was coming to us for treatment earlier, she would be very particular. She would always come every 15 days or once a month whenever she was called. She would always reach before time, sit in the clinic and wait. So we knew that she was regular and disciplined in that way. Suddenly after about say 8-10 months she disappeared. We were surprised.

So when my assistant called her up and said that we wanted to speak to her, she called back and asked what was it regarding? My assistant said that it would be nice to see her at the clinic as we really wanted to know how she was doing. She responded by saying, "I am doing very fine and you know I am doing things just as any other person would. I am handling everything fine so I don't feel that I need come anymore. I don't need the medications". So my assistant asked, "How are all those feelings?" She said, "I feel absolutely normal. I don't feel I am weak. I don't feel anything of that sort. Those issues are not there anymore. So why should I keep coming to the doctor all the time?"

Her sensation had now eased and she felt – 'I am normal. Now I am healthy, health is not an issue anymore. So why should I visit you? I am not dependant on you anymore.' We felt happy to hear that.

IV. Summary

So all in all she received only about 3 doses of Ringworm 200C till September 2004 which was the last time we saw her.

 # A CASE OF CARSINOSINUM

I.   Case Introduction

II. The Case

III. Two Ways of Case-taking

IV. Remedy and Case Follow-up

V.   Summary

Cases always clarify what you have learnt. Most times we learn things from cases in the first place. But when we are coming up with a concept or a theory, cases give us a deeper understanding. This particular case that we are going to share with you is a very interesting one.

I. Case Introduction

This case is of a 21 year old boy who came to us with complaints of hay fever. His description about the complaint is very peculiar. While we were trying to capture him in our camera, he said something very interesting. He said, "I must sit forward sometimes, because I fidget. I may be all over the place." What an interesting way to start the case! We then went to the complaint.

II. The Case

P: I might sit forward sometimes because I fidget. I may be all over the place.

D: Tell us your complaints.

P: The main thing is hay fever. It's bad; it's just started since last few days. It usually starts earlier on, in the summer. Recently it has only just started to get really hot and humid, so it's just started in the last kind of two-three days and that's my main complaint, yeah definitely. And it's really kind of annoying when you get it because what happens is you've either got a problem with your eyes or a problem with your nose and you never really get them at the same time; it's either the eyes or the nose. One will stop and the other will start. It seems that way. It seems like you've got some kind of seal that breaks. Like your nose will be fine and then like you won't be able to breathe very easily but it'll all be bunged up so it won't annoy you. And your eyes will be going and then you'll sneeze. Something like the wind or something will kind of break the seal and it'll feel like that'll start something and that's just the way I can describe it really, it's strange. It's just something that'll come out. The main thing that'll happen is that as soon as I wake up, like this morning when I woke up, my eyes are really swollen and red and they look a lot different to how they are now. Umm, that kind of hurts and it was kind of hot I guess. And then that slowly wears off during the day like now it's kind of stopped. Well it's probably still a bit red but it's stopped right now and then what happens is through the day it'll kind of come on every now and then. But then my eyes usually settle down during the day and my nose usually kicks in at some point and will start running and then I have sneezing fits. You know I'll have five or six sneezes all in a row and then it will stop and then it comes on again at night. So it's kind of morning and night that are the worst times really. It's strange because I can go outside and I can be sitting outside and I can be around loads of flowers and I probably just go around and run around in the grass but I won't get it at all. And then later on in the day when I am inside, I usually get it when I'm just sitting around or just before I'm going to bed.

So he is talking about his complaint, the hay fever, the sneezing and that he experiences his complaint like a seal. We dig into his complaint further and ask him to describe the seal.

D: Describe this a little bit - You said the seal…

P: The seal. Well I mean it's coming from my past experience of hay fever as well. Like my last year but it does apply this year as well. It will feel as if everything is blocked up (*hands are coming closer, narrowing inwards*) but in a good way like my nose won't run. It'll all just be there and I won't notice it because nothing's actually happening. It's just all blocked up. I mean my breathing, I will be slightly uncomfortable and stuff like that but it'll feel like this thing has clogged it together (*hands are coming closer, narrowing inwards*) and it's all stopped. And my eyes will be you know if I rub them or something touches them or something happens, then the seal would be broken (*hands going apart*). So it feels like they're fine now. They are really comfortable and just normally functioning. But if for instance something I don't know started like raining or the wind blew into my eyes then it might feel like it triggers something and something changes. Then my nose might start running. It takes a little while you know. Then you have to blow your nose loads and just relax. I think if I'm doing something and not concentrating on the hay fever, that seal will kind of reform and it'll all settle down. I'll know it's still there but it won't affect me. So it feels like there is some kind of seal that can be broken like barriers of a dam (hand gesture making a wall). You know what I mean? Like it'll be holding it all back and then something will break it and then it will start. That's what it feels like. Other things are…

D: No no no. Just describe this little bit. What you were doing with your hands? That is very important.

P: Well what it is with the seal? It feels like it's up at the top of my nose so it'll be there and in my eyes. The seal will feel like its right in the corner of my eyes, here. It is all around the edges of my eyes not actually in my eyeball.

I can feel it just tingling and right now it's just fine but then something will happen like I say and this tingling sensation will come on quite a lot. Then something might happen and my eyes will start to redden or like gunk will come out of the corners or they'll just start to water. They can really swell up quite a lot. So much so that they kind of swell out of my socket slightly so that when you look left or right it kind of squishes up to the sides so that the side actually ripples. It's completely mental.

He is talking about the seal, the barrier. It's all clogged up and there is lot of irritation. He is talking about a whole lot of things. At this point of time we pose him a question.

D: Can you describe this seal, the barrier, it's broken and something will start? Just describe the experience of the whole thing.

We ask this because it looks like his complaint is not just a small thing of hay fever but a complex thing. So we give him the entire complex back and we take him further. Also note that the complaint has already taken the form of an image of a block or a barrier.

P: It can feel almost good I suppose because when the seal is there, when it's blocked and everything is there it can feel like all the sinuses are blocked. So you've got it all through your head, your ears, your throat and your nose. That'll all feel slightly swollen and it can be painful but at the same time just nice because it's not running. But then as soon as something happens everything will kind of freeze up and in all sensations loads of feelings will happen. So all my skin will become really tingly and that's the main thing. It's from a relaxed kind of blocked up sensation where you don't really recognise anything but your breathing will be difficult to that kind of sensation where everything is at full awareness. You're at full sensation so everything will be tingling, itching, running and kind of sore. So there are kind of a few different modes to the hay fever you know, a few different stages.

So what does he say? There are a lot of things but mainly he talks of two different things in the chief complaint - one is the blocked up sensation where he feels all blocked and the sinuses are heavy and sore and the other is the flow when everything is on high alert. Both of them trouble him. He is not very happy with this blocked and sore thing and neither he is very happy with this flowing thing that is happening. So in my mind, Cruciferae is out. He doesn't talk about being blocked that 'O My God!

The sinuses make me feel blocked. It's terrible. I need them to flow.' He is not talking about Cruciferae. Both these things - this blocked and flow are a part of the same chief complaint and it tells me that this chief complaint is far more complex than just these two things. There is a lot more to come. This person from a calm relaxed person suddenly gets transformed into a nervous fidgety person with this change in his complaint. So in order to know what his experience is and what is it that he is talking about, we encourage him to talk by consoling him.

D: You are doing very well in trying to explain what's happening because you are giving us your personal subjective symptoms right. As we go on asking you, there might be times when you might repeat certain things because that's what you feel. You might find our questions repetitive which is absolutely fine. It is all a part of the process. I just need to understand this a little bit more. So you said that it's relaxed and blocked. Then it changes to everything aware and too much sensation. I just want to understand this relaxed and blocked and then this change, the whole experience of it.

P: Well, as I say, it's a subconscious thing so I'll be sitting there and I'll be doing my work and I'll have absolutely no awareness of the hay fever at all. That's when it's blocked and that's when it's relaxed and that's when all the barriers are up and there is nothing happening. It's absolutely fine and then it will change and quite quickly! So something will start itching like my nose and I'll know it within my mind. I'll know even if nothing has physically started happening. I'll just know it and I'll immediately get ready like – 'Oh, ok. I'm going to get hay fever for a bit', so I'll accept it. I'll just try and relax and take it as it comes. You know the best thing that I've found is to try and absolutely forget that it's there because it goes from being a basic subconscious thing to a very conscious thing. It will feel like everything is wet.

From a subconscious thing it suddenly gets transformed into a very conscious thing. So what is this transformation and what is he experiencing, what is happening to him? This is what we ask him and he explains it a little bit more.

P: I guess nothing actually is wet. My nose will run a little bit but my eyes aren't wet. But everything is just tingling. It feels like it's free and your sinuses start to just move around and you feel like everything is connected - like your ears, nose, mouth and throat, as if everything has got this. I'm trying to think about it now. You can feel it deep within your ears and maybe it's like some kind of ball in your ears. Like there is some kind of actual thing which is there that wasn't there before and that has just kind of forms and pushes things out of the way and makes your face feel like a bit bigger than it is (*hands moving outwards*). That's when everything is going on. It's a case of sitting and relaxing so that everything dries up again and goes back to normal. But what happens is when everything is free flowing and as I say moving, it is ok. But once it dries up again and forms this seal, that's when everything can go sore; really sore. As I say I'll be very unconscious of it but because it's all dry instead of being wet, that's when it's all sore and red round the very brims of your eyes. But you're not bothered about that as much when it's running. So it's that kind of thing. I feel because....

Complex things! Now the ball is coming into picture and what is interesting is that either way it is painful - the block makes him sore and the flow makes him alert, irritated and agitated. There is a swelling and there is a ball but there is no place for that. This tells us that he is talking about something that we have not heard before, something that we need to explore further. Where are these balls coming up from? A completely new dimension is that the balls are pushing. We would like to explore what he is talking.

Do you notice how quickly from the complaint he goes a little bit to the level of the fact describing the complaint and he jumps to the delusion, to the image of the complaint. Isn't it interesting! So we asked him to talk about it and let's see what he has to say.

P: It takes over my mind completely it takes over everything. But in this case of everything being free flowing and moving I think what happens is that it feels as though everything slightly swells, gets bigger and inflamed. So there's heat and as a result, from my neck down, it'll all be really itchy. I'll just want to scratch it on the outside of my neck and inside my throat. So what happens is inside my throat it's a bit like my ears, it feels like there's a ball or something which grows (*hands coming together making the shape of a ball & then making it bigger*). It just grows big and pushes everything that was there originally, out of the way. So it feels really uncomfortable, like you've got something slightly alien in your ears, throat and nose. And you know even if it doesn't swell physically because you can't tell it swells, it feels like it swells. Then because it swells, your throat is blocked up and you can't breathe very much so I do these incredibly deep breaths.

*We started talking about his hay fever but it has taken a completely
different direction into the aliens. This is the word of delusion and we
explore this delusion further. He is giving you the delusion of the
complaint and is going deep into it very easily and quickly.*

III. Two Ways of Case-taking

*Something that we need to keep in mind: case taking is of two types - one
when there is a patient like him: they start with the complaint, go into its
facts, into the delusion, into their sensation and finally maybe to the
source. In the second type, the patient goes from the complaint to the fact
and then the fact takes you to the emotion in general or to the situation.
From there it takes you to the delusion in general and then to the
sensation and finally to the source.*

The Direct way of case taking

*In this type of case, we have the complaint which the patient mentions
and describes like here the patient said, "I have got a running nose. It
makes me feel irritated and angry and as if my nose has a ball inside
which is growing. It's like an alien inside." Maybe this alien will take us
to the sensation that this patient belongs to and that sensation along with
this energy that we see along the case, helps us confirm and clarify the
sensation and takes us to the source or the remedy that the patient
requires. This is one way of case taking, which is direct like a straight line.*

The Indirect way of case taking

*But not all cases are like that. There are cases which take a different route.
They finally come back to the same source, the same remedy but they take
a completely different journey. Let's see that. The patient starts with the
complaint of hay fever. You ask him to describe more. He will say that
there is a runny nose with a discharge which makes him feel very irritated
and upset and that he always gets upset. This upset will make us wonder
why he is being troubled and tortured. He feels that somebody is pursuing
him, both because of the complaint and in general too. Then the patient
goes into an incidence of his childhood or a completely different story. We
then ask him to talk more about that. He says that the childhood incidence
makes him feel as if 'they' are attacking and troubling him; they are
cornering him and are going to finish him. So that brings about the*

87

sensation of a 'me versus you'. Then you see some hand gestures in the case that gives us the energy of the case and finally the patient goes to the source. It's like the spirals; the patient takes a long route before finally coming to the source.

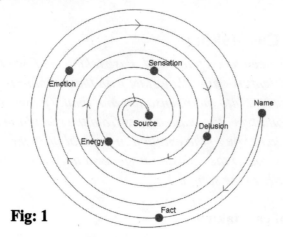

Fig: 1

But in our case the patient goes directly into the complaint. He is already in the level of delusion, as he continues describing the chief complaint. Probing that further will take us to the sensation and finally to the source.

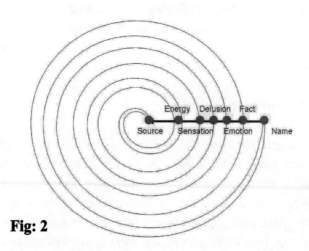

Fig: 2

We will give the delusion back to the patient. We will make him elaborate and take us to the final destination. So we ask him to describe the balls that are growing, swelling, pushing and everything that is happening.

D: So just describe this - there is a ball that grows swells and pushes everything.

P: Yes, well that's how I can describe it. I think because when it's all full, I feel as though it's all connected. So there'll be sensations that run all the way through my eyes to my ears and down into my throat. Especially my throat, my throat's a fairly new thing. The idea that its swelling happens, I can't really remember it happening in my original hay fever. So what will happen is that the outside of my neck will start itching and it will feel as if there is something blocking my airways (*hands coming together and making a wall*).

D: What are you doing with your hands?

P: What am I doing with my hands? Well I'm a notorious fidget, people call me the fidget. I love throwing my hands about. Yeah so this ball, I suppose you've got your Adams-apple there and that feels like a ball. I guess the shape of it.

D: No don't, forget the eyes, the throat and everything and the experience of this ball swelling and pushing everything.

P: It's hard to relate it, not to take it all back to physical terms.

D: Of course you relate it to what you feel but I'm not asking you why you feel all that. What is the experience like to feel it?

P: Yeah yeah yeah. Well it's debilitating. So it's as I say at the very fore-front of my consciousness, of my conscious mind. I'm just absolutely aware of it and it's a sense of agitation. It feels its pushing stuff out of the way. So it's actually where everything is normal, it's pushing all that stuff out of the way and bringing in this new bad thing.

Something is coming in and is pushing his normal self away and bringing something which is bad. This delusion is getting a little bit more serious. It is something which we haven't heard and cannot follow. It is something which one normally doesn't say.

We need to understand this more because we have to explore this entire phenomenon that is happening in him. Sometime back we asked him what he was doing with his hands. He said that he is a fidget and he is all over the place. We didn't know what question to pose at this point of time.

We told him to describe it because we needed to understand this a little bit more. We wanted him to clarify it and take us to the next deep level and finally to the destination. The final destination is always in our minds. For that we needed to go in deeper. What is it that he is talking about at this point of time? How is it going to help us towards the next step? What's the next step, where is the final destination?

D: Describe this. You are doing very well; we only need to understand this.

P: Yeah. Well it's like everything's normal, so everything's there and everything will be absolutely fine. Then there'll be something that happens. I don't know if it's a ball, I think it's a round shape. It feels like that. It's the same as it is in my ears especially in my throat. It feels like a round shape that pushes into the space that was already there. So it blocks up the space and the space being the free space that's supposed to be there i.e. like a windpipe or whatever, that ball impedes on that space and the space impedes on my mind. So it impedes on everything, it's like an enemy I guess against me. It swells and the idea is that if I relax and I don't let it hurt me, if I don't let it swell and I don't let it kind of affect my mind, then it will piss off again and disappear.

His hands were moving, making a shape of a round ball when he spoke about his space. He said that it's like something which is going, which should not be there. As he talks about this ball like an enemy, it brings up the 'me versus you' in our minds. Okay he is having that battle with the ball, something against his mind but what is interesting is that his 'me versus you' doesn't take us further into something that is going to be very fatal but takes us to a point where he says that if I don't pay attention it will just disappear.

So his 'me versus you' is very peculiar. If you see how the case has gone so far - we started with the hay fever we went to a seal, a barrier and something is blocked. Something blocked and sore makes him fine but when it is flowing it makes him nervous, fidgety and all over the place as if it's like a small ball, which is at a place where it is not supposed to be there. The balls are growing, become like aliens and now the balls are like enemy. Look how much we have travelled with this ball. We have travelled so far and as he is going further, he is telling us something very important. The pattern is getting clear. Something that is not supposed to be there is there. This pattern needs to be established and taken further. It should be clearly seen in the case all over. We ask him to describe more about what he is saying.

P: It's that kind of thing yeah… It's something that affects everything about me and pushes my normal self, pushes myself out of the way and replaces it with this very conscious, agitated, annoyed, frustrated and fidgety person that doesn't want to be there. I don't feel like myself when I've got it. I am kind of very relaxed but when I have it I'm all over the shop. I'm a mess mentally. It's just this thing that stops everything from being normal. Rather than everything happening as a mental thing it feels like a physical thing; like I say this big round shape or this ball.

Can we appreciate the pattern which is repeating itself especially because all this is coming back again to the ball – a big round shaped ball? Yes we can appreciate this pattern because it is taking us one step further every time that we probe it. Hence we need to explore this description of the ball more. So we ask him to describe it further.

D: This round ball that you are experiencing, what does it do to you?

He says, "Whatever it is, it pushes my normal self away and it's making me into this something nervous, agitated, fidgety…" He doesn't say it pushes him away or something is coming and pushing him. This is a very peculiar way of describing, isn't it? We all homoeopaths must be aware that we have to see what is peculiar and what has been told at this point of time. Every line spoken by each patient is important. Every line is giving us the kingdom, the miasm, the sensation and the entire story. So we have to be alert and aware to see what is peculiar.

Now what we are going to probe into is something very peculiar. It might open the door to something more important. As we investigated further, we kept a close watch on his hand gestures because his hands are moving all the while. He said he is a nervous, fidgety person but we also saw a pattern in these movements that was coming up.

D: Just keep describing this ball and physically what it does do to you?

P: It is certainly a sense of everything getting bigger so it will actually expand on things. So there'll be something there and a lot of it will be there and the thing inside you is absolutely normal. So say you've got your heart, a normal thing that's inside you, it'll feel like that heart is going to get bigger. So in my throat especially what I imagine is that my Adams-apple looks like a ball and it'll feel like that ball gets taken over and it swells into a bigger ball.

And in my ears I feel like this round shape; my ears are in a normal shape but when the hay fever happens something attacks that natural physical shape of the ears. It makes them all swell up and pushes all the other things out of the way. It's that pushing sensation...

Amazing! We will see this pattern getting crystal clear as it goes further. As we move further in the case we realise that he elaborates more at the delusional level and he moves further into the sensation and then finally to the source. Many times all these components that he is speaking of don't make any sense to us but they play a very important role at the end when we come to the source of the remedy. These are very important things which we need to explore and take into account. We are not going to probe them at this point of time because they are very peculiar and important. It might be the language of the source. We have no idea. We are open and eager to know more about it. So we need to elicit it, make it more lucid and then take it further.

"So what is this that you are talking about? Make this thing more clear to us. This non-human language and delusion that you are talking about... make it more understandable so that we can prescribe..." This is exactly what I tell him in my mind and we let him talk further.

P: Everything feels like it's touching everything else. So where there was nothing touching everything's there with your hands like this and then when it swells, everything touches so that will swell and my hand will swell. Then if I touch that hand and that will make that hand have felt in and therefore it does the same thing. So in my nose there'll be a swelling. When in your nostrils there's supposed to be a hole that goes open to your head, it feels like everything starts to touch because of this ball and this swelling and therefore everything starts to tingle because it's touching everything else. Everything is inflamed and kind of irritated. It touches and therefore all this sensation happens.

'Everything is touching one thing or the other. One ball is touching the other ball; it is getting inflamed and is passing on to the next thing.' It sounds like a chain reaction that goes from one place to another, a kind of transmission that is going on.

P: That's how I can describe its touching. So this ball makes things touch each other and therefore when this sensation happens in my ears I'll feel like I really don't know how to describe it. But it's deep within my jaw, deep within the whole structure of my head. I just feel like everything is connected and because everything is swollen so that everything touches. It's that connected like before when I'd say I'm in a relaxed time and it's the seal. There's nothing touching, there's no swelling. I feel as if everything is just kind of you know, it's yes, it's not touching everything. It doesn't feel connected anymore and everything feels relaxed and they're not bothering each other. You know if my body parts were like that…

He says that everything is touching and getting swollen and everything is getting connected and that this should not happen. 'Connection, touching and swelling' looks like a problem which is troubling and bothering him. It makes him not his normal self. We let him talk more.

P: They're fighting against each other to get space. So you know in my throat it feels like there's a fight going on between trying to get space for the air to go down into my lungs. So because of the fight there, there is the irritation. It is the same with my ears. It's not even in my ears, its deep within my head or it's around where my ears are.

Then he goes further to describe in the next paragraph… You will see it's this kind of a roundish ball which is coming in - "In my eyes, in my sockets." So he kind of generalises this entire ball phenomenon that is going on within him.

P: It feels separate when we're talking about balls or you know shapes. I don't think it's exactly like a ball but it's some kind of a roundish shape. And I can feel two of them, one for each ear; one in my throat, in my nose and then my eyes. It is just generally the whole of my eyes not just my eyes but the socket itself, everything and then...

D: So what's the experience like to have these balls?

P: Well that's the time when it really comes on. That's what I mean when I say that everything is connected. Everything because these balls appear to connect with each other because they're pushing everything out of the way and therefore everything starts to hurt because it's trying… It shouldn't be where it is. I mean it's pushing.

It's pushing and trying to be somewhere where it should not be. Do we see the same pattern coming up again which we saw some time back? This is what we say – when the pattern repeats itself in the case in the same way, it helps us to establish that this is the phenomenon that is going on and as the pattern repeats itself at different points in the case, it also brings along some more issues which at the end of the case make a lot of sense - that they are not just mere images but actually source mechanism and information. At this point exploring every point takes you a step closer to the destination (source). We believe this understanding keeps emphasising with every case we see.

P: All the things go out of the way. So the sides of my throat would actually feel like touching each other. It's just not natural and it's the same with my nose. So the sensation is the sense of a very, very physical thing. Everything is connected in a bad way so it's a complete sense of frustration. So you've just got to relax and it just heightens you up completely like makes you feel you know absolutely mad and angry because you wonder why this certain thing happened. As if it is because of hay fever and so you kind of think why you have got that allergy? Why does it just attack certain things? And certain things just grow you know, what's that all about? So you kind of feel a bit frustrated because you don't know why it's suddenly changed. You know there's no real reason why.

So it is connecting in a bad way, something which should not be there is there. This pattern is what we are looking out in the case and this comes in every line that our patient is speaking. What is his experience in this? What is he talking about? What's happening inside him is what we wanted to ask him.

D: So just to understand this a little bit more describe this whole thing - This attack and then it grows and this sudden change and that everything is connected. What is the experience and what is the feeling like to be in such a situation?

P: The most important thing that I can tell you is the fact that it stops me from doing what I want to do, that's the thing because I will be doing work. I'll try and forget about it. I've got to push it at times and forget about it and when I'm doing my work I just suddenly go, "Damn, I've got to go!" And I blow my nose. You know it just takes you away from your concentration. So it's very hard to get back into that concentrating mode of working. Then it makes you very scattered and very jumpy. You know your moods kind of just

94

jump around the place so you'll be happy. Then suddenly you will be very unstable and then suddenly very afraid and suddenly very comfortable and concentrating, then completely conscious of everything. That's going on and it's really tingly and that's the thing while I've got it, it makes me you know, really on the edge like kind of angry with myself I guess.

Now you see some emotions coming up. He feels scattered, angry, jumpy and edgy with this problem. What is the experience? We let him talk and go on. We noticed something very important that he spoke now. He brought the aliens back into the picture and his experience with the aliens. What is this alien for him?

P: I feel like its alien. I do feel like it's not a part of me, the actual thing. So when I say it grows that's what I mean. Actually I think it might have been there already but it might not have. I suppose when the seals…

So there is one point - he is saying something might have been there and might not have been there and this alien is not a part of him. This is what he said so far.

P: You know it's there. Although when I've said it's unconscious, it's there but when it grows it feels like it's not a part of my body that's growing you know, it's something else. It's something that appears and grows and its absolute main aim is just to piss you off and to make you angry and to just completely stop you from doing what you want to do. You just want to focus on the floor all the time therefore and that makes you feel like…

Something that he could not decide was whether it's a part of him or whether it's a part from outside. He is not very clear about it. Then he further goes on to tell us that it is a part of him. It might have been there. It grows and becomes big and its only aim is to just trouble and bother him. We think of these questions in our minds - What's the experience of this alien? What is the alien making him do?

P: Not communicating with people feels like you have not been a nice person or you know that kind of thing. When it's runny and everything is going, everything is sore. But it's a different type of sore like a sense of itchiness. It's a real sense that yeah everything is just touching each other, it's just like everything is connected in a really bad way. So it's all communicating this thing that's inside me, it's all within my head but…

95

D: Keep describing this.

P: Well what I was talking about was that it builds up to my anger levels to a time when I feel like hell, why it won't just stop! And it's that point when I feel like I want to stop what's going on and therefore if it was an alien thing, if it was a person, if it was some kind of maybe… it's like I can't think about what it would look like. It would look like maybe spiky because what it does in my nose is that it feels like there are loads of little hair that have stood up at the end of my nose and this thing kind of touches those hairs. So everything starts tingling and it's like a fizzing in my throat. So everything is just moving really fast.

So I'd want to itch in my throat because it feels as if loads of little hair are just on the surface and they're just all brushing about the place. And that's exactly what it's like in my nose; but then in my ears it's this real strong thing, a real object. It is an absolute object. There's an itching inside my ears but then deep within it feels like the object is like a block or a ball that I could actually feel yeah. It feels like it shouldn't be there. Like it is absolutely moving everything else out of the way and it's just there to infiltrate. It's just there to… your body and your mind is telling you that it shouldn't be there and therefore you get so annoyed with the fact that this thing is there.

How beautifully he brings out the same pattern – 'Something is telling your mind that it should not be there; that it's there and therefore you are getting annoyed.' And in the process of telling this he again gives us a whole lot of things. His hands were moving. He then said, "It's so hard, it feels like it takes me over but I could easily control it if I could."
So - 'The whole thing takes me over, there is no control but if I had the control, I could control it.'

All along if you see this pattern which we have been establishing is that, something which should not be there is there and is troubling. This pattern is very nosode like and this nosode like pattern is getting established very clearly for us. In our minds we are very clear that yes, this is a nosode case. We will establish this very clearly in the next few paragraphs.

P: It doesn't feel like a very strong... it feels like it takes me over but I could easily control it if I could. It does feel like a physical thing, I know it's not a physical thing. I don't think it's within my nose, it definitely feels like it is

96

pulsating. It's this you know like well, what you'd imagine - some scary kind of alien blob thing to look like. It's in there and its purpose solely is just to produce as much feeling you know. It's sending out loads of signals all over the place to generate as much mucous as possible.

'The issue is within me, there is a problem within me. It's like a scary alien blob...'

P: I just get this feeling that something is touching, something that shouldn't be touching you know.

Again it comes to – 'Something is there which should not be there.'

P: That's especially there in my eyes because they swell so much that they touch the inside of my socket. They touch where they shouldn't be touching and they come out of my eyes slightly. So they're touching and therefore this touching irritates the thing next to it. This feels like that would then touch the thing next to that and therefore everything will start touching each other and will be annoyed, jostled into position and shaken around and really be agitated.

This one is touching this person, the other person is touching the third person and then the third person touches the fourth person. It's touching everywhere - the eye, the ear, everywhere and everything gets agitated, jostled and shaken. What a beautiful mechanism. These all could be the words of the source he is telling us; the exact way in which the source could be representing. Good! We are taking it and motivating him to tell us more.

D: How do you experience this little thing move here, move there and agitate you?

P: How do I experience it? I just experience there is something that shouldn't be there you know. It doesn't feel like a part of me. It's like something that's different from me and therefore something that I could get rid of.

If it was something that should be there like just a pain, say like my heart, it's there and therefore if it was inflamed I wouldn't want to rip it out. But because this thing doesn't feel like it's a part of my body, it does feel like it could just be taken out and thrown away and therefore just gotten rid of;

especially when it's in my nose, because it feels like this spiky little blobby pulsating thing inside the nose. Therefore if someone did just open my nose, take it out and threw it away it would be gone, it wouldn't be there anymore you know. It doesn't feel like a part of me that's why I feel so annoyed because it's like why can't I just get rid of it. If it's not actually something that I need, I don't need the sensation and the thing that's inside me.

He gave a beautiful example of the heart and the nose. 'There is something over there that is not supposed to be there and I want it out to get myself back again.'

P: It feels like I've got this layer all over my face. As if I can grab it and put a slit in it and pull it all off. So it's like a mask. I can get it off and then I'll be back to me again. So it's that getting off of something. So there are the shapes that I want to pull out physically; just want to rip them out and then there's this kind of tingling all over me that I want to scrape off, especially on the inside of my nose. I want to get in the inside of my nose. It feels like it'd be red you know, really red and raw and tingling and you want to get just, it'll hurt but you want to get it and scratch it off (gesture); so it's just all off and it will reveal your normal working eye. So if I get my eye and I get that thing out there and I get my nostrils and I get that thing out there and I take that thing out of my ears and out of my head then I'll be back to normal.

The summary here is that –'These things being over here make me abnormal and once they are out they are going to get me back to my normal self. There is something wrong within me. I need to correct it to get my normal self back again.' What is he doing in that process?

P: You want to do damage. You want to hurt it, it's hurting you and so you want to stop it from hurting you. You feel like the only way you can do that is to take it out. So it could be like a tumour, something like that. I know there's not anything physical there but it feels like something that could be taken out. It could be taken out quite easily. It feels like you've got this centre of hay fever and this centre of a little hay fever demon, a little hay fever monster. It was inside your head like right deep within your head and it just makes everything itch so you can actually just go, "Oh, you've got one of those hay fever tumours. Oh don't worry, we'll take it out for you." You could go to the doctors and they'd take it out for you and throw it away. So it feels like there are things that are irritated by pollen or whatever it is and those things are alien. You know those things are things that your body doesn't need. So why have you got them in the first place? Why was I not born without those things that will get irritated?

D: Sorry, "Why was I not born without…?"

P: Why do I have those things inside me that are allergic?

What a beautiful example to give. We never thought of a hay fever tumour but it gives us the beautiful example of the remedy that this person requires.

If you read this paragraph very carefully the last line was amazing. "I was born with those things with these irritants which get irritated. I was born with those cells which got hyperactive. I got this hypersensitive allergy and which is like a tumour; which if it is out will help me get my normal self back again." He is giving us the entire complex of the pathology, the sensation, the remedy all in one paragraph. This is a unique case where we have not moved away from his pathology and we have been tracking his hay fever and the symptomatology - the sensation and the emotions coming along with it which led us to the sensation so quickly. There is no story. We have absolute no clue of what he does, about any family situation, about anything else in his life. We have only the main core focus. Very few clients move in this direction.

We let him speak more about it because he is going to clarify it to us and then we are going to confirm it again. So let's read these last few paragraphs before the remedy is clearly established for us, before we nail the remedy.

P: Say your eye is allergic to pollen right, it doesn't feel like my eye is allergic to pollen, it feels like there is something on my eye and that's the thing that's allergic you know. So it doesn't feel like my throat becomes allergic to hay fever, it feels like the thing in my throat becomes allergic and then that triggers my throat to hurt. So it's like why was I born with these extra stupid things inside me that annoy me. Why can't they just be taken out? It doesn't feel like my eye. There is something on my eye, something which should not be there but is there and that is causing this.

D: Describe this – "Why was born I with these stupid things?"

P: Extra stupid.

D: You said extra... Sorry what was the word?

P: Yeah. Why was I born with this extra stupid thing? Um... well because it feels like something added on to your body. Like everyone has got similar things inside their body and it feels like you were born or you know you developed or you have inside you, an extra thing that's just there to be bad. Like you know your appendix or whatever, if that's got appendicitis, you just take it out, and you don't need it. So it's exactly like a tumour. I suppose you know you don't need a tumour, a tumour is a bad thing and if you take out the tumour then hopefully this illness will stop. It's that kind of thing where you feel like you've got something extra that other people haven't got. That's one of the reasons why it's annoying; I say this to my friend as well who's got hay fever. We say, "Why the hell have we got this thing? Why the hell we have got hay fever and other people haven't?" It's like you've got this extra thing that you might have been born with i.e. these extra things in your throat and your eyes and you think that's become allergic and you think well if they're not doing anything for me if it's not good to have them, why have I got them? So why not just take them out?

D: Acha!

Acha means 'Got it' – like 'Oh, ok.' What did we get? We got this extra thing and something that our patient doesn't want which makes him feel abnormal. So what is characteristic about this extra thing? It is that this extra thing has been a part of him all along. It's not that the extra thing came from outside like being attacked by a virus or a bacteria but that extra thing which should not be there is there, which is irritating and causing the trouble like a tumour, which is the pathology.

So, where did the spiky balls and alien take us to? 'Why was I born with these extra stupid things?' All along we saw his hands which were moving, making the gesture of a ball being scattered all over. It was the whole energy of the Cancer miasm, the Carcinosinum and finally it was the source - one touches the other, infiltrates, the tumour needs to be ripped off to get back to the normal self.

To put it in one line we got this case through, right from hay fever to the pathology of Carcinosinum - cancer. The pattern here directly pours into the source and as the source begins to speak, the sensation reveals itself. Note that a number of times in between in this case some words didn't make any sense to us. It was something beyond the level of delusion but as we have mentioned earlier these could be source words. We weren't jumping on what source he was talking about at that point of time. But it was telling us that it is something very important which will be helpful in understanding the source per se.

The sensation of a nosode is normal and abnormal, correct-incorrect. 'I am abnormal and I need to be normal'. We knew it by this time. The characteristic of this nosode is that there are abnormal cells within the body which when irritated wage a war against the body. This was beautifully shown by our patient at different levels. He used beautiful words of this alien blob touching one another and infiltrating. Cells of the body start going against it; one cell touches the other and the abnormal cells proliferate, infiltrate and the tumour begins to grow. A nosode in which there is self antagonism or alienisation, there are some cells which are perverted or abnormal. They keep multiplying and more and more cells of the body start behaving like aliens. This is the process of growth and metastasis that you see in cancer. This is the state of total chaos which you cannot control. You are overwhelmed by this chaos. There is chaos going on within him with the hay fever which he said. The moment there is flow, there is discharge everywhere, "I am irritated and scattered. I am this fidgety person". A usually calm and quiet person gets completely agitated and on alert with the chaos going on within him. Now we saw the case go straight in from the hay fever to the sensation and then to the source. Now let's see this spiral on the next page.

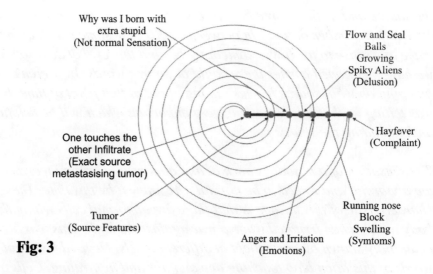

Why was I born with
extra stupid
(Not normal Sensation)

Flow and Seal
Balls
Growing
Spiky Aliens
(Delusion)

Hayfever
(Complaint)

One touches the
other Infiltrate
(Exact source
metastasising tumor)

Tumor
(Source Features)

Anger and Irritation
(Emotions)

Running nose
Block
Swelling
(Symtoms)

Fig: 3

When you have a case which has connected so well & come to the same pattern, everything else in the case must follow the same route. So to confirm the same from all angles we ask him to describe "I am very calm and collected."

Let's see the general aspects of his nature and confirm the same pattern and be dead sure of the remedy that he requires. So let's take a detour and see whether the same pattern repeats or brings out something new. For us this is just a confirmation. We are very clear of the prescription but it's always a good thing to reconfirm the prescription.

D: So let's now go to the other side a little bit where you said, "I am very calm and I am connected." We want to understand this.

P: Well I'm usually much centred. I'm very collected and understanding and I like that I suppose. I do my best to try and keep it up and so it's that kind of sense of being happy within yourself, being really happy with whom you are. That's the thing that switches so that you become agitated and annoyed.

D: Right. Let's leave the agitated. Describe this, much centred, collected, understanding that you are. Describe this a little bit.

P: I feel like I am driven and I have a goal, I have within me a lot of creativity and calmness, I am much centred.

His hands came together making a ball like thing. We asked him to describe - 'I am calm' and his hands were moving like this. (Hands coming closer together and going away)

D: What are you doing?

P: When I do this I feel very connected and collected. This is the centre and the core that I was talking about. When I say I am calm, it is a protective shield behind which there is a lot of activity going on. The activity of creativity and the things I have to do. So when I have made this gesture I am driven and I am in my centre and the opposite of this gesture would be when I am not calm. The opposite of this is when I'm really annoyed. It's when I want to be creative but it's that want that makes you not creative because you're just driving too hard to do something and therefore it makes you really the opposite. It's just annoying because I can't do what I want to do. So the opposite is when I am all scatty, I am just like I can't concentrate and I lose track of time. I'm a mess and I piss people off because I miss deadlines and stuff like that. When I am scatty and messy then I do not achieve anything. It's like I am all over the place at different levels.

D: How does it feel to be separate, to be all over the place and at loads of levels.

P: Um, it feels unlike me, it feels like what I want to be...

D: And what do you want to be?

P: Focused, I want to be focused. I believe myself to be focused, but then sometimes I'll be looking at what I'm doing and think you're not actually that focused. You're not actually that good. You know that sense of I want to be good, I want to be really good! And then suddenly I go from into utter mood swings; not mood swings as in anger itself but mood swings where I feel centred and then feel separate, I feel together and then I feel messy.

D: Scatty and messy... What is it that you are talking?

P: Yeah but my mood swings are kind of like they won't affect me on the outside as in when I feel scattered I won't obviously look a mess or go and be angry with people but it's like sometimes I'll be sitting there and I'll be like - 'Oh great! I know what I'm going to do now, I know what I'm doing, I feel really happy with what's going on in my life. I'm there and then something will happen, not necessarily anything big but something will happen. I'll get into this sense where I'm like oh shit everything is all over the place again. Oh! I need to get this thing sorted. Oh no! I need to get this thing sorted' and those kinds of blah blah things.' That's the scattiness that's all over the place. So it brings those things together because the way I work and the way I talk is quite scatty. You know I'll talk about one thing then I'll talk about another thing, I'll talk about everything else and be all over the place. I like being like that but then that's controlled, that's my creative side just letting ideas rip apart but then that's controlled.

So all along we could see the issue of Carcinosinum of being scattered and wanting to have that control, to do extra-ordinary things and not having that makes him feel scattered and chaotic.

D: So describe this control a little bit more.

P: It's certainly a concentration thing. Actually when I think of a word, the one word I would use is organisation; see I have to feel like organised disorder in a way. The way I work is very kind of... I'll be thinking about this for a bit or something like that and then I'll go and see my mates or go and see my girlfriend and I'll enjoy that. I like to think about those things and get involved in other things, but it has to be organised, it has to have a structure. Like I hate routines and schedules and yet I have to have to have schedules because otherwise I won't do my work. I find it very hard to stick to my schedules. I don't have regular sleep patterns you know. I'll get up early some days and not other days and whatever and so it's this organisation. But it's an organisation physically like scheduling day by day what you've got to do in diaries like you've got to do this and this by this time; but it's this mental organisation that I find really difficult. I want to be able to just organise my thoughts into this one thing that I can then take and use.

What words to use – organise and disorder! Both are two sides of Carcinosinum. You want to be organised which is the control part of the Cancer miasm or the Carcinosinum and the disorder is what is happening inside. He is sensitive to order and chaos, which are two sides of the same Cancer. Usually he is disorganised but what he would like to have is focus. He wants to have control and structure because everything is chaotic. Hence now, we asked him to describe the experience of being disorganised.

D: Describe disorder.

P: Well I think it's because I can't keep still and I see that as a disorder. Not disorder as in like a bad thing but disorder as in chaos.

D: Chaos?

P: Yeah, chaos in a good way. As in you know you're furiously active. It's not chaos as in everything's destructive; it's like organised chaos. As in, in my mind when I sit and I think, my mind is all over the place. It's really active and chaotic but in a very open, just let it go free kind of a way. But when I need to be organised in the sense that I need to then take that chaos and use it and put it down on paper...

His hands were all over and randomly, chaotically moving as he was saying all this.

P: ...and put it into a schedule, use it and talk to people and... So it's like I'm happy that I'm quite chaotic in my mind I'm happy with that but then I need to have some kind of structure to that chaos. So I don't just think loads of things and never actually do anything about it, because for me when I think about things and I don't do anything about it that's a really annoying thing. So it needs that organisation to bring it down to a level.

What does he say? 'Chaos', that's the word we would expect in Cancer, in Carcinosinum. And what does he want? He wants to put chaos in order to organise that chaos that is happening in him, to be in control of the chaos. This is Carcinosinum. Chaos is a thing that we will find in every case that we require Carcinosinum. Many times they want to put order in the chaos, there are so many things that they want to do and there is such a lot of chaos that they need to put that in order. That is what a Carcinosinum will constantly strive for.

Here, he is very happy in this chaos because he can put some order whereas when he was talking about his chief complaint with his hay fever, the barrier, he seal and the aliens that were moving inside him that chaotic and that scattery feeling gave him no order. It was something which he could not put order to and that's why his whole state has come out. So it is this that we try to understand and clarify. Organisation is difficult but what about organisation was our friend looking out for?

105

P: Yeah I'm a messy person, my room's a mess. I'm just not very clean. Not as in not clean but as in not washing but just organisation and stuff. But then it's this longing to be organised.

D: It's the longing to be organised?

P: Yeah I think it would be the feeling that I am trying to constantly obtain. You know I feel like I'm searching for a feeling or searching for a... whatever it is. It could be a physical or a mental thing, anything. Just that I'm searching and when I'm organised, if I get organised and I can organise everything, then that will be the time when I'll produce the best of me; whether it's work, relationships or all that. That's the time when I can really be me, the best of me.

D: What would it make you feel to be the best, to be organised?

P: It would make me feel very excited. I'm excited about the idea of being organised. I feel like if I was organised, I would be better, I'd be... and then to be the best I can be. You know it's hard to describe what the feeling of being best could be because it's yeah, just efficient but at the same time it's free. I suppose I will be free when I'm organised. Although organisation can bring a sense of structure, routine and no freedom, I think that when I become organised then I'll be free. At the moment everything is taking over everything and everything is kind of impeding on everything else. So I'm not free to actually be really (gesture) who I want to be you know. I'm creating all that. So if I organise my freedom, if I organise so that I can really concentrate on certain things and just you know like feel where everything is whether physically or mentally in order. I'd love to have my room ......and people go "Oh! Where's your red t-shirt" or something like that and I could go, "its right there, three foot to the left." Or something, or someone would be like, "Have you got a pencil sharpener?" and I'd be like, "yeah, it's in that drawer just at the back." I'd love to be able to say that.

D: You would love to be like that?

He would love to be like that, how interesting. What does he say? I would be free if I am organised. He wants to have that freedom because organisation gives him that control where he can do things the way he wants to do. So that allows him to control the chaos and be free. As pathology in cancer, you will see the cells getting haywire, proliferating,

106

infiltrating, taking over others and creating a complete chaos. They are so free that they are everywhere. This needs to be in control so that the normal self can be preserved which does not happen. This is exactly what is been spoken by our patient through a human language.

P: Yeah I'd love it. I've got a friend who's like that. It's absolutely great with people like that. But I find it really difficult. I usually just have everything in a big pile. My work place is just my desk, I just like to be free you know. Just having piles of stuff and having all your work messed around and getting …. but it has to be organised so that I know where it is and I know where I stand and I know...

There are two striking poles in this person. Chaos and organisation or control. One leads to the other and vice-versa. This according to us is the picture of Carcinosin

IV. Remedy and Case follow-up

We gave him one dose of Carcinosinum 1M in June 2006. The remedy helped him tremendously. We have a couple of email follow-ups to share with you where you can see the changes that the remedy has brought about in him.

The patient has been in touch with us via email. We prescribed the remedy to him in the month of June.

First follow-up: August 2006

About two months after the remedy, he emailed us. His parts of the email have been put under 'P' as in the patient's words.

P: I apologise for my lack of correspondence. The most noticeable thing after taking the remedy was how my hay fever cleared up. In the week after taking the remedy my hay fever persisted in annoying me and became quite intolerable and then without me really noticing it, it almost suddenly stopped.

I realised a few weeks later as I looked back that it hadn't been bothering me which was great!

So after the remedy there was an initial aggravation and after that the complaint got better. This is the ideal response that we would expect after the right remedy. He goes further to write something more to us.

P: I still have small symptoms such as occasional blocks or runny nose. But the whole controlling and attention grabbing nature of it has gone.

P: My eyes haven't itched or swollen up at all and the blocked up feeling has gone. My nose has still been blocked and sneezy from time to time. But it hasn't made me feel angry or frustrated or stopped me from getting on with things.

So we see that the remedy has helped him a lot at the physical level, at the level of his complaint and at the level of his emotions because the irritability and the trouble that the complaint had caused him which had really bothered him, that's not happening now.

Let's see what more changes came after the remedy.

P: Soon after having the consultation, my work load increased and I became quite busy working on few different projects at the same time. I found this to be very positive and exciting. But also quite hard to manage because I still found it difficult to focus on one thing at a time. I also found it difficult to switch off from work in my spare time and relax. I haven't found myself to be any more organised than before. It remains frustrating as it doesn't feel like I am in complete control of my work and day to day life.

So the remedy has really helped him at the physical and at the emotional level but deep down the sense of wanting to have control and multi-tasking, the disorganised feeling and being in complete control of himself has not yet been touched by the remedy. This tells us that the remedy needs to work more and we need to repeat a dose. So at this point of time we repeated the second dose of Carcinosinum in about two months of time. Since his pace is very fast, we expected at this level as well, the remedy to touch much more than what it has done till now. After repeating the dose we heard from him again in September.

Second follow-up: 21 September 2006

On 21ˢᵗ September we hear from him. He says,

P: I took another dose of the remedy as you suggested. One major thing that has developed over the last month has been my recurring migraines that I think you should know about. When I had the initial consultation with you I didn't mention my migraines. I hadn't had one for about a year and I believed that that they had gone forever. However in the last month I have had two migraines, which is worrisome. So the hay fever settled down that got better and the migraines came up.

This is good for us at this point of time because it tells us that the old symptoms are coming back, which is a very good indication. But at the same time when old symptoms are coming back, we expect the deeper state to be calmer. Let us go to the next part of the mail and read what he had to write.

P: Regarding my initial complaint of not being able to focus and generally feeling disorganised, I believe certain aspects have got better and certain things haven't changed. For the most part I do feel more solid and in touch with what I have to do when it has to be done and I do feel I am on top and in control of my life. My feelings and thoughts can change quite wildly. I can feel quite weak and confused and my major problem is getting on with things, usually.

So now the control which wasn't there is coming back. He feels himself to be at the top. He is able to do it though there are times when it goes into a swing; he goes to the other side but his capacity and the capability and the fact that 'I am being in control' is coming back which is very important. He further writes.

P: Now, I can plan things whether it is work or whatever and I know what I have to do and how it will work. This excites me overall. I do feel less confused and more focused.

Now this is very important because not being able to focus was one of the main aspects of this person for which he had come to us. Now he is able to focus, he is able to do that. His hay fever is better, his migraines have come back which I am sure will settle down and that did happen. We

109

heard from him in the later follow-up. His migraines went down.

The next step was to move to a 10M to make further change in the sensation. We adviced the homoeopath observing him to prescribe 10M the next time. So this was about this case - A case which was chaotic and all over the place and now is focused and in control. How wonderfully the entire cancer pathology was speaking and giving us the picture of the pathology! We are thrilled!

V. Summary

This case was somebody who was giving out through his words, gestures, explanation, and language, the entire phenomenon of the disease as it happens. We didn't need to look into any book. It was right there in front of us, the whole phenomenon of metastasis, how everything grows and how there is no place left for the normal self anymore. That was the time we realised that this is the first case where actually we saw so much of chaos. The whole chaos that cancer brings with it was in this patient from point one. This was very interesting because you often find in different plants, minerals and animals the Cancer miasm and you recognise it as one of being in full control. The control is the compensated or the successful side of the Cancer miasm. The chaos, the disorder, the feeling of being overwhelmed by everything around and that everything else takes control over you, is the failed or the decompensated side of Cancer. So this patient was actually a decompensated or a completely failed Carcinosinum where the sensation was – 'I am abnormal within' and the intensity was – 'I am just so abnormal, there is such a feeling within me that I am totally in chaos. My whole system is in chaos. How can I control this chaos?'

Naturally when you are talking of a failed or a decompensated Carcinosinum, the picture of chaos and the source itself of Cancer will come out because that's the phenomenon from where the remedy has been derived.

SECOND CASE OF CARCINOSINUM

I. Case Introduction

II. The Case

III. Remedy and Case Follow-up

IV. The Difference between Niccolum and Carcinosinum

V. Summary

I. Case Introduction

Now we want to talk to you about another case which is a controlled Carcinosinum case. It's a case where the chaos has not come up. We had to really dig for it and it's only through the whole journey of control that we understood the other side of the chaos.

So it's a completely opposite journey than the journey we had in the previous case where we understood the control through the chaos. But in this case you will understand the chaos through the control. Also it's a case taken very long ago, almost along with the Ringworm case somewhere in 2003 where we had just begun working with the nosodes. It's interesting to know how in this case we understood the repeated pattern, the polarity of correct and incorrect, of abnormal and normal and then after understanding the polarity how we understood the extent, the intensity and the coping of this polarity through every situation. Here the feeling was – 'I have to do superhuman efforts to control this mistake.' That's how the Carcinosinum emerged in this case.

II. The Case

It's a man about 43 years old who had come to us with complaints of essential hypertension, high blood pressure and symptoms like uneasiness, discomfort and nausea. When he came to us his BP was 180/100 mm of Hg and all his family members were our patients. He was the last one to have come to us from the lot. His wife told us that in fact it was she who pushed him to come to see us. She said that she had to tell him, "It's about time that you see them". She told us that not only does he have hypertension but he also seems to have a whole lot of business pressure at the moment. He has disturbed sleep; he mutters in his sleep, is always mumbling something and then he also grumbled that his sleep was not at all refreshing. The first thing we asked him when he came to us was of course to tell us about the problem. As he goes to explain us the problem you will see what it is all about.

P: The first thing that you can say is a problem which is bothering me today is the state of business. Previously for five years when we got separated we were doing a great business. For five years I had minted money you can say according to whatever standards we have. But now you know what has happened is, my perceptions have changed and the business is also changing. Suddenly the things which I was doing and I have always been doing are changing. Now what is happening is basically that the item is going, you can say out of fashion or out of sale or something. People are not interested in that type of business which means I need to change my line of business. I have also already started. I have a good eye and knack over it. The only thing positive is that I have good customer base which I can exploit to change to items. So that is a positive side.

P: I mean I am very positive about that but still that anxiety is there of whether the switch-over will give me ample time of breathing or not. It's like one thing is dying and one thing I am generating. Now before this dies I want to regenerate my customer base and my sales so this is the only worry. Another worry is that how much I mean for X's (son's name) financial things. I feel that whatever God has given us, my child has got this illness. (The child has an autoimmune problem.) Now what I want is that financially whenever I leave, at least he should be in a state where he is very comfortable with his life. It's like suppose you know if he does not work for his life still I can provide for him. Now that thing is always behind my mind. Today I think that whatever I save it has increased in X's (son's) account so I like to live a simple life. I don't spend so much. Though I can also afford a good car, but I restrict on my...it's not like that I restrict on my hobbies just because of him but my personality is like I feel it's a crime to buy a expensive car and just show off.

What we have asked him is actually his chief complaint. He could have said its nausea, its headache, its anxiety, its pain or whatever. But what he talks about is two different things - one is some kind of a business worry where it looks like he is changing from one kind of a business to another and he is worried if he has enough breathing time between the two. The other is that he is worried about his son's future which he wants to secure. He went on describing this for a much longer time. Nowhere in the talk had he spoken about his physical complaints that he had come to us for. At some point he spoke about what he wanted to do for his son.

P: The other worry that I have is that I want to set up a good business for my son, the way my father gave me his business. But you see nowadays the business scenario is changing, the market is becoming very competitive and you know you can't have a staff of thirteen or fourteen people under you. In about six months I think I will recover my cost expenses but I don't get the return on my capital. So I need to bring about a lot of changes in my business. I think I am going in the right direction. I perceive things in a very balanced manner; just like a partnership, an outside business. You know I am thinking and I am very strongly trying to take a decision. I never take my decisions with my heart. Like okay you put your money into anything and I don't have

113

any money.

You know my father, since we were very small, he never pushed us up-front and now all the responsibility of the finances is on me. I think I am doing a very good job. I have earned a lot of money, supposing say you take the last five years. The money needs to be taken care of, nurtured and invested in a manner that it grows like a fruitful tree for the family. Sometimes I feel I don't have enough time to think about all the money I have earned. All my decisions... I mean, it could be normal that everybody has these kinds of pressures. But it's not such a big pressure you know. This basic changing over from one business to the other and of course as I told you, X's (son's) finances.

We were just looking at this patient surprised and trying to figure out what is he talking about. Where are the symptoms that he comes for? The business aspect does not make sense to us.

But we got some very important points in the case, from the way in which he was talking about his business issues. He says – 'I know that there is this, I know that I have a problem here. I know that I am changing over', but he is also showing confidence there. 'I know I can perceive the problem and deal with it.' Isn't it a very interesting manner of talking? It is also very important that he has not given us a single chance to stop him and ask him a question. He is going on non-stop about this problem and about the ways in which he can solve this problem.

It's so easy you can literally pick-up any remedy like Niccolum or Arsenic or Calcarea flour, because there is anxiety about future, doing so much for the family and there is anxiety about money. You can easily pick up these things and give these remedies to him. It's very tempting to do that. Probably the case might lead us into the whole story like that who knows. But at this point of time we were keeping our fingers crossed. We knew that the issue is with this whole business. We knew that the whole delusion, the sensation and finally the energy lies in this entire complex that he is trying to give us because he is talking of nothing else except that. But what is the sensation? What is the pattern that will come up? I don't know at this point of time. I only know that business forms an integral component of this pattern. So, we go a little further into all these things to understand a little more about him.

Also see how this case is completely different from the earlier case you saw where there was the complaint, the delusion of the complaint and the sensation from the complaint. Here there is no complaint. Literally the complaint itself is only the entire story. It seems he is going to take a roundabout turn and a roundabout way into the case unlike the first guy. We go a little further ahead.

P: You see our life style is terrible. I go to work at 7 in the morning sometimes 8 or 9 but I am stuck up till 9 in the night. 12 hours of work. Look at you guys. You just keep travelling everywhere, you take holidays. Look at you, you enjoy your life, you do so much. Our business is like we get money out of it but we are stuck with all these efforts and in the traffic and we are stuck for 12 hours a day. This is not what I want to give my son. I want to give my son a good quality of life, maybe a higher education or some kind of a good business so that he will have a much easy life-style tomorrow, a much more comfortable life. But I don't think this is a big worry on me. I don't think it's putting any kind of pressure on me.

Pressure, this word comes at couple of times in the case. His complaint is high blood pressure but here he is talking about a different kind of pressure. So we go to a point where he describes this pressure a little more.

P: I want to give him (son) a business which gives him enough money to sustain his life, a good quality of life. Where you have money and quality of life; here we have money but we don't have quality of life. So I am passing through that phase that I want to settle something for X (son) today or tomorrow. Either I can give him high education so that at least he gets a good job and a comfortable life-style. That is my worry. But I don't think it's that big a worry that will put me in pressure. (*His voice becomes loud when he said the last sentence*)

'I don't think it's that big a worry.' So there is a denial, there is a spontaneous denial. Definitely there is worry, there is definite pressure. But there is a denial and compensation. 'I don't think it is there' is a need to overcome that worry. The worry and the pressure will take us to the sensation. The fact that he is trying to overcome it is his attitude to the sensation. We haven't asked him anything at this point. We will go a little further.

P: The other thing is that our business is on credit. We give a lot of credit to

115

people. A huge chunk of my money is invested with others. You can say that it is out of my control. So I feel really bad you know when people don't pay you back. They don't give you back as their family condition is not so good. So I feel that this man is not good morally. He should pay me. It's not ethical that you have taken goods from somebody but also his condition is not good. So we write 2-3 letters to him to give us our money back. That is I think the main cause. It is like this - you make money, then you invest it in business then it goes out of your control. What is the meaning in life? So we should not invest money in things where it goes out of your control. Money should be under your control.

How many times he used the word 'control'? It's very interesting. The next important part of the pattern is that there is this business pressure and the feeling with the business is that money is not under your control. At this point we didn't know the kingdom, the sensation or anything else. But we just knew that this bit will take us further down in the pattern. Why does he want money within his control? What about money being in control or not being in control is an issue for him?

Also just making a comparison with the previous case, you see in that case there were gestures. He was all over the place with his chief complaint. Here there is no gesture. There is just folding of hands and sitting behind as if you are in control.

Remember that he has an answer to all his problems and that we have not asked him a single question as yet. This entire narration, he is telling us on his own. He further said slowly that - "This year I gradually withdrew some money which was unnecessarily invested in the business. Now I feel okay. I can take the money from business and let this business slowly go down. I don't mind. I feel I must change my line and change my status such that that you have a very good control over your money."

Yes, we have understood that the next component of the pattern is control over money. But we need to know what the feeling behind this control is.

P: You know what happens when you ask people for money? They say that they are sending it to you but actually the money does not come. But if you owe me money and if I demand it from you, you must give it to me. That person is not in a position to give me back my money, so how does that feel? It feels as if we made a mistake that we gave him such a big credit. We should have restricted him to a point.

So he is talking about when you have given money to people and then when you ask them back for your own money, they give excuses. The pattern that 'money should be under your control', is getting clearer. The feeling he has is that it is his own mistake that he give money on credit.

P: But generally I feel I have a good control over my business. Also after I computerise everything, it will bring my own stress down. You know what's happening at the moment is that you are ignorant about the situation as to how much money is due from whom? So every time you get tensed up. When you look at the books, (*he is talking about the account books*) you don't know how much money other people owe you and so you get tensed that your money is not in your control. But now I have designed a system.

Now he is giving us the solution for his mistakes as well. He is giving us his anxiety but he is also giving us the fact that he has made amendments.

P: I have designed a system by which I can get my whole accounts computerised and every 15-20 days I can get a reminder. This is going to be my next system of working and I am very positive that it will work. I have ways to do this. I have plans to do this and I never feel trapped.

It's interesting, again there is another denial – 'I never feel trapped.' His feeling is – 'If my money is out of control, I have made a mistake somewhere and I feel trapped.' We can understand the statement 'I have made a mistake somewhere' but what is this trapped feeling? We don't understand. He went on to say -

P: You know what? I am even telling myself nothing will happen if a situation arises where I have nothing with me. I am satisfied with what I have earned. My present lifestyle is good. I am very philosophical. Many times however, there are some negative points like fear. Everybody gets fear. I also get fearful. What's so abnormal about it?

He didn't say that I have the fear of responsibility.

P: And one thing that I have marked is when I feel tensed up I don't ever feel tensed up for my own problems. The only time I ever felt tensed up was when my son was not well. About my BP and all, I never feel tensed about it. I have the courage. I can completely manage it myself. I know how to control it. Both body wise I am quite aware of my problem. Like you know I had a breathing problem sometime ago. I know when to take my medications. I know when not to take medications. I don't take too much.

It looked like he was having a monologue here. He was giving us his problems and his control over his problems. He was giving us the fact that he had solutions to the problems. It was like a one act play or a monolog where we were not interacting with him at all. I think he would have might as well sat in front of the mirror and talked. He didn't need anybody to be there, he wasn't aware of what we were doing. He wasn't aware of whether we were listening to him or of the fact that we want to interrupt or we want to ask him something in between. Nothing! It was just a one way dialogue. He was completely engrossed with the problems he had and how he was trying to make amendments and find solutions to the whole thing.

P: I can give you an example. One day I came home and my body was warm. I had a very heavy sinus. My wife told me to take some medication. I said, look I know what's happened to me. I told her to give me some hot water put some salt in it as I will gargle once and then I did that. I gargled twice before I went to sleep and you won't believe it that fear, no I mean that fever which was approximately 38.06^{0}C, immediately cleared!

Did you notice – 'That fear, no I mean that fever?' It is very interesting to see him at this point. He was talking about how he knows his whole system and where to correct his system. He knows how to get out of the fever. But he couldn't stop himself from saying fear.

P: I took some warm water and I took it at 10 and then at 11 or 12. I took it twice. The fear, I mean the fever was cleared. Everything was cleared. I slept well and got up in the morning absolutely ok. So I know what is happening in my body.

So what is his feeling? 'I know what is happening to me. I know my body.' By this time we had still not understood the sensation. We had not understood what is behind his fever, the trapped, the responsibility, the pressure. It could still be a plant mineral or an animal. We had no clue. He is only giving us human situations but what we understood was that there is an immense control over his sensation. There is an immense need

118

to be completely in charge, completely responsible and completely in control of the whole thing. So his miasm was clear but his sensation was not. We will go a little bit further. He was still talking a little bit more about his body.

P: I have high blood pressure. I will need to take some help. So I started morning walk and right now I am on three ayurvedic medicines which I take like a tonic. One is like garlic, some tablets I take for reduction of cholesterol levels and keeping it under control. I like garlic. I have a craving for garlic. Means my mom makes garlic chutney, spicy. I can't tolerate much.

D: You can't tolerate tikkha?

P: Tikkha means?

D: Spicy.

P: But cloves I can eat ten at a time and nothing will happen. Even garlic nothing will happen. I will not complain of 1% acidity even if I eat a lot of ginger. So I can tolerate these hot things because I know my body type is 'Cough type' (Ayurvedic way of body types). So my inner linings are very powerful that is the reason I can tolerate anything.

In a way he is very chaotic and erratic. He is all over the place with his complaints. Now where are those business tensions and the son's finances? Now we are on this garlic and on his blood pressure and his fever. So you see he is all over the place. But in a way there is consistency in the things that he is saying. Everywhere he is saying the same kind of thing that, "I know the problem. I know how to get in control with it. I know how to tolerate it." Right now he literally jumped from the fever incident to we don't know what… ayurvedic medicines and the kind of food he eats. He just jumped without any rhyme or reason. But what he is saying here again is the same thing. So his feeling of how he can cope with the situation is really the same, consistent pattern. 'I can handle everything. I can tolerate anything whatsoever' and also along with it the same thing – 'I know what is happening to me.'

P: Even this blood pressure, I am just passing through a phase when I am a little stressed out. But I don't think it's something I can't overcome. I don't think I can overcome, no I am sorry, I mean I don't think that I can't overcome

119

it. I have never felt this in my life.

So he is constantly trying to tell us whatever the issue is 'I have the resources or I have the capacity to overcome it.'

P: I never see a glass half empty. I always see it half full.

And now back to his business problems.

P: When I computerise, everything will be perfect. I have the perfect calculation. There is no tension that somebody will take away my money. Whatever is in my destiny I want to run this business but I want to run it with control. It should never go out of control. It should be in control. I think what was happening there with my business earlier was that it was going a little out of control.

It was very important to understand what the experience is for him when things go out of control. What is the need for him to be so much in control? Now if he feels going out of control means being vulnerable to the attack, then it could be an animal with the Cancer miasm. 'You know you are so much vulnerable you could be attacked but you never get attacked because you are always on the alert.' In fact you get back, if feeling completely out of control feels that maybe you could be scattered, all over the place and you don't know where to go. Maybe you are in a state of complete chaos and you are sensitive to just the whole scatteredness of it. Who knows, it could be Leguminosae. If the money goes out of control, I will lose my house, my security, my children, come on the streets. So it could be all about row four. To understand this, to understand the sensation and fear behind losing control, we asked him to describe this that 'I don't have control' and what is his experience with it.

P: It's that you are trusting the people who don't keep their words. Their words are not kept so either I have to pump in more money which I am not ready for or I have to tighten my credit. Or I feel the great reason is the system of accounting because you know as I go on talking and as I think the great fault lies over there that if you are not perfect with accounting how are you doing a perfect business?

Isn't what he is saying very interesting? You see we are asking him what is the feeling of control and he is giving us how he looks inwards.

He is not trying to tell us that you lose control and you lose everything. He is trying to tell us that I try to see why it happened. He is not trying to tell us that you can't trust other people or that people can cheat you or that people are not worth trusting. He is trying to tell us that why did he put his money with untrustworthy people. He is insightful, he is looking inwards. He says that 'The problem lies with me'. He is not looking outwards. Then he goes to say further -

P: The great reason is that I go on talking to myself and as I think the great fault lies in the fact that if you are not perfect with accounting how are you going to do a perfect business? You won't be able to do it.

So according to him, the problem is not with anybody else but within his own system, his accounting is not perfect and so his business won't be perfect either. He blames himself for the situation and nobody else. The feeling is not that the situation has a problem outside the person, but the problem is within. The intensity is strong cause he is looking for perfection and nothing less will do. And because the problem is within himself he is looking for answers within himself.
This is why in the case he hardly allowed us to talk. He did not need us at all. He was seeing his own faults, talking to himself and trying to change it. And he wanted so much to be in control of the situation that nobody else's help was needed. Not even the doctors. He was never looking at us for advice though he was mentioning his faults, his worries and all his problems. He wasn't looking at us for any help. The next few sentences are just a perfect confirmation of that.

P: ...very soon I will start my computer accounting, and I should be clear with that. Then what happens... see it is like if you need to be reminded, it's your duty to remind others, people are not that bad.

What is he trying to say? Referring back to the example of business he says, I don't think I am going to face any problems again. The feeling is that I will be able to handle it. He has the fear of losing his money.

But what does he come to? 'It's not them who are bad. It is you who couldn't do your duty. It was your duty to be perfect. It was your duty to check and decide what kind of people you have to give your money to. 'So the problem is not with the people, the problem is with your own self. Listen to a few more sentences. Let's go ahead.

121

P: I called a man yesterday I wrote him a letter that you have to yet pay me Rs.100,000. I demanded approximately Rs. 50,000-70,000. Immediately he gave me a call. He said, "Mr...... (Patient's name), I got your letter. I will send you Rs. 30,000 today. Within ten days I will come and give you 20,000." Very good, so now I think that problem lies with my system. If I develop a good system to work, I don't think I will face problems.

The sensation here is deeper than the trap, the fear of the money loss and everything. Deeper than all these things, the sensation is of 'there is a problem within me'. The problem is within and the coping to this sensation is that – 'I have to do superhuman things to correct this problem and amend my system. I have to be in total control of every problem'.

Now it's getting really very interesting and clear. What was his last sentence? "If I have developed a good system, I will not face a problem." So, the controls are within me and the issue is within me. Do I have enough control to solve the problem which is nowhere else but within my own system? When we understood this case from this light it was really interesting because it was the time we were working with nosodes. We were trying to understand this abnormal phenomenon just as you saw in the Ringworm case.

Here what you also understand is that this is a compensated Cancer, a successful Cancer. This is a guy who is in control of his chaos. The earlier guy was in no control of his chaos. His presentation was chaos. But this man's presentation is control. In both the cases the sensation is that the problem lies within me. In both cases the polarity is chaos and control. That guy is on the chaotic side of control and this patient is on the controlled side of chaos. This is the difference between the two. Let's go further.

P: So once that system will change, even I will feel that I have staff to work and all this is in my control.

D: How does it feel? Just describe this.

P: I feel that now I have changed everything in the system and I have control over my business.

D: Describe how it feels to completely lose control over a situation.

Now we really want to be sure of it and bring out the chaos.

I want to remind you another thing that we have only taken bits of this case for the simple reason that we want to differentiate the controlled Cancer miasm, the Carcinosinum in this case from the previous case. The case went on for a good two, two and half hours and all the issues - the responsibility, the fear and the trapped were well probed into. It all came back to the same thing that the problem lies within my system.

P: In that loss of control I feel that again there is a slight fear behind that. If I don't have control, (gesture hands shaking / shivering) then the feeling is...

His right hand clenches as if he is holding a ball tightens it and loosens it, this gesture goes on all the time as he speaks this paragraph. He is talking about what is going on behind. He says that in that loss of control, the feeling is of slight fear. So if he cannot do things in positive energy, his life is not in control. Rather his thoughts are not in control. So he is not able to put emotional control over his thoughts.

P: I feel that there is no control over the mind, no control over my health. Why did I not have control over this? When I have loss over here, then I start feeling fear that I will lose in two-four other fields also. So then I will lose in every way. My calculations will go wrong and again I think no, no how can that be possible. There is a problem and I will try to get in touch with it. Pressures do come, but I don't succumb to them. I never get erratic or you can say 'out of control'. I control it. I reason it as "Okay I will see to it".

Then he suddenly began to speak in the third person, he started giving us an example of a man who is not in control of himself. He started telling us about the life of this man, who has no control or has gone out of control. He said that such a man would have erratic thought and that he would never want to be a man like this. So we asked him to describe what happens to this erratic man or this man who has no control.

D: So what will happen to this man, if his thoughts are not in control?

P: His thinking is haphazard, so his life will also be haphazard.

What did he say? 'I never succumb to pressure; I never get erratic or out of control.' Then he gave a certain example that you know if a person

123

seems to be out of control, his life will be erratic. Here the issue was - 'I have to be in control or everything will get chaotic.' The sensitivity was to chaos. This is exactly what happens in Carcinosinum. The body loses control over its own self and there is chaos. Everything has to work under the control of one single body so that the functions are normal. But in cancer some cells begin to defy that and go against it. This is what is happening in this entire case.

He is trying to constantly keep his own system in his own control and look for loop holes in his own system. What happens with the failures, the business loss and the money loss? What happens with all these financial losses? With everything he gets a feeling that he is losing his control. He feels that everything will go haphazard and this whole system will get faulty which he needs to control.

III. Remedy and Case Follow-up

At this point we gave him one dose of Carcinosinum in 200C. The potency we gave this person was 200C because he was talking only in terms of his entire situation and all the emotions. He was compensated; he looked as if he had control. But from the fear, from the dreams and the muttering that he is getting in his sleep it was also evident that he lived his chaos in that emotional to delusional level. The result that we got in this patient was really amazing. In total he received two doses a year for a period of two years. We will go to the follow-up, but just before the follow-up I need to differentiate this case from Niccolum.

IV. The Difference between Niccolum and Carcinosinum

With our understanding of the periodic table, we see Niccolum also in a Cancer miasm. He is very much in control and wants his security. He is a very good father and task performer. He does his duty and everything well. His money, his security, his finances, his house, his family, everything is well in control because in Niccolum he feels scared that if he is trapped, if he loses his money and that safe secure position, then he can be vulnerable to attack. Then he can lose his structure and crumble and fall down. It can be a situation of Row 4 -You cannot lose that well-protected harmonious structure that you have formed with so many efforts. But that doesn't come up in this case. When we ask this patient what's the feeling when you lose control he says that you look inwards to find the fault in your system. Thus though he does mention trapped, fear, money all the time, his sensitivity is not to the money, the threat or the position. What comes up here is that I look back and I see how I can change my computer works. How can I decide which person to trust, where did I go wrong and how can I change my faulty system? If I lose everything my feeling will be – 'What is the problem within me that I lost this control? I cannot lose this'. That's the difference between Niccolum and Carcinosinum both of which belong to Cancer miasm.

First follow-up: 2 months after the remedy

He developed boils in the first follow-up and he said, "I always had a pustular tendency in the past. With your remedy all these boils came back again."

He went to the parlour for his hair cut. Somebody told him there, "Your face looks terrible with all these boils, can I bleach it for you?" He said, "O No. Don't even touch the boils. My doctor said that more boils should come. As your hypertension reduces the boils will increase so don't touch the boils".

His hypertension reduced remarkably with the dose and he felt much more balanced after the very first dose.

P: Basically you were telling me the way you started the treatment and everything. I have gone through this homoeopathy treatment before also. So I generally knew the symptoms. I mean first aggravate the situation or the symptoms and then you try to... So I was thinking that day you asked me whether I had lot of pus in the body. So immediately I said yeah because I have a history. So I was relaxed, I don't bother about it now. I bother that I don't have to go to the beauty parlour as it shouldn't leave black stains. My barber told me, "Can I bleach it for you?" I told him, "No. Don't touch it. The doctor has created them."

D: One thing I wanted to ask you is if you can just repeat that generally emotionally how are you?

P: Emotionally I feel much more balanced. Rather I mean you can say that the impact of the things has... I take things lightly. Now as I am also thinking, so I mean the medicines are working in the manner that whenever the things come on, I feel that it's ok. I see the positive side because I am myself, I think, trying to change the patterns of my thoughts. There is no need to fear so much. We'll see later. I will give you a precise example of how I think.

Somehow with the remedy we couldn't change his loquacity. We don't need to go into the examples. But he has already started to feel much more balanced, his sleep was better, the muttering in the sleep had reduced and the fear that he had about his business and the changing in the business all that reduced to a very large extent. In fact there is a beautiful follow-up which we saw some months later that we want to share with you. Here he actually starts talking about how this -'need to control' had eased out and he felt that nothing can ever be in any human control; that we have to just be easy about it. The words he uses are very interesting.

Second follow-up: March 2004

D: How are you doing?

P: Good. Good.

The boils have already reduced and even the marks are not there anymore. He feels much better as a person.

P: I feel the best part is the one thing that I can measure the difference with the medicine. That once you have that fall of the thoughts or the negative pattern of thoughts, I feel the bouncing is quick, very quick; means immediately you kind of get relaxed. I can take care of everything. That sinking feeling, I mean is not there. At a point you stop and immediately the next day it's alright. Earlier I used to get the negative thoughts, keep thinking on them and get fearful. But now it's quite less. Maybe it's there a little bit, but it is quite less.

What is he is trying to say? The gesture in the first consultation of hand clenching as if he is holding a ball, tightening & loosening it, which came often as he spoke about the need to have the control has eased a lot. The gesture came up at every point when he was telling his sensation, but the moment he said that it had reduced the gesture eased out too. Although he talked about a lot of control, there were a lot of negative thoughts as well. Now he admits that there were negative thoughts. However with the remedy, those negative thoughts and the sinking feeling has reduced. He feels much more balanced. You see if the intensity of control is too much,

126

whether the patient mentions it or not, it's obvious that the intensity of negative thoughts must also be very high because it's that dip down which helps you to bounce up. Similarly, when the patient says that the intensity of the negative thoughts has reduced, the need to control which is the upper bounce will also reduce. Which is why in this pendulum which goes up and down or you could say side wise, when that distance that it travels on either sides, when that oscillatory movement reduces on one side, it goes only a shorter distance on the other side as well. See if you have a pendulum which is swinging to the far right, it will swing to the far left. If you have an intensity which is very severe of sinking you will have an equally high intensity of control. (To know more refer to page 6 in Homoeopathy & Patterns in the Periodic table- Part 1, by Dr. Bhawisha Joshi)

What he mentioned was tremendous control on one side which automatically meant that though he always denied it, there was an intense chaos on the other side. In his follow-up he says that he is more balanced and that the sinking he felt earlier has significantly reduced. What you expect now is that the control will have reduced as well.

P: When I first met you, when I came here, my belief was that 'which medicine can help? I feel man is capable enough of helping himself. That was my belief. That okay you people are telling me to take medicines I will take but my strong belief was that 'whatever my mind, I can have a good control over it and I can divert it and change it to the positive thing.' That was my concept. But to a great extent I feel that ultimately you have to do it. But still I feel when a person needs some kind of support, he should take it. That is the thing which has changed in me.

What has changed in him is the immense need that 'I am the ultimate; I have the control. I can do everything myself.' That intense need to be constantly in control or feel constantly super powerful has also reduced. 'I can understand that sometimes if I need support I have to take it.' He has eased out as a person. He is going to say something very interesting now.

D: You constantly had the need to keep everything under control and you had a fear that things would...

P: ...Go out of control. That is correct. That 'control' word was very much

127

there. Now it is not like that.

Just as we said to him that he had a need to be in control and had a fear, he immediately completed the other polarity that - things would go out of control, that's what he felt. He said that control was too much for him. Let's see how much it is for him. We'll go on.

P: Okay fine. I feel that now I am at a stage where I can leave it and I know that I can get it back. So that control feeling is still there but I don't think it's so tight that I won't leave it only. I don't think I am holding it so tight anymore. I can even loosen it and I know I will get back my control. That feeling, that need to really have things so much in control is not there anymore you cannot control everything.

He said that his fist was so tight that he needed so much of control that he was not even opening it for a second or something like that. But now he has decided that this is the way it is going; because he won't be able to change the events at any point of time.

D: So you can't control that?

P: No. Events you can't control but you can have a better way of looking at them.

D: You have learnt the right statement.

He said that earlier the fist was not even loosening for a minute but now it can keep it open because he has understood that he can't control events. He was almost going to say that he can control his mind but then he didn't even say that. He said, "You cannot control your mind. You can have a better way of looking at things." Hence his need to control has reduced a lot.

What this means is that actually the chaos deep down has reduced. It's only when the chaos reduces that the control will reduce. They are both two sides of the same coin.

V. Summary

This is the change that we could bring about in this person. He is now no longer so held up or tied up. He no longer has the pressure of holding things. He can loosen and ease out. He can now say that it's okay, there are different ways of looking at it and I don't need to be in control all the time. Naturally if the pressure of all this and of his sensation has reduced, his hypertension is also going to reduce. This is exactly what happened. His blood pressure was also very well in control for quite some time beyond this point.

He was this way until 2006 when we saw him again. That's when there was an intense situation in the family and he started to develop certain pathology again. His wife said that this time it's like a skin blackening and there is eruption behind in the nape of his neck. But when it was examined it almost looked like that area was dry. It was the same thing again where he felt he was losing control over the situation in the family. His father was sick. He felt he was really losing his father and losing the control that he had on the situation.

We repeated Carcinosinum and again saw a dramatic result. We repeated the dose about five times in these three years till finally we decided that this is too much of a repetition. What we would like to do is jump to a higher potency and so we jumped to 1M. This is when he has done very well and now he is on the 1M potency since the end of November 2006. He is much better with it since that time.

So this was a case which I specifically wanted to share with you to differentiate with the earlier case. A case like this is what you would commonly see in the Cancer miasm. The earlier one was an extraordinary case not seen often.

A CASE OF MALARIA NOSODE

I.   Case Introduction

II. The Case

III. Differentiating the Sensation of Nosode from Animal Sensation

IV. Remedy and Case Follow-up

V.   Summary

I. Case Introduction

She is a 19 year old girl who came to us with complaints of polycystic ovarian disease and ugly massive sized acne all over the face. So we asked her to tell us about her complaints.

II. The Case

P: I am not getting periods regularly. Sometimes they come after three months I get lot of pimples and they don't look normal. They are very large in size and it's very uncomfortable that's it.

D: So tell me about - it's very uncomfortable.

P: When I get pimples they are very large in size, they are not normal size. So I feel very different. Then I feel that I must not go out of the house till the pimples are there. They normally last for one week, then there is pigmentation, after that the skin gets cleared. When they come, the size is very large.

D: Tell us little bit more.

P: The place where the acne comes looks very odd, so when it comes its one at a time but it's very big. It comes only in this part. This is the area where it comes out the most and also on the back. But on the cheek they are very big in size.

She showed the area. She gets acne on the forehead, on the face and on the back. But the ones on the cheeks and around the nose are very big and ugly. What does she do with the complaint? She does not go out. She stays indoors.

D: When they come you don't feel like going out of the house?

P: I feel very awkward. I haven't seen anything like this on anyone's face. So I feel very different that it's only on my face. And everyone keeps on asking me that why is this happening? Then I have to explain to them that I might be having some kind of hormonal problem that's why. So I explain everybody that I could have a problem in me, a hormonal problem and that's why I have this problem.

So what's interesting is that these acne make her feel that 'she is different, she is not normal.'

D: Describe this - 'I haven't seen this on anyone else's face but only on my face'. What is the feeling?

P: Describe means?

D: What is that feeling that it's on nobody else's face but only on your face?

P: Means what's the problem in me exactly? I have seen a lot of girls whose periods are irregular but they don't have pimples. Then what is the reason for that exactly?

'What is the reason, what is the problem, what's the problem in me? There is something wrong in me and that's why I have these acnes, these pimples. There are so many girls with PCOD that is polycystic ovarian disease and irregular menses, they don't have it but I have it. I have a problem within me.' It is the same pattern coming up again. Good.

D: Describe this - What's the problem in me that I am getting it? What is the feeling within?

P: I feel like crying at that point of time. I feel that why is it like this? I cry every time I see an acne. I cry a lot when it comes. I just avoid going out.

Her mother says that she cries a lot. The girl again insists that she has seen pimples on a lot of people, they are not like this. The mother says it too. Here we get the hint of the coping as well. What does she try to do? She just avoids going out. She just does not want to face it. This gives me a slight Sycotic taint. But we let her speak more. She says that she only goes for her exams and her college.

P: Only if it's compulsory that if I have to give an exam, I go out. During the exams I pray to God that I must not get pimples. I cannot concentrate every time. I am looking at the pimple in the mirror. I keep thinking that which cream should I apply? There is no effect with any cream. Every two minutes I will go and see my face in the mirror. Pimples make me look ugly. I just got it last month in June before getting my periods and after that I haven't got that big a pimple. I apply compact, foundation and all possible creams just to

133

cover up that big pimple. I go to a girls' college. Even in a girls' college everyone stares at me and keeps on asking me. Instead of asking what it is, they ask why it is like this. Maybe they haven't seen something like that. Therefore they keep on asking me why it is like this.

Now we re-emphasize our question.

D: Tell me more about – I don't feel like going out. I just avoid going out.

P: I don't want to show it to anyone that I have something like this on my face.

The obvious question now is -

D: How does it feel to have something like this on your face?

P: I feel different. It feels as if I have some disease. So I am different, there is problem in me and I don't want to go out and face people.

By now, we had caught the sensation of the nosode which is that 'There is a defect in me. There is a problem in me'. And the coping is – 'I completely avoid people'. So this tells us that it is a nosode of the Sycotic miasm. We ask her to tell us more. We explored this phenomenon to establish this nosode very clearly. She says something very interesting...

P: I feel like **avoiding** everyone at that time. I feel that no one must look at me and it's not a disease. I cannot tell them. It's always that I get pimples and everyone knows that I get it. But still they keep on asking me again and again whenever I get those pimples. They don't ask purposely but still I feel that I must not go or show them that something has happened, it is something different.

'There is a something in me which I need to repair, which needs to be corrected.' So we get the confirmation of the same pattern.

At this point of time the mother said, "She tells me all the time that I have never even seen anyone on the road with such big pimples. I have seen small pimples but not such big ones. So then what's the problem in me? After that she tells me that we will go to the gynaecologist but then I avoid it because then she will get reactions or get side effects of the

134

medications since she already has a lot of hair on her hands. "

So the constant problem the daughter has is that 'What is the problem within me? Why me. Where is this problem? I want to avoid going out whenever I have this problem.'

D: What is the feeling within to be different or to have something different? Can you think of anything that comes to your mind? Just tell us the experience of being different.

P: Means I feel that they will think that this is really a disease. If we stay with her then they will also get it. So they will start avoiding me because of that.

The acne are all over the face - around the nose, on the forehead and the big ones come on her cheek. So what did she say? "People will think that I have a disease."And as result what will they do? "They will start avoiding me." This is the theme that we have seen in nosodes because finally what are nosodes? Nosodes are diseased products like abnormal tissues within the body. Hence this thought can come in a nosode's mind that I am diseased, so I can be contagious and I can be infectious.

So at his point of time we ask her - What if this is contagious. If it's a nosode it has to come back to the nosode. If it's something else this question can open many directions.

III. Differentiating the Sensation of Nosode from Animal Sensation

If we ask her what is contagious and if it's a plant, her reasoning will go like this – 'I feel that people will start avoiding me. I will feel so bad it will pain me over here; it will make my heart shrink! I don't want people to avoid me. My world will get smaller if I don't go out. Staying in the house is claustrophobic. It is like being tied and bound and you cannot do anything in such a narrow place. The walls of the house begin to close in on you. I hate any place that is narrow and I need to break free and make space.' So this will take us to a plant's sensitivity something like that of Cactaceae, Hammamilidae etc.

If it's an animal the response will be different. When we ask her to tell us

135

*about avoiding and the feeling that something is contagious, she will say -
It is contagious. People will say – "Oh! She is contagious leave her away,
let her out. So I will be left all alone. If I am all alone then people might
just finish me up. I will be all alone standing over there with nobody to
protect me and that will be the end of me. This world is very competitive
you know so I cannot afford to be alone. I need to be with the group."*

*A mineral might say that, "If it is contagious it makes me feel incomplete
because it kills my identity. I need to have a particular position. I have
respect; people respect me and my position. If I have something which is
contagious then it will really put down my image. I can't go in society like
that. It will make me feel very incomplete."*

*So this contagious question can bring into picture all the kingdoms.
Hence we pose this question to her. Let's see what she had to say.*

P: It has not happened ever. What will you feel? I won't be able to bear it.
When I have the pimples I am not so confident. I cannot talk to anyone or any
unknown person. I will feel what will they think about me? Who is she? I
avoid facing the class, the lecture room all the time. Mostly I don't go out
until it is completely gone.

*The mother says that she only goes to her college when necessary and just
with a few friends of hers otherwise she just doesn't go out in the evening.*

D: Describe this - I will not be able to bear, what if they avoid me. What
comes to your mind that you will not be able to bear?

P: If everyone avoids me I will not like it, it's such a big problem. Everyone
has some problems. But my problem is very visible. There is something
wrong in me and so people are avoiding me. I will never come out of the
house.

*The coping if you see, is coming more clearly. This question of being
contagious is not taking us to any other kingdom. It is coming back to the
coping and it is giving us the hints of the nosode.*

*Her mother said, "She never comes for any functions. If I have planned a
function and the acne appear she will just refuse to come out. She will just
be at home and she will remove all that anger at home; the anger about*

136

the fact that she cannot go out. All the frustration that she has in her mind comes out as anger and tears. I explain to her but she feels very bad. She feels constantly angry that why is this problem coming to her, why does she have this problem and what is wrong in her."

This is how she complains to her mother bitterly all the time. Her mother tries to console her by saying that it's fine, that she will look good but she is just very upset about it.
She repeated, "I don't like going out. If I go out then people will start avoiding me." We asked her again –

D: What is the experience if people will start avoiding you?

P: People of my age group love to go out. All my friends go out; they go for movies and have fun other than the college life. People have boyfriends and friends to interact with but with such a bad face I will not have any one. I will be all alone.

D: How will that make you feel?

P: No it's not good; it's not a good feeling. I want to feel normal. Normal like everybody else; everybody has boyfriends; everybody has friends even I want to feel like that. Why should I have something wrong? Why should I feel in such a situation where I cannot go out and make friends? So what I do is that I just completely avoid. I go out of my house only once in a week so that nobody will see that I have this kind of a problem with me. I just completely stay indoors and then when it's gone I am normal. That's when I can go out, meet friends and have some fun.

D: What if you cannot have fun?

P: She said I would love to have fun, enjoy my life it doesn't make me feel normal, it makes me feel different. Why has nature made me like that? Why hasn't nature made me something like all other people are; like normal, like all others? Why has nature given me like this on my face which I just cannot go out with? That dirty thing on my face! I need to be out; it just troubles me a lot. I do all the things... I have a healthy and proper diet. My dietary habits are very good even then my periods are not regular. There are people who have such a bad diet, people go out and eat anything but yet they get their regular periods then what is my problem? I eat all the vegetables. I eat all the nutritious foods but even then my periods don't come on time and I have this kind of a dirty, ugly thing. I don't know whether I will be able to get married. Will I look good after marriage? Will it affect my pregnancy?

So you know her thinking went to that direction and level where she constantly felt that there is something so strongly wrong and abnormal in her which she needs to set right. She started thinking at such a deep level, right up to her pregnancy when she is just about 19 years old! She is nowhere close to getting married as of now. But still that's the way her mind has been running. Then she went on further to say that her mother read an article in 'Times'- newspaper about people with such complaints. It said that they have got lot of problems. Her feeling remained the same – 'Why do I have this problem? Not many have this problem, like such big acne. Why do I suffer from this problem?'

D: What's the experience to have this problem and what is the experience if it affects your pregnancy?

P: There is something wrong in me. That's why I will not have a proper pregnancy. So I will not like it. I will feel that because of me things are not going properly.

D: Something wrong with me and that I cannot bear?

P: Means if someone points out at me I don't like it. Even in small things, like when I don't score well in exams and my mother points out at me that I didn't score well then I tell her that I will study when I will feel like or I will score well whenever I will feel like. Also this problem I have not created it. It's natural; nature-wise it has happened so what is my mistake in that?

There is a fault in me because of which I am having this trouble but that's not my mistake. What should I do? These thoughts and feelings really trouble her. This confirms the nosode in her. 'Correct-incorrect, mistake in me, I need to correct it. There is some abnormality in me, I need to be normal.' The mechanism, the coping, was the Sycotic way of coping – completely avoiding, not facing the situation and not thinking about it.

IV. Remedy and Case Follow-up

So the remedy that she got was Medorrhinum. She received a couple doses of Medorrhinum 200C when she had visited us at the first time and after that we could see a change in the eruptions in just about a month's time. Her period complaints improved as well –they were regular and with adequate flow. She responded well to Medorrhinum but the acne though very few now were still persistent and she was very dependent on the medicine. We felt that something was missing here.

Then after about eight months her mother visited us in a panicky state. She said that the girl did not have her period this time and that she had totally stopped going out of the house for the past eight days since this time the acne had returned. The mother complained that she was crying and lamenting all day and night. The mother said that she was screaming and yelling at everyone and throwing tantrums all day long. She had become very touchy and irritable and kept complaining that nobody understood her and that she was singled out for this kind of an ailment and that no one in the world was as abnormal as she was. The mother added that since the remedy this was the first time that she had thrown such a tantrum but before eight months this kind of behaviour was seen every month. This information from the mother revealed a trait in this girl that she had not mentioned before. She was definitely hiding herself (Sycotic behaviour) but there was also a very clear acute, complaining and childish trait in her which is the trait of the Malarial miasm. The Malarial miasm is a combination of Acute and Sycotic miasms and has the feature of Acute episodes over the background of Sycotic behaviour.

The periodic complaining, whining, lamenting and feeling persecuted by her complaints were a perfect trait of the Malarial miasm. Immediately we changed the prescription to Malaria nosode in 1M potency. The improvement after this was remarkable. The girl's face cleared completely over the next one year and her periodic cycles have been regular ever since. It is now five years and she has been off our medicine for the last three years. Her sister, her cousins and several others are our patients and she comes to meet us sometimes. Her face is still clear and her periods are absolutely regular.

IV. Remedy and Case Follow-up

She has had about six doses of Malaria nosode 1M in the three years till she was with us. The tantrums and her nature have sobered down considerably. The most important thing is that she does not feel inferior, abnormal or singled out from the rest anymore.

10

 # A CASE OF MEDORRHINUM

I.   Case Introduction

II.   The Case

III. Remedy and Case Follow-up

IV. Summary

You have just seen the case of an uncompensated Malaria nosode, which has a Sycotic behaviour as well, where the sensation was – 'What is wrong with me? Something is wrong with me. I am different. I am diseased.' She was open about the fact that she is covering up or hiding her complaint. We have another case of a compensated Medorrhinum. These compensated cases are very difficult ones.

I. Case Introduction

This case was taken way back in about 2002. His complaint and his feeling was that there is something wrong. He had some kind of a muscle ache and he felt as if one muscle which was hurting was completely different than the rest of the body. It was very hurtful, very painful. But despite the pain he continued with his work and with everything else. He wouldn't go one bit beyond this much information. It almost looked as if he was trying to not go into all of this at all. Since he is a very successful person, he didn't want us to have the cameras on and didn't want any assistants in the clinic.

We requested him several times to tell us a little more about the pain and the feeling that this bit is different from the rest but he would not say anything further.

II. The Case

P: Otherwise everything in my life is normal. I am such a successful person; I don't need to have any problems. I don't have any problems. I am absolutely fine. There is nothing going on in my life. There is no kind of emotional stress. There is no kind of physical stress. There is absolutely nothing going on.

Everything was a complete no no no. There was no way we could even get a glimpse what he felt. All we understood was that he is compensated and that he is really covering up. We asked him to describe this that there is no problem and he said that's what it is.

D: How would it be to have a problem?

P: That wouldn't affect me either.

He simply didn't in any ways, either negatively or positively want to go into his case. So the next attempt we made was by asking him about his dreams. This was the only window that was left for us. His dream was very

142

peculiar. He said -

P: I have a dream where I am flying by a parachute. I am flying in an airplane and then I jump out of the airplane with a parachute. I am supposed to be doing a fantastic landing. Everybody is waiting for me to see how he lands on the ground. But as I come closer to the ground I realise that the scene changes. It's not that people are waiting now; instead, there is a little party going on - maybe a birthday or some evening party. And I have then realised that I haven't worn my pants. So I am coming down with this parachute and I don't have my pants on and that's where the dream ends.

So we asked him to describe the whole feeling with this dream but he would not go a wee bit beyond this. He said that's all that was there. So I went to my next question.

D: How does it feel to be without pants?

P: I don't think it matters. It really doesn't matter to me.

D: Okay if it doesn't matter to you, how would it matter to somebody else to be without pants and to come down like this by the parachute?

P: That is somebody else's problem, not mine.

What we realised in this case was that he was covering up the problem – 'That I have a problem within, that I haven't worn something and that something is wrong with me.' But even that covering up was a very compensated covering. It was absolutely in the form of denial like - where is the covering? I am not covering up or hiding anything. I don't have any problem with my dreams. I don't have any problems at all.

So the hiding or the covering up which we saw in the previous case was a very open hiding like - 'I know I have a problem. If I hide or cover it, I end up avoiding other people and I sit in my room for ten days. Then I think it will be okay'. This is an open Medorrhinum. A closed Medorrhinum says – 'I have a problem. Do I have a problem; do I need to cover it? I don't need to cover a problem. I don't even have a problem'. So when everything is being covered up and the problem or the issue both get into a negative mode, it becomes a compensated, covered up Medorrhinum. Let's go back to the case and see what happened beyond this point.

D: Just keep describing that this person is going down with this parachute and that he is in this crowd.

P: This person who is going down the parachute, he covers his eyes up and if he covers his eyes up he knows that it's almost as if he knows that nobody is watching him.

III. Remedy and Case Follow-up

It's almost as if you blind yourself to the situation so you feel that nobody is watching you. At that point we gave him Medorrhinum because the covering up was also a very compensated kind of a covering up. You cover up and you deny that covering up. At that point it was not clear to us that his feeling was that he is different from others. It just looked like this is somebody who is completely covering up every issue or problem that he has. The dream itself is showing that he is coming down and he is in an awkward situation.

A few months after we gave him Medorrhinum, his wife called us saying that he has completely changed as a person. "He used to be very outgoing, friendly and social. He is usually very successful with the kind of work he does. But you suddenly changed this man; he is very different now. He is quite fearful and anxious about everything."

Then when he came back, we asked him to describe his fears and anxieties. In a compensated case when you give a remedy, the things that they were denying always come up. So it always looks like a massive aggravation.

D: Describe the fear, describe that dream again.

P: While I come down it's a feeling of utter shame. It's a feeling that you have something which is so completely different. You are the odd man out and everything is extremely different. You are very different compared to others. You are abnormal and the weaker one. You know you have your weakness. You know that you have a problem within you and therefore you are covering it up and acting as if it's not there. Knowing that you have a problem, you do your level best in other spheres so that it does not become obvious to others.

At that point we were sure that it was Medorrhinum that brought about his whole state back. We told the wife not to do anything. We continued him on placebo. Couple of months later all those fears and anxieties had settled. All that extra covering up, extra social behaviour and the friendliness had reduced to a very large extent and of course he had changed as a person. He was very grateful to us for bringing out all his fears. The patient also got rid of his muscle ache completely.

P: You brought out all my anxieties but now they have settled to a point where I feel that I am completely normal. I don't get those dreams again, those dreams which have haunted me all my life which I would almost have every alternate day. I don't have that dream anymore.

IV. Summary

So that was a case where we gave Medorrhinum in 1M potency with the feeling that there is something abnormal within me. There was even a denial of the sensation, a denial of covering up the sensation and feeling abnormal. Now we will go to the next case.

11

 ## A CASE OF TUBERCULINUM

I.   Case Introduction

II. The Case

III. Remedy and Case Follow-up

IV. Summary

I. Case Introduction

This is another very interesting case. It is the case of a woman who came to us in a very desperate situation. Her mother called us saying, "Please do something for my daughter, she is pregnant and really suffering with this nasal congestion. She can barely breathe and it's almost become a panic attack for her." Her daughter had also called us up in a rather frantic state. She said. "I cannot breathe, it's almost like I am choking to death. It's such a fragile time of my life!" So this woman came to me in the 2nd trimester of pregnancy.

Her mother also called our family (out of earlier acquaintance) and requested them to convince us to take her case and that too on an urgent basis. So there was a lot of pressure on us from different sides to help this person out. But of course we would have helped her out anyways. However, it's important to know that this is the situation in which the case came to us. We had to fit her into our appointment schedule with some difficulty because otherwise it would have been delayed to maybe a week or two later since we had no time till then. But because we were told that she was in such a terrible state, it looked like she needed immediate attention. We were told that she could hardly breathe. She hadn't slept for several days altogether, that she was taking some steroid sprays and was panicking all the time. So the next day, we squeezed her in between two appointments.

II. The Case

P: The problem is basically nasal polyps. I think this has been the case since I was 16, 17. I lived with it for a while without knowing what it is and then I went to a GP (general practitioner). She told me to start using something that was like a nasal Otrivin …. So I was on it for a while. After that I discontinued. Seasonal coughs and colds auto correct themselves and when I started working, I think it was for a phase of 2 years where I was continuously using it. I had got addicted to it like somebody who is on drugs. If it got over, I sent out people from my office to get me Otrivin. But later I saw an ENT and she told me to stop it. Then she gave me some decongestants and that resolved. After that, since I was always into working out I didn't really require it because you know with exercise itself every morning it would sort of autocorrect.

So she is talking about her complaint. She said that the nasal congestion is not related to the trimester of pregnancy. She said that since 16, 17 it was there and always needed Otrivin, as good as some drugs. This shows her dependence on Otrivin which is a nasal decongestant. Finally she said that the working out or the exercises that she did every morning helped to autocorrect this complaint. Let us go on.

P: The real problem used to be in winter and in the monsoons, summer is a very good time. I don't remember having a problem in summers. I also tried pranayam and things like that and it was auto manageable but once I conceived, the congestion increased. I was told that yes it does increase after conception. So I put up with it for about 3 months. Every time I would sit in the car with the ac (air condition) on, it would get totally blocked and I would wait to get out of the car. Then again it would get blocked in the office because of the AC. So this went on and on and then I think after my first trimester I got back onto Otrivin. It just got aggravated after that. It is constantly in a state of being choked if I am not using it.

So now she says that with the second trimester it has really worsened. In fact from the first trimester, every time the air conditioner started, it came back again. She mentioned it as a severe congestion which gets her choked if she is not using Otrivin. She is going to tell us more about this choking now. Let's go on.

P: I was continuing that for some time and then this whole thing started. Many people said – "Oh you mustn't use this, it's very bad for you." So then I panicked, I said let me do a check. But most doctors said that Otrivin is quite safe, it doesn't harm the foetus but it also doesn't do any good to you in the long term. So then that is when the search for something more permanent had started and especially when I have to live with it for another 6 months… pregnancy is supposed to be you know an aggravated condition.

Now parallely, what happened about a few days back is that we have another house which is closed most of the times so we just went to check it. Of course it's a little dusty. Since it's closed it tends to be mustier. So when I entered inside I started sneezing. I mean I had that rhinitis kind of condition. We spent about half an hour there; by the time I came out, I had a complete throat ache. I said that this can't be a cold, it has to be dust. So then there was a full blown you know cold and throat infection that happened. This congestion got so severe that it sort of stopped being just physical. It got a little psychological also because I was too scared of that sensation of being you know constantly choked.

D: Go on

P: I was using more Otrivin but it wouldn't help. Then I was up all the night. In the last four - five days something else happened while I was sleeping. I would feel the wall of the throat vibrating. I have never had a snoring problem, not that I am aware of. So once that started vibrating I woke up with the biggest scare of my life! I thought somebody was choking me. I thought there is something like an apnoea happening. I didn't know what's going to happen to me. That memory just wouldn't go. It became maybe so larger than life that I spent the next three nights just being scared thinking what am I going to do? Despite all advice I was still using Otrivin and so then that continued; and I think the night before yesterday was when I had a severe panic attack. I just sat up through the night and I was totally wired. I was pacing up and down and I said I can't sleep. I changed like a hundred locations in the house - I couldn't sleep here, I couldn't sleep there. I could make out that it was all emotional. I mean I just told myself that look if I just fall asleep with the Otrivin I would be okay. But I was totally scared and wired. Then last evening I got an anticipatory panic attack in the evening. So it is not just restricted to night.

So this is the situation with which she has come to me. To begin with, there was choking, then there was this throat congestion and then along with the throat congestion, the nasal congestion got so bad that she felt choked to death and got a panic attack which was larger than life and now she doesn't have the panic attacks only at night but also in the evenings. The entire day goes in thinking about the panic attack, the choking and the fact that she can't breathe. This is the reason that brought her to us.

P: Then I went on the pump. I had to see a doctor. My gynaecologist took one look at me and said, "You need something right away or you are going to almost collapse here". So she sent me to an ENT surgeon who put me on a steroidal pump. He said I also have acidity and blah blah blah. So now I am having antacids and I am also having a steroidal pump. But I don't want to go through all this. I would rather like homoeopathy.

She said all this with intensity and energy.

D: Describe this entire state to me that you are in - the choked up, sat up, wired, panic and constantly choked.

150

P: It's like you know it is a state where if the Otrivin effect is worn off then both sides of the air passage are like vacuum tight. There's nothing I can do to even get in a milligram of air.

Look at the intensity of the whole complaint!

D: Go on.

P: So then its so choked that you know even when I say certain words those words also can't be completed because of course some part of air has to be throw out with the nose to complete the pronunciation. So my MIL (mother-in-law) will ask me what I said again and again. Then I have to write it down because it's so choked. I understand that it is a panic attack because I have a psychology background. It's kind of where I just anticipate the worst, my heart races terribly and I can't sit up. I have to pace up and that's where I find a sort of release. So this is what happened for three nights in a row.

D: Describe this whole experience – 'It is vacuum tight, not even a milligram of air can go in, you cannot pronounce, you are panicking and pacing up and down.'

P: It's pretty scary because maybe, it weighs on your mind. I mean you're not supposed to be conscious of your breathing right. It's supposed to be the most automatic activity. But when this happens, you are so conscious of it and there's nothing else you are thinking of. And at work I have a task ahead of me; I have to think of the presentation ahead. I sit with the slide in front of me and I think I can't do it. So it's that much… I don't know whether I've blown it up so much in my head.

D: What's this experience 'I can't breathe, I can't do it?'

P: It's very scary. It almost like my husband was asking me - what are you so scared of ? I think I finally pinned it down to, "Look I am so scared that I am going to die." I mean nothing can be more debilitating for us.
The situation is very desperate. Its intensity is very strong. You are choked; you are panicky, you almost feel like you are going to die in this situation.

D: Describe this more. Go on.

P: You just feel so weak, so helpless, so worn out. I can't relate to all of this because that's not me as a person because normally I like to be on the top of things. No matter what happens I find a way to deal with it. I shared this whole thing with another friend of mine and she is like but I can't relate this to you at all. You and scared?! I said, "Yeah, I am." Somewhere at the back of my mind is the feeling that maybe I am harming that child so that double pressure is there too. I also live up to that. Whereas another part of me is like I really don't care what happens to the child, I must think of myself first. All these kind of mixed feelings are in the head. That's about it. I was thinking if there is something that sort of helps me tide through the pregnancy? I can restart my yoga or if I am working out every day like a 30 minutes run on the treadmill, I will be ok. But I am not allowed to do any work at this time.

So at this point it went to her generals along with the panic attacks. It is a feeling of being weak and debilitated. 'I am scared, I am going to die.'

D: So describe this feeling of being weak, helpless, debilitating, dying and scared.

P: How else can I describe this to you? You have to see me. I don't know how do I describe that?

D: How are you at that time? Can you enact and show me?

P: It's like I am sitting up, people are talking to me but I am not paying attention to them. There's a lovely humorous program on TV yet I won't care. Somebody is putting on soft music for me but my mind is not on it. All I think of is how scared I am and how is this going to go. The night becomes like the scariest part. During the daytime ten things are happening around you so you don't really care.

Then in a couple of minutes she did more of this gesture of her arm coming downwards and the hand clenching in a tight fist as the arm comes down. This gesture came quite often while she was speaking earlier on in the case too. So she says – 'I am choked, I am constantly choked, it's vacuum tight' and things like that. This was even coming up with the last paragraph. But this is the feeling she portrays even through her gestures.

D: What is this? You did this a couple of times. Can you show it to me? What is the experience of it?

P: I don't know. It's just one of those things.

D: What is this one of those things? I am trying to understand more about you as a person.

P: I don't know what could this mean, how would you interpret it?

D: How would you feel to do this?

P: How would I feel? Maybe more in control?

D: I am sorry?

P: A little more in control.

We wanted to know how control came up in the case.

P: It's like finally maybe you think that you are on top of the situation with more and more of strength perhaps.

D: Describe that.

P: It's the opposite of how you feel otherwise. Yes, that's about it I think.

D: Describe this - it's the opposite of what you feel otherwise.

P: Like I told you, I feel quite weak and helpless you know and I'm always looking at other people around. They seem to be functioning so normally. I mean why is this happening to me?

D: Describe this to me – 'weak, helpless and others are functioning normally.'

What does she feel with the panic, with the scared, with the death and with the dying? She feels weak and helpless. She would like to be strong but she feels weak and helpless and questions that why is it happening to her and not to others.

D: Describe 'Why is this happening to me?'

P: Weak? I mean how else can I put it?

D: How is this experience of it? Describe weak and helpless.

P: You are totally sapped of your energy. It's like I can't go on for even one more minute. But there is no option. You have to go on even though you feel drained.

D: Describe this more.

P: That's it.

D: Describe this experience to feel completely sapped off and drained. How does it feel to be in that situation?

P: Very scary.

D: Describe scary.

P: Scary is scary. How else can I describe it?

D: Scared of?

P: Scared of what's going to happen to me and when is this all going to end? So it's like you are scared of the uncertainty. If you know the answer, there are 100 issues you go through when you're pregnant. For example in my first trimester I had a lot of trouble. I had a lot of urination but I knew that at the end of the three months I'll be ok. So when you know a certain thing, when you know if either you have the information or you have the way to deal with it you can deal with it. But in a situation like this you don't know why your body reacts like that and so it's like a state of zero. Then you don't know where you are headed after this, so that's the scary part. I don't like that; I like to know things, to be informed and to get out of situations very quickly so that I can function normally. I've got a hundred other things to do. I have work and I'm setting up my home so that is there too. All of that must go on. You can't just be with one problem, totally incapacitated! I don't like that.

She says that if you know what the problem is and if you have the resources to deal with the problem then its okay. In nosodes this is another important theme. To know the answers and to know how to deal with problems. Dealing with the disease is the attitude of the source or the diseased tissue itself. She also says that she likes to do hundreds of things

154

at a time and does not like to be bound up by just one thing. What was peculiar was that her fear led her to feel that she needs to know and get out of the situation very quickly.

D: Sorry can you just describe to me what you just said? You talked about uncertainty; you said, "I need to know and be informed, I need to be able to get out of situations very quickly." Describe this whole thing.

P: I am a very active kind of a person and I am a desperate multi-tasker. At the end of the day I need to know that ABCD list has to be completed. Even my husband teases me because I always have tasks like that. I feel very nice if I can tick off things from my list. So I like to do things. I mean you can't just waste your time sitting being physically so sapped. There is so much you can do by being well and healthy. That's when you will then function on all cylinders and that's how I would like to be.

D: 'You would function on all cylinders'. Tell me about it.

It is interesting that she came to us with such a desperate state of collapse. She is somebody who is a desperate multi-tasker, wanting to do things all the time. Can you imagine her complaints put her in the exact opposite state! There is desperation on either side. When she is normal, she has a desperation to multi-task and to work on full cylinders. But when she is in the complaint, the same desperation puts her in the exact opposite state – the state of collapse. 'You can't do anything, you are sapped. You cannot go on even for a minute more.' Isn't this interesting that both of these are two sides of the same sensation which we haven't got yet. But we are trying to go there.

D: Describe this a little more - You function on all cylinders and you do everything very well.

P: You can do so much! You can achieve your full potential. Now the reason why it's so difficult to deal with this is that I'm not used to this state of affairs. I've always been able to work out and do a lot of work. For a good amount of time I've been a consultant at work. So there are times when I take up work, there are times when I have my personal life, all of it. It's a nice experience too... You know you are young and there is so much to do and you are enjoying all of it. Then suddenly you get pregnant and it's supposed to be the happiest time of your life and everybody is telling you to be happy and not to

155

worry. I wish I could just buy that off the counter! I have a problem; I wish you could understand that.

So she feels that she is young and full of energy and hence there are so many things to do and to enjoy. She has a personal life and a private life. But when she gets pregnant, she is suddenly bogged down by all these things. This makes it difficult for her to go on.

P: And there are other things I have an answer to. Luckily I have never suffered any morning sickness. So in that sense you know it never kept me away from work. I could work and travel. But the doctor told me not to travel that much because I work at Churchgate. So neither the train, nor the car was an option. That's why I switched gears and decided to work from home.

So in this complaint, there are things that she has an answer to. But here with this choking it looks like she doesn't have an answer to anything. Then she says she decided to work from home. Implicit is her message that the decision was a major mistake because at home she is thinking of a 100 things. 'Now that I am home, I am just constantly thinking about this one problem...'

P: That is one mistake I made. Since I was working through home I had more time to think of my nasal condition. I wish I kept continuing going to office because then there wouldn't be a hundred things I would be thinking of.

By this time we actually realised the miasm of the case - the intensity, the pace and the desperation with which she took the appointment, gave the complaint and with which she lives her life everyday. The pace is extremely hectic.

Remember the pace is not chaotic and she is not trying to control anything. She is just trying to achieve a lot of things and in the process she is feeling drained and sapped which is her chief compliant. It is the exhaustion of overdoing. You hardly have the resources but still you have to keep going on. It's almost like a last ditch effort.

So by now we had figured out the coping in this miasm. The coping towards her state is a very Tubercular pace but what behind this panic and sensation is making her so Tubercular? We don't know as yet and that's what we are going to track down. Now she started talking more

156

about her situations, examples, her work and office. We went back to the point of her desperate feelings. We needed to know the reason for this desperation. What is behind the need to get out of things quickly? We asked her to describe this need to get out of situations.

D: So can you describe this a little bit? You said 'I need to get out of situations quickly', and you did this.

P: Yeah. Because I think this comes from my mum. She's a desperate multi-tasker.

D: Go on

P: This, that and the other! All of it has to be done. Sometimes just looking at her is a very exhausting experience.

She is saying that, "You just can't look at my mom." But she is the same as her mom.

P: It is okay. I mean if you can't do this, so what. But no, she is not like that. She expects that you must do all that and be a full person. So that sort of rubs off on me. I like to do a lot of things. It could be house work, maintenance work, office work or socialising and all of that. The need for that is even more now you know because sometimes I feel it is probably the only window that I have of footloose and fancy free kind of life. After this baby I will get sort of tied down so let me do as much as I can now. So it's about more than getting out of things. It's like… I don't mean in an escapist sense but I like to tick things off my list and [hand moving as if ticking on paper] finish off the must do this and that list and then look at something else.

The Tubercular pace gets heightened even more. 'I like to do lots of things and there is very little time I have for my own freedom. So I have to make the most of it and I have to do everything. It's not like I want to get out of this situation but I must do all of this.'

Just a second, let's go back to that point where she mentions that, "You want to be fancy free and footloose because otherwise you are going to be tied down."

Now we want to understand what does this tied down meant for her. What

157

is this feeling of being tied down? So we asked her to go slow.

D: Let me understand this a little more clearly. Describe this that you feel tied down.

P: You know pending forever.

D: Just one minute. I need to ask you something before we go on this track. What's the experience to be tied down?

P: It's not a pleasant experience.

D: Describe that.

P: Tied down could be in so many different ways. There is some tied down which you are ok with. Everything in life can't be so buoyant. Sometimes you have to be tied down.

D: Everything can't be so…?

P: So buoyant. Sometimes things… like see for example when you are going to get married, in that sense you know that you are a little more tied down but that doesn't worry you because it's a part of life. That's life, it happens. But to be physically tied down is like you want to break free.

It's very interesting - tied down and break free. We are getting almost two opposites here. But we are not getting any gestures. Anyways we need to know where the tied down and break free is going to take us.

D: So describe this tied down and break free. Go on.

P: It's like, uh, it's like if you're tied down it's like a zero. There's nothing in it for you and if you are not, then there is so much you can do. (Her finger makes a circle in air)

D: Describe this gesture. (Finger makes a circle in air)

P: It's a zero.

D: No, what's the experience when you do this?

158

P: I'm just trying to draw the zero.

D: So what's the experience when you draw zero?

P: Nothing particular. I am just drawing a zero.

D: What's the experience?

P: It's just that it's not a very pleasant feeling. It feels very heavy.

D: Describe heavy.

P: It's heavy on you. It's like maybe some weights are tied to your feet. How would you feel when you can't move?

D: Describe that.

P: It's a total helplessness.

D: Just elaborate on this a little more - Something is heavy and tied on your foot.

P: I can't describe it any more.

D: Just about this experience. Supposing I do this to you - I tie something heavy to your legs.

P: It would make me very angry to be the object of the person who does that to me. I don't deserve to be tied up. Why should anybody be tied down?

D: What's the feeling? Describe it.

P: You feel like crying. I don't deserve to be tied down. It's not fair.

So at this point it almost looked like an animal to me - being tied down and you are angry that somebody is doing this to you. We wanted to understand where this is going to lead us. What does this tied down make her feel? Does it make her feel tied as an issue of survival, as a wanting to break free or tied as in tied and wanting to be explosive? Who knows what the tied means here?

159

D: Describe this a little more – "It's not fair; I don't deserve to be tied down."

P: I think it boils down to why me? I look at my peers. I look at my family members, they don't have a problem. Why only me? So there is this sudden feeling of resentment and feeling deprived. You could well not be so... you want to be as trouble free as everybody else and you must know how to deal with it. Earlier I knew what to do. You know people told me that work-out and aerobic activities are good for me, so I did that. I had a way to deal with it but now I don't. And hence I feel tied down.

It is interesting to hear about her feeling. The tied down should have brought out something like the image or the delusion of tied down and break free. But what it brings out is – 'Why do I have a problem that others don't have? You want to be as problem-free as everybody else.' It's again a comparison between the abnormal and the normal. Are you seeing it? Then the very interesting thing is that you must know how to deal with it. That's the other side. So the intensity here is – 'I feel like I have a problem and I can't deal with it so the problem is kind of tying me down.'

Now what we did was that we gave her back the entire complex of things that she mentioned to us.

D: You had a way to deal with it but now you don't. So you feel tied down. Now can you describe this to me that you could be as trouble free as others but why only me?

P: Yeah, I mean I look at some of my friends. In fact we were having a conversation with a colleague of mine. She has similar respiratory sort of problem so we were sharing those. She has a twin sister who was laughing and telling me that her sister is fine and has no problems. Then she said that I am like a defective piece. I am wheezing all the time, my nose is running all the time and when winter comes I'm supposed to get myself so many medications but her sister does not have to do all this. So it's only similar I would think. It's like, my friends either have a baby already or are in the process of having one but none of them suffer from this kind of thing. Why me? Then I think it's so individual. Like somebody goes through horrible morning sickness while I was spared of that so maybe this is one of those things.

So what's the feeling that she has? She feels deprived and she resents her helplessness. A feeling of resentment is another thing that we have seen with nosodes because that's the resentment of the diseased tissue. There is a feeling of being deprived in comparison to others. There is a feeling of being born with this abnormality and being defective in comparison to others. These are also very important nosode themes. Anyways, we shall go a little further.

D: So describe this - I am a defective piece, why me? Somebody goes through this, why me? What's this experience?

P: You resent the whole thing.

D: What do you resent?

P: Being different and being ….of … having a condition which stops you.

Because the nosode has been derived from a source which is diseased and different from the normal tissue, it often comes up with this I am so different. I am so defective. I am so abnormal as compared to the others.

D: Describe this whole thing - being different and having a condition which stops you.

P: You're looking around and you're constantly comparing yourself. Look at her, she doesn't have this. I look at my husband sleeping peacefully through the night and busy snoring. Look at him, he is so happy.

D: Describe this - you're constantly comparing yourself, look at others and look at you? What's this experience?

P: This experience is not a happy one. You could well be spending your time doing so many more productive things than just thinking of this.

D: Completely agreed. What's the experience to see your husband happily snoring while you are like this?

P: It's again that I feel helpless. I sometimes feel that you know maybe I am a little too sensitive to the environment and you know too sensitive to my own body. Some people who go through life you know… this is happening, that is happening but they say its okay and they go through it. But I don't. I am just so in tune with everything that happens to me. That way I'm almost on a corrective mode you know like let's correct this and let's correct that.

Helplessness is another thing with the nosodes. 'I am helpless that I am this defective piece and I am trying my level best to correct it.' That's exactly what she comes up with. 'I am so much in tune with everything going on inside me'. They are very much looking inwards. 'I am always on a corrective mode. I must correct this, I must correct that. I am always correcting myself.' Here comes the issue of correct-incorrect. We will go a little bit further. She is going to say something very interesting here.

P: My husband he snores and sleeps happily. I don't think he cares. I don't think it ever bothers him. See for example my friend who has kids. She had warned me much ahead that you might start snoring and I laughed at her and I said that I hope I don't and then that night I had that vibratory sensation and I felt like you know… I don't know if I would have started snoring. It just didn't stop there. It went on to wonder… is it apnoea? Is it going to choke me? What it's going to do? Whereas somebody would have just happily snored away and finished it off but no not me, I must correct this.

The whole feeling within is that there is something incorrect within me, I must correct this and that is how I will function.

P: So that's what I mean by being little more sensitive and little more conscious of every sensation.

D: Describe this - 'I must correct it', 'conscious of every sensation'.

P: I can't describe it any more.

D: O! You're doing very well. In fact we are almost there.

P: You know in my line of work we call this emotional laddering. I often bug my consumers with this kind of laddering which goes on and on and finally I feel that I am on the ceiling end of it. I tried my level best. I thought I was articulate but not enough.

D: You are doing very well. It's just that I want to confirm it from different angles. So even if you repeat something it's ok. You don't have to fish for new words for me. I just want to see that I have not left a stone unturned; something like that. So that's helpful. What was it, describe that.

P: I am always on a corrective mode.

So we asked her to describe this - I am always on a corrective mode. She said, "Yes, I can give you parallels, with work. I feel I must be as good as any other person."

D: Because what's the experience?

P: It's a feeling of maybe… you could say it's an inferior feeling at least in the context of my work. You know that guy does so much better. I wish I could do as well as him. So then I am always on a corrective mode. Like let me get better. Let me start to think from this angle, that angle and every angle.

D: Describe this experience that the guy does so much better at work and let me get as good as him.

P: I know that I have the capacity to do that. If I can't be as good as that, I have to find a way of doing it better and better you know. If others can do it why not me; let me try.

So we asked her to describe this experience and she kept repeating that it's a feeling of inferiority.

D: So I said what's this experience to be inferior?

P: I don't like it and I don't feel good about it at all.

D: What's the experience?

P: I don't know how to describe it. It's not a very big thing but you know it's just for that fleeting moment.

We were going beautifully with the nosode. Here we were getting the miasm and this sensation that 'I am a defective piece, something is abnormal within me, something is wrong here, let me correct it.' But at that point she decided to switch the kingdom and she said to me – 'It feels like I lack something.'

D: What's the feeling within?

P: The feeling within is that I lack something.

D: Can you describe that I lack something?

P: It stays at the back of my mind. That there is possibly one area I'm not good at. And again I am talking you know purely in the work prospective. I wish I knew how to… I wish I could grab *(hand grabbing something pulling towards herself)* that skill so that it just makes me a little bit more complete.

> *Not only does she say that she is lacking something but she says, "I wish I could grab it so that it makes me feel more complete." It's very interesting now that it's going in a complete mineral language. This is a beautiful case. It exactly differentiates the nosode from the mineral. So we asked her to describe this experience that you are lacking something. We wanted to know if there is an issue here of one of the rows.*

D: What's the experience to lack something or not be complete?

P: It's not good. You have some expectations of yourself and sadly they keep increasing. Every time you see that there is a benchmark which is better than you, your expectations of yourself rise. You know there is so much more to do and go higher. But it's not always very frustrating because I know that yes not everybody has everything. So there are some things that you lack and there are some things which somebody else might lack.

> *Again she is into a corrective mode. Then she said something very interesting.*

P: I have never been happy with my body. I always had a tendency to put on weight. So again I feel that why should this happen to me? Somebody else eats like a quantum, four times more than what I eat and yet they are in a good shape. I have to be conscious of every gram that I consume and I have to be so active. I have to be in the gym everyday for an hour and somebody else gets away with it.

> *Again that corrective mode wants to do something about it.*

P: But somebody else might be totally happy with ….like I have this very good friend who is three times my size and it doesn't bother her at all. She goes through it with life but not me. I must correct it.

Isn't it interesting that when we asked her what's the experience to lack something and to not feel complete, she gave the weight example. Her sensation is – 'What is it that's wrong with me?' Very often in a nosode you see a lacking feeling as another expression of the feeling that, 'I have a problem within me'.
Similarly for a mineral - 'Something is wrong. I need to do better, I need to correct it,' might also be an expression of - something is lacking in me. Are you getting this difference? But the point is you have to see what is coming up repeatedly.

For example in a mineral if you ask to describe the feeling of being incomplete and lacking, they will automatically go into – "I feel like I am not as good as the other person. I feel like I can do much better which will give me my own recognition. I feel that I can do so many different things and more challenging things in life." Or they will say that "I can do much better by way of which I will feel more independent. I can stand on my own two feet." So they will give you a specific issue related to their incompleteness.

Whereas in the nosode the feeling of lacking is - What is wrong with me? Where am I going wrong? What kind of a defective piece am I? What kind of an abnormalcy is inside? How can I correct it? They are not sensitive to a specific issue of separation, independence, existence, challenge, power, or materialism. They are not behind any specific issue. All they are behind is how much can they be compared to the others. How much normal, healthy and proper; how much correct, how much a full person can I be because the feeling inside is – 'Actually I am a defective and diseased person'. This is what our patient keeps coming back to. She starts with the lack and incompleteness but she ends up with - I feel what is wrong with me? I must correct it. So this incompleteness doesn't lead us to a specific issue like an incompleteness of identity or image or any kind of a further example like that. But what remains is still this feeling. Then she gave another example.

P: See, I will give you an example. In my work I sort of have a reputation of being good at what I do. So then it's an expectation that every time whatever project or task I take up, it must be good. So it's like a tall order all the time.

You just can't slack. I guess it happens to everybody not just me. So it gets you to work that much harder on it. It's like a real constant work out.

Now you see that the miasm is very clear. We have a patient with a Tubercular miasm or just the Tuberculinum nosode itself. You see the intensity is much deeper. The desperation of the situation is – 'I am almost there'. You know when they are sick or when they are in the depths of their negative feelings, their feelings are – 'I am almost so close to Syphilis. I am almost so close to death.'

The other side of that is how much better can I get? I must go on doing and put in every effort. Tubercular comes after Cancer. So a successful Tuberculinum is somebody who is a very well achieved person because he is really putting in a lot of efforts and doing so many things because the desperation is much more and that's what you see in this paragraph. She says, "Whatever task I take up, it has to be good." That's the Tubercular pace. They are constantly regularly, hectically and continuously doing things.

As you go further down in the miasms from Psora to Syphilis on the successful side, you see people far more successful. For example a Tuberculinum or a Carcinosinum might be far more successful than a Sycotic, than a Medorrhinum. Similarly, when you see the levels of desperation, the desperation of a Tuberculinum or a Carcinosinum might be far more than the desperation of the Medorrhinum because the intensity at which Tuberculinum, Carcinosinum, Leprominum and Syphilinum see the situation is far more desperate, fatal and far more destructive. Hence, the amount of efforts that they put in to come out of it is also much more intense. As a result, their successful side is far more successful, far more achieved and far more challenged. This is the other side.

Let us go back to the case.

D: Describe this tall order, high expectation and reputation

P: I love challenges. Some people thrive on challenge but you know the challenge also makes you feel that you have to work much harder and the stakes are high so you could also fall. I see people in my profession thrive on the challenge. This is tough. It's like let me see how will I get on top of it.

166

First she said I love challenge. Then she said I don't like challenges and then she said no I do take up challenges. The very fact that she mentions about challenges, thriving and the stakes that come with it, shows that the challenges are automatically an issue for her. So she said that when you want it easy, you look at others and you feel that they are doing it and so you want to be as good as them.

D: Describe this that you feel you can do it as well.

P: If they can so can you. What is wrong with you? Nothing is wrong at all. You have achieved so much in the past. My self-image is very important to me.

D: Describe that.

P: I am someone with a very high self-esteem. I am capable of doing a lot of things, not just doing but I am capable of multi-tasking. Everyone knows that my image is that of an efficient, capable person. If I am not all these I am not with the flow of the others. Something in me is different from the rest and I am always in the doing mode. Like something is wrong within and I have to be MISS FIX –IT. If anything goes wrong I am in the corrective mode. But I am doing so much more. I am struggling with things and managing it because there is so much multi-tasking involved. If you cannot do all of this, multi-tasking and struggling and doing this and that, then it feels like a part of you is getting eroded. Diseased and eroded because a part of you is not functioning well.

Then she said –

P: You know for instance, I took a lot of responsibility for managing the home front. Then I started working and I took great pride in doing my work and managing it along with home. So then that image continues for me that I am capable. I don't care what somebody else thinks of me but in my mind I know I can do it. But if you can't do it then it's like a part of you is being eroded. Something that was yours now it's getting in a way decayed and eroded. So you must do something about it. I told you that I get on to the corrective mode and multi-tasking begins.

You know what was interesting was that we were thinking in our minds that if she feels so much about image and capability then why is it not

167

coming up? What is she capable of? Maintaining her identity, her position, her power or her independence? What is the issue that she is capable of? But that never came up.

We wanted to know that what exactly is getting eroded - her image, her identity, position or status? To know this, we asked her to describe eroded. It was interesting to hear what she said.

P: It's like a part of you is getting decayed, rotten and eroded. It is as if that everything was fine and going well and is now becoming eroded. It is as if your body cannot do all the functions and abilities. It feels very confident if you can do all these things.

So the eroded again was not coming back to anything else. It was in fact coming back to the fact that your own body is getting decayed and eroded. These words can also be used by a nosode.

Coming back to that again - it's a diseased tissue and once there is an infection, parts and cells of the body are going to die. There is going to be some sort of a structural change, some sort of pathology. So, decay rotting and erosion will also be part of a nosode. Already the miasm that has come up in the case is Tuberculinum, the Tubercular miasm.

If you look at the Tubercular pathology then what happens? It is quite a destructive pathology; it is pathology where parts of the lungs get fibrosis by the end. If you survive through it, that part of the lung is not going to function anymore. It's like a part of you is getting decayed, rotten and eroded like the patient mentions. So a Tuberculinum can often feel like this - that if the condition is not corrected, it will decay. That's what happens to the Tuberculinum if you don't give medicine at the right time. It is a feeling of defectiveness.

Then the other side comes in where she says 'I feel very positive and confident. It makes me feel how can I correct it?' So she is constantly thinking in terms of only one thing - how can I correct that what is incorrect.

We want you to note that successful Carcinosinum, Tuberculinum, Leprominum and Syphilinum are often in this corrective mode. We have cases of the Leprominum nosode as well. So what will come up very often intense need to prevent this erosion because it's the last effort. In Leprominum there will be a constant need to keep up the isolated top position and shun others and in Syphilinum there will be a constant on-guard corrective mode, a one small mistake will cause ultimate death and destruction.

So rather than 'I am defective' or 'I am abnormal' coming up in the case so much, what comes in the Tuberculinum and the Carcinosinum case is 'How can I prevent it from happening; how can I correct it'. The coping of the miasm comes out more strongly than the sensation because they are making desperate efforts to come out of the situation. The sensation does come up too but less strongly. It is – 'I feel what is wrong with me? I am a defective piece. Why am I not like the others?'

D: Describe I feel positive and confident.

P: Much more confident that's it.

D: And if she doesn't think well of you?

P: That's what I said, I worry about it.

D: What does it make you feel?

She comes back to correcting.

P: How can I correct it?

D: How can I correct it?

P: How can I change the impression which she now holds of me or?

This feeling of being tied down, we have seen in 3 cases of Tuberculinum and in this whole need to come out, they start to feel as if the situation is really very narrow and suffocating and that they really want to break free and somehow want to come out of the abnormal situation and feel normal like the others. Thus, in the Tubercular miasm and in Tuberculinum especially, you often find them using the words narrow, suffocating and restricting.

D: Describe this.

P: It's as if you are in a tunnel, in darkness and you want to see light.

This is another interesting thing of the Tubercular miasm - to feel as if you are in the dark. You know that the amount of efforts and desperation brings in a feeling that the situation is very dark and narrow. You can't see any light in the situation. You need to break free from the situation. So these are all parts of the Tubercular miasm which is what she will come back to. What she says is very interesting.

P: It's a dark situation, it's narrow. I need to break free from it because I am constantly thinking how this situation can be improved.

The intensity of the situation is that it is so close to death that there is absolutely no way out. There is not even a milligram of air that can go in. So these are kind of words that Tuberculinum often uses because it shows the intensity and the gravity that is felt about this sensation of being abnormal.

We asked her to tell us more about this darkness and freedom and this desire to break free.

P: It's a situation; you have to be there even if it gets worse. It's like being in darkness and you want to see the light.

D: Can you describe that?

P: No I can't …you're scared, you're vulnerable you're uncertain, what lies ahead?

D: Little bit more. What is this scared, vulnerable, uncertain?

P: I can't describe it any further.

D: 'Dark and you want to see the light.' What's this experience that you are in the dark and you want to see the light. Imagine if you're in dark, what's the experience?

P: You are very scared. I just want to be out of that situation. You want an

170

answer. You want to know how your situation can be improved. It's dark and uncertain, you feel vulnerable and scared about what is it coming down to? You are only trying to think of how you can improve this situation.

So it's coming back to the coping again and again. Her entire focus is inwards, only on her attitude and towards the problem.

D: You are always thinking of how to improve the situation. How do you improve the situation?

P: Yes, that's what it is. I am always thinking of coming out of it. I am always thinking of correcting the situation.

D: You always think of how to improve the situation and how to correct it?

P: Yes.

D: Just last. What would be your experience if you are scared, vulnerable and in dark?

We wanted to know if there is anything else that's going to come out of this scared, vulnerable and dark. But the whole focus remains on how she can manage to come out of it.

D: What's your experience in that?

P: I feel helpless.

D: And?

P: I want to be out of that situation.

D: You want to be out of that situation?

She does not say that she is attacked, she is losing something and or that she is sensitive to anything. It's just that she is helpless. She must come out of it in any way. 'I am helpless' - in it the focus lies within, somewhere the problem is within. And her whole concentration is on the coping mechanism which is – 'I have to be out of the situation at any cost.'

I. Remedy and Case Follow-up

We gave her Tuberculinum in 1M potency because it was a very desperate situation and she was giving us the entire image of the Tuberculinum at the delusion level. Also the situation was that of intense panic and choking. Within about a week or two she was so much better. The panic settled immediately and she was back to her own house. She could sleep and she had started to breathe. Her nasal congestion was still there but she was far more relaxed than what we had seen her. So we will see her follow-up a month later, after the first dose.

First follow-up: March 2007

D: You look very different than what we had seen you a month ago.

P: I relaxed my hair. Maybe that's why. Also I am feeling much better. Last time I guess I was little more panic stricken. Now I'm ok.

We give her a remedy. She goes and relaxes her hair.

D: So tell me on the whole, how much better are you? And how is everything so that I know.

P: I am about 90% better. The only issue I have now is that it feels very dry inside and therefore when I am in an AC environment it gets very uncomfortable. It means like every time I take in, it burns and then it's like I'm trying to constantly fidget with my nose, so if I switch off the AC, it's much better.

D: You want me to switch it off for a moment?

P: No it's ok. And when I lie down at night, sometimes the congestion is more, particularly towards the morning. So when at around 5 o'clock I can hear myself breathing, it's like wheezing, wheezing, wheezing. But I'm OK. It lets me function. It's not like... I guess that much constriction in pregnancy is normal.

D: And how are the panic attacks and everything?

P: Panic attacks have gone down in the sense that I'm okay now. But the panic had become a generalised panic - it was nothing to do with my nose.

172

D: How is that generalised panic?

P: That I have actually not tested because what I have done is that I don't sleep in my house. Now we have another house. It's like a bare bone house but I like sleeping there. So I don't care. I just decided that I will test that panic thing sometime later.

D: So you're still scared of that?

P: I'm maybe not very scared because what used to happen is that if you start anticipating that thing towards the evening as the day would turn into…

P: I know that I am much better because I used to anticipate it by evening and that itself used to make me restless. It doesn't happen anymore. I think we are at home till around 11- 11.30 and we just go to the other place to sleep.

D: Ok. You are saying that earlier the panic would start by evening whereas now you are still in the same environment till 11 or 11.30 in the night. So the panic would have set in by then?

P: Yeah and couple of times I have even slept there and I have just been restless because it's towards the road. So the traffic keeps me awake and I'm generally a light sleeper. In fact, pregnancy has made it even lighter. So it doesn't help my cause. I told my husband that let's not sleep here. We will sleep in the other house. It's okay.

D: So tell me how those feelings are when at work you constantly need to do this and that and you need to get out of things and solve them immediately?

P: That's the way I am. That doesn't change.

D: Is it the same intensity?

P: Maybe not.

D: What do you mean by maybe not?

P: I am feeling much more relaxed. At least I am making a conscious attempt to.

D: Generally how much has the medication been able to help you?

P: Emotionally?

D: In every which way?

P: 90% -95 % or so. It's just made me calmer. I mean I'm not thinking about it all the time. Otherwise it used to be on my mind all the time. I told you, last time I would think of nothing else but this. Now I know I have things to do. I am functioning. I am thinking about my work, I am thinking about other things. So it's much better.

D: It's much better. Good!

So you see she is much better and relaxed. The generalised panic as well as the nasal congestion, both of them are not there. We had given her almost about three to four doses till now because we had seen the situation as really very panicky but the moment we saw this much of an improvement, we stopped the doses. So actually in that one month that she came to us, she got two doses and then beyond that it reduced.

Second follow-up

We saw her in April 2007. We took about an hour's case taking again because this time she came up beautifully with the whole situation in her family life and how she feels completely constricted and that there is no way out. We could also see her intense need and the immense efforts that she puts into this problem to just completely break free. This time her entire explanation was about suffocation and breaking free.

We repeated Tuberculinum at that point because the last trimester of pregnancy had started and she had developed some kind of a bad throat infection ...because of the stress of it all. So we needed to give her something. Then of course it eased out and she is far better now. She is still in touch with us. She is more relaxed as a person today. She has two children.

IV. Summary

So this was the case with the Tuberculinum 1M. What we realised and learnt from this case are some common themes of nosodes which have to do a lot with a feeling of being abnormal and defective. But there are other themes and other words which can come along in all our nosode cases. Before we go on to those themes, we would still like to do one more very short case with you to differentiate Tuberculinum from Bacillinum. This case is where we gave the patient Tuberculinum to begin with, only to understand later that this was a better picture of Bacillinum. Hence we shifted to Bacillinum. We will go to this case.

12

 ## A CASE OF BACILLINUM

I.   Case Introduction

II. The Case

III. Remedy and Case Follow-up

IV. Summary

I. Case Introduction

For this case we are not going to go into any details. We will not go into the chief complaint of the case or even the sensation as it has been explained in earlier cases.

Just keep in my mind that the sensation was – 'How can I change what is going wrong in my own system.' But here we are going to show you the efforts that he is making and the way in which he is seeing this sensation. In the paragraph below, he is talking about losing his job, losing everything and feeling insecure. He said his mind was running faster to just come to a good position. So we are at that point in the case where we want to show you the intensity and the sinking that this man comes up with. In the earlier case we didn't see so much of the sinking. We saw it in the chief complaint but not beyond that. We just saw somebody who is multi- tasking, doing many things and is on full cylinders.

Here in this case what we have focused on is somebody who has the same intensity and who is talking about the same things of doing this and that but what we see in him is the fear of losing, the desperation and the failed side or the side that you are so close to death that you are sinking.

II. The Case

P: Insecure means just losing a particular thing. I am insecure about it. I will tell you how it is. Losing means if I am on a particular job or with a company. If I am not doing well, I am insecure about losing my job. I am you know, afraid and because of that I try to put in more efforts which is not required. My mind runs faster than my own activity and I try to bring it into a better position. Doctor, if you remember, I have told you all these things previously. And also that it goes in the same cycle. The only way to relax is if I am not insecure. Then I feel good means I feel happy. I enjoy things.

P: Just give me a minute.

D: Take your time.

P: The experience is very bad. I feel you know this experience doctor, I can best describe as feeling helpless. I go through an experience of helplessness or sometimes I hurry-burry things and try to be street-smart. Like trying to do something street-smartly and try to just work around things and get things to a comfortable position.

We see the same intensity here – 'I try to hurry burry. My mind works faster than my body. I try to do all these kind of things to come to a comfortable position.'

D: Go on.

P: That is what I can say experience is about. It means trying to pull something inside, trying to process my thoughts and trying to bring them to some comfortable position. And then I feel relaxed, "Aah! Good." That is how I feel - relaxed 'aah!' You know like very relaxed. I feel relaxed. Yes relaxed once it gets over. Then the load is suddenly gone. I feel once all that has happened then after the situation subsides I feel relaxed. I feel completely comfortable but when it's happening I don't take anything inside. I am in my own world of hurry-burry (*hands moving, jumbling motion*) and trying to... too many thoughts come and all the thoughts go inside at the same point. I just try to decide something. I am trying to decide faster and faster and everything gets collapsed.

D: Just go more into this.

P: Yeah, I am going more and more. I am trying different things and all of a sudden when I get something, a way out like a tunnel coming to an end, then I feel relaxed. I can see the tunnel light coming in and I feel relaxed about it. "Ah! I got the solution" or "I got the thing which I wanted". I cool down you know. Then I can take things. Then anything else can come in. I feel good.

He was making gestures (hands moving, jumbling coming closer, going away, lot of rapid movements). Finally he comes to – 'I am going to feel fine when I see the light.'

D: Describe this whole experience, the other thing.

At this point of time in the case we were constantly differentiating Typhoidinum and Tuberculinum because if you see the pathology of Typhoid then the nosode Typhoidinum should also carry this interesting crisis-collapse kind of a situation but if you come out of Typhoid, you come out unscathed, absolutely free, fine and normal. So the feeling in Typhoidinum is - You make an intense effort in a situation of complete crisis but once you come out of it you are fine and this person is trying to say something like that. There is hurry, there is collapse, there is doing this and that but at the end of the tunnel when he sees the light, he feels a little better.

So we wanted to understand just how desperately he feels his situation. Tuberculinum is between Sycosis and Syphilis. The intensity, the desperation of the situation, the fatality, the way in which he looks at death is much more severe than in Typhoid. In Typhoid which is between Sycosis and Psora which has such a large component of Psora, the element of hope is very high. So it is like – 'I rush and I try and I really make all the efforts and once that situation tides away I feel fine.' But in Tuberculinum it is as if the situation is nearly going out of my hands. 'I am trying and trying, I can collapse, I can almost die in this situation. However what I do is I still keep on trying.'

Now this person was also talking about a safe comfortable position which is why the doubt was in our mind of whether this is Typhoidinum or is this Tuberculinum? So we go a little further in the case. We asked him to describe this hurry burry, tunnel and collapse.

D: 'Hurry-burry, tunnel, collapse.' What is all this?

P: I get stressed. Doctor, I get just totally stressed and my whole body energy is like towards only that experience. I feel my whole body concentration goes to that particular point when it is like that and my thoughts go in and come out very quickly like something is running with the thoughts you know.

Now this intensity, this running, this going, this coming, this kind of a pace is what is not seen in Typhoidinum. It of course takes a lot of efforts before you reach a comfortable position. So there is an impulsiveness and impatience in Typhoid. But this kind of relentless intense effort is a far more desperate picture than just Typhoid and that belongs to Tuberculinum and Bacillinum both because both are nosodes of the Tubercular pathology. So this intensity belongs to the Tubercular miasm.

We will go a little further and know a little more about tunnel and collapse. The other point is that tunnel and collapse are again a part of Tuberculinum and Bacillinum. See why they feel this need of a tunnel?

180

This is because they are so close to Syphilis. They are very close to destruction, to death. They feel that time is really very short. So, they have to make large amounts of efforts in a very small time. Hence this time constraint is really very demanding and constricting on them. This feeling that they are near death gives them this image of a tunnel; that they are into something from which they have to really come out and the light has to be there. Whereas in Typhoidinum it's not a situation of time constraint; it's only that there is a situation and you have to make effort, and you are very hopeful that you will come out of it. Therefore tunnel is a very important part of the Tuberculinum.

D: Describe the tunnel and collapse more.

P: I will tell you. I am getting into (*hands making a shape of a tunnelling, narrowing, jumbling hand movement, very rapid movement*) a tunnel of thoughts and I am trying to work out around things. I am just thinking and thinking and then finally once that is over, I come out easily, relaxed and cool. Once that full cycle is over to achieve something, I feel relaxed and good.

Now the moment he said that once it is achieved, I feel relaxed, it brought us back to Typhoidinum. You see what he is trying to tell here is not that he sees his situation as something which is achievable and fine.

Otherwise, any person can say that I feel relaxed once the situation is gone - whether it is Cancer miasm, Medorrhinum, Tuberculinum or Psorinum. So it's not as if the moment he says that once the situation is gone, I feel relaxed that you automatically think of Typhoid. You must look out for the feelings of the person in that situation. If his feeling is, "O my god I have no time at all", then it is Tuberculinum but if it says, "O my god it's a chaos, I need to have total control over this situation", then its Carcinosinum. If the feeling is that I have to struggle and struggle endlessly, then it is Psorinum. So the way he looks at himself in that situation is more important and that's exactly what we did at this point.

We understood the tunnel and the collapse but this comfortable position kept coming time and again. So we asked him to describe his feeling and experience when he is in that situation. We wanted to know how much is the level of hope? In short, we were trying to evaluate whether he is Typhoidinum or Tuberculinum.

P: Even though I know that I am losing a battle, I keep trying with the same energy. Probably sometimes the energy even goes up. I try to put more and more efforts.

D: I just want to understand this a little bit more – 'I am losing the battle, but still I am trying'.

P: Yeah. I know that I have got less time. I know it is difficult to achieve, but I keep trying and every time I try, I try to put more efforts and in a channelised way. I try to study my previous efforts. Then I put my efforts or I take external help to understand where I am going wrong. But I keep putting more and more and more efforts.

D: I understood that you are putting more efforts. Can you describe this – I am losing the battle and I am trying?

P: Yeah, I will just say in one line. I am losing. The thing is going away from me and I am trying to achieve by putting more efforts.

Here you see the level of hope. The feeling he has is that, 'I am fighting an almost lost battle' and that is the Tubercular pathology. In the Typhoid case the battle is not completely lost and so there is a whole lot of hope. If you can battle with the Typhoid you can come out of it and you can defy. But in the Tubercular pathology you know that's not the case. Here, the body has contracted a disease which is much more difficult to fight. Even if the disease leaves the body, it is going to leave marks on the body which it will always have till death. Hence you can always find out on an X-ray if the person has had tuberculosis in the past. The fibrosed patch is always seen as an old scar of tuberculosis on an X-ray.

When Typhoid infection leads to perforation and death the miasm changes from Typhoid to Syphilis because it happens in immune compromised individuals. Mostly it's easy to come out of a typhoid infection. So the pathology here is much less fatal and much more hopeful than the pathology of Tuberculinum. We gave this patient Tuberculinum and he did respond but not to the point that we would have liked him to. So, we looked back in the case and saw what he was trying to say.

His efforts were still the same - his whole thing was about a person who has to speedily correct himself and find where in his system he is going

182

wrong. So where were we going wrong? Then we decided to read Tuberculinum bovinum and also the other remedies of the Tubercular miasm. One of them is commonly known as Bacillinum. Now Bacillinum is the maceration of the lung affected with tuberculosis whereas Tuberculinum bovinum is taken from the infected gland.

III. Remedy and Case Follow-up

We gave the patient Bacillinum 1M with the thought in mind that the feeling of collapse and sinking would be much more in Bacillinum than in Tuberculinum. Interestingly, what we saw in the follow-up was that he improved much more on Bacillinum 1M. Earlier, he had a history of thyrotoxicosis. His gland was irradiated. When he began treatment with us, he had developed panic attacks, following the irradiation. There were joint pains, tremendous weakness and a feeling that he couldn't achieve much. All these panic attacks and the sinking and collapse feelings improved with Bacillinum 1M.

Bacillinum:

Bacillinum is taken from a collapsed lung and therefore the feeling of collapse, drain, exhaustion is much more in Bacillinum than in Tuberculinum. In other words, if we have a case where the efforts are extensive and there is a feeling of suffocation and breathlessness due to these efforts we think of Tuberculinum. But in a patient where there is exhaustion, a feeling of no escape and total collapse we think of Bacillinum.

IV. Summary

It is clear from this case that cases can be tricky. It is important to be vigilant. We need to keenly observe the theme and sensation that is being depicted by the patient. Of course, practice makes us better practitioners!

13

 **JOSHIS' TAKE ON
MIASMATIC RELATIONSHIPS**

I.   The Ten Miasms

II. How the Miasms Differ

III. A Renewed Understanding of the
Miasm Categories

IV. Comparative Table of Miasms

V.   Successful and Unsuccessful Side of each
Miasm

I. The Ten Miasms

There are three main miasms or pillars, namely Psora, Sycosis and Syphilis. The Acute miasm lies even before the Psoric miasm. It is more or less like a very acute infection or situation. The rest six miasms are interspersed between these main miasms or pillars.

Since we see miasms at the mental level or the state level, the Acute miasm does not remain an acute infection but becomes an acute, intense way of dealing with the situation. Hence to understand miasmatic relationships we have made two halves.

For the ease of understanding our concepts, we have segregated Acute to Sycosis as the first half and Sycosis to Syphilis as the second half. Psora here still remains as the main pillar. Hence according to us there are four main pillars on the miasm chart. So there are two main miasms Acute and Psora in the first half and Sycosis and Syphilis in the second half.

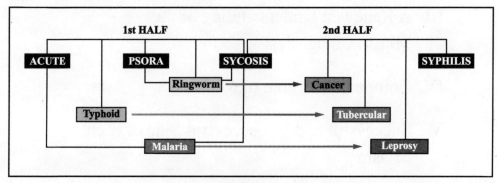

Fig. 4

There are three miasms in-between the main miasms. All the in-between miasms have a combination of at least two of the four major pillars. We have seen that there is a definite relationship between the three miasms in the first half and the three miasms in the second half of the compartments. According to us, the second half is an intensification of the first half.

To illustrate:

★ Typhoid is a combination of Acute and Psora

★ Ringworm is a combination of Psora and Sycosis

186

★ Malaria is a combination of Acute and Sycosis

★ Similarly Tubercular, Cancer and Leprous have the traits of Sycosis and Syphilis but in varying intensities. They become uniquely different from each other.

When we looked back on our cases and our common mistakes, we often found that we had confused the Typhoid and Tubercular miasm, the Malaria and Leprous and the Ringworm and Cancer miasms respectively. Eventually this got us to think about the relationship or the similarity between these sets. Then when we studied our cases and the miasms, we found something interesting -

★ The Typhoid miasm has something common with Tubercular: the pace and the efforts.

★ The Leprous miasm has something common with Malaria: the harassed and persecuted feeling.

★ The Ringworm miasm has something common with the Cancer miasm: the constant trials.

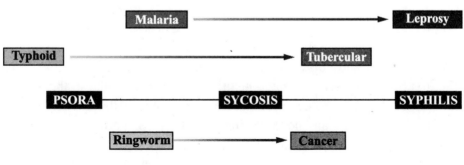

Fig. 5

II. How the Miasms Differ

The difference in the two sets of miasms is in the desperation and hopelessness. According to our theory, Psora is closer to health, Sycosis is mid-way and Syphilis is closer to death.

Psora

When you are closer to health your hopes are high, your efforts are positive and your desperation is not intense. You don't even see death but you see health and you make efforts to go towards it.

Sycosis

Sycosis is mid-way between health and death. It is like a plateau state where one feels too far away to be able to reach health and too far away to even die. In this state, the individual accepts his abnormality thinking that he can do nothing about it but at the same time, there is some stability because the individual is not expecting to die so soon either. In other words, there is not much hope to reach health but there is not much danger from death either.

Syphilis

Syphilis is the closest to death. Here one feels very close to one's own destruction. Hence the effort to prevent this or save oneself is frantic, hectic and with an intense desperation to survive.

Health is too far away, as a non-reachable goal and death is too close. Therefore here one is making efforts to avoid death.

On the Psoric side there is an effort to be healthy while on Syphilitic side there is desperation to avoid death.

III. A Renewed Understanding of the Miasm Categories

The similarity and difference between Typhoid and Tubercular miasms:
Typhoid and Tubercular both share a hectic pace. They both have restlessness, frenzy and impatience in their efforts. On these lines you can understand that although Typhoid and Tubercular miasms share this fast pace Typhoid being in the first half, is closer to life and health whereas Tubercular in the second half is closer to death and destruction. The experience of the Typhoid man is one of falling in a pool and not knowing how to swim. He will make efforts to call for help, move his hands and legs and do something to reach the other end of the pool. But the experience of a Tubercular man is one of falling in an ocean. He is all alone and he cannot see the shore. So he cannot call for help. He is exhausted; he knows that he has little time and resources left. He knows that he is nearing death.

The similarity and difference between Ringworm and Cancer miasms:
Similarly, Ringworm and Cancer share a similar feature of trying constantly.

But Ringworm in the first half is closer to life and health and has a pillar of Sycosis safeguarding him. So he gives up trying and alternately tries again while Cancer on the other hand tries relentlessly, exhaustively, endlessly, without losing any control or any chance because he is closer to death. He knows that if he gives up, he will be dead and gone.

The similarity and difference between Leprosy and Malaria miasms:
Leprosy and Malaria both feel harassed, persecuted and singled-out but while Malaria throws a tantrum and then settles down, the Leprous patient walks away because he knows he is shunned, singled and punished.

Malaria has the base of Sycosis and so he hides for a while and then throws a tantrum to attract attention and call for help. This comes from the acute element which it has within itself. But in the Leprous, the hiding is extended to the point where the person shuns the entire world. He feels so close to death that he feels extremely hopeless and disgusted about himself. He feels defeated. He thus exits or walks away from everyone because he feels that no one can help him or will help him in such a desperate and destitute condition.

In this way you see that there is a rhythm or a cycle that is seen in the miasms. It is as if there are two halves where the same cycle of the first half is repeated in an increasingly desperate, intense and destructive manner in the second half until Syphilis.

Malaria	Leprosy
• Accepts the problem but the problem not life threatening but not solvable either	• Resigned to fate because the problem is fatal and unsolvable
• Blames fate vehemently but childishly	• Death is too close
• Feels unlucky and singled out	• Feels isolated and thrown out
• Hampered and hindered	• Disgusted
• Will do nothing about it except complaining and whining	• Can do nothing about a hopeless situation so blames himself, bites, cuts himself, resorts to stealing, etc.
• Appears like a nagging, irritating child	• Appears like an abandoned beggar or leper

Typhoid	Tubercular
• Feeling as if drowning in a pond	• Feeling as if drowning in an ocean with no one is sight
• Childish, impulsive, impatient	• Hurried ,hectic, frenzy, multitasking
• Highly hopeful	• Collapsing and hopeless
• Everything is achievable and hence the impatience to finish things quickly	• Running against time as everything is unachievable and one is close to death
• Goals are achievable	• Death is close, destruction - evident that makes it suffocating
• Hopeful	• Desperate

Ringworm	Cancer
• Hopeful since the situation is not fatal.	• He is very close to hopelessness since the situation is progressing towards fatality
• Accepts the problem but wants to try to get rid of the problem	• Cannot accept since if he accepts he will die
• Alternately resigns the fate and tries with hope	• He wants to make superhuman efforts to come out of the problem
• Try and accept alternately	• Try relentlessly till you get exhausted Perfection is must or death is evident Endless efforts and trying
• One tries to improve the situation and then gives up since he knows it is not so bad	• If one gives up situation will become chaotic and completely out of control

The above tables point out the relationship between different miasms.

- Tubercular is a more intense miasmatic state and desperate than Typhoid.

- Leprous is more intense and desperate miasmatic state than Malaria.

- Cancer is a much more intense and desperate miasmatic state than Ringworm.

Having found these connections between the miasms, we now have a deeper understanding of miasms. It helps us immensely to understand the reason for confusion between certain miasms. This new insight also helps us differentiate the miasms correctly by looking for their intensities in the cases that we get confused.

IV. Comparative table of miasms

Name of the Nosode	Family sensation of nosode	Sensation of miasm	Specific characteristic of that particular nosode
Lyssinum	SOMETHING INSIDE ME IS WRONG	• Sudden onset and sudden recovery from the situation • Panic and insanity • Overwhelmed by everything happening around him	• Feeling of going insane • Feeling of having suffered wrong • Intense anger and rage • Destructive • Biting • Cursing and swearing because one is overwhelmed by the situation and has no control over what to do • When situation passes one settles as if nothing has happened • Confused • Maniacal • Yelling • Screaming
Typhoidinum		• Must work immediately and almost impulsively to reach health and eradicate whatever is wrong with me	• Hurried • Impatient • Quick and then resting peacefully • Childish • Impulsive • Urgency
Pyrogen			• Septicaemia, septic, toxic feeling, feeling that if nothing is done there will be disaster which is sudden • Sudden collapse but one can come out of it by effort but one is exhausted and toxic to make efforts
Malaria		• Intermittently angry due to the feeling of being harassed or attacked at intervals • In between these attacks the attitude is to be lazy, to just avoid or accept the situation	• Acute bouts of anger and complaints coupled with periods of avoidance and acceptance • Feeling intensely chilly • Nagging, complaining character of the person • Feeling persecuted, troubled, unlucky and harassed • Whining, loud complaining, childish complaining

Ringworm		• Trying and giving up alternately • Will always try and make efforts but as soon as there are hurdles will give up all efforts and accept the situation but will try again sometime later	• Alternate trying and giving up • Itching • Dryness • Spreading slowly and gradually and resistant nature of complaints • Therefore what is the point in trying and person gives up in between attempts of trying and making efforts
Psorinum	SOMETHING INSIDE ME IS WRONG	• Work continuously with hope	• Hopeful about one's faults and want to change them and works towards improvement but never gives up the continuous struggle
Medorrhinum		• Avoidance, hiding character	• Avoiding inner issues by either denying or putting up a false bravado
Carcinosinum		• Working too hard • Perfectionist • Detailed • Isolated because of too much work, • Cannot tolerate the slightest mistake from fear of chaos • Highly controlled • Non expressive or suppressed and controlled • Ambitious	• Metastasis, spread of the wrong elements causing chaos, need to control every fine thing to avoid chaos • A sensation of having born with a weakness or a weak cell which when triggered by external stimuli turns alien towards one's own body • Feeling of body turning against its own self • Feeling of complete chaos within the body
Anthracinum			• My insides are giving away there is necrosis and I am losing all control over my body, over situations over everything • There is putrefaction, decay and it is my fault • My own misdoings, my own faults make the situation beyond repair and control • Lot of suppressed grief, bitterness, sadness which turns inwards on the body as necrotic changes

Tuberculinum			• Multitasking, hurry, restlessness lack of time, claustrophobia, as if in a tunnel, exhausted, suffocated, time is running out, panic as if death is close and time is running out
Bacillinum	SOMETHING INSIDE ME IS WRONG	• The desperation is nearing to Syphilis and death • There is poor hope • Time is running out, hectic efforts, hurried, restless, doing many things at one time since there is no time left • Exhaustion from this frenzy • Suffocation • Choking	• Feeling of collapse, exhaustion, collapse after having hurried quite a lot • Need to move out of narrow places, need to move out every time, tunnel, gasping, breathless, panting, tired form running fruitlessly • Picture like a failed Tuberculinum and similar to Diptherinum
Pertussinum			• Force, push, power, strength, suffocation due to a feeling of a wall • Needs great force to push this barrier or wall which is very strong like a wall, restlessness, panic, hectic, hurry, fatal condition and time is running out • Picture similar to Tuberculinum but the feeling of wall or obstruction is the key point
Diptherinum			• Exhausted, completely tired and collapsed • Sensation of membrane, layer in parts or sensation of a layer, which he has no strength to go through • He has lost all strength and he has made mistakes and is so much at fault that he will never be able to get up and go over that membrane or layer. • Gasping and panting and cannot breathe • Picture similar to Bacillinum • Wall like sensation is similar to • Pertussinum but the sensation is like a layer or curtain hence more soft than Pertussinum

Leprominum		• He is shunned by the society and feels treated as an outcast There is a self destruction. • Given up feeling, as if there is no way out	• Feels very ugly, disgusting, monster like, contagious, isolated and extremely hopeless, feels deformed and handicapped • Desire to hurt, bite, scratch one's own self
Variolinum		• Very close to death Suicidal because rectification will not help any further • Have been isolated, pushed out, abundant and exiled because others think they are so infectious, contagious that they will ruin the whole society	• Sudden collapse to fatal condition, if I survive I will be deformed and handicapped and ugly and disgusting • Deformed suddenly, isolated and shunned suddenly • Overnight becoming a beggar or loser
Syphilinum		• The feeling is beyond hope, there is no way out and death is inevitable • There is a lot of anger and a desire to destroy others as well as desire for self destruction due to this hopelessness • Perversions of all kinds	• Fatal, homicidal, suicidal, destructive, problem is fatal, putrefied, necrotic, deadly, no hope, no chances for recovery • In successful Syphilinum there is no room for making the slightest mistake as every little mistake will prove fatal • Perversions, overindulgence in every way

SOMETHING INSIDE ME IS WRONG

V. Successful and unsuccessful side of each miasm

Every miasm has a successful or an unsuccessful side but the basic pattern of the miasm is the same on either side. Both sides can be present in a person and these presentations may vary like being two sides of the same coin.

Miasm	Successful	Unsuccessful
Acute	Who has help and can come out of the situation	Collapse and cannot come out of the situation
Typhoid	Who has reached his point of safety, who is at a safety zone	An acute, sudden collapse, feeling unsafe
Malaria	Who manages to get attention by throwing a tantrum	Who feels victimized, harassed, and throwing a tantrum doesn't bring help
Ringworm	Trying	Giving up and failing
Psoric	Struggling with hope	Constantly finding one weakness after the other and tired of this struggle
Sycotic	Somebody who is covered up, he knows his faults and does nothing about it but cover them or hide them	Somebody who feels all his faults are exposed
Cancer	Control	Chaos
Tubercular	To do every activity, multitasking	Collapse and suffocated
Leprosy	Isolated but very famous, Rude, arrogant, insulting	Disgusted and shunned by the society
Syphilitic	Someone who has a high political career, manipulative	Somebody who is a terrorist, serial killer, psychopaths who go on rampage killing

14

 COMPARATIVE ANALYSIS OF NOSODES WITH IDENTICAL REMEDY GROUPS

I. Introduction

II. The Case

III. Remedy and Case Follow-up

IV. Understanding Sarcodes, Fungi and Bacteria

V. Comparison between Fungi, Nosode, Bacteria, Sarcode and Lac humanum

I. Introduction

There are other group of remedies that come very close to nosodes like Sarcodes, Bacteria and Fungi. Sarcodes are remedies made from healthy human tissue or discharges – like the hormones, glands etc. Although we can say that bacteria are a completely different kingdom, they come close to nosodes since they are the ones who cause diseases. Fungi are also a different kingdom by themselves (Monera) but they come close to nosode sensation since they have the common themes of invasion and disease which are shared by nosode remedies as well. Due to their parasitic nature, fungi cause several diseases to man. We also feel that Lac humanum comes very close to nosode remedies in its sensation. Some important bits of the case have been highlighted for easy understanding.

II. The Case

Let us now look at a case which has similar traits to nosodes but is different in many ways This is a case of a 13 years old girl, who came to us with the complaint of viral warts all over her palms, knees, and a few large ones on her forehead. She was also suffering from recurrent upper and lower track infections which sometimes caused episodes of breathlessness. During the episodes of breathlessness she would have to use the inhalation pump. But her main concern was the warts and so we started asking her about the warts. She kept insisting that they were symptomless but that the appearance bothered her. She started to weep almost instantaneously while talking about their appearance.

Given below are the most vital parts of the case and the conversation between us and the patient

P: I don't like it. It feels very odd. (weeping)

D: You are crying, means it's troubling you. What do you feel?

P: Why this has happened to me only? None of my friends have it, then why only me? Nothing else.

D: Tell about this – "None of my friends have it, then why only me?"

P: My sister also had this but they went away and one of my friends had got corns but they also went then why my disease is not going?

D: And how does it feel?

P: Weird, I mean it feels odd. Everyone gets fever but this, only few people get.

D: How does it feel – "only few people get it?"

P: My friends know that I have warts but they don't react, so it's good with them but still it **feels very odd.** Nothing else.

D: Describe this –"it feels odd" – elaborate it further. What is the experience that it feels odd?

P: Means other people have a very supple skin and mine is like this. Only in few fingers. **Weird.**

D: So how does this weird feel?

P: I mean it's jutting out. **And its colour is also different. As if some kind of bad thing has come in or a fungus is growing on the skin.**

D: Yes.

P: Nothing more.

D: See what you describe, is very good. This is what we need to know. Just elaborate it a bit more – "feels like a fungus growing."

P: I mean kind of **different from all the other people.** And then I don't usually get pimples and all but this all is very different.

D: How does it feel – growing like a fungus, different?

P: No, usually it gets rubbed so it gives that feeling. Means like when you touch here, it feels natural but this is not that natural. Nothing much.

D: So how does it feel, it is not natural?

P: Means everyone doesn't get this, so it feels as if...**that it's very odd**.

D: So how does it feel - it's odd, everyone doesn't get it, it's different from other people.

P: Everyone's skin is smooth, not rough, if so then it's only on soles and that is because of thorns going into their legs, sometimes, but there is no possibility of thorns going into the hands. So it becomes clear.

Until now she has mentioned weird, odd, different so many times. Her main concern is that these warts set her apart and make her different and weird than the rest. This is very similar to nosode language that you have seen in the book so far. In fact at this stage we too were thinking that she could probably need some kind of a nosode. We now had to see if this feeling of disease and different was a global phenomenon and present in every aspect of the personality or was it leading to something different. Though she mentions that the warts look like fungus growing on her palm at this level itself I know that the feeling I am different because things grow on me is not the feeling of the fungi kingdom. The fungus feeling is that something is growing slowly, spreading and encroaching into it. Here the feeling and the stress is more on being different and diseased from within - more like a nosode.

D: Describe this little bit more it's like a fungus growing, it's little different.

P: It's a hard fungus growing. I mean fungus is usually soft and all; this is very hard and does not match with the skin.

D: Go on, you are doing extremely well.

P: I don't like it.

D: Yes. Because tell me more what are the things you don't like about it. You are doing extremely well. You said it's a hard fungus, growing, doesn't match with the rest or doesn't match with the skin. Slightly elaborate on it.

P: Something new because I have never suffered from something like this. So….

D: It's something new, it's something different. How does it feel to have something new, something different?

P: As if something bad is there, doesn't feel good and if you touch it you know it.

D: See your feeling is that it's different, right? It's novel, right? Suppose if we have something like this – that is new, different, like fungus, hard… hmm.

P: **You feel kind of like germ (HG), something dirty, pus you know something like that.** (weeping)

D: You feel like a germ… Describe this to me – "you feel like a germ, like a dirty person", you leave the warts.

P: I always clean myself and keep myself very clean. But …how ever much I take care, it starts growing only, it does not stop.

D: Doesn't stop. Now just describe "feel like a germ, like a dirty person"

P: I mean… look insects have those spots and they have kind of hard skin so it feels like them.

D: No, I didn't get this?

P: **Insects have very not very smooth skin. It is very crooked and I mean, very hard. So it feels bit odd.**

D: Feels like the insect's skin?

P: Yes (nod).

D: Describe that – "feels like the insect's skin"
– it feels like a germ, it feels like an insect, it feels like a dirty person."

P: I feel very odd.

D: Ok, let me put it differently – "how does it feel to feel like a germ or like a…."

P: It feels very bad.

D: I understood everything about the warts. Now leave the warts aside, I think you don't like to feel like a dirty person or like a germ or like a different person or insect that is hard. Am I right? So if you were to feel or if you were to be this germ or dirty or insect or hard skin or fungus or whatever that you are saying. How would it feel to feel like this or to be like this?

P: Dirty, again that's what is coming to me. It feels very odd.

D: How does it feel to be dirty, to be odd.

P: Because of something different from other people.

D: So what is the experience in that – "that we are different from others?"

P: Because of these warts.

D: Completely agreed. Because of these warts, you are different from other people. Correct?

P: Different, I am different from other people because I don't like to…. I mean go on laughing and laughing or jesting all the time. I am very…. I am a book worm, I keep reading books and I enjoy with a small company of friends, I don't have a very big group and I am not a very interactive with other people. I don't like people teasing me because of my spectacles or anything else.

D: "I don't like people teasing me."

P: Teasing for fun is good but I mean I feel very hurt. I know that it's a joke but still it feels very hurt.

D: Describe that – "people teasing you makes you feel hurt."

P: Weird, dirty

D: Describe this – Weird, dirty

P: Just because they don't have it, they can't tease others, because I have this hereditary problem so it's my lookout whether… what I must do, so they have got no right to tease me.

D: How does it feel to you – to be teased?

P: I don't tease people so when somebody teases me I don't like it, I just don't like it.

D: Describe this. When we are weird and dirty then how does it feel?

P: Feel bad. I mean I know I am not dirty but if others pinpoint then it feels bad.

So again and again it comes back to feeling weird and different and dirty, we asked her things a bit differently to see if anything else would come up.

D: Just leave everything aside for a moment. I am giving you some words, you tell me when the words come, what is the feeling the words generate in you. So, tell me the feeling when you say – "dirty"

P: **Garbage.**

D: So say garbage.

P: **All dirt lying around**. A **mess.**

D: What's this experience – 'dirt, garbage, mess, dirty?'

P: Something **different from the surroundings**.

D: Just elaborate more, just stay with this feeling. – 'Something different from the surrounding.'

P: Something different from what the other people are.

D: Very good. Just stay with this feeling, different than what the other people are. What's the experience to be different than what the other people are?

P: **Weird.**

D: What's the experience to be weird?

P: I can't explain it properly. Something out of the box.

D: Keep telling this experience –'Something out of the box.'

P: Something different from other people.

D: Describe this – 'different from other people.'

P: Something different from the other people in a bad way.

D: Describe the experience – 'different from other people in a bad way.'

P: When somebody teases you, it's actually, what… they are pointing out some of your minor mistakes or something and making a mountain out of a mole hill. So it's bad.

D: Describe this – 'somebody pointing out your mistakes.'

P: I mean some mistakes happen by themselves and we don't do it and still we get blamed. So… doesn't feel good.

D: Describe this – "if somebody blames" you said – "some mistakes happen and somebody blames for something you have not done and it doesn't feel good."

P: You feel like a culprit even though you haven't done anything.

D: Describe that feeling – 'culprit even though you haven't done anything.'

P: That shows that the other person does not like you.

D: So what's this experience? Describe this – 'the other person does not like you.'

P: It feels like I am not good.

D: 'I am not good' - Please describe this.

P: It's like I have done something real bad to hurt that person. Something like that. Even though I have not done anything personally, I may have been done something abstract or something like that but still if the person is hurt, so you don't feel very good.

D: So this is…I have done something really bad to hurt the other person.

P: I try to be better.

D: Ok.

P: Try to be better but still they are hurt then I tell her, "please, please forgive me, if I have done something wrong."

D: So describe this – 'I am not good and I have hurt the other person' what's this experience?

P: Not a nice one. **As if you are isolated from other people. (HG as if shooing away)**

D: Show me what did you do?

P: You feel isolated from other people.

D: Describe this feeling – 'you are isolated from other people.'

P: You feel lonely and... When a person doesn't talk to you (HG), you will naturally feel that he is trying to avoid you and all that.

D: What is this (HG) you are doing? Describe that. Do it again. This (HG). Just do it and see what comes to you when you are doing it.

P: I feel angry (HG) I don't know little. But those incidents I keep remembering.

D: You keep remembering them? You are isolated from the rest and you are lonely. So what if you are isolated.

P: It is as if they don't care about you.

At this point now we tried to take a completely new direction in the case. We asked her about her dreams. This would be a good way to enter into her subconscious. This would also be a good way to see if there is anything else that is coming in the case apart from the different, isolated and dirty feeling.

D: Can you tell me some of your dreams?

P: I want to be successful in life.

Sometimes patients start to tell us about their aspirations and their ambitions instead of their subconscious dreams when asleep. But we do not correct patients; we let them speak about whatever they want.

D: Describe that.

P: I don't want to do some ordinary job or anything. But be something different from other people in a good way.

D: Tell me more about that. **Different in a good way.**

P: I want to see the world and do something good for the world. Something that can help mankind.

D: Describe that– 'I want to do something good for the world. Something that may help mankind.'

P: I want to... I mean... this all terrorism and all is happening everywhere, so I want to like... want to contribute to stop it in small way but if it's possible, small way but I want to make a difference, little difference. Not an ordinary, middle class life but I mean…

D: How do you feel – 'to make a difference.'

P: I will feel good.

D: Describe that a little bit.

P: I mean it will. I guess show mankind to hope again.

D: Show mankind?

P: **To hope everyone is losing hope** and everyone is thinking that our end will be near and all that, so it's not good. So we have to be optimistic, search... and try to find happiness even in hard times.

D: Describe this a little bit.

P: In terms of relations between people. You stop this caste system… try to at least stop all this non-sense that is happening in the name of religion. **People are killing each other. I mean that will lead to their own destruction.**

D: Describe that – 'it will lead to their own destruction.'

P: What are they getting from killing other people? Getting nothing, I mean the happiness is short lived no. What happiness do you get from killing other people, **it's inhuman.**

D: So how will you feel to make this difference and to help and to..?

P: I will feel very good.

D: Describe good.

P: I will feel that my life is a …. Is it a waste? Just thinking… I am not only thinking about myself, I am also thinking about other people, so that will give me a better feeling.

D: What feeling it will give you?

P: That I am helping others.

D: What's that experience?

P: It will be a nice experience.

D: Describe this…. what's the experience to be different, to do something, to show hope?

P: To help mankind progress and me progressing it.

D: Let's put it like this, you said "I don't want to be a simple middle class person" because what is the experience to be just a simple and middle class person?

P: I mean... …millions of people are living a plain life; I don't want to live the same life.

D: What's the experience to just live the same life? What would be the experience? Because if you just live a middle class life?

P: I will be disappointed in myself.

204

D: Why? Describe that. What will it make you feel?
P: Because I won't realize my purpose in life if I lead a very simple… I mean… I want to live a simple life but not extravagant or anything but… **not an ordinary. It should be different.**

This is interesting. On one hand at the level of the physical complaint she does not want to be different but at the same time on the level of emotional development she wants to be different. Our task was to find out how do these two come together in one person. Not wanting to be different and isolated in one way and wanting to different and special in another way. At the same time it was also important to understand what would being different make her feel. What was the sensation underneath being different? Was it a sensation of achievement like a mineral, superior in comparison like an animal or what?

D: Describe this 'something different.'
P: Make me feel better.
D: How would that make you feel about yourself.
P: I will feel proud of myself. I will feel happy that I am a help to other people.
D: Where will it place you, what will it make you feel happy, proud of yourself, better than other people, to help other people, sorry.
P: At least I will feel proud that I have tried to do something for… good for the people.
D: What is the need to do something good for people?
P: In today's world everyone thinks only about themselves, not about other people. Even there are … bad means like cheating and all for earning money and all that. I don't want to be like that. I mean depriving other people of their happiness. So I don't want to do that, stop the others from people doing like this.
D: So what's the experience when people are doing this?
P: It feels very bad. I mean… **I never thought that human kind could be so… mean… animals…** behaving like animals, killing each other and depriving others of their happiness, for their own greed.
D: What's the experience to be like that, just like animal, depriving others?
P: I guess I don't do that but I wouldn't feel good if I were in their place. My conscience would have hurt me. Conscience may bite me.
D: What would it have made you feel?
P: Ashamed of myself.
D: Describe that – 'ashamed of myself.'

P: I mean I don't have the right to seize other people's happiness. Everyone has got their own shade of happiness and they should enjoy as much they have and not be greedy.

D: I don't understand these feelings about mankind. I want to know exactly what is your feeling about all this and what do you want to do. I want to know....

P: I want to change. I want to make a better world. Where there is sadness I want happiness and I mean… no terrorism and all that. But all people will be happy.

D: You want to make a world like that?

P: Yaa.

D: So what would be the experience – all people are happy?

P: It will make me happy as well.

D: How will it help you to make people better and to make the world happy? What will you benefit out of it? What will you gain out of it…?

P: It will… It will make my mind peaceful and happy.

D: Hmm.

P: By cheating people of their happiness and...

D: Because what will make you feel happy that what have you done? What have you done?

P: I have done something good,

D: What is the need to do good?

P: For other people… because if someone would do something good for me then I will feel happy as well as that person will also feel happy that he has done something good for me. So like that.

D: What will be your experience to do something good?

P: It will make me proud of myself. Then I am not… I am not cheating other people.

D: Cheating?

P: Some people, like politicians who go to villagers, they give them a day's meal and ask for votes so they are making profit for themselves but in this those villagers are also suffering. They think that we have done something we have got food but what do they know about that person? So I will… I don't want to do something like that.

So she does not want to be different like a mineral where her achievements and her completeness matters to her the most. But she also does not want to be different like an animal. In fact she says people all over are behaving like animals and I don't want that. She does not want to be an animal. Her feeling of being different is not wanting to be superior but rising

*above all bad, inhuman and animal like qualities. This is something we have
not heard before. What is this quality?*

D: You said – they were behaving like animals, right? Describe that.
P: **Killing our own... own race is like cannibalistic... so it's not good.**
D: How does it feel?
P: Those people don't understand that if they had been... they had been
killed by other people how would they feel? That they don't understand and
they are just selfish and do everything bad in the name of God.
D: When these people do this, what do you think, what's the experience of it?
P: I feel ashamed that someone of my own race is doing something so bad.
Hurting... I mean...
P: We should all live in good harmony. Harmony and respect other people's
feelings.
D: Hmm. More. What would be the experience to live like this or to be like
this?
P: **It will be a unique experience. Something new,** something good for the
people too.
D: How will you feel when you will be able to do that?
P: I will feel happy.
D: Happy that... what... finally what do you want to achieve? What would
you...
P: Eternal peace.
D: Sorry I didn't get that word, what it means?
P: Eternal Peace.
D: What is that?
P: Means, don't want to be disturbed. Want to be happy that I have done
something good for the mankind.
D: Eternal peace
P: and Internal Peace.
D: Describe that – 'internal peace'
P: Peace of mind that is internal peace.

III. The Remedy & Follow-up

**This is not the essence of an animal but a super-animal. We thought this
could be the source talking to me. It is not a nosode, not an animal. It's a
super animal-Human. This could be Lac humanum talking at source
level.**

207

Let us look at Lac humanum or man in an objective way. What makes man different from the rest of the animals?

Though man started as an animal he now considers himself as the king of the land.
As an animal he is weak to defend himself by virtue of strength and yet by virtue of intelligence he is the most powerful animal on earth.

He is always trying to improve himself, to progress and go further. In the process he has laid rules for himself. He has made laws. He must obey them and yet he is the only one who breaks them. Other animals obey the laws of nature but man makes his own and breaks them too.

Man claims that he is the protector of this earth and the guardian of all the flora and fauna on this planet yet he is the one who misuses his position the most. He made religion, law and yet he is the one who is the most unlawful and violent and destructive. No other animal digs out earth in quantities like man does or explodes mountains for gems, minerals. No other animal makes bombs and weapons of mass destruction to protect its territory.
Other animals behave as nature wants them to. Man thinks he knows better and makes his own rules. He causes maximum destruction to appease his ambition. He who considers himself the most sane and intelligent animal, the most evolved one creates the most havoc and destroys nature's balance. And then he tries to correct himself and his actions all the time.

He is the only one who sees his emotions of anger, rage, hatred, revenge, jealousy and his actions of killing, cheating, cannibalism as bad and inhuman. All of these emotions are present in animals too. But Man feels he does not need them and must rise above them.
Hence remedies from animal kingdom do not feel guilty to be jealous or revengeful. They feel they have been victimized and hence they have the right to feel these emotions. But Lac humanum being a human feels jealous like animals and at the same time he feels he must not feel it, he must get rid of it or rise above it.

Nature is no longer in control of these instinctive emotions in man –he is himself in control of these emotions and on the other hand he wants to get rid of these negative qualities in him.
He is the only creature who wants to overthrow nature –who feels he has the right to destroy, build or save nature.

His negative feelings are way out of balance and so is his need to become positive, spiritual, peaceful etc.

The feeling in Lac humanum therefore is one of
    Immense guilt, remorse, awareness of man's negativities and a
★ **burning desire to come out of these negativities.**
    An immense desire to break this polarity of negative and positive or
★ **to break this circle of life and death or to become self - balanced so that nature is not needed for this balance anymore.**

This shows the eternal conflict of humanity - the good and the bad side. The polarity of the human core is thus - I have within me the evil and I must rise above this evil.
I have within me destructive power - I have to bring eternal peace.
The one person who has brought harm to this planet is man and yet he is constantly trying to help the earth.

Let us look at man's concept of diseases.
He is the only animal who wants to correct, prevent and overpower disease.
He is the only one who thinks - 'disease is my own doing and the power to correct it lies within me.'

Also as we advance more and more, infections are getting lesser and iatrogenic diseases and idiopathic and autoimmune diseases are more on the rise. The use of several chemicals and toxic elements in our day-to-day life has caused an increase in malignancies affecting humans. Stress is another important cause of diseases today. There is more and more awareness in humans that we are responsible for our own illnesses and hence we feel the burden of our disease. The feeling of guilt and burden also causes a feeling of isolation. Another human nature is to feel dirty about one's excretions, discharges, odours.

These emotions are similar to that of a nosode as well but what makes Lac human different from a nosode is this need to rise above negativities – not just return to normalcy but rise above the whole concept of disease and health, rise above all the bad things and emotions and to bring to oneself and to this earth eternal peace.
You could say while nosode is a particular phenomenon Lac Humanum is a grand phenomenon.

Like the nosode Lac humanum feels he is different, isolated, dirty, abnormal, different from the rest but the nosode thinks that by returning to health or normalcy his problem will be taken care of. Whereas, Lac humanum sees this problem not just at the tissue level - he does not want to just get rid of the disease but he wants humanity and mankind to be rid of these emotions, these negativities that are plaguing and decaying our times. He feels the responsibility of not only the self but of the whole universe. It is up to him to restore the planet to peace and harmony to rise above health and disease. With this responsibility on his head, he is bound to feel different, guilty and isolated from the rest.

Let us go back to the case now. The best way to know more about any remedy is to learn it from the patient. We then asked the patient to doodle or draw anything she wanted.

D: Just close your eyes and then open them and hold your pen…. just do whatever you want to do on the paper. Don't think. Just feel that peace, that you have done something for the mankind, you are feeling it, you have achieved it, you have got it, you have done what you wanted to, those internal feelings, just with those feelings put the pen to the paper.

D: What was that?

P: It's a **flower.**

D: Now look at this flower and don't think about anything of the past. What's the experience?

P: **Flowers make all people happy** by their beautiful colours fragrance and it makes me feel happy and it's so little and yet it makes… it makes us feel… I mean we experience nature's beauty and its power.

D: Come again, come again.

P: Nature's beauty and its power. It expresses through its little petals, chlorophyll colour. That's why I like them very much.

D: You said something about nature's beauty.

P: Nature's beauty and the power of it that it's so huge and yet it created something so delicate and yet it can be so devastating, if we anger it, like tsunami, I mean…… it is all a part of nature and…..

D: And…

P: We sometimes make nature angry by causing pollution and all and yet in spite of all that it gives us happiness through these little flowers and little birds and all. It……..beautiful songs birds, butterflies fluttering around you, the sun-set, the moon, the hills and yet we are hurting it, so I guess including ourselves we should take care of the nature which has created us as well as protecting us through all means, even though we are hurting it.

Since her name was something unusual, I asked her casually about the meaning of the name. She said that she liked it a lot because it was a very peculiar name and different from the rest.

D: What about it you like?
P: It is a sweet thing and different from other people. I like to be different and unique.

This is also the conflict in Lac humanum. To be different from the rest on one side and yet to fear being lonely if one is different.

Follow up

We started off with Lac humanum 200C, as that was the potency available with us and in a month's time we switched to 1M. After the two doses she was better in every way; her chest cleared completely, there was a significant change in her breathlessness and the tendency for the upper respiratory tract infection has also reduced. There was a marked change in her attitude and her outlook towards life as well. The feeling that mankind is terrible reduced. Her desire to do something good for society did not change or reduce. But she now she wanted to do something out of choice and not because of the strong pessimistic feeling for the human race.

However the warts didn't clear up with Lac humanum 1M, they kept disappearing and reappearing again, so we decided to change the prescription and give her Lac humanum 30C once a day for 7 days since she was so much better in every other plane but the physical particulars of the warts remained. This did the trick and all her warts felt off in a week's time.

The miasm of Lac Humanum

The miasm of Lac humanum is Ringworm. This is because Lac humanum has the desire to try and overcome his negative feelings constantly, however every once in a while he gives in and succumbs to the negative feelings which are part of him as his normal animal instincts. This alternation between trying to overcome all negativities and giving up intermittently is of the Ringworm quality. One could argue that the dirty, isolated feelings make it look similar to the Leprosy miasm, but in Lac humanum the feelings of being isolated or dirty or different are part of the sensation and the person is constantly trying to overcome these feelings, with the hope that someday mankind will be a

211

better race.

IV. Understanding Sarcodes, Fungi and Bacteria
A quick note on sarcodes to differentiate them from nosodes.
A sarcode is made from healthy tissue, discharges or hormones of the body .
The main difference between a nosode and a sarcode is that while the nosode
is from an unhealthy source a sarcode is from a healthy source.
A sarcode performs more or less the same function in every species.

E.g.: Adrenalin in every animal has the same function and effects.
Testosterone in every animal performs the same function. Thyroid gland in
every animal performs the same function.

**The main issue with a patient needing a sarcode is that they see the world
or their reality only in the light of that one phenomenon or function.
Their life is governed by this one function.** Everything for them is either
overwhelming stress, or rush or growth or fight or flight response. So
everything is one function or another. The issue here is not about achieving
something by performing a function or proving one's superiority by
performing the function but merely keeping on performing in a certain way
and living that way. Like they have only **one goal or one motto** that regulates
or rules their lives. Everything is centred around that one kind of response or
reaction or motive in life.**There is no battle with anybody outside of you as
you see in the animal kingdom. The situation is here and now -- this is
how I need to feel, act and react.** It is like a **pure sensation** - or **pure
energy -** the situation brings no feelings, or not much description or images
but pure energy which **you cannot compare to an image like tied or caught
or bound or light or buoyant .**

It s more like
* **whoosh**

* **vow, go for it**

* **move**

* **act**

* **body is getting ready**

212

* **gear up**

* **react or act quick**

* **quick**

It's all about an action or an act or the energy behind the action

As any sarcode is from a tissue or gland or secretion, it is not the whole but a part of a whole. It is basically a chemical – an amine or a protein or tissue which has life because it is part of the whole and it gives its contribution or feels some bits of the whole and acts accordingly. The whole (individual animal) feels a combination of many things but the sarcode only feels one section of that whole as it does only one or some functions for that whole organism and for every organism that it is a part of. It is goal or function or action oriented.

The other thing that comes in picture here is the theme of **Regulation** or control. Hormones are controlled by certain other hormones and they in turn regulate or control the functioning of certain glands, tissues etc.

* **Am I in control of my function?**
* **Am I performing the function very well?**

Here it feels like a **nosode** – but the nosode feeling is - **I am diseased and weak and can be attacked like in a nosode.**
In a sarcode -- the feeling is I have to work or function at my level best.
E.g.: In this situation or set of events this is expected out of me or **this is how my system responds**. Is my **system responding or failing or acting or reacting?** It's like **a computer system in function.**

A short example of a case of Adrenalin

Here the main themes are rush, danger, stress since Adrenaline is a hormone released at times of fright and flight or stressful situations.
A patient who did well on this remedy in our clinic had been given some tubercular remedies in the past. He would often talk so hurriedly that it was impossible to understand what he said. He was always in a panic stricken state and moving restlessly in the clinic every time he visited us. One day we reassessed the case and he said that everything in his life, every situation was a do or die situation. He knew he should have the capacity and the know how

213

to face these times. Every situation gave him a thrill or a high or a feeling as if he was facing death. He said my body must always be alert and on guard to be able to handle these situations. At this point we thought of giving him the sarcode adrenaline because his whole life was about facing stressful life and death situations and wanting the ability to handle such situations. He mentioned that he liked to think of every situation as an adventure. He dreamt that his boat is caught in a whirlpool in the sea or that he is in a jungle and is being attacked by a big bear or that he is being followed by a snake and is trying to run or escape or figure out what must be done in such a situation. In this case the attack by the snake or bear or the drowning in the river were of no significance. But the importance was of the thrill behind a situation, the whoosh and the fight or flight response behind the attack.

Fungi

The fungi group have the main characteristic of growing and spreading gradually and insidiously over or within the host. Hence in the fungi group the main sensation is that of being encroached, invaded by something or somebody else. The nosode on the other hand has the feeling of being abnormal from within. The nosode stresses on his own weakness and need to correct it while the fungus stresses on invasion and encroachment from the outside by another organism (animal like).

Bacteria

We are now beginning to explore some remedies of this group as well. Some of the cases we have of this group talk about being attacked. Here too like the fungus there is an invasion but it is not a slow insidious invasion. It is an attack where someone attacks and breaks your boundaries and comes within your wall. Since most bacteria attack and invade the cell and dissolve its nucleus the feeling in bacteria is that of being attacked by a stronger one (animal like). Wall or barriers are broken and the enemy comes in and destroys and dissolves everything within to change one completely.
The nosode is a diseased tissue affected by the bacteria or any other organism and hence the nosode stresses on one's own weakness and the bacteria stresses on the mechanism of the attack (animal like).
The difference between fungus and bacteria is that in the fungus it is always slow and insidious and then becomes deadly while in the bacteria it is a sensation of attack from the very beginning.

V. Comparison between Fungi, Nosode, Bacteria, Sarcode and Lac humanum

	FUNGI	NOSODE	BACTERIA	SARCODE	LAC HUMANUM
Main sensation	• Invasion	• Abnormal	• Me vs. you • Attack and defence	• Performing the function • Experiencing situations purely as an energy not emotion purely • Overwhelming stress, or rush or growth or fight or flight response	• Conflict between animal instincts and spirituality • Rising above all negativity and animal instincts
Kingdom and source	• Fungi	• Diseased animal or plant kingdom	• Monera	• Animal tissue or hormone	• Animal or super animal
Main sensations words	• Encroachment and invasion	• Weak, • Diseased, • Abnormal	• Fight between invader and victim	• A situation where how you function is of utmost importance	• Rising above negativities. • Saviour • Humanity • Human race • Spiritualism • Conflicts
Themes	• Encroaching to take away space • Decay • Destroy • Smell • Disgust • Necrose • Decompose grow, spread and take over • Kill	• I am weak, incapable, wrong, at fault, system is deranged • How can I try to overcome my weakness so that I am just as normal and at par with the others	• One invades or attacks the other and the stronger one survives and overpowers or invades the weaker one	• Control, • Regulation, • Balance must be maintained so that the right response is got • Energetic, functional or dynamic description of the situation	• The split between the right and wrong, power and powerless, awareness and desires, greed and generosity, destruction and creation, disease and health, life and death, power and spirituality

	FUNGI	NOSODE	BACTERIA	SARCODE	LAC HUMANUM
Themes	• Invasion, • Suffocation, • Spread, ever growing • Fermenting eating from within	• Main focus of symptoms and feeling of inner wrong or faults and fallacies and weaknesses	• Attack at the cellular level-quite like the animal kingdom • Mention of words like weak and abnormal and disease like nosodes but main focus on the attack • Mechanism of the pathogen	• Description of the entire function of the hormone • Excitement • Control	• Focus mainly on the entire race of mankind, • Global effects • Global destruction • Global warming, etc

COMMON WORDS AND
THEMES OF NOSODES

I.   Common Nosode Words

II. Common Words & Themes of Individual
     Nosode remedies

I. Common Nosode Words

Weak

Abnormal

Diseased

Mistake

Error

Nutrition

Deficient

Incorrect

Faulty

Defective

Broken

Irreparable

Different

Singled out

Shunned

Disgusting

Contagious

Infectious

Disharmony

Unfit

Victimised

Attacked because I am weak

Hypersensitive

Hyper reactive

Why me?

Tumour

Decay

Rotten

Amputation

Eroded

Fibroses

Repair

Correct

Autocorrect

Change

Rectification

Normal

Strong

Comparison

Others are strong

Want to be like the rest

Healthy

Fit

Harmony of the body function

II. Common Words & Themes of Individual Nosode remedies

⋆ Typhoidinum
Quick
Impulse
Hurry
Intense
Help
Childish
Impatient
Hopeful
Quick result
Instant relief
Demanding

⋆ Psorinum
Struggle
Constant
Itch
Irritating
Normal and healthy
Continuous
Hypochondriac
Anxious

⋆ Ringworm
Trial
Giving up
Alternately try and give up
Start impulsively and then give up
Nothing works
Optimistic periodically
Lazy
Inconsistent
Irresolute

⋆ Malaria Nosode
Nagging
Why me
Singled out
Tormented by the disease
Nothing can be done so let it be
Periodicity
Comes up time and again
Harassed
Complaining
Persecuted
Troubled

⋆ Medorrhinum
Anxiety
Anticipation
Hiding
Weak and hiding the weakness
Cover it up
The complaint is where it is
Fear of being exposed of his weakness

★ Carcinosinum

Total control

Constant efforts

Tremendous superhuman control and effort

No fear

Never give up

If one gives up → total chaos

Haphazard

Tumour

Out of control

I have some trigger cells within that must be controlled or checked

If control is lost then chaos and disease will take over and it will be end of me

Within me is a chaos and calamity waiting to happen and I am making superhuman efforts to control this total breakdown

★ Tuberculinum

Narrow	Time is running out
Suffocated	Breathless
Tunnel	Burst out
Dark	Break away
Closing in	
No way out	
Trapped	
Enclosed	
Escape and breathe	
No time at all	
On all cylinders	
Hectic	
Hurry	
Desperate	
Mulitasking	
Exhausted	
Drained	
Collapsed	
No reserves	

⋆ Leprominum

Monstrous, hideous, ugly
Contagious
Shunned
Singled out and thrown out
Stinking
Decayed
Amputated
Disfigured
Rotten
Maggots
Insulting to others
Isolated
Given up
Beggar
Rags
Love white and spotless since everything else can be dirty

⋆ Syphilinum

Explosion
Destruction
Body is at the brink of death
Nothing left
Want to kill, destroy one's own body
No hope
Murder
Destructive anger

Beyond The Horizon

As a child when he would go to the shore
He would wonder more than often
What was beyond that orange hue?
Where the water met the sun

Said his father to the child
That's the horizon my son
But you can't reach it nor can you go beyond it
Cause the more nearer you go, the more farther moves the horizon

From that day on
He'd go to the shore and dream
Of reaching the horizon and beyond it
To a land all meant only for him

In his childhood this dreamland was full of joys
Lots of fun, happiness and toys
In his youth it had fame in store for him
Beauty & love enhanced the wilderness of his dreams

Over the passing years, he grew older
Less of a dreamer and more of a doer
Yet his dream was one thing that never ceased
He thought of his dreamland whenever he pleased

And as an old man
The sight of the shore brought back all those
dreams and fantasies
Of his mystical land never seen by anyone
And when he died on his grave was engraved
This man has now begun his voyage
To the land beyond the horizon.

1993

By Bhawisha Joshi

16

THE POLARITY IN IMPONDERABLES

I.   Introduction

II. Summary

I. Introduction

We have categorized two types of remedies in the Imponderable group. One group is remedies made from non-matter, i.e. energy and the other is remedies made from the energy or rays from magnanimous matter like stars. If we look at energy by itself, it can be converted to matter and matter can be converted to energy but energy can be experienced only in the presence of matter.

This is true of our homoeopathic remedies as well. As the material substance in remedies gets lesser and lesser by potentisation more and more energy is liberated, the effect of which is only recognised by the human (matter) using it.

The Big Bang theory proposes that energy condensed into matter and that's how the universe came into existence. Hydrogen atoms and Helium nuclei were the first forms of matter to be formed during this energy condensation.

If we were to consider the dual nature of things the basic duality or polarity of imponderables is that of:

Energy vs. Matter and Materialism vs. Dynamism
In our earlier book and even in the earlier chapters in this book we have put down this duality in nature in the form of 'I' and 'U'. I is the basic individuality of anything and 'U' is everything else that is not 'I'.

In terms of the **'I'** and **'U' in an imponderable** this could be seen as -
* 'I' influence 'U'
* 'I' am noticed by 'U' / 'I' am unseen by 'U'
* 'I' transform into 'U'
* 'I' am much more than 'U'
* 'I' do or do not want to change to 'U'
* 'I' am energy and dynamism and when 'I' change to 'U', 'I' become heavy, lifeless, matter

II. Summary

It is very exciting to explore this kingdom. We want to start with a case which shows you clearly the deep sensation or polarity of energy and matter. The case is in detail so that you can appreciate the derivation of the polarity and the way in which an imponderable kingdom differs from other kingdoms. We intend to take you through the complete journey to the source via these

Imponderable cases.

Before we begin, I thank the patient for allowing me to share this case.

17

 IMPONDERABLE CASE 1: SOL

I. Case Introduction

II. The Case

III. Remedy and Case Follow-up

IV. What are Imponderables?

V. The Formation of the Sun

I. Case Introduction

He is a 54 year old man who came to us with complaints of migraine. We started by asking him about his complaints.

II. The Case

P: I will start with my teeth, previous spring I had a problem with my teeth. In technical terms it was the nerve dying and it was very painful. It was an abscess above the root of the tooth. Sometimes there is a problem on my right side, the right arm, the right leg, so it's the entire right side. My dentist did a root canal filling, but it wasn't successful. Finally I had to take the tooth out. A year later I had the same thing happen on the left-hand side. Again the nerve was dying and it was very painful. One thing is that I don't like having anaesthetics. I like to feel what's happening inside? But on the left-hand side this time I let her use the anaesthetic. On the right-hand side I didn't use it. So that's been done now and that work is complete. So that's the dentistry part of it. I still have the neuralgic pain however. It comes down and it goes right down to the right side of my foot. To me it's sort of a mystery and I can make all sorts of conjectures at my end. That's not an issue, what's crucial about this quadrant is my experience of the world but that's my speculation not yours.

This was just the first paragraph of the case. He had started to speak about his complaint. He spoke about his tooth ache, the root canal and the filling. It was interesting to know that he did one part of the root canal filling without anaesthesia.

He already knew that we don't need emotions, delusions and facts but we need his experience and his sensation. There are so many things that have come up in the case just in the first paragraph.

We just asked him to describe more about the pain, the discomfort that he had with the tooth. In cases where the patient can open up and talk a lot of things, we can get lost and lose sight of the case. So to make things easy, to take the case step by step, we asked him to talk more about the complaints.

D: Tell me more about your pain.

P: Yes. I had great difficulty locating which tooth was sore. I couldn't be sure because I noticed sometimes it was the bottom, sometimes it was the top.

Sometimes it was more of just a sinus pain. Sometimes it was more of a head pain. It's a rather dull pain but in quite a small location there and my arm is like there is slight heaviness and sometimes I am tired. I feel it is hard to be dexterous, to pick up things with precision. It's easy to fumble with things. So the pain is quite acute and down the leg. Sometimes I get pain in my heel as I have been walking a lot but I couldn't say that the intensity is the same.

So the pain from the root canal went to his sinuses. From there it went to his head and then the arm and finally the heel. We could see the same pain getting generalised.

D: Describe this a little bit more - the character of the pain. What is your experience? What are you talking about when you say that there is pain anywhere, everywhere?

P: As far as the tooth is concerned it's sort of a continuous pain. Normally it pains like one has in a normal everyday life and also I have hurt myself a lot. My hands are quite warm because I do most of the things with my hands all the time. Inevitably my hands get grazed and they have scratches in the garden, a jab from a thorn or whatever. So those kinds of pains are very transitory and I have awareness there. Maybe it's a prick sensation but I think or there is a sharp pain which comes, which dulls, which fades off. But I think this dull one stays for very long time.

D: So that's about the continuity of the pain. Can you describe the character?

P: I have difficulty with the term character there because I think character has to do with personalities of people but if you want to say to me what is the character of the pain then what I can say about the pain is for some reason you are not able to explain. Maybe something is nagging you like thap, thap, thap, thap. If the pain is personified that's the character I would give it. It's like someone who wants you do something that you don't want to do. Like you are a small child and someone is getting you to do what they want to do; like you request small children to do.

'Character has to do with personalities of people.' This shows the awareness of this individual. It shows how sensitive he is and how deeply he thinks about things and brings them out. He immediately connects the character of the pain to a childhood experience or to a child as if, the child has been forced to do something that he does not want to do. Here

231

we see a direct jump from the complaint level, the fact level, to the level of delusion when he uses the words - as if. Now we just ask him to describe this because it has come in direct connection with the pain.

D: Describe the experience of this child. What does this child go through when he is made to do something that he does not want to do? This *thap, thap, thap,* that is happening to this child. What is his experience?

This will take us to this delusion which will get clearer and then finally to the sensation. So we asked him to describe that and if we have to elaborate on the question, we say - just describe this child.

P: No, I think the sort of the thing I wouldn't want my children to do. Normally as a child you are living in your own world and you are engaging. It's as if you are in your inner world as a child and that's where I like to be - in my place. So in a way you don't want to be drawn from your inner world and someone else is requesting you to go there. That's how I feel that I don't want to be drawn from this inner world.

D: Can you describe this?

P: I guess giving character to the pain and trying to understand what it is saying. It seems to be saying – "Come out of your inner world" but I don't want to. I am quite happy doing my own thing. I don't think I can describe anymore. This is my own inner world. I don't want to come out of it.

This was interesting – 'Come out of your inner world but I don't want to.' What is his experience when he is asked to come out?

D: Can you describe this more - I am in my inner world and someone wants me to come out?

P: The nearest I can say is that I am an artist. I don't like being continuously nagged. It's because the nagging persons are being persistent in their own terms. They are nagging you to do something that you don't want to do. They want to change your life and behave in a way that's appropriate for them. They want you to act in a way that they are choosing. It's not of your choice. So for me that's being nagged. I wish to tell them – "Go away this is my world. If you have to get something out of me better come clean. Let's negotiate it. Don't tell me what to do! Don't force me into your world."

232

If I am a child, I don't have the resources or the sophistication to put it like this to that person or to put that person away. In a way as a child you are defenceless and the adults make you do what they want you to do. Pain is also very similar. It's something you can't do much about. So it's as if it's a third direction. You can do your own thing or you can do what the other person wants you to do. Similarly, you can do your own thing or the pain won't allow you to. As a child you don't want to do what they want you to do and they don't allow you to do what you want to do. So as an adult pain becomes the third direction.

What we understood is that the same thought process is going on since childhood - as an adult you are defenceless against the pain and as a child you are defenceless against the adult; so both are narrating the same story of feeling defenceless . We wanted to understand this more by probing into the child's feelings? What is the experience of this defenceless child?

D: Describe this a little bit more. What is the experience of this child who does not want to do and the nagging person does not allow him to do?

P: My experience is that I am quite happy and delighted with my world. My world is very…it has a lot of beauty, fun and enjoyment but someone wants to come and stop me from doing it. I want them to go away.

D: What's the experience?

P: The experience in terms of my inner world or my relationship to that nagging person?

What a beautiful response. We asked him to describe both – the inner world and the relationship to the nagging person because for us both are the same. We told him to explain both.

P: Well, once they started nagging me, they prevent me from my inner world. Instead of doing that thing or even showing my inner world to that person they are setting the terms of reference. They are setting the grounds for what I can experience and I don't like that. The sort of things required as children are very ordinary and unimportant things to ask. Like why should we be concerned about putting our socks in the drawer or in the washer or turning up in school on time? These are not important things to us as children. I guess we have got many more important things to do. I guess that's the experience. It is a resentment that someone is putting on their agenda onto you but without negotiation. As a result, I would experience it as bullying, like someone wants me to do something the way they want it. Stupid person! We can come to an agreement, its manipulation.

Someone is trying to manipulate or use words to make reason or rationalise such that this is the only course of action that is allowed. You know there are different levels of bullying. Do this or I will hit you or this is the course of action or you can do this or you can do that. And it's not that you can simply say a no. The world is much more complex than that. There is more choice than just this or that. There might be bullying at even the emotional level like "You are no longer acceptable if you don't do things my way; if you don't do the things that are required from you." So all this puts you in a conflict. Nagging is more a sort of a physical assault. I know the words, those sharp words. They can feel like an impact for me, like a blow.

The gesture he made with the words impact and blow was of the swish or sway of his hand. This is an unusual way of showing it. What he actually means to say is that they are forcing him to do something which he does not like. That sounds a lot animal like. But when he brings out the words impact and blow, it shows some plant sensitivity.

So at this level where we are, that is the delusion level, we can fit the case in any kingdom.

D: Describe this – 'sharp words feel like a blow'.

P: In a way that's exactly it. It is like the words almost become a physical thing like a slap or sharp hitting. It's that sort of an assault - a combination of the physical pain and the emotional rejection. It's a sharp point like that.

D: What's the experience when you do this?

We needed to understand this gesture of the swish or shove of the hand.

P: Its rejection isn't it? It's like saying – "Go away, become unimportant. Dissolve into space."

Wow! How come a shove or an impact leads to dissolving in space –this

234

can't be animal, mineral or plant. It is an unusual description. It is something that we have not heard of before. Once again it came with the same gesture.

D: Describe this more.

P: I could resort to maiming in this case. Maiming is much easier than this. For me, one of the important things is that sharp words always feel like an impact. In a way it's not addressing. It's like the lowest common denominator.

Before we go further and before he describes more about this, we must note that the gesture of the swish of the hand has been coming time and again at different levels. At different points in the case, every time he describes this feeling, he brings out different words like rejection, go away, dissolve into space, sharp, blow and that the words are like an impact. So you see he is bringing out so many different expressions. We need to understand the core and the source of these words and feelings. So we are not going to probe into these words. More than the words, what is important for us is his experience of the gesture that he is making which will take us to the next deeper level.

D: Describe this gesture.

P: It's a denial of my inner world. The way I work in the world, understand things and engage with. That is being denied. Someone is just saying do this or move this. For me obviously it's a very deep thing. For me it's how I make my world. It's the entirety of my experiences of the world. It's at different levels. If someone just comes in and strikes me or uses a sharp word then all that is denied in a way. It's quite a serious matter for me.

D: What's the experience?

P: Being denied? I guess it's really on an ontological level. I mean how do you know that you are awake or you are alive? It's a summation of your experiences, your memories and all those processes. That's what for me makes me. If somebody just goes past that and whacks you, it's the denial of everything that I would be. It's the denial of who I am!

At this stage we can't figure which kingdom he belongs to. He talks about dispersal, bullying and identity. He is bringing out so many things. Like we told you some time ago, we are at the stage of delusion. So this is what we ask him.

D: What is the experience when someone whacks you? How is the experience when you are being whacked?

P: For me the impact is as if someone has hit me physically with the hand. I would feel like a sharp pain maybe on the cheek or in my head and the head would move back and if the pain was more intense it would really hurt. The experience would be that my eyes start to water and I would have a response to hit back automatically. That shock feels similar, it's like a sting. So very quickly and almost instantly I defend myself with a counter attack like "How could you do that!" What I experience then is much on a kinaesthetic level. It's on the physical level; an impact to which I want to rebound. It feels like an attack. Someone is physically attacking me and therefore my response would be to attack back.

D: Because?

P: Someone is attacking me. I am in danger.

He is talking about attack and danger. So finally it looks like the animal kingdom. This makes us happy. So now we ask him – "What is the experience when you are in danger and that someone is attacking you?" If he is an animal, he has to bring out deeper animal sensitivity of 'me versus you.' Like someone is attacking me, I am in danger, I could be finished, I need to counter attack and finish him. Or that somebody is attacking me, I am in danger and I need to flee otherwise that will be the end of me. Or it would be that someone is attacking me, I feel cornered, trapped and suffocated and that's going to be the end of me. Thus I need to do something because either it is me or him.

We are at the delusion level and the next level has to be at the sensational level or as we call it, the level of the deepest polarity. When we pose this question to him, his reply is very interesting.

D: What is the experience when you are in danger and that someone is attacking you?

P: The experience is like someone is attacking me. It's like a physical push,

236

like a shove. Someone is going to push me away. It's that pushing and that dispersal that I was talking about.

The attack doesn't bring out the 'me versus you' sensation but it brings us back to the same words which he had used earlier. Not a stabbing, but a push, a shove and dispersal. The same gesture comes in again. We wonder what this is and thus ask him to describe it further.

P: For me to hold my experiences, my memories and the way I interpret the world together, is actually quite a tight thing. That's what I am and if someone disperses that it's like an ink in a large glass of water.

Wow! This tells me that this is something non-human. It's some kind of a phenomenon that he is talking about. We have no idea what it is or from where it is coming. But we are going to probe this experience more. We gave his entire phenomenon back to him to make it clearer.

D: How does it feel when you say this is shoved, it is a tight thing which is dispersed like ink in a glass of water?

I have a feeling that this is going to lead us to something very interesting.

P: At a different level, it's almost like your identity is a tiny coherent drop. That's the way I bound it together. That's the way I make 'Me' and everything that I understand in the world. What I want to do is this thing and this is the reason for me to be bound up in this. Then there comes a physical assault which threatens to disperse me and disperse that coherency - things that make no sense for me. So this would be what I perceive as an assault. Either it's an assault, a harsh or a sharp word or that sort of a nagging pain. Or it could be that someone is trying to dissolve my identity - whatever I thought to be me. It is as if they don't want to be engaged with who I am. Somebody is trying to dissolve this thing.

He is exploring the phenomenon and he is talking the language of the source. We have no clue of the sensation and the source but we know that this is something non-human and related to the source. It is something that has got some life to it. There is a process involved in it. We need to understand this source, this process to be able to get the entire perspective. We are eager to know what it is because it is something that we have not heard before. So we let the patient talk and explore it for us.

P: So they don't see me as a person but they see me as an instrument or a piece of furniture. As a passive part of the world which can be pushed here and there. They even move me like a table or a chair - now put it over there. It's like they are engaging me by saying that this person is in my way so just move him out of the way, There is an interesting bit in you know Lewis Carroll's 'Alice in Wonderland' book. I would like to tell about a part in the book where they are actually trying to play croquet with flamingos and hedgehogs.

The flamingos are the mallets and the hedgehogs are the balls. Now if you play croquet you use mallets and balls. These are physical things and they operate on the simple laws of physics and you can play with them. But in the book they can't seem to play croquet at all because the hedgehogs run away and the flamingos that they are using as mallets, look up and say - "Hey guys, what the hell are you doing?" So you can't treat the flamingos and hedgehogs like physical objects. The importance of this part is that we are all people; we are not physical objects in that way. We all have volition. For me to be denied that I have volition is to tell me that I am a physical object like to think that I am a hedgehog or a ball that you can kick hard which goes in the socket. You take a swing and you use it as a hammer or you knock it to a certain distance. So the sensation is that my identity which at the moment is a spherical thing as bound together in all three dimensions is in threat. It is that someone is just denying this identity, knocking it off and dissolving it. My instant response is that I will come back and counterattack. How could you deny me as a person? How could you treat me as an object?

D: How does it feel?

P: To be precise, it feels like you are not alive anymore. You don't have your own volition.

D: So can you describe this? You are this somebody and someone shoves you and you get dissolved. Can you describe the whole experience? It's very important.

P: It's a sort of visualisation. I know that I am being in my processes. These processes could happen anywhere in my mind or in my spirit. This is important and this is very handy because this is the way I say that I am in space. At that moment within it, I have memory and light. I have a connection and a history with all the people I know and with all the things that I am hoping for my future; all that is there. And if someone treats me as an object, that's just so offensive because it denies any of all those memories, history, past and light. It's as if I don't exist. And if I were to let someone manipulate or treat me like this, like an object, I wouldn't be anything. For me to be the experience of something I need to have a sense of identity, a sense of relation to everything around; it's like a process.

Again, we see a process coming up and when he is talking about who he is, he uses lot of important and interesting words like – "Within this I have memory, I have light, I have connection, I have history and I have people." Wow! So it's not just him but there are lots of things along with that which we need to understand. It is not making any sense to us. This far, it makes pure sense only to the patient.

D: Tell me a little bit more about this.

P: In a way, how do I know who I am or what I am? I know it by these things. I know it by my memories, by my intensity, by the way I relate to others and to other things. That's the way I know who I am and that's my strength in defining what I do. In the world for me, if someone denies it they deny who I am; they deny me. And by denying what I am, I will no longer exist. For me, my sense of experience knows that I have got boundaries, relationships and relationships between my history and my future which would get dispersed by denial. It would be as if you have no boundaries, you have no volition and have no will.

D: So can you describe this experience of no boundaries, no volition?

P: I would say it's tricky because I think I describe everything in terms of boundaries. So it's half the sense of being free in the air, like a bird flying in the air. But no, a bird flying in the air wouldn't make sense because you are flying and you have feathers which support you in the air. So you have your own boundaries. No that's not how it should be. You would have to be like a balloon; a balloon that bursts. So whatever air is inside this balloon gradually goes out and vanishes. Or in terms of light, you could have a little candle in the dark which is burning and has flame. But when the sun rises and the daylight builds up and gets stronger and stronger, the candle is harder and harder to see until it is completely gone.

D: So what happens to that candle?

P: It's still there. You just can't see it. For me the experience would be that it's there but you are not quite sure. You might be just in all that haze and you are making it up or perhaps it's not there. So it's almost the dispersal or dissolution that I was talking about. It's dissolution into something larger. You are dissolving until you are unaware that you exist but obviously what you are interested. In there is the experience of the sound itself which becomes fainter and fainter. I don't know if it's a valid thing without pre-supposing what that experience might be. But to turn that around and say that if I were an identity of that candle or that flame or that sound, it would be like having a loss of identity. It's no longer having a will or volition, a shape, a history, a future or a memory; it no longer has all these things.

Wow! He talked of so many things. What was interesting was when we asked him to describe about his volition and no will he started talking about the space that he was in and then the space went further. Then he gave the example of a balloon that goes up and it bursts and that air gets dispersed everywhere. Now he connects it to a candle which gets over-taken by a sun such that one is getting dissolved into something that is larger. He says that it is larger until you are unaware that you exist from outside.

He is saying a lot of things at once. This is an entire phenomenon; something like a source language.

D: Describe this dissolution into something that's larger until you are aware that you exist from outside. What is your experience in that? Please tell me.

P: That spins off and I don't see then at that point, what's the connection of all that to the nagging and the toothache. But you see it's a rather wonderful thing because if you dissolve and become the background sound of the world, you experience the world and everything is there. You have dissolved into the last trace of cent. It's as if you have become everywhere. The dissolving… if I become that air in that balloon and that air dissolves all through the entire world, there is one molecule of that air from that balloon in every room in the world. For me that's an absolutely wonderful thought.

Wow! What a wonderful dissolution he is talking about. He doesn't say that it leads to a loss of identity. Instead it takes us everywhere. It's a powerful dissolving and this dissolving is a very happy thing for him. It's not the end of him; instead he is larger than what he was.

D: Good. What is the experience?

P: You have had the totality of the experiences of the world. You are everywhere. You have been everywhere in the world and heard every sound in your hearing; every cent, every experience. You would be so diluted that you don't have the ability to process it but just being in that thing of that complete dissolution, it's amazing.

We wanted to understand this more so we probed further. We asked him to describe more about this dissolution and this entire totality of the world. What we realised is that this dissolving is a very powerful one. So what is the opposite of this? We are not very sure whether it's the same thing that is going on in our patient's mind. So we pose the question in such a way that the patient is free to take any direction that he wants.

D: What is the opposite of this experience that you spoke to me?

P: It's being tightly focused. It's knowing...

This is what we had in my mind. It had to come back to being tightly focused. Now somewhere our line of thinking is going along with the patient's and we are able to follow him at this point of time. On one side is something which has an identity, volition and structure and on the other hand this something dissolves and becomes so all pervasive that it becomes part of everything. So we let him go further.

P: It's like you know where your boundaries are and having a place to put them in your future and being certain in the mental processes of reduction and deduction, the synthesis becomes very crystalline. You know what your experiences are and it's like being aware in many ways of the different experiences put together. It's like having a strong identity. It gives you a way of understanding the world. It gives you intention and volition. You have something to exchange with the people and people have something to exchange with you. For me also, if I am in this, I can see the dance of the world. If you are ever in this frame and you are like this here and you look down upon the crowd of people there, they think they are all separate but that's not true. You could see a crowd moving around and they are all aware of each other. But you know they are like one large living entity. So in a way you need that strong career or that strong position to see the world around. You are making the world coherent. You are making sense from up there. You

241

are seeing people in their own individual processes and how they are making the world. So that's the reverse of being dispersed. It's not necessarily being tight. I don't think tight is the right word to use because it's more like a contained structure. It needn't necessarily be tight. It is contained and it is separate from the world.

Now he says that this things must have exchange with the others, it must have a strong position from where it watches the world. It is itself so great that it is making the world coherent and making sense of it. This thing he is talking about has a very high position! We are sure you must have realised that he is speaking about the source. We yet don't know what the source is but we have got beautiful information about it. It's like we have got such a nice description that all of us can prepare an impression as to how the source would be. We ask to him to describe this more by saying that we have not understood it because we were very ignorant at that point of time. If we say that we are able to follow it, we might miss out the source.

D: I didn't quite understand this. Make it more clear for me.

P: So this is the reverse of being dissolved. Having burst as a part it contains the reverse and that's a coherent structure. It is something that's got an identity, a history, a future, relationships and processes. Because of that, I have the awareness of observing the world and seeing people. So I get to see how they were and how they relate and how things that people make, reflect what they are; what these people make, why they make this? It's like seeing all this that the people are doing.

Now we need to know where the polarity is. Polarity is something where you need to have two clear opposites like positive and negative, sensitivity and reactivity, me versus you or complete versus incomplete.

In this case we see something which is unheard of. On one side is a small coherent structure with an identity and the other side is something of such magnitude that it dissolves and becomes the background sound, it becomes a lot larger and unfathomable. Both sides are formative and productive but different in a certain way... One side is coherent, matter-like and the other is incoherent yet so enormous, something that is very dynamic and larger than matter. So here we see the polarity of 'matter and energy'. This is the polarity of the imponderables where we have matter on one side which gets transformed into energy on the other side, which can get transformed back into matter.

Although we do not know what the source was but by this time we know that we are dealing with an imponderable. So, we need to now take the imponderable sensation that we have obtained right up to the source. The description of tight and dispersal is what is going to take us to the source. We ask him to describe this.

P: [Laughs] Oh! You are looking for dialectic. First you ask me one and then you ask me the other. First you ask me the tight then you ask me the dispersed and now you ask me both.

Our patient started laughing at that point. He himself could perceive the phenomenon of tight and disperse and that we were trying to elicit the two and make it more clear.

P: It's a synthesis that you have pre-supposed. You have elicited one side. Let's say this is the side of the dissolution and then you say what's the reverse of that? So then you have the coherent side. And once you go up to coherent side, you go back to dispersal. So for me, it makes me laugh. It's such a wonderful thing; this idea. It's so lovely!

D: What about it is so lovely?

P: It's lovely because that's where the beauty is. That's the aesthetics of the world for me. And for me sometimes the world is a bit too beautiful and sometimes it's very ugly. I don't know what to do with myself? It's something that I am not necessarily in control of.

Interesting! After that he explained some phenomenon which we did not understand at all. So we asked him to describe that once again.

D: Sorry we didn't get it.

P: You can't have a perception or a structure or an identity unless there is a world to perceive it. There has to be a world out there and it can't be a part of a structure because the structure has to then dissolve.

So the structure needs to be separate from the world. It look down on the world it needs the world to perceive it.

D: What is the experience of this structure?

P: If I have to think about a structure, or if I have to think about something that explains this structure, this dispersal and this identity, it's the way I process the world. It's that position which I take from where I can see what's happening in the world down there. When I say structure, I am thinking of a structure like making a garden. But a garden is not self-contained, it's not tight. The garden draws light from the sun. The plants draw elements from the soil. And I as a human get fruits and flowers from the garden. So in a way there is a process there. But it's not self-contained. There are other elements that come in as well.

I am trying to think of a working dynamic structure that explains this experience that I have. Maybe a crystal would explain it. But I am not sure if a crystal would either because if I think of a crystal it is tight and tight is not what I am looking for. I am looking for something which is coherent but not necessarily tight. But I am also looking for something where there is dispersal and an open process going on.

But if I think of a crystal, a crystal cannot disperse. If you start from that first geometrical structure of the crystal, it's just the same structure which gets bigger and bigger. So the crystal atom has the same structure as the larger crystal itself. But I am not talking of something getting bigger here. I am talking of something getting dispersed so there has to be a process involved. I can think of several crystals that I like - I can think of galena which is lead sulphide, quartz, feldspar or marble and many more but they will not disperse into everything. Frankly, I am still looking and trying to understand this kind of a structure which has tight and coherent on one end and dispersal on the other end.

You can see that while he was telling us about the source he gave it a little bit more depth. It's something which is coherent with a dynamic structure, a working structure where there is a process involved. It's not confined. We continue to probe him.

D: Please tell me more.

P: I think the best that describes this whole dynamic process is a garden. Yeah, I think a garden is something that I would think about because you always have a process in the woodlands or in the forests, in nature. It looks like in the garden there is some kind of an entire process going on. It's taking light from the environment and it's growing but how can I think of this dispersal? Maybe opals... why did opal come to my mind? I think if you look at an opal closely and if you are looking through, you will see there is fire within it. The light goes in and it is dispersed. It is very, very bright. Probably, it has a mineral like structure. So yes, the opal does have a structure. And then it has this fire in it. And the light goes in, it gets reflected and when the light comes out its dispersed and it brings out so many colours. It's something like this ring which has the opal here. So maybe I could think of an opal which has structure and dispersal, maybe I could give it a thought.

He was fascinated by the opal. And all along while he spoke, his hands were as if holding a ball or some circular object between them. We wanted to tell him that the source was right here but he was holding it back. We wanted him to reveal the source so that we could potentise it and give it to him. So we asked him, "What is it that you are doing with your hand? What is the experience when you do this?" The reply that came at this point of time was crystal clear for me! He too felt happy that this was something which explained it.

P: Maybe the visualisation that comes to me is that of a small ball. Perhaps it's the size of a cricket ball. Its fiery, it's glistening. It's pulsating. It's a structure that you could just see inside it. It's the most extraordinary thing. I just thought and I did that exploration of whether I can hold this structure and maybe put it here (gesture of putting the ball near his heart) or somewhere else. What happens then to my feelings? They need to go back to where they belong (back to his heart). This is where they belong and where the feelings need to be. And that's my exploration. It's just sort of wonderful.

It's the visualisation of a fiery red ball. He is indeed speaking out the source.

D: What comes to you when you describe this fiery red ball?

P: It's just this size, it isn't bigger or smaller. It is this size of a fiery red ball. It's my subjective creation of this ball. And if you ask me if there is anything that you imagine that could be like this then the most obvious thing I can think of is of course the Sun. Why? Why not? It's a fiery red ball. For me the Sun has got a structure. It has got all the sub-type of processes that can make power, heat, light, energy and even life. It brings joy and life through the entire solar system especially on our planet.

If I explore that a little bit more then the Sun starts off as atoms which are spread all through space and the solar system, in the Milky Way and in our galaxy. It has been formed like that. Usually because the galaxies are revolving, there is a rotating motion to everything and so all those small gases and atoms coalesce. Then they start to form the solar system which will start to spin after which you see planets condense and assume life. It is as if you could see this entire process of five billion years in just a matter of ten minutes. It would be so dynamic to see all of this happen from the gas and the atoms, to condensation, to the planets and then to life on our planet. Then the sun would be the centre and it would get hotter and hotter and hotter. As the fire builds up it starts to provide life, light and energy to the entire solar system. So for me, I think it's the Sun and it's the size of a cricket ball in my imagination and it needs to be here.

So what he was holding all along was nothing but the little fiery red ball, the size of a cricket ball which is the Sun and by talking about the Sun he explored and explained a lot of things. Let us do a quick case-analysis.

★ *He started with the complaint of pain which is nagging, troubling but which had a character as if he was talking about himself.*
★ *It forces him to do something that he doesn't want to do, like he is a child.*
★ *How does that feel? It feels like a sharp blow, an attack which came with an interesting gesture. This was at the level of delusion. He feels that he has been shoved away.*
★ *Pushed, dispersed and dissolved in space.*
  It's like your identity and your sphere has been dissolved.
★ *That thing has then dispersed everywhere, in every room and become the background sound of the world. It watches the dance of the world from a position and makes sense of it.*
★ *By probing further, he reached an open process, a working structure along with the gesture of the ball all along.*
★ *All along he was holding a fiery red ball - the Sun, which has matter and energy both. It was the highest, the best and the most important example of matter and energy responsible for life. It was a perfect example because the sun is that fiery red ball which has history, volition and all the processes that he spoke about. The Sun is a very thrilling model*

indeed. It is a ball but at the same time it is the background sound or the ruler of our solar system and it is dynamic and it is the creator of a process. There is nothing closed or structured about the Sun. It is a very open, dynamic process which has triggered life on our earth. And the concept of time mentioned in the case matches exactly with the concept of time in space.

P: Yeah, it's extra-ordinary as a process. It is one of the most stupendous processes that we have in nature. How can you diffuse that power? How can all that power come together in a space of few years? Mind you I am talking of five billion years here. Can it make trees, plants, animals and everything that we experience in the world? And then at the other end of the process there are different stars that get finished in different sorts of ways. Some of them just fizzle away, some of them explode and then all those atoms just disperse and go into space. And in sometime in the future they come back together to form a new star, maybe a new solar system.

III. Remedy and Case Follow-up

So he gives us the entire formation of the solar system - Our Sun, the planet and the entire thing that we have around us; the whole process. Of course we couldn't give him the sun per se but the closest that we can get to the Sun are the sunrays which travel and reach us. We gave him Sol 1M, 1 dose. He was right at the level of delusion and 1M was the best potency for him. It was interesting to see the changes that came into him after this remedy.

First Follow-up, 26th March, 2009

This follow-up was taken about 8-9 months after the remedy when we chatted with him on Skype.

D: How are you doing?

P: My migraines have gone down. They are becoming very good. I have migraines for a very short time and I don't get as tired with the migraines as I did in the past.

D: What are the changes that you have seen after the remedy?

247

P: I think instead of the migraine being a special event it is just there; you know something that happens. Instead of doing something special, worrying about it and getting visual disturbances like before, I don't bother about it anymore. I have to take it easy. Or it is like a message to me to stop doing what I am doing with my left side. It's fine.

D: How have the visual disturbances been?

P: The visual disturbances have been just occasional. They start very quickly and then they settle down. The migraine is not a big event. It's just a part of the whole process.

He said something very nice.

P: It's not part of my identity you know. I can make things out. It doesn't trouble me.

D: What about the pains that you had in the past? Are they nagging and troubling you and not allowing you to do the things that you want to do?

P: It's not nagging any more. It is simply a gesture that you can work on if you want to. It's only like a message. It's no more a nagging thing.

D: So it's more like a message now. It allows you to do something. It's not nagging and stopping you and telling you don't do this?

P: That's right. It doesn't stop me from doing my day to day things. It's very interesting because it's an awareness that there are so many messages that pass me from different parts of myself to be aware of another sort of information. I am very okay with it. It's just like being hungry. The migraine just comes and tells me that its there and I can easily pass it over.

D: What about your cold and coughs?

P: I am okay. They are not troubling me.

The headaches have also changed considerably.

D: Tell us something more.

P: I could resolve the issues that I had within me and with others - somebody very close to me. I could connect to that person and resolve those issues which I had been holding on for a very long time. I am very happy about it.

D: The previous time you talked about the sun...

P: O Yes!

D: Tell us a little bit more about it.

P: My experience now is that the sun, where is it? It's over here, it's over there, it should be somewhere over here. It is back in its place (gesture of pointing to the heart). The sun which was everywhere has come back to where it should belong to. I think it was a surprise that somehow it had got separated. So I think for me, the process has been going on for years. That feeling that it should be in its proper place, which is inside me, had somewhere gone out but now I feel it has come back to me. The sun is a very important part for me. It's something... I don't know if you can separate my cognitive presentation of my feelings. It's like all the warmth and life and the world arises from the sun. It's such a bright thing!

Other follow-ups

We saw him again in March after which we saw him in June. In total, three doses of 1M in two years have been given to him.

This case was very interesting. We could see the source coming alive so early on in the case even though we didn't know what it was. The source came out so beautifully and along with the source it gave us the entire derivation and understanding of the imponderables which is energy and matter. It showed us how the perception is different in the imponderables.

IV. What are Imponderables?

Let us understand imponderables in detail.

Imponderables mean something that cannot be pondered upon, that which cannot be fathomed or easily understood in our material or earthly world. So we feel that the imponderable kingdom includes everything that is larger than matter like stars and it includes those things that are extremely minute like electromagnetic waves - electrons and positrons. So, all those things which are way out of the range of the normal material world come into the kingdom or the group of imponderables. And the sensation in imponderables is therefore matter on one side, or fathomable structure on one side and a completely unfathomable dynamism on the opposite side. Like you saw in this case you could fathom structure, you could fathom the idea that there was something coherent. There was something bound or contained. But it was unfathomable to understand how this bound thing could disperse into every space to become the background of the world. So there was matter of fathomable things on one end and there was absolute dynamism, energy, unfathomable force on the other end.

Sometimes as in this case right from the point of delusion very often the patient is actually already beginning to use the source language. However it is too early for us to understand the source at that point because we are still at the delusion and so the image is not clear. As we explore this image further, the client gives us the sensation. Once we have understood that this is the sensation or rather the polarity of matter and energy, the image that was brought at the delusion level can be understood as the source or the sub-kingdom itself.

The image of being broken into thousands of particles could make somebody think of mitotic division of cells, it could make somebody think of the dispersed of Leguminosae plant family or just about anything. But when one understands that the deeper polarity under the dissolution is that of matter and energy, not me versus you and not sensitivity-reactivity then it leads to the Sun and its powerful energy.

So the energy and source words start to come up much earlier in the case almost at the time of delusion when the person is giving the image of whatever his perception is. But until we understand the polarity and the sensation, it would be wrong to pinpoint or cash onto these kinds of words. Of course we pick these words only to go further ahead in the case. We pick these images, these gestures as a yard stick to travel further down. But at that point before the sensation is established they cannot be held onto and the source cannot be pinned down on because at that point if we are trying to pick on the source then you are interpreting it.

The other doubt that could come to our minds is that Sol is just sunrays. How can they be given to a case where you need Sun? But remember for a case of

Lac leoninum you don't give him the whole lion, you just give the patient the milk or the blood of that animal. So the discharge of that animal carries the entire essence of that animal.

Similarly what's going on in the Sun is a gamete or a complex of several processes. The light rays coming out from the Sun not only carry the light from the Sun, they carry the dynamic energy of that huge star and that's the only way to get the energy imprint of the Sun.

The Sun is not a quiet place but one that exhibits sudden releases of energy. One of the most frequently observed events are solar flares that are sudden, localised, transient and increasing in brightness that occur in active regions near spaces called as Sun-spots. So you can imagine the dynamic processes and the dynamism that is associated with this huge fiery ball.

V. The Formation of the Sun

How was the Sun formed? The Sun like other stars was formed in a nebula.

The obvious question is what is a nebula?

It's an enormous cloud of dust and gas, mainly hydrogen. Dense parts in a cloud undergo a gravitational collapse and form a rotating gas globule. This globule is compressed by gravitational force and also by the pressure of any adjacent supernova. So what's happening here? It's just a gas cloud which comes together, starts rotating by itself and there is an adjacent supernova, meaning a collapsing star somewhere close by, which comes and puts more pressure on this gas cloud which is already rotating. These forces together cause this globule to rotate further and collapse even more. This process of collapse can take anywhere from ten thousand to ten million years.

Remember here we are talking of absolutely unfathomable limits. As the collapse proceeds, the pressure and temperature in this globule increases and the globule begins to rotate faster and faster. This spinning action causes an increase in the centrifugal force and therefore causes the globule to have a central core and a surrounded flattened disc of dust. The core becomes the star and the surrounding dust eventually coalesces to form planets, asteroids, etc. The core heats up further due to friction and it forms a glowing proto-star. This is a stage which lasts for fifty million years. We are now on the stage of the Sun. When the temperature is about 27 million degrees Fahrenheit, there is nuclear fusion that begins at the core of the Sun. Hydrogen atoms convert to helium and energy and this energy further prevents any contraction of the Sun or a star. This is the most stable period of the star where the planets formed rotate around the star and the star glows as the centre of the solar system.

So the formation of any star is the process of coming together from a dispersed dust and gas globule. This process could be enhanced by the shove or push of another dying star. Then again the dispersal of peripheral elements of this star forms the planets that then revolve around it forming the whole solar system. And the end of a star is the process of dispersal again. Now you can relate this entire process to the above case. These were the exact words of the patient. "You are shoved and you disperse to then dissolve and become the part of the entire world. You dissolve like a drop of ink in all the water and you become present in every molecule in every room. So you are nothing but this dust and when somebody shoves you, you end up forming the solar system".

So out of nothing which is just the dust, you have the capacity to form the whole solar system. This dust, this contained thing eventually ends up forming the whole solar system - the centre which is again contained and everything around it which are the planets. And then slowly over billions and billions of years it once more ends up into atoms and disperses again.

18

 ## <u>IMPONDERABLE CASE 2: SOL</u>

I.   Case Introduction

II. The Case

III. Remedy and Case Follow-up

Here is a short summary of one imponderable case from our practice which illustrates the polarity clearly.

I. Case Introduction

A woman, about forty-five years old, came to us with borderline schizophrenia, heavy menstrual bleeding and severe menstrual cramps. She, however, was bothered about the 'out of control' state she always was in.

She had symptoms of schizophrenia - various kinds of hallucinations, people talking about her, people pointing at her, people becoming liquid as she gazed at them and people appearing from nowhere.... people appearing from a gas-like cloud and talking to her etc. She had a recurrent delusion that, if she focused on anything for a while, the whole space would get dark as if she were in the universe and there were galaxies around her for millions of miles and she was travelling in space. Hence she had to quickly shift her focus or attention. This made her restless physically, although mentally, she was not a restless person. With all of these complaints she felt as if she was in a state of 'auto-pilot' and that felt awful.

II. The Case

P: I feel completely out of control with my state. I never know who I am. What my next reaction will be and what I will say next. There is no control over my mind. I can know when I am losing my mind – when I am going insane. It's a terrible feeling. It is a feeling as if I am on auto-pilot. I do not know whether I want to be on auto-pilot or not. To be in control of destiny or some other force of nature beyond you, beyond your imagination, beyond what you can fathom. There is always a dilemma in my mind - to be heavy in this blob state or to be light (without any weight). It is a feeling of having such gravity and such an immense load of some matter within you. This is not what I want to be. I want to be lighter than this immense load. I feel like I imbibe this energy but it puts me on auto-pilot and then there is no control. To be on auto-pilot is to be light, as if there is no gravity. As if you defy all the laws of gravity. One has substance hence one is, but the mass comes with its own shortcomings. I am me because of this blob. This blob can have any shape or size. That is not the point.

The point is not how big it is or how small it is, or how it is, or what shape it is. The point is what it is. It is this mass and heavy load and you are, because you are that, and then you want to be not that, but something that

254

does not have this blob or this mass. But then what are you if there is no ....if there is no substance and there is no ... blob .... I think I am confused ....well not really ...Do you get what I mean?

We wanted to say to her that we were as confused as she was. But we kept a poker face and said, "You are doing really well go on... we can understand every word of what you say but please explain it in more detail."

Our intention was to encourage her as this information was the core of her deepest feelings. Only this non-sense had within it, the potential to take us to the remedy she needed.

P: It is almost like my complaint - maybe that's why the doctors term it borderline schizophrenia. I am on the border, or on the narrow thin line, that differentiates sanity from insanity.

Before we go further in the case we want to say what our thoughts at this point of time were – 'She is someone who has the polarity of heavy and light. Heavy is matter, substance, load. And light is when you can be fast and light and moving. But when it is so fast you feel like you are losing control of yourself and you are not matter. This is not merely the opposite of heaviness and lightness. But here, on one side is something that is heavy because it has substance, while on the other side is something that has no substance yet the energy to move. Could this be a case needing imponderable, a remedy where the source has no matter but pure energy?'

Then she said ....

P: Auto-pilot gives one the freedom to move and be wherever you want to. It gives the body the freedom to not have the body, and when the freedom to not have the body comes, there comes the feeling there is no body. That I think puts me in a feeling of....what am I? Do I want to be this load for the world or do I want to be the energy within me?

We asked her to describe this energy further with the intention of finding which energy remedy she needs.

P: It's a feeling of, feeling that immense energy stored within you. It has no matter and it just moves and flows in the world. It is self-propelling and it

255

goes whoosh and it does not have any gravity so there is no 'I'.

At this point we were sure that it was a case of an Imponderable with the basic polarity of matter and energy. The feeling within was that 'I am energy and the other side or the worldly side of it is matter'. We knew that this was the source speaking to us.

On one side is heavy matter which gives the feeling of substance but on the other side is the need to defy matter and gravity and be this energy. Our experience with Imponderables over the last couple of years has shown us that all of them talk about this basic polarity.

P: The energy has a flow and rhythm. This flow is very important to me. The flow makes you feel in balance and in rhythm. When the flow is there, there is an ease and there is no tension. No flow is like being a blob. You could say it is like these circuit boards and capacitors. I hate them. I look at them and the feeling I get is all that energy there is trapped and it goes buzzzzz through my whole body. There has to be this sine curve to the flow. I was a very poor student of physics but this is all I remember from my school days. I loved the sine curve. I loved it.

Here we realised that this was a case of an electromagnetic radiation where the electrical and magnetic components of the wave move in a sine curve at right angles to each other.

We thought to ourselves if this was a case of electricity? It was as if she read our minds and she said-

P: Sorry electricity is not what I like. I am an energy that gives birth and warmth to the world. I have the power to create lives and the heat to destroy them. There is a nurturing element there. There is warmth in its heat. In the electricity wave there is a resistance. Here there is no resistance. They flow from a centre and they go far away. The centre takes care of everybody. At this point I realised this is the light wave from the Sun.

Then as if she read our thoughts again, she said,

P: Yeah, one could say …the Sun. It takes care of everybody connected to it. He is the father. Life works around the Sun; the entire solar system! The Sun has beautiful positive energy and the rays flowing out have the same intention.

You are fed by the Sun's positive energy and it feels organic and natural.

III. Remedy and Case Follow-up

We gave her Sol 1M one dose to find a remarkable change in her disposition within a very short time. Her feeling of being completely out of control and her symptoms of hallucinations and her attacks reduced remarkably quickly. Her complaint of menorrhagia was well taken care off and a few months after the first dose there was no complaint of the cramping pain during menses. The first thing to improve was the conflict between matter and energy and her 'out of control' feeling. She no longer felt that fear of being on auto-pilot. She said because there was no fear of losing control anymore she knew in her heart that the schizophrenia would be helped. We started doubting whether she even had this complaint in the first place. In the first few follow-ups we kept asking her about the hallucinations and she kept telling us that they are a result of the state within.

That state had lost its balance. With the remedy, the balance was restored. The symptoms would definitely go. We have had some experience with cases of schizophrenia. All of them are still under our care. Some of them have been with us for six or eight years now. I must say that we were shocked with this kind of a quick response. By the end of the year she reported that her feeling and fear that she could lose her sanity any moment, this fragile feeling, had reduced and she felt far more grounded within herself.

19

 UNDERSTANDING THE NATURE OF IMPONDERABLES AND THEIR THEMES

I.   The Homoeopathic understanding of Imponderables

II. Common Themes of Imponderables

III. A Cure from Within Outwards

IV. A Personal Note

V.   Time Phenomenon in Imponderables

I. The Homoeopathic understanding of Imponderables

To understand homoeopathically the sensation of energy we will have to understand imponderables at the source level. In other words we will have to understand energy at its source level. Magnetism is a force and the rest of Imponderables in our Materia medica - light, electricity, x-ray, laser beam, lunar are electromagnetic radiations of varying wavelength. So let's understand the nature of these electromagnetic waves in brief. This will help us to understand the basic polarity of imponderables and the core issues of these cases.

An electromagnetic wave or radiation is a wave with electrical and magnetic components both at right angles to each other. Electromagnetic (EM) radiation carries energy and momentum which may be imparted when it interacts with matter. EM radiation is caused by electrons moving in space.

Once we come to the basis that electrons carry charge or form electric current, we come to one of the basic particle – the building block of the universe - ***the atom.*** Atoms are so small that millions of them would fit on the head of a pin. Atoms consist of protons and neutrons in their nucleus and electrons revolving around this nucleus. The protons and neutrons are very small, but electrons are much, much smaller. If the nucleus were the size of a tennis ball, the whole atom would be the size of 100 storied building. Atoms are therefore mostly empty space. If you could see an atom, it would look a little like a very tiny centre of balls surrounded by giant invisible bubbles (or shells). The electrons would be on the surface of the bubbles, constantly spinning and moving to stay as far away from each other as possible. Electrons, as we know, are held in their shells by an electrical force.

The electrons in the shells closest to the nucleus have a strong force of attraction to the protons. Sometimes, the electrons in the outermost shells do not have this attraction. These electrons can be pushed out of their orbits. Applying a force can make them move from one atom to another. To put it simply these moving electrons form electromagnetic waves or fields.

Why the electrons should remain in their orbitals, was not completely explained by Newton's laws of motion and by classical electromagnetism. Consequently what came into picture was the **'Quantum theory' of the atom**. This brought in the theory of **'Probability'**.

Probability in the context of quantum mechanics predicts the likelihood of finding a system in a particular state at a certain time, e.g. finding an electron, in a particular region around the nucleus at a particular time. Therefore, electrons cannot be considered as localised particles in space, but rather should be thought of as "clouds" of negative charge spread out over the entire orbit. These clouds represent the regions around the nucleus where the probability of "finding" an electron is the most. This probability cloud obeys a principle called **'Heisenberg's Uncertainty Principle'**, which states that there is an uncertainty in the classical position of any sub-atomic particle, including the electron. So instead of describing one specific place for the electron, it provides an entire range of possible places of distribution of the electrons or any sub-atomic particle.

So at this sub-atomic level or this Imponderable level of electrons, the concept of finite and constant ceases to exist. What prevails are the concepts of **'uncertainty'**, **'probability'** and **'relativity'.**

In 1900 Max Planck described that the energy of waves could be described as consisting of small packets or 'quanta'. Albert Einstein explored this idea further to show that an electromagnetic wave, like light, could be described by a particle called the photon. This led to a theory of unity between sub-atomic particles and electromagnetic waves. It was called **'The wave-particle duality'** in which particles and waves were neither one nor the other, but had properties of both.

Hence at the subatomic level certainty gives way to the concept of probability and uncertainty. In a healthy way one learns to accept that nothing is constant or certain or fixed and rigid. Everything is relative and ever changing and ever evolving just as our entire universe. Therefore humans with Imponderable states have a knowledge and awareness of this probability, uncertainty and duality of existence in general. They usually have an acceptance of the fact that things can be this way or that way. They are more tolerant of others views and they believe in the interdependence and relativity of things.

II. Common Themes of Imponderables

Matter & Energy

* ✶ Since all of them have a tremendous power and potential to transform, destroy or create matter, they possess a sense of having no matter yet possessing the power to change, alter and transform all material things.

261

★ There being no matter in these remedies, the ego is minimal. Their self-esteem is very high yet it is sans authority or egotism.

★ Since the basis of Quantum physics is the theory of Probability and the Heisenberg's Principle of Uncertainty, it is reflected in these cases as well.

★ They are often very receptive and respectful of others views and opinions as they feel everybody can have their own perception. They believe in the relativity of things just as is their behaviour in nature.

★ Their concept of time is very weird. They talk in terms of past as being millions of years ago or they talk of issues like anti-time.

★ They also talk of speed and velocities so tremendous that it comes as a flash of lightening.

★ Their concept or the experience of space and its description is magnanimous. It is indescribable and unfathomable.

★ They often describe their own encounters with UFO's, their experience of their past life, out-of-body experiences, etc.

★ They indulge in a lot meditation; have a strong sense of ESP, clairvoyance and everything that connects to dynamism and energy experiences of any kind.

★ They are usually very polite and humble but also very determined and well-achieved or well-respected people in society. The awareness, the potential and the high energy within them allows them to reach great heights in their professional fields. They are people who are very well achieved in whatever field they are. They also are seen to play a major role in social service.

★ They believe in the interdependence and relativity of things just as the presence of energy can be perceived only by perceiving its effects on matter.

★ We do feel that quantum physicists, astronauts, astrologers, monks, scientists and inventors might have states that need these remedies.

A word of caution!

Just because somebody talks of UFO's or out of body experiences it does not automatically mean that the patient needs an imponderable remedy. However patients which imponderable states often talk about these experiences.

III. A Cure from Within Outwards

We also feel that these people come with deep pathologies but with an awareness of their inner state. When the remedy is given, unlike the other kingdoms, imponderables improve in their state followed by a reduction in the pathology or the physical symptoms.

They come to the homoeopath seeking an improvement in their state, not just the pathology. We had a case of Vacuum and one of Sol where both patients specified that their states needed and help not their symptoms. It is as if the patients needing imponderables are aware of the fact that the energy within is more important than the material body. They are aware that the energy within, gives rise to the problems of the material body. One case of Sol said that his symptoms were nothing but a material reflection of his perception of his reality. In the follow-up he stated that his perception of reality had changed and therefore his symptoms had changed. It was as if the Sun outside had integrated with the Sun within his soul; the two had merged. In both cases, the pathology took quite a while to settle down and the state was much better after the first dose itself.

During our initial experiences with Imponderable cases we were hesitant that the pathology showed no improvement. We were unsure whether we were on the right track. It was a patient who said that she felt such amelioration that she was sure we were on the way to health. She taught us about second prescription and follow-up criteria of these cases.

IV. A Personal Note

It has always been a great feeling to learn from our patients and our cases. It is true that our patients are our best judges and critics. Most of all they are our best teachers! We feel that our association with these cases taught us a lot about life. It strengthened our belief in spirituality. The more we read and understood about the micro cosmos the more our belief of the world being a finite, constant and fixed entity started giving way to the existence of infinity, relativity and uncertainty. It was then that the often-heard phrase that 'the only thing constant in life is change' made so much sense to Shachindra and me. Therefore, the well-known idiom among all religions 'live in the moment' made more sense than anything else. The need to 'hold on' eased. There is nothing to hold on to if there is no past and no present. There is nothing to hold on to if everything is relative and ever-changing.

We have had an interesting experience with our Imponderable cases and it has proved true for all cases since then.

Every time Shachindra and I have reached mid-way in the case, it appears fuzzy and our energy dips down. We feel muddled up and sleepy and that we cannot carry on. When we cross that point, things begin to fall into place and the whole circle is complete. A spurt of energy fills us up. Needless to say, the patient also feels understood and gets to understand something about himself.

The whole process of case-taking, when complete, is a rejuvenating experience for the homoeopath but when the case is left half done it is a draining experience.

V. Time Phenomenon in Imponderables

A woman who needed the remedy Vacuum felt that her present life was merely a continuation of her past life. She believed that we could cure her 'pain in this life' only if we healed her 'past life'. It was a strange expectation from us. We prescribed Vacuum 1M and a few months later she felt that her death experience of her past life (which was very painful) was healed and taken care of with the remedy and now she was on the road to cure. Though her state was much better and her symptoms were also showing a significant improvement, she was not concerned with them. She believed that it was her past life's experience that was healed by our remedy and hence she was better in this lifetime.

If we look at it this way - *The only truth is the present*. It encompasses the past, present and the future. A patient might talk of past life or present life or re-birth or out-of body experience or whatever, we could come to the remedy from any of this information.

It really does not matter which route we take. Rather, the patient decides which route to take. His experience remains the same. The vital force carries within it the information of past, present and future. What each one of us experiences in the moment, at the deepest level, is the same as our experiences as a child, in the past life or in the future.

Imponderables have the understanding of this aspect of time. Time for them is not constant - it is a relative phenomenon. It takes a while for a homoeopath to understand the concept of time and matter in such cases.

The experience of the moment is what matters as there is no truth other than the very moment we are living in. Everything else is but a delusion. Today scientists and physicists are talking of anti-time, parallel time and cyclical nature of time. What we feel as past, is what is happening somewhere else at the same time in some other universe. The moral of the story therefore is that what matters is NOW. What matters is the experience of the patient in that moment while he is sitting in front of us irrespective of whether he speaks of it as his past, present or future.

20

SPECIFIC CHARACTERISTICS OF DIFFERENT IMPONDERABLES

I. Sol: Sunlight

II. Lunar: Moonlight

III. Electricitas: Electricity

IV. Thunderstorm

V. Magnetis poli ambo: Magnetism

VI. X-ray

Before we go further please note that the basic polarity underlying all these cases is polarity of energy and matter and this must come out in your case clearly. Once the polarity, energy and matter, has been established you can then look for information that can tell you the source of the remedy.

I. Sol: Sunlight
Here the feeling is I am/possess an energy that has:
- ⋆ Supreme power
- ⋆ Power to disperse and emanate to the entire universe
- ⋆ Power to penetrate and travel and effect large masses over large distances
- ⋆ Power to produce life
- ⋆ I feel neglected when that power is denied or not noticed
- ⋆ I have the power to destroy

II. Lunar: Moonlight
I am / I possess an energy that is:
- ⋆ Radiant, cool, calm
- ⋆ Works in unison and co-operation with others
- ⋆ I need others, and I reflect the good work of others
- ⋆ I work under others, and I spread light and happiness just as moon reflects sunlight but cannot produce its own
- ⋆ I have the power to pull, attract and unsettle others worlds

Lunar can also reflect these features:
- ⋆ Others have the power to attract and unsettle me - Comes from the gravitational forces of moon causing tides in the oceans
- ⋆ Reflecting, being in harmony with others
- ⋆ Beauty
- ⋆ Marked periodicity in the symptoms and periodical aggravation of state

III. Electricitas: Electricity

* Flowing of my thoughts and values is important - just like the flow of current
* I have the power to change reform and do wonders to the world

We know that electricity flows between two points of unequal resistance. Displaced free electrons carry electrical charge as they flow.

This is seen in the cases as:
* Against resistance, I will not give up my individuality
* Against resistance, I shall flow. Rather, the moment I face a resistance I begin to flow
* I have a feeling that they are moving and displacing me, and I flow

Although it looks like an animal, the feeling is not that of survival and death. The feeling is of flowing and maintaining one's own individuality.

IV. Thunderstorms

* I am powerful, and will not give in to resistance from the others
* I have the power to destroy as well
* Range, anger, uncontrollable
* Destructive rapid force like lightening
* Aggravation from/aversion to loud noise
* Fear of/aggravation from/love for rain
* Fear of thunderstorm
* Aggravation in cloudy weather

V. Magnetis poli ambo: Magnetism

Magnetism is a force. In most objects, all the forces are in balance because half of the electrons are spinning in one direction and half are spinning in the other. These spinning electrons are scattered evenly throughout the object.

Magnets are different. In magnets, most of the electrons at one end are spinning in one direction. This uni-directional spin of electrons causes a magnetic field and therefore forms the magnet. The magnetic force at one pole is the opposite of the magnetic force at the other pole. A magnet is labelled with North (N) and South (S) poles. The magnetic force in a magnet flows from the North Pole to the South Pole.

The theme here would be:
* ★ Imbalance causing a pull
* ★ It is a feeling of a force or a pull
* ★ I am in my sphere or in my world and there is a disturbance that pulls me towards it.
* ★ There is a force that pulls me or pushes me and I am so much affected by this force.
* ★ Others pull me towards them. I feel pulled towards things or people. I feel pulled by some unseen forces.
* ★ I am being pulled into a field and I cannot resist it
* ★ I am repelled by the others or I repel the others

It is almost a physical force or a physical push. We do not have much experience to be able to differentiate Magnetis polis arcticus (North Pole) from Magnetis polis australis (South) at this point.

The proving symptoms of Magnetis polus australis show a kind of repulsion to other people and other things. Hence we would use this remedy more where the experience is that of being repelled more than pulled or attracted. As the flow of charge is from the North towards the South Pole, the South Pole appears to be more at the receiving end of the charge.

Magnetis polus arcticus could be used where the experience is that of an active force, a more aggressive one. The patient experiences that he can pull and push while Magnetic polus australis, would have the experience as being pulled or pushed by the magnetic forces or the people around.

Ref:
Magnetis polus australis
Vermeulen's Synoptic II
"Wild, hasty, harsh, violent in word and deed (which he is not himself aware of); he asserts himself with vehemence and despises others, with distorted features."
* ★ "Society is disagreeable to him, he wants to be alone."
* ★ "He dislikes cheerful faces."
* ★ "Wants to say something hateful or make up a face." [E.E. Case]
* ★ "Aversion to anyone who comes near, even persons fond of." [Case]

VI. X-ray

X-rays are electromagnetic waves of much shorter wavelength hence are more powerful and penetrating.

X-ray themes:
- ⋆ I am strong and penetrating
- ⋆ I can pass through matter
- ⋆ Others can resist my efforts or whenever there is resistance, I will be single-minded and I will penetrate thoroughly, finely and surely
- ⋆ I have the power to pass through, permeate and be myself and stand against resistance

Please note that a person who has X-ray as the source could also say the opposite. He could say that he experiences everything in this world as a thing penetrating him. He would say – "Everything has the power to penetrate me or see through me like an X-ray." This kind of passive component is best explained by the next case.

21

 ## IMPONDERABLE CASE 3: LASER BEAM

I. Case Introduction

II. The Case

III. How did we Prepare Laser Beam?

I. Case Introduction

(**L**ight **a**mplification by **s**timulated **e**mission of **r**adiation = Laser). While in regular light the beams are random, in a laser beam there is stimulated radiation causing a monochromatic beam of light. In homoeopathic language this would mean that laser beam has a focus, single direction, a clear target or goal to achieve and is powerful as compared to the ray of light coming from any other sources. This is exactly seen in cases that need Laser beam as a remedy. The remedy Laser beam was made for us by Helios Pharmacy, England.

II. The Case

P: Sinus headaches as if a needle is penetrating the temples, and as it passes from one side of the temple to the other, it cuts through the head and fine pieces are scattered all over.

D: What is the experience?

P: I don't know what to say – whether to say it is pleasant or unpleasant.

D: What do you mean?

P: I like it when things are focused and single or uni-directional. So in a way, this pain - when the needle comes in is much focused and I like it that way. I would not be able to bear a burning or a lancination, or a dull, spread out and scattered pain. This is how I am focused and uni-directional, and there is no doubt that my pain too is the same.

D: So what is the problem if you are happy with the pain?

P: No. It's the fogginess it causes in my mind. It leaves me dazed – as if I have been hit, and my entire mind – my coherent functioning mind has been thrown back or scattered into pieces. I hate to appear confused and out of control.

D: Describe that.

P: When you are confused, people can take advantage of you.

D: Describe that.

P: They can confuse you further. I hate to be in a spot where I cannot make sense of what is happening around.

D: Describe that.

P: As a child, I remember my father would drink a lot. He would come home a completely different person. He would be sober every morning while leaving for work. We would wait in anticipation as to what the evening would have in store for us. When he would come home, he would be drunk, and he would beat us all up including my mother. I was the eldest sister of the four children. It was terrible.

D: Describe that.

P: He would throw things and beat us up and we were all scattered in pieces. My world was scattered in pieces. I had to get up the next morning and pick it up and start all over again. There was no fixity, no direction to my life. I hated to be scattered like that.

D: Describe the experience of scattered.

P: As if somebody has poked you through and through and the whole world is scattered into thousands of millions of pieces. It sounds very out of the blue, but I can see that happening now in front of my eyes.

D: What is happening?

P: I can see a beam – a red laser beam cutting through a fleshy body and making pieces all around it.

D: Describe that.

P: The beam knows where it has to go. It has the focus I was telling you about; but the body is lying there lazily, and has no aim. It knows not what to do next. It is dazed and the beam is single minded. That's what I want – focus in my life. I like to act with a plan. I like to keep things in order. When I work, I plan the entire schedule and the route and then I start; just like the beam. Funny! But that's what comes to my irrational mind – the beam.

III. How did we Prepare Laser Beam?

The remedy was prepared in a dental clinic in England. The remedy was made using the Ruby laser. Four different energy settings were used from 100 mili joules to 500 mili joules. It was the 500 that gave the best temperature rise. The liquid was first directly exposed to the laser energy but since the dental laser uses compressed air it simply blew the liquid. Eventually the liquid was exposed through a clear glass test tube for about one minute until there was a temperature rise of approximately 10 degrees. This vial was then sent to Helios pharmacy, London for further potentisation.

22

 POSITRONIUM
(We consider it among the Imponderables as it is anti-matter)

I.   Introduction

II. The Theme of Positronium

III. A Case of Positronium

IV. Remedy and Case Follow-up

V.   Summary

I. Introduction

Positronium is an anti-particle of the Hydrogen atom. It has a positron and an electron. It has almost no mass. It has been proved by Misha Norland. We have used it in a patient to palliate her in last stages of intestinal carcinoma. However we did not come to the remedy from the proving symptoms. We came to the remedy from what we understood of Positronium from the source information.

Some information about Positronium and anti-matter:
* In 1930, Paul Dirac, in an attempt to develop an equation for the electron, ended up having an irreparable mistake in his calculation which proved that for every particle on this earth there is an anti-particle.

* If any particle came across its anti-particle, they would simply nullify each other and create energy. The anti-particle is the same as any particle and has the exact opposite charge. It moves in anti-time.

* One theory believes that in the Big Bang, matter & anti-matter co-emerged. It is also postulated that there could be a parallel universe somewhere. This parallel universe is identical to our universe but it is composed of anti-matter and things move in anti-time in this universe.

* A positron is mathematically anti-electron. So, it is an electron with a positive charge and moving in anti-time. Positronium is anti-Hydrogen. It has one electron and one positron. It has almost no mass. Since the Positronium is made of electron and anti-electron it is extremely unstable and quickly annihilates itself.

II. The Theme of Positronium
* Converging of polarity of any kind into nothingness and a oneness
* Conversion and explosion
* One nullifies the other
* Creation of immense energy and power
* Does it all really matter?
* Close to nirvana or enlightenment
* Two states
* One opposes the other
* One is the anti-matter of the other
* Annihilation

- ⭑ Explosion
- ⭑ Energy release in this merging
- ⭑ Small and yet powerful
- ⭑ Anti-time
- ⭑ Before time

Note: It is not necessary for every case of Positronium to have an explosion but I believe the conversion of polarity and nullification of the two poles would definitely be present since this is the theme of any anti-matter.

III. The Case of Positronium

This is a case of a woman suffering from cancer of the colon, terminal stage. She was a Jain monk. She was 47 years old. She appeared very peaceful and strong. I was amazed as to how she could bear all her suffering. She was vomiting continuously. She was almost bending double with the pain but she had a smile on her face when I met her. I was asked to see her as I am from the same extended family. I asked her to tell me about the pain. She smiled and then, what I got was a sermon on Jain philosophy.

I had to understand the patient and separate her polarity from the intermingled threads of her state and religion.

P: You are asking me about the pain. You are asking a Jain monk about pain. This is my Karma. And I have to negate all Karmas before I leave this earth. Why did we come to the earth? Do you know something about the Jain Philosophy? We are all souls with Karmas attached to our souls. Karmas are negative energies that make the soul heavy. The soul is an energy that actually gets more and more materialistic with Karmas. The material prevents us from getting back into the pure energy form that we always were once upon a time. You know the theory of Big Bang is all about energy being transformed into matter. The Jain philosophy is the same. We are all souls and we come into the body (matter) only because of these Karmas. God has also shown us the path to negate these Karmas so that we can go back to energy; the pure energy which is all encompassing. It is one. It is the state of Nirvana. It is the state of enlightenment or detachment. It is called Vitrag or Anashakti.

I am washing out my Karmas with this pain. I know I must bear it all so that Karmas can be washed and the soul becomes pure. If the soul becomes pure it unites with the all encompassing almighty. You can call it cosmos, cosmic energy and anything you want to. It is difficult to bear the pain. I am trying my level best to.

You may call it Brahman in Sanskrit or Yin-Yang in Chinese philosophy. You know, even Quantum physics today believes in the Jain philosophy. It is the theory of observer and observed and the relativity between the two. The two are one and the same. When one separates from the other, there is life and matter. When the two unite there is oneness.

D: This that you say is really very interesting and I would love to listen more but more than the philosophy, I need to understand you a little bit more.

P: The philosophy has been a part of me before I became a monk. I was 14 when I picked my first book on the Jain philosophy. I do not believe in rituals, chants and ceremonies. I never did. But I always wondered as to what is the reason for all this pain and suffering we must go through. I was around 10 when I asked my mother as to why I was born. She never answered my question. She just laughed it off. I asked her why I was born to her and not to my friend's mother. She said it was my Karma. I was 18 when I decided to be a monk. My father was shocked. I was always the quiet one in the family. They would call me a day-dreamer. I could look at the vast ocean, the mountains and the trees and the flowers and go into deep meditation. I wondered why and how the universe works. I could never find a reason for the existence of things.

Then I learnt about Jainism. I am a Jain by birth. We often went to the temple and those sorts of things. But one day I got my answers from a discourse by a Jain monk. But my questions were different and needed different answers. I teach people the way to live, the good and bad deeds and Karma but these are stepping stones to a much deeper philosophy. They are stepping stones to the final oneness of things. I wanted the answer to my question - why should we enter into this cycle of life and death? I was very young when I realised this was all futile, which is why I chose to be a monk. I want release from this cycle of life and death. I have to have a soul that is without any Karmas and then it will be capable of uniting with the almighty or cosmos.

I am the first born among three brothers and one sister. My mother did not have any children for 11 years. Then my father went to Mount Abu and performed a few rituals.

He promised to offer his first child to God. I knew nothing of this. My father had no intentions of making me a monk. When I chose to be one, my mother told me this story. She said that it was written in my destiny. God had given them to me only on one condition – that, they give me back to him. Since my father broke that promise God himself chose to take me away from them. I was destined to become a monk. I was destined to (.....silence ...)

D: What is the most important thing in this philosophy that touches you?

P: Dwandwa or Pratipaksha. Nothing can exist without its exact polar opposite. I read about the polarity or duality of things in the several religious books. This is most important of all things. The idea that two opposites annihilate each other and then there is absolutely nothing or in other words, there could be everything. It is so ironical and yet it is the only existential truth. There is no light without darkness. And when the two meet there is neither light nor darkness. There is everything and yet nothing. Everything that exists has an exact opposite to it and when the two merge there is a collision where matter is extinguished and all that remains is pure cosmic energy.

D: I would like to know what attracted you to this path since childhood.

P: (Smiling)...You want to know about my childhood ....

D: Whatever, I want to know about your experience as a child before you knew about all this philosophy. Not what you read or learnt but what you felt.

P: I felt pain, intense pain! I could not understand the reason for so much pain and pleasure in life. I felt things very intensely as a child. I could get hurt easily, I could feel excited easily. I would feel every little thing for days together and I could not get it out of my mind and body. I felt so caught in this circle of pain and pleasure, life and death and highs and lows. I don't think I knew so much about life and death but I saw my grandfather's dead body when they brought it home. He was bed-ridden ever since my birth so I did not have a special bond with him. But I felt that he was a member of the family. When he died everything came back to normal in a few days; everything and everyone but me. I could feel his presence in the room every time I went in. I had a feeling that I would be able to see him if I wanted to or if I strongly desired and I was scared of this feeling. I can feel so many souls around me at any given time. I live on a different plane than you. I am not trying to brag about it but I just want you to know that I feel very different. I feel I am soul and you feel you are body. I felt the pain of the body and its pleasure when I was a child and I wanted to get rid of it. I think what shocked me the most was the polarity of things and emotions. I felt as if every time I was very happy a sad moment would follow to nullify the happiness. Everything always nullified or negated everything else. I feared one emotion as I knew the exact opposite would follow. I was caught in this trap of opposites and I needed to be free.

D: Describe caught in the trap.

P: In Vipassana (Buddhist form of meditation) one is supposed to concentrate on one's breath and observe the sensations that the body feels. We call it Sanskara in Jain philosophy and Sankhara in Buddhism. It is called Karma in Hinduism.

D: So what was the sensation?

P: You really know how to keep me on track ....Laughs ....I feel every molecule of my body vibrating. As I concentrate more and observe more, the molecules feel like they are being caught ... Each molecule feels caught in between two exactly similar traps on either side. There are millions of such small traps within the body.

D: More about this caught,

P: Yeah every little molecule is like a spurt of energy caught between these two exactly similar but polar opposite traps and the two traps come closer and closer and annihilate each other and there is a spark of energy and there is release.

P: There are several sparks all over the body when there is this collision of the two sides of the trap. With every spark, I feel a release from the trap. The trap does not open to bring release of energy, but it closes in and the two opposite sides meet. Then there is no trap and there is freedom and there are energy sparks.

D: Describe this trap and these two opposite sides and this spark, etc.

P: They are part of one thing. As if two opposing petals of a flower that

282

come close. As if... but the two petals is not the exact description since they are part of the same flower. No, what I am talking about is two objects which are very similar and kept facing one another. Like me watching myself in the mirror. So there are two things but one is the mirror opposite of another.

D: This is what you feel ...

P: At the level of the Sukshma or micro cosmos or at the level of Annu which means atom in your language. But this is what my reality is. I had an intuition of this as a child. I did not have the words to express it but I always had the feeling in my heart or somewhere embedded in my soul. I think in this life I have come here to clear these or annihilate these karmas. I am sure it will take a few more lives till I am completely devoid of any. I do not want to be cured of this cancer. The cancer brings all the Karmas on the surface and if I observe the pain I will be free of it. It is a philosophy difficult to practice but I am trying my level best. I hope you do not discuss this with any students. I learnt that you teach all over the world.

D: Yeah, but I think people will learn a lot about the remedy and also about the philosophy if I talk about your case.

P: You may do as you wish.

IV. Remedy and Case Follow-up

I had Positronium 30. I gave her one dose and sent her a couple of doses. I saw her for about three months after that. Her pain had reduced markedly. She then travelled to another city in India and wrote a letter to me once that she was still doing fine. The vomiting had reduced and so had the pain. She had even been able to give a couple of lectures. The very fact that she could travel and was not bed-ridden anymore was a miracle. The doctors had lost all hopes. I was in touch with her for about seven to eight months and then had no contact with her or any other monk.

We then got a message that she peacefully passed away last year. She was active, had resumed her lecturing and was quite at ease till her last days. We were happy to know that.

V. Summary

The reason why I gave her Positronium:

The polarity that ruled or governed her life was that of matter and energy – 'Matter transforms into energy and that is where I belong.'

And what kind of a source was she talking about?

She was talking about a source where there was an opposite of everything. Everything had equal opposites to them and the two opposites annihilated each other to create energy. The trap she felt at the molecular level was a trap of two similar particles which are actually polar opposites (mirror images of each other) and when they meet they annihilate each other and there is a spark of energy.

That must be the theme of anti-matter as anti-matter is opposite of matter. When matter meets anti-matter, the result is an annihilation and release of tremendous energy. This was exactly the pattern that she was talking about.

The only anti-matter that we have in Homoeopathy is Positronium, the anti-matter of Hydrogen. We had a feeling we would cause 'killers aggravation' with any potency higher than what we gave her.

23

 ## <u>IMPONDERABLE CASE 4: VACUUM</u>

I. The Case

II. Remedy and Case Follow-up

I. The Case

D: Tell me about your problems.

P: I was diagnosed with ischemic heart disease and anginal pains ever since my menopause. I think once the hormones stopped working, my heart started to show its weakness. I feel it in my body. I know when the pain comes, that I have to relax. I am not taking the sorbitates or aspirins but that's not so important. I think my problem, what I want you to solve is what I said to you - the theme of shock. I see it in my life I suppose, sometimes heavier only a bit. I am sure there must be a connection to this shock and also my headache. There is some point in my back that hurts a little bit as well but it's not so heavy. So I have come to you to speak about the shock in my life.

I have done a lot of psychological work. I think it was good work and it helped me a lot to have a very good life. But then oh! I know I have to cry now. I can't, I can't talk about the shock unless I cry. Five years ago I got the shock of my life. My son took away all my property. It's unbelievable that one can do this but I think the most important moment was when I get to know that there is something fishy. I asked him and he said, "Yes it's true. All your property is mine now." I was shocked! That was the kind of shock. I know in my life it's the same reaction ever since I know and then I had it again and again. I had it again when I was with my husband and the things he did to me. It's the same reaction when something happens that I don't expect. I couldn't imagine it would be possible. No, I didn't expect it. I see it. It's like a flash that comes in and I can't think anymore. I get lame or heavy. I can't think anymore of what I can do or why it is so? Or what happened to me at that point? I don't think anymore.

The worst thing is that this shock, this reaction has no end. This was also in my childhood with my uncle. He was loving and kind and then one fine day when no one was home he came and he abused me. It was the same shock. I was numb and stunned and then he was absolutely okay as if nothing happened. I wondered if I was day dreaming about it. It's that shock that stuns you; it's the same reaction every time. When I got on to the plane to come here I saw that I lost my passport. It was at that moment of shock that the flash came. It was like "O God!"

D: Describe this more - the shock and flash comes in.

This shock and flash had come with this kind of a gesture quite often in the case so far. Hence we thought it was important to know more about it.

P: I have the feeling of becoming dead and heavy like a stone. There is a cramp of hurt in my heart. I can't breathe and I am shocked and I am choked. And I am like a stone. There is no life. I am almost as if a carved stone statue. I have this feeling often when I have had a dream or even when I am awake sometimes. This feeling is here. I have a stone on my heart. Ah! It's the feeling like it's the end of my life. This idea that it's the end comes nearly in every shock, always.

The attitude was almost Syphilitic. The shock is like this flash is coming.

P: After the shock with my son I told him, "Now you are dead for me." After the shock always I am like a zombie, a robot. I think I do it only mechanically. I just lay down. I have no energy left. All energy is out and I ask myself what should I do to come out of this state? I need to go to a warm place or take a walk or do exercises or yoga for a long time. But in the state of zombie I can't do it anymore. I try to do everything to feel that I am alive again because otherwise in the shock I feel completely dead and numb. There is nothing I feel with this shock. I think I am a person who likes to live. I like to do a lot of different things. I like to make the best of my life. I like to enjoy with my children and grand children and friends.

When I was thinking this morning about what I had to tell you, I had the idea that my life just goes away somewhere. I have ideas and plans that are important for me and I do it rather enthusiastically and sometimes perhaps I do too much. Then I am a little bit tensed. Perhaps, I cannot feel when something I didn't expect and it comes. The whole energy is put down and it takes a long time in the bottom. Then I have to start all over again.

D: So just describe this - I didn't expect and then it comes. This whole energy and I didn't expect and...

P: What I don't expect is that it doesn't lie in my spectrum.

D: What do you mean that it doesn't lie in my spectrum?

P: My spectrum is what my life should be; also what I can expect.

287

D: Just describe this feeling - It didn't lie in my spectrum.

P: It's out of my range you could say. It's out of me. It doesn't belong to me. This shock, it doesn't belong to me.

D: More.

P: That's it. I think its something; I think it can poison me.

D: What do you mean?

P: It can destroy me and take everything from me. I need to have a good life. In this statue feeling there is a feeling to be completely empty. Everything is taken away from me. Of course then I feel very sad. I cry a little bit about this empty feeling. At times it's like a computer that's crashed. Then I have to start the computer again I think. I have to start to give it all the information. Whatever text I had in the computer before, I have to gather all that information and start all over again.

D: So describe this empty feeling; this feeling that you have of emptiness.

P: Lost. Just lost; no connection to the outside world anymore.

D: Describe no connection to the outside world anymore.

P: It's like a satellite and you send it out in the universe.

D: Describe this.

P: And the earth's station has lost contact with this satellite. What does the satellite do then? I have to redefine me, who am I, where am I in this space? Do I exist, do I not exist?

D: Describe this - I have to redefine, do I exist, do I not exist?

P: Where am I, where am I going? There is no road map; you might be anywhere in the universe. There is no map to orient you. There is no orientation here. I can only see here I am and time is gone. That's an important aspect somehow there is no feeling of time when I get this shock.

D: How does that feel?

P: If you have no time its senseless to do something. You can only do something if you have the concept of time. Actions and everything we have on this planet is somehow embedded in time. It lasts for a while. It is as if there is no time. The usual life has just gone. It's the only life as I am. I am shot out of my person. I am shot out of my body. When I have this empty feeling I am just shot out. I am not in the person any more. I am afraid of this feeling. I have only the feeling I am part of the universe. It's as if there is no connection and you are really dead. It's perhaps the feeling of when somebody dies. And he doesn't know that he is dead. He is out of the body. He can't make any connection with his family and he doesn't know where shall he go now, what shall he do now?

D: How does it feel, out of the body, somewhere in the universe?

P: Lost, totally lost. Perhaps this was the reason I did past-life therapy. It was very important for me to know how dying goes. I can remember how it was the last time that I died and how it is to be out of the body. Three or four times I have had out of body experiences. This has happened sometimes in the night.

D: Can you describe those out of body experiences?

P: It's not so, you know that you will go back to your body so it's not really frightening.

D: Can you describe this?

P: It's a good feeling to be out of the body.

D: How do you feel that?

P: I feel free from all this heavy stuff. You can move everywhere you want. You can think you are out here and you are out there. You are out of your body. That's when I feel that you are a soul not only a body. What is it to be a human being? What is soul, what is spirit? At that time I know I am soul and I have left my body.

D: That doesn't feel like a trouble at all?

P: No. That's not a trouble at all. As long as I know that I am here, I can get back into my body. Once I had a …I woke up out of the body, I flew over and through the trees with such a good feeling. I flew very fast almost as if I am in an airplane, better than in an airplane.

D: What's the feeling like?

P: Totally free. I think it's even better than a bird. Better than an eagle perhaps.

D: What's this feeling?

P: Flying? It's as if an eagle to the wind. You feel like the wind is in your wings. And you can do only a small movement with the wings and then it goes up in the wind and down, this is the feeling I have. You can fly across the sky.

D: What is this feeling of going fast, going through the trees?

P: Do you want the sensation or a picture?

D: Everything.

P: It's a feeling like perhaps intruders from the other world have come to planet earth. They have an aim. They know where they go. They know where they can go back. That means it's like a God like feeling. God is a being that doesn't need something and is not vulnerable. I think I am very…

D: No, no, no you are just perfect. Just go on. What do you mean by not vulnerable?

P: Yes these two feelings are very similar or they are the opposites - The eagle and the intruders. Intruders, is that right? Is there any other name for intruders? Yes, aliens! I have to say.

D: Describe this whole thing and the feelings.

P: I think they took me with them. This is the feeling everyone has who has been with them. It was a shock, they took me with them.

D: What do you mean they took you with them?

P: They did. Perhaps you have heard that in America, in the States, they have a lot of these cases. People say that they come; these aliens and they take some of your tissue. Perhaps they know DNA analysis and then they bring you back. All these people tell that they have lost some time. All these people tell that there is one hour, half an hour, two hours where they don't have any memory. They have the feeling that time stopped. When I saw these creatures it was the same for me. Time stopped and then I am on this road again and then life goes on. And you can't remember anything. When I talk about this experience now, I never thought that there would be a connection with the shock but now I see there must be a connection.

D: So describe this feeling of being shocked and afraid.

P: It's the same feeling as I said before. You stay here and you see something that you didn't expect because it doesn't belong to your spectrum. It doesn't belong to you at all and all that you knew that did exist for you.

D: And what is it like? Just go into this feeling.

P: It's so confusing you can't take it in your mind or integrate it. You have to just let it be there. I can't connect myself to these feelings at all.

D: Describe this a little bit more.

P: I can't open my mind to let it in.

D: No, just this feeling - it does not belong to everything that you exist.

P: It does not belong to anything that existed till now in my world. I am simply over challenged by this thing. I think am challenged.

D: I don't get it.

P: I can't handle it. It's a kind of helplessness. Of course it comes from a world that I didn't know before.

D: So what is your feeling with all this? Because it's like this - it's unexpected and it doesn't come from a world that belongs to you. What is your feeling?

P: I am nothing.

D: Describe this.

P: Perhaps I have the idea that I am... because I have a lot of experiences. I know myself through my past and my present. The experiences I have gone through make me, me. So it is to say that I am nothing. I am empty. There is nothing inside me that can give an echo. I am not me.

D: Very good. Just describe this - I am nothing, I am empty, I have nothing that will give an echo.

> *What is important over here is that as this case was going, the thought of Hydrogen as a remedy was coming to our minds. 'Whether I exist or I don't exist.' But as she goes further she kind of cancels out all those things.*

P: Echo is a sound. Echo is to give a response. There is something out of me, out of my spectrum that is challenging and I have nothing in me that can respond with a reaction or a word. It's a kind of helplessness.

D: How do you feel at that moment?

P: I don't feel anything. I just don't exist anymore in that moment.

D: How does it feel to not exist?

P: The feeling is felt in the deepest of my body. It is felt in the deepest of my core.

D: How does this feel to not exist?

P: It's not to be a part of this planet or life here.

D: Describe this - not here.

P: I am dead now, I have lost my body. I have lost everything that belonged to me, everything that was the idea that I am. Everything is extinguished as a fire and you put water on it. It's a fear that somebody can extinguish you. I am dissolved, I am really dissolved, I am everywhere completely dissolved.

Hydrogen has not developed or gathered anything. The feeling of the Hydrogen patient therefore is not that everything existing is lost but that nothing is formed in the first place.

D: What are you doing? What is this that you just did?

P: The energy is spread.

D: Very good. Just describe this.

P: There is no solidity anymore. There is no frame, no border. Here I am and here are you. The energy is just spread out and this whole sinking feeling.

D: Describe this a little bit more – I am dissolved. What is your experience? How does it feel?

P: Here I am and here are you. There are no frames or borders. It's like anything that you can experience at this moment; anything. Can you ask me some more questions?

D: Yeah.

P: So that I can clarify this.

D: Just go on. Describe this a little bit more. Make it clearer to me. What is the experience when you say this is all dissolving?

P: It's actually a good feeling. But it's also full of fright and shock that I must not experience once more. I don't want to experience this fright and shock. No it's really not good I think. The next time I could die because the first time the shock happened I was in delirium for four to five weeks. My reaction was very intensive. Fevers came and went. I was in the shock. I had the feeling of being a zombie. I was feeling like a robot. And I just lay down for hours and hours and hours. Time didn't exist for me. It was a feeling of being in the universe. 'Everything was over, I don't care and I must not care about everything here. I would like to die now.' This was my feeling of a zombie.

D: Describe this feeling in the universe. You said time does not exist. What is this universe? Is there anything that you want? What is this that you are experiencing?

P: I would like to die now and go to the heaven. Go out; merge with my soul and with my higher self.

D: How does it feel to merge with the soul and higher self? What is the feeling like?

P: Wholeness.

D: Describe whole.

P: Totally at home, to be one with God, with my higher life and my real home.

D: What is your real home?

P: Where I belong.

D: And where is that?

P: Where there is love.

D: Where is that?

P: Love.

D: Your home?

P: My home is full of love and light.

D: Describe this - my home is full of love and light.

P: Unity, joy and flowers and everything. No, not flowers; I mean colours, totally free not alone.

D: Describe this - free and not alone.

P: That's what I try to live here in my life all the time; with my partner and with my children, to be free and together as a being and an identity to live with respect and love. Perhaps such a little bit heavenly feeling I tried to bring in my life here.

What's happening, where are we going? The patient went on talking about so many different things at the level of delusion. It didn't make any sense. We were as lost as you guys are at this point of time and more than lost, we were just spaced out. What's going on? We talk about her complaint, about this shock thing. The shock thing took us to past life, regression, to aliens, DNA and what not; shamanism. And after this time point she went on talking about shamanism. We had no idea of what was going on in the case. But we needed to focus on this to find the essence of what she was experiencing. We asked her what was happening to her at that point of time. What she said took the case further into much more sense in terms of prescription. But she went into her jumbled talks further more.

D: What's happening to you at this point of time?

P: I feel like a complete zombie. That's the feeling, I feel like a total zombie.

D: Zombie? How does it feel like a zombie for you?

P: Empty, without anything, without a feeling of wholeness. Is it broken? Yeah! Perhaps it's broken, it's damaged. There is a part of me which is taken away. There is a part that is light and the rest is body. What's the name for the second body?

D: Describe this body is there and the light is taken away.

P: The light belongs to the wholeness. The light is shining through this wholeness with the shock. This connection to the light is interrupted with the shock.

Wow! This shock interrupts the connection with the light. This wholeness is interrupted by the shock. This tells us that the patient is making some progress. So we ask her describe this light.

D: You said, 'That light can't come in again in my body'. Just describe this light.

P: If you keep asking me to just describe this light, the light is this. This thought that I took from the universe, from my soul, from my source. The light is all that. It's my universe, it's my soul.

D: Sorry go over it once again.

P: In this incarnation, this part I took from the…I don't know what to say? This light I took with me when I was incarnated. When I was incarnated my soul was full of light. The light and the spirit I think. I know the light is… I know that I am the consciousness. When I incarnated, I had this consciousness that I am the light, I am life, I have energy, light is energy.

D: Describe this light.

P: Light is the highest energy we know on this planet. It's what we have from our Sun. The sun sends light and I think there are other sources and other stars. We can't live without light. In this shock the light stops, time stops and light is cut away. Everything is simply cut away.

D: Cut away? What is this that you are talking?

P: Its cut. I have to go forward as a zombie. I am just doing things, exercising, eating, but just like a zombie. There is no light, there is no life. And then the light comes again in the next few days.

D: Just describe this whole phenomenon that light is not there. What is this experience that you are shocked and life is stopped?

P: Life is stopped. That's what I am trying to tell you. There is only darkness in my life at that point.

D: This experience is extremely important, shock and…

P: Before being in connection, you are in life, joy, energy, in light and all this. Then the shock comes in and something happens and everything stops. The light stops and there is darkness. There is no feeling of who I am..

So the experience of our patient is as if light is stopped.

D: What is this when light stops? How does it feel? What is the experience that life stops, time stops, energy stops? What is this experience? How does it feel?

P: Block, stuck and immobile.

D: Right you are getting over there. You are just getting there, tell me the experience.

P: No, you give me the word. I don't get the word. It's almost like you know life and death. Its cold, it's hot, it's to work in a cave down below. It's lost. I don't know what the word is but it's that deep, deep point where there is nothing, there is no light. There is depth, it is cold. It's that point.

D: Very good, go on. Describe this and you will reach there.

P: I have lost connection to life and to God.

D: Yes this is it. Just this feeling, talk about it.

P: It is as if you are nothing; just nothing.

D: Describe this nothing, just the experience of nothing.

P: It's like a dark black spot in the universe. You know there are black holes. It's as if I am a black hole. I feel I am a black hole.

This makes some sense to us now. Stop, nothing, light stops, time stops, something stops and then she brings out this picture of black hole. Now we try to explore this black hole and the source.

D: Describe this a bit more – the black hole.

P: I could never understand it when people said it. I don't know what it is? I only know this word. Physically I can't explain what I am feeling in this black hole.

D: What comes to you?

P: The Black hole must be something totally without energy. The universe is full of energy but in that spot where I am, there is no energy, there is no light. It's like a hole of full of nothing. There is nothing in it. There is absolutely nothing there.

D: Describe the hole full of nothing.

P: Because it feels like that. It tries to hold things, it tries to bring in things and it tries to suck things. It tries to bring something, where there is something some warmth, something to fill this empty hole but there is nothing that can fill this hole. This hole has a tendency to suck, to fill and may be its like black holes. You know I know that they can take in stars and the entire star systems. It's something like this, its trying to pull.

D: What is this that you are doing?

P: I am trying to reach out. This hole in me is trying to reach out, trying to take in something, like a star system. It's trying to take light and fill up that emptiness within it with some light.

D: What's this emptiness?

P: Nothing, nirvana.

D: What's this?

P: I know a word 'nicht' in German. Or you could say Null

D: What is 'nicht'? Describe nicht.

P: Nicht is nothing and the opposite of that is anything. Anything is the whole. There are books written on nicht. It's like a sign to be or not to be. It is the feeling that I am this null or nicht or not just this empty thing.

D: Describe this not to be.

P: I have a feeling or a phobia that there is no black point or maybe I have a phobia of this black point.

D: Yes, what is this nicht? Don't think. What comes to you? Just tell me the experience of nicht.

P: That it's not there. It's like this black hole. But empty. I know black holes are stars and they are full and dense and yet they pull. I feel empty like a Null.

Here you see the source is different from black hole as black holes are dense and full of matter while she is talking of being empty.

D: What comes to you when you feel null?

P: It's the feeling I said before. It's a feeling that I am completely extinguished. There is nothing there. No, that's not good. Yeah, null. It's null. That's what I feel - completely empty, and null. I want to suck in something to bring some light. It's completely empty.

D: You have really done a good job in describing what your experience is. I am sure the remedy is going to help you in a very strong way.

P: It's an experience for me, this case taking. I never thought I would come to all this stuff that I spoke to you about.

D: How does it feel now that the stuff is all out?

P: It's in my deepest inner being. This is the polarity in me. This is what is there in me - nothing.

D: What's this polarity once again?

P: Yeah it's the polarity between wholeness and nothingness. I wonder why I never reached till this level before doctor. I have done a lot of psychological work with my dreams and with my past life and so on. But I have never reached this point. Somehow today I have understood that it's all about this null, this empty feeling and I want to fill it up with some kind of wholeness. I want to fill this emptiness with a feeling of wholeness.

So this was the case. It was difficult but then persistence helped. It is important to be patient and focused at that point of time when we feel completely lost and confused. After the confusion comes clarity. And that's exactly happened here. That zombie opened up and took us right to the source, giving all the words of the source. Nothingness, lack of light, null and that is what we thought she requires.

II. Remedy and Case Follow-up

The black hole that she was describing was not really the energy of the black hole. She wasn't describing that power of a star of the black hole. What she was describing was a total emptiness. The black hole for her was an expression of that emptiness. Deeper down was a different kind of emptiness which was trying to suck in some light, some life and something. The polarity here was totally empty and vacuum on one side and totally full and whole on the other side. And that's what we gave her.

We gave her the remedy Vacuum in 1M potency because she was completely in the image of this shock and this vacuum and all the different things in the past that have stuck with her like the UFO, the abuse, the shamanism and the past life experiences.

The result was that this tremendous shock that she felt reduced to a very large extent. She said, "This shock which has been such an important part of my life is absolutely not there anymore. The shock that I was carrying for so many years with me has finally left my back." The remedy helped to heal this theme of shock that was so all-pervasive in her life.

But it also helped her to a large extent with her physical complaints – her pains and her hypertension. The deep sensation of shock and emptiness was the first to be cleared up and then over a period of three months the hypertension started to respond and after six months for a period of four years till she followed-up with us, the hypertension was in the range of 120-128/82-86 mm of Hg. Her earlier pressures before coming to us were of 160-210/ 100-120 mm of Hg. However she was more concerned about her shock and empty feeling, etc. rather than her BP.

24

THE THEMES OF BLACK HOLE

I.   Introduction

II. Themes Given Elaborately With Connection to Source Characteristics

III. The verbatim of our Cases of Black Hole

IV. How is a Black Hole Formed?

V.   Making of the Remedy

I. Introduction

Every time you make a remedy or come across a new remedy that has never been made, it is a complete euphoric and enthusiastic feeling where you feel you have unravelled something and have come one step closer to truth.

We have now three successful cases of black hole and we would like to put forth the complete picture of this remedy including the source description, the themes of the remedy and the phrases used by our cases.

The entire theme of the black hole energy is the **'Polarity of matter and energy'. The specific sensation of a Black hole is that of an experience that one is pulling in, drawing everything around oneself into one's own depths and in the process getting oppressed, dense and small. It is a feeling of extreme gravitational power or pull within oneself that draws anything and everything around it. It's a feeling of being huge, magnanimous and powerful yet dark, invisible and sometimes having a negative energy.**

II. Themes Given Elaborately With Connection to Source Characteristics

Just as the names suggests, black holes are black and dense because even light cannot escape them. Hence they are actually invisible or visible as black spots in Space.

The themes of black holes relate to the entire Space/universe including all matter and huge amount of unseen and invisible energy that pulls matter within it all the time. Black holes are known to pull matter into them and known to suck like vacuum, everything that reaches a particular point or distance within their reach. This activity of sucking or pulling matter within is not because a black hole is empty. Infact black holes are extremely dense. Matter within them is collapsing on itself and coming closer and closer.

As such, a black hole would be able to pull stars and galaxies and anything that comes within its way. However, this does not happen. If it did, all of space would be one black hole. This does not happen because everything needs to be within the reach of its gravitational pull. There is a limit to this pull, to this force and the limit is called an 'event horizon'. Till one does not reach the event horizon, one does not get pulled into the black hole but once one reaches it, there is no going back!

Hence, the event horizon is a kind of a boundary that gives the black hole its limit or its definition or boundary so to say.

Hence feelings that are common to black holes are:

* Pulling
* Drawing
* Sucking
* Feeling like a vacuum, but denser not empty
* Attract
* I feel I am pulling things in like a dark black hole within me
* Black
* Black mark

Other themes that are commonly seen in patients with black holes:

* I am small
* I am dense
* I am pulling
* Great speed
* I am taking in and actually getting smaller and denser and I don't believe it
* I am pulling in and things come in and never leave
* The smaller I get the denser I get
* Like a pull that one can never ever get out of

Feeling of Containment:

* A sense of a boundary
* A sense that separates me from the rest of the world
* I do not have the sense of container
* If I do not have this I will suck everything into me

Since black holes mark the end of magnanimous stars and are also responsible for the beginning of new stars in galaxies, patients also have this part of the story in their expression.

* Universe

* ★ Galaxy

* ★ Big

* ★ Magnanimous

* ★ Expanding

* ★ New Birth

* ★ Stars

* ★ Explosive

* ★ Power

* ★ Shine

* ★ Light

III. The Verbatim of our Cases of Black Hole

* ★ Connection is bigger

* ★ Want to move upwards, expand

* ★ Universal size

* ★ Expansive, powerful, creative

* ★ Fiery force, big, powerful

* ★ I am drawing

* ★ I am invisible, I am this force

* ★ Dense, heavy, dead

* ★ Need to have container

* ★ Ball that has identity

* ★ Things can come in and go

* ★ Growth and no growth

* ★ New ground to be created on higher level

* ★ Big, powerful, fast, explosive, expansive universe

* ★ Evolutionary force

* ★ They are invisible

* ★ They are dying stars

* Dense, compact
* Stars are creators
* Stars are fiery forces
* Black holes create grounds for new stars and galaxies as they give away dust
* Fire
* I was taking into the sky going high & then plummeting downwards
* Snuffed out
* Oppressed
* Dead
* Something that is dense, drawing and dark
* As things get drawn into it and enter it
* This thing itself becomes narrow, more dead and constricting
* Something within me is receptive to the fault of others
* That is drawing negativity
* But also someone who has the desire to life and create and give birth to things
* Something that is a fiery force
* Fire
* Lots of space
* Expansive
* Explosive
* Expanding universe

IV. How is a Black Hole Formed?

A black hole results from the remnants of a massive star which is dead and has collapsed. There are black holes at the centre of most galaxies, including our Milky Way. A black hole is usually so strong that nothing can escape from it, not even light. However, our solar system is so far away from the black hole that we do not get influenced by the pull of its gravity.

For a star to turn into a black hole it must be at least three times the mass of our Sun. The next question that arises is – how is a star born? Why and how does it shine? Does a star live forever?

The Process of Birth of a Star

All matter from the tiniest microscopic particle to the biggest galaxy begins from atoms. The same is for a star. The simplest and the lightest element is Hydrogen gas. Enormous clouds of Hydrogen gas and dust particles form in space.

Gravity draws the dust and gas close together, forming a huge clump or mass. As more and more matter is added to the mass its gravity increases. This pushes the atoms of Hydrogen gas closer to each other. The mass begins to contract and gets denser and hotter. The hottest area of the mass is the centre due to the squeezing effect of the atoms. The excess heat gives rise to tremendous energy! This energy becomes the power house for making things happen.

So what happens next?

As a result of excess energy, matter gets packed so tightly that the force of gravity pulls the star into itself. Finally the crowding of the atoms, the heat, and the violent energy forces the Hydrogen atoms to combine. This produces Helium. This change of Hydrogen to Helium gas is called **'Thermonuclear Fusion'**. When this happens, a star is born.

The Life of a Star

Throughout a star's life, thermonuclear fusion goes on in its core, creating enormous energy. This energy gets converted into light and heat which makes the star shine. This is a very stable state where no further contraction occurs. At this stage, the star is called a **'Main Sequence Star'**.

It takes 10 billion years for a star of about one solar mass to convert all the Hydrogen into Helium. When a star has finally turned all its Hydrogen into Helium, it is nearing the end of its life. Helium then fuses in the core to form Carbon. The outer layers of the star expand and cool. At this stage the star is called a **'Red Giant'**. When all the Helium is exhausted, the outer layers cool and drift away causing the formation of a gas like cloud around the core of the star. At this stage the star is called a **'Planetary Nebula'**.

At the end of its life, a star with the same amount of mass as our Sun will shrink to about the size of Earth, which is a million times smaller than its original size! At this stage, the star gets so hot that it turns white. This small dead star is called a **'White Dwarf'**. When the star completely cools down, it dies and shines no more. It then gets addressed as a **'Black Dwarf'**. The black dwarf contains ice, carbon and oxygen.

Bigger Stars

This entire process is slightly different for bigger stars. Here we are talking of stars that are more than three times the mass of Sun. The mass and gravity of these stars is much greater than other stars. Such a star rapidly converts its Hydrogen to Helium. It remains stable for a million years after which this massive star gets altered into what we can call a **'Red Supergiant'**. When this happens, no space is left between the atoms. The electrons and protons inside these atoms get pushed together and turn into neutrons. All the energy of this giant star gets used up. It collapses and shrinks into a very small size, even smaller than a white dwarf. At this stage the star is called a **'Neutron Star'** with a diameter of only a few kilometres. Although it is very small in size, its mass is so much that even a tiny bit of this neutron star (lesser than a teaspoon) would weigh about half a trillion kilograms! We could say that would be as much as a long freight train loaded with bricks!

The process of deterioration continues. In the core of this massive Supergiant, Helium fuses into Carbon, Nitrogen, Oxygen, Silicon and finally Iron. Around the iron core the outer layers drift further away. There comes a point where the core collapses within itself, causing an explosion and throwing the gases even further away. During this collapse photon like particles called neutrinos are forced out of the atoms. As the neutrinos burst from the dying star, the star shines even more brightly, brighter than any other object in the galaxy. This enormous sparkler is called a **'Super-nova'**. This star finally becomes a black hole.

Event horizon

An event horizon is the threshold at which things get pulled into the black hole. It is only few kilometres away from the black hole. But black holes are invisible. Researchers detect black holes with the help of a binary system and by observing visible stars in the orbit of a black hole. Black holes create tremendous gravity in a rather small sphere of space. The matter that is pulled into the black hole goes in so fast that energy in the form of x-rays is released.

Matter spiralling into a giant black hole emits copious amounts of radiation which is seen as a very bright object called **'Quasar'**. The gas going into the black hole causes emission of radio-waves and visible light brighter than even many galaxies put together. The gas that spins around the black hole while entering it is called an **'Accretion Disk'**.

Astronomers hence detect a black hole by noticing the effects of gravity like tracking the x-ray emissions and the quasar. Although a quasar is smaller than the solar system, it can outshine an entire galaxy!

How big or small can a black hole get?
A black hole can be as big as 18 billion solar masses and the smallest that a black hole can get is 0.0000000000000000000000000000001cm.
Astronomers theorize that coupled black holes exist, and that black holes sometimes merge and form **'Super massive black holes'**. Super massive black holes are areas in space that are so dense and massive that they contain up to billions of stars and continually suck in more stars, further building their mass and gravitational pull. Even light cannot escape the pull of gravity in such a black hole.

Once a black hole reaches a critical mass and becomes too large for its host galaxy, it zaps away nearly all the gas needed for young stars to form. On the other hand, during its formation, the gas and dust thrown out can go on to form new stars in future.

V. Making of the Remedy
On Monday December 3, 2007 at 7PM a Santa Fe, NM astronomer, Peter Lipscomb and Homoeopath Rowan Jackson went out to Peter's backyard and began the process of affixing a small bottle of Ever clear 100% grain alcohol to his Meade LX90 8 inch aperture telescope. As they were assembling the platform, a bolide - a large and low meteor came out of the SW. It was the most interesting green and blue colour which Peter said was very unusual. It was a great omen for the procedure and it was unique as binary stars are usually seen as yellow/white by astronomers in some capacity.
The binary system concentrated on was CygnusX1 for the Black Hole with the star number HD226868. Cygnus was a Binary Star until its companion became a Black Hole. At 7:50 PM they taped the bottle to the eyepiece and exposed it to the aperture and left it there until 9PM. Peter explained that as

the Black Hole transited the sky because of the air mass and degrees above the horizon, they would no longer maintain the same strength if it was left on longer. This is a phenomenon known as **'Atmospheric Extinction'**. The equipment used was an 8 inches compound reflecting telescope. They exposed the grain alcohol to the CygnusX1 which coordinated for 80 minutes through the aperture, tracking uninterruptedly in the clearest part of the night sky.

Rosie brought the bottle of exposed alcohol back to her house. Rosie then experienced an unusual depression for a while and she felt like she was in a black cocoon. She made it up to 6C and then sent it to Helios, London for further potencies.

We have used Black hole up to 10M potency in three cases.

What is Cygnus X-1?

* Binary star system that is a strong source of X-rays. It provided the first major evidence for the existence of black holes. Cygnus X-1 is located about 8,000 light-years from Earth in the constellation Cygnus.
* The primary star, HDE 226868, is a hot super giant revolving around an unseen companion with a period of 5.6 days. Analysis of the binary orbit led to the finding that the companion has a mass greater than seven solar masses.
* A star of that mass should have a detectable spectrum, but the companion does not. From this and other evidence astronomers have argued that it must be a black hole. The X-ray emission is understood as being due to matter torn from the primary star that is being heated as it is drawn to the black hole.
* Discovered in 1971 in the constellation Cygnus, this binary consists of a blue super giant and an invisible companion that revolves around one another in a period of 5.6 days.

25

 IMPONDERABLES AT THE MICRO & MACRO LEVELS

I.   Introduction

II. Imponderables at the Micro Level

III. Imponderables at the Macro Level

I. Introduction

The word imponderable means something that cannot be pondered upon or cannot be comprehended so easily. In this category we include everything that is unfathomable or imponderable. While x-rays, electricity, sunlight are all energy and are rightly put into this kingdom, stars that emit these rays, galaxies, the Sun itself, black holes etc. are also included here. They are matter in such large magnitude that their mass or their power is almost unbelievable or unfathomable to the human experience. We therefore categorise them as well in this section of imponderables.

We would want to simplify it further and say that we see imponderables as having two extreme levels – **Micro level and Macro level**.

At the micro level there is no matter. Only energy can be felt and experienced. Whereas at the macro level, matter is so huge and gigantic that it is beyond human understanding or experience.

Let us take a look at the remedies and themes in these two major groups.

II. Imponderables at the Micro Level
At the micro level we have remedies like:

* ⋆ X- Ray, Light, Electromagnetic waves, Vacuum, Electricity, Magnetism, Laser beam, etc.

The Themes:

* ⋆ I am small, invisible, pure energy
* ⋆ I am dynamic
* ⋆ I belong to and am part of the energy of the Universe
* ⋆ Connection to Cosmos
* ⋆ I initiate or I am responsible for transformation
* ⋆ Matter converting to energy
* ⋆ Small and invisible yet powerful
* ⋆ Speed – I travel with great speed
* ⋆ They do not talk of being a creator, being so large, magnanimous

II. Imponderables at the Macro Level
At the macro level we have remedies like:

⋆ Sol, Lunar, Pole star, Black hole, planets, etc.

The Themes:

⋆ Stars, galaxies

⋆ I am huge

⋆ I am magnanimous, enormous

⋆ I am the universe

⋆ I create

⋆ I have huge and unfathomable power and force

26

THE DIFFERENCE OF IMPONDERABLES FROM OTHER SIMILAR LOOKING REMEDIES

I.   Noble Gases, Lanthanides and Actinides

I. Noble Gases, Lanthanides and Actinides

Noble Gases: These elements belong to Column 18 of the periodic table. They have a complete and stable configuration hence they are called inert or noble gases. Helium, Neon, Argon, Krypton, Xenon and Radon are the six known noble gases. The core issue of noble gases therefore, is that they have resolved their issue of incapacity and lack within. Hence they are ready to rest and withdraw or look into something completely new and cosmic.

Lanthanides belong to Row 6 and Column 13 of the periodic table while actinides belong to Row 7 and Column 13 of the periodic table. Lanthanides are heavy elements belonging to the same row as Gold and Mercury. They are self-igniting and are used as catalysts in several chemical reactions. The core issue of lanthanides therefore is that they are trying to find their hidden powers within themselves. They want to be their own masters and this is their mission.

Actinides are very heavy radioactive elements. Most of them are explosive in nature. The core issues of actinides is that they are hungry for power and at the same time they feel everything is slipping away from their hands. In their need to keep everything under their control and authority they become even more destructive and explosive.

They share the following themes with the imponderable remedies:

Connection to stars, space, planets etc.

Explosion, energy, power

Out of body, rebirth, past life experiences

Love for astronomy, astrology

Please note that lanthanides, actinides and noble gases are all minerals (matter) and they are concerned with completion of their configuration in some form or the other. Hence their deep issue would be of completing, feeling complete or incomplete about their own inner capacities. This basic duality of complete and incomplete does not form the basis in imponderables. As has been discussed in detail earlier the imponderable duality is that of matter versus energy.

Lanthanides	Actinides	Noble Gases	Imponderables
• Masters of their own self	• They want to rule others	• Resolving all issues and completing everything to finally let go	• They have the polarity of matter and energy
• Autonomy • Searchers • Researchers • Therapists	• Powerful • Explosive • Power within oneself	• Need to experience peace, contentment and serenity within	• I do not want to be matter • Other side of me is matter • Transformation • Creation
• Power over self • Their issue is search for an inner power or boss within	• Heavy • Explosive • Authoritative and powerful • Radioactivity • Disintegration	• Need to give up every struggle and pass on • Searching for something more hence they get interested in social work, astrology, etc.	• Understanding the futility of material things and material concepts
• They want to have control and power over self or within the self	• They have a fear that their power is slipping away	• Understanding the futility of achievement	• Feel themselves either invisible or very magnanimous • Feeling of power to change and affect and create matter

MIASMS OF IMPONDERABLES

I.   Joshis' Concept of Miasms

I. Joshis' Concept of Miasms

We have already discussed miasms in detail. In very short, this is how we look at miasms: Psora, Sycosis and Syphilis in an increasing intensity of despair but in a linear manner.

Health			**Death**
Acute Psora		**Sycosis**	**Syphilis**

After going through our energy cases and the understanding of electromagnetic radiations, we have now come to the conclusion that miasms are not linear but circular. So if you put any matter (physical human body) between Psora, Sycosis and Syphilis, we see imponderables on the other side of the line. It is almost like a circle wherein the imponderables come between Syphilis to Psora and matter comes between Psora to Syphilis.

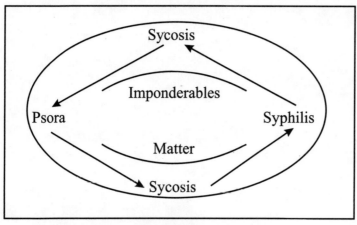

Fig. 7

What do we mean by this? Let us look at Psora, Sycosis and Syphilis first in a linear fashion where the attitude or the coping gets deeper and deeper and closer to destruction.

If we look at the classical theory of chronic diseases, Psora progresses to Sycosis, Sycosis progresses finally to Syphilis. This is how matter progresses towards destruction. We know that as the pathology increases, the energy or the energy pattern in an individual gets further and further depleted. In Psoric miasm you have maximum functional or emotional symptoms. As you come to Syphilis, the pathology increases further and further. It is as if energy converts more and more into fixed matter and into pathology. Hence, in Syphilis we observe more pathological than functional symptoms.

The Physics point of view

Energy is what is released when matter undergoes any kind of change or transformation. So energy is the other polarity of matter itself. It is that which makes matter function. For example, when you heat matter it changes form and it liberates heat and light. So in the process of changing and destruction of matter, energy is released. If you look at it from energy's point of view, energy has not undergone destruction. In fact it has been liberated.

The Process of Creation of the Universe

According to the Big Bang theory, the universe was created about 20 billion years ago from a cosmic explosion that hurled matter in all directions. The early universe was filled homogenously and isotropically with an incredibly high energy density and concomitantly huge temperatures and pressures. So initially there was only energy. This energy expanded and cooled as it went through phase transitions analogous to the condensation of steam or the freezing of water as it cools (here it's related to elementary particles). So, just as you would say that gas condenses into liquid and liquid condenses into ice, energy started to gradually condense to form matter. Approximately 10-35 seconds after Planck's epoch, a phase transition caused the universe to experience exponential growth during a period called as 'cosmic inflation'. After the inflation stopped, the material components of universe were in the form of quark-gluon plasma in which all constituent particles were moving relativistically.

Now let us look at it as Homoeopaths

In the beginning there was only energy. It started to condense into the first particles which were nothing but quarks which is even smaller than the atoms and electrons. As the universe started to cool and grow more in size, the quarks and gluons combined to form baryons like protons and neutrons which somehow produced the observed asymmetry between matter and anti-matter. Lower temperatures led to further symmetry breaking phase transmissions that put the force of physics and elementary particles into their present form. Later, protons and neutrons combined to form the universe's deuterium and helium nuclei. Over time the slightly denser regions of nearly uniformly distributed matter gravitationally attracted nearby matter and thus grew even denser. This formed gas, cloud, star, galaxies and other astronomical structures that we observe today.

The very beginning of the universe appears to be a condensation of energy into matter which makes the attitude of energy extremely constructive. Yet if we look at it the other way, it was an explosive big bang. So, an explosion actually lead to formation of matter, life and everything .

Therefore here if we now look at the map of Psora to Syphilis linearly energy does not fit into this line. It rather fits in the opposite direction which means that the miasm is destruction leading to formation. It's the other side of the circle where Syphilis is going towards Psora. What do I mean by this?

With the energy cases that we have had in our practice we see that whatever pathology they have, (it's usually a serious one) their attitude is very Psoric and somewhere the development of that pathology has helped them to develop this Psoric attitude. The pathology is at a constant state and their attitude is helped by that pathology. They could be living comfortably with the Psoric attitude over a destructive pathology. It's not a cover up or compensation where they say that I don't have a problem. It's a kind of a realisation where they say, "Look I have a problem which means my perception needs to be altered. So it's the perception change that I am looking for when I come to you doctor. The problem may or may not remain. But I know that if my perception changes I will be able to lead a much healthier life."

What we have also seen with energy cases is that their perception changes when you give the remedy although some part of the pathology might even remain. That little destructive pathology in a helpful way stays at that stage, relatively constant, not harming or increasing further. It stays almost benign at that stage and allows the patient to change his perception and lead a more comfortable life. When we give the homoeopathic remedy in these energy cases, their perception changes first. They feel far more happy and healthy in their situation emotionally and functionally first and then they physically improve.

Important Note
There are cases which are mainly Psoric or Sycotic in imponderables but it means that they might have had a background of Syphilis in the past or in the genetic history. However, there isn't an impending danger that they will move to Syphilis. In fact they have moved away from Syphilis to be Sycotic or Psoric or the smaller miasms in between.

A CONCLUDING NOTE BY
BHAWISHA AND SHACHINDRA JOSHI

We have introduced these ideas but we think we still have a long way to go with many more imponderables and nosodes waiting to be explored. There are many more interesting things about these kingdoms that are to be understood. These topics are subject to evolution. So these topics and themes will evolve and will expand more in the future.

Meanwhile, we are happy to have initiated this process of going into new kingdoms. We feel a sense of profound satisfaction of having opened the window of these new kingdoms to the Homoeopathic world from a completely different viewpoint. Slowly and gradually with more cases, we will all learn more about these remedies which have not been prescribed so much in the past and then hopefully we will prescribe them far often in our practice.

Notes

Notes

Notes

Notes

Notes